I0578335

Mommy's Top Drawer 2

A romantic lesbian MDLG and ABDL novel collection of 6 in 1 kinky BDSM age play stories

Tina Moore

© Copyright 2019 by Tina Moore

All rights reserved.

The content contained within this book may not be reproduced, duplicated, or transmitted without direct written permission from the author or the publisher.

Under no circumstances will any blame or legal responsibility be held against the publisher, or author, for any damages, reparation, or monetary loss due to the information contained within this book, either directly or indirectly.

Legal Notice:

This book is copyright protected. It is only for personal use. You cannot amend, distribute, sell, use, quote or paraphrase any part, or the content within this book, without the consent of the author or publisher.

Table of Contents

Mommy's Home, Princess

An ABDL and MDLG story of a middle girl who needed a Mommy more than she knew, and the perfect Mommy to teach her how to be a good girl

Tina Moore

Chapter 1

"Well, well, what do we have here?" Samantha quietly said as she sat down in a café after work, opening up the newspaper. Samantha was a regular at the café and would stop in for a caramel latte after work most days. She worked downtown in a busy office as the HR manager. After being at the company for over ten years, she had become bored with the day to day tasks that awaited her every morning. She took comfort in the fact that at least her job was easy and gave her time to get her nails done during her lunch break or go shopping with her friends. At 45, her figure was beginning to show her age with her hips having gained a few extra kilos over the last year, and her large breasts starting to grow heavy. Yet apart from this, she still looked like a glamour model and never had a hard time finding women to share the night. Her hair shone chestnut and chocolate brown through the window of the café as she looked out the window and sighed. It was Friday, and she had nowhere to be. She thought about heading to the gym, or giving the new girl she was chatting to online a message, taking her phone out just to put it back into her long felt coat.

"Can I get this to go?" She asked as she stood up. The

waitress hurriedly put the slice of black forest cake into a paper box and handed it back to Samantha.

"See you Monday," she happily said to Samantha, who smiled politely.

That's a bit tragic. I need to find somewhere else to go. Samantha thought to herself as she pushed the glass door of the café open and walked out onto the street.
She pulled her coat tightly around her body as she felt the crisp bite of the afternoon on her lips. Being the tall woman she was, it wasn't long before she found a quick rhythm and paced quickly, wanting to warm up as the cold air began to settle in for the night. As she turned the corner, she saw a girl that she just knew she would love to take home. The girl was lean, wearing the no-label type of clothes Samantha herself hadn't purchased in over two decades. Her hair was a light blonde, and her green eyes looked up at Samantha as she passed her. Samantha couldn't help but get turned on by the girls' big eyes and sad face, wishing she could have scooped her up and held her tight like a lost little puppy needing love.

Sweet little thing. Samantha thought to herself as she opened her apartment building door and walked inside. She walked across the lobby and pressed the elevator button to her penthouse.

"I should probably take Holly out for a walk actually," Samantha said out loud as she rode the elevator to the top floor. Holly was the black Belgian Sheepdog Samantha had bought two years ago. Samantha had a wood cabin two hours from the city where Holly and her would escape to most weekends so that Holly could run around, but during the week, she had to settle for a walk and run around the off-leash dog park three blocks from the penthouse.

"Come here, darling," Samantha said as she walked through the door. Holly jumped up from sunning herself in the living room and almost knocked Samantha over in delight and excitement.

Walking down to the street, Samantha numbed out the strangers who passed her, wishing that the emptiness in her heart would leave her alone. Samantha and Holly reached the dog park only to find that they were the only people out that afternoon.

"Well, Holly, I guess you have the run of the park," Samantha said, finding a wooden bench and sitting down, her heeled knee-high chocolate brown boots crossed over her thighs. Samantha sighed and watched as Holly sprinted around the park. She closed her eyes and rolled her head back, trying to feel the last of the sun before it went down, only opening her eyes when someone sat down next to her on the bench.

"Hi," came a soft, gentle voice. The sun went down, and Samantha saw the girl before her shiver, making Samantha lick her bottom lip seductively.

"Hello," Samantha replied, eyeing the young woman more predatorily than she meant to. The black-haired woman with piercing blue eyes made Samantha bite her bottom lip as she turned her head to look away.

Fuck me, Samantha thought, her body instantly tingling. She rolled her eyes at herself, deciding that she needed to get out of there before she was even more tempted to lay the girl down and have her way with her right there on the bench.

"Are you from around here?" The girl asked, her eyes wide and innocent-looking looked up at Samantha's face. Samantha couldn't help but smile down as she looked into the girl's eyes, pausing a moment before replying.

"Yes, but I haven't seen you before. Is that your new puppy?" Samantha replied, tilting her head towards the small golden retriever with the big puppy dog paws trying to keep up with Holly.

"Yep, I got her three months ago. I try to take her out when there are not so many people here because she's so little," she explained.

"I guess I'll be seeing a lot more of you then," Samantha said, the suggestive tone in her voice making the girl giggle.

"Maybe," she replied, looking out toward the dogs. Sensing the girl pull away from her, Samantha extended her hand.

"I'm Samantha," she offered, smirking a one-sided

smirk when the girl's smaller hand fit sweetly into her larger one.

"Nelly," the girl replied, a wicked gleam in her eye intriguing Samantha.

"And I'm 26. You know, for when you invite me to have a drink with you," Nelly replied, holding her breath and biting her lower lip, her eyes sparkling with mischief.

"That's very presumptuous of you," Samantha said, holding onto her hand a little longer than necessary. Nelly just shrugged her shoulder, the wind picking up her shiny black hair and floating it in the breeze.

"I'm free tomorrow at 7. I'll meet you here," Nelly replied, getting up to walk away. Samantha quickly got to her feet, enjoying how she towered over Nelly, making her pussy instantly wet. Samantha's older body was soft and curvy, and Nelly's mouth was in perfect alignment with Samantha's large, thick nipples.

"I wouldn't usually take orders from someone so little. But I will see you then," Samantha said, whistling to Holly, who came bolting over to where the two women stood.

"I wouldn't have had to if you had backed yourself," Nelly teased, before clipping her baby, pink leash onto her puppy and walking away.

What the fuck just happened? Samantha thought as she softly chuckled to Holly as they headed in the opposite direction. Holly looked up at her, and Samantha could almost swear she was smiling at her.

Samantha took her time getting ready the next day. She had gone to the salon and gotten her hair freshly blown out, her nails done, and her body massaged.

Even if baby girl stands me up, at least I will look divine, she thought to herself as she laid out multiple outfits on her king-sized bed. She had decided that even though Nelly had made the first move, the bar they would go to was going to be Samantha's choice. She wasn't interested in going to a loud club with dance music and instead had made a reservation at an expensive cocktail lounge which overlooked the glittering lights of the city. There was a particular table which Samantha had requested, knowing that it was secluded and private. She was secretly hoping that Nelly wouldn't be appropriately dressed, making it look like Samantha was her sugar Mommy. She liked it when her girls didn't match with her. She also liked it when they were either under or overdressed. This mostly made them slightly self-conscious and feel vulnerable and made Samantha feel like she was truly protecting them because they would instinctively lean into her and be more open to her affection.

She looked over her-self one last time, running her hands over her voluptuous body, the red satin dress hugging her full-figured curves perfectly. Her silver heels giving her extra height she didn't really need, and her hair, nails, and make-up looking flawless. She sprayed her body with perfume before heading out the door.

Nelly was already waiting at the dog park when Samantha whistled at her, causing her to turn around, and her mouth gape open.

So you fucking should, Samantha thought to herself, seeing the desire in Nelly's eyes. Samantha smirked, her eyes taking all of Nelly in. Her hair was tied and slicked back in a flawless pony-tail, her black leather skirt had a loose white t-shirt tucked in, and her heeled combat boots made her thigh muscles stay flexed. Her silver sequined jacket lay on the bench next to her small red clutch purse.

"Hi sweetheart," Samantha said, pulling Nelly in by her wrist and wrapping her arms around the smaller woman. Nelly held her breath, worried that her knees would give way if she let herself relax into Samantha's cuddly embrace.

"Hi," Nelly replied when Samantha finally let her go and took a step back.

"I think I should go change," Nelly said, her gaze wide and untrained, looking over Samantha's body, not sure where to rest her eyes.

"No, you look lovely. Come on. I've made a reservation at a place I know you'll like," Samantha said, reaching out to take Nelly's hand in hers. Nelly whipped her head around and looked up at Samantha, Samantha seeing this out of the corner of her eye and smiling.

There's my cheeky girl. She thought to herself as she saw the gleam of mischief in Nelly's eyes.

"How do you know what I'll like?!" Nelly teased her playful giggle at the end of her question, making Samantha's heart warm.

"Because, it's the perfection influencer spot," Samantha knowingly said, silencing Nelly.

"I've got nothing for that one," Nelly said, somewhat impressed that Samantha wasn't letting her take the lead.

"I know you don't," Samantha laughed back, pulling Nelly into her as they walked past a rowdy sports bar as a group of men were coming out. Nelly giggled and wrapped her arm around the older woman's body, resting her head onto the side of Samantha's breast as Samantha pulled Nelly closer as they passed the group.

"You know, I can defend myself," Nelly said, pulling away from Samantha as they turned the corner.

"Oh, I am sure you can. But when I'm around, you won't have to," Samantha said, looking Nelly dead in the eye and unnerving her once again.

"Ok," Nelly replied, her first moment of surrender written in her eyes. Samantha loving smiled at Nelly and continued to walk up the street and toward the cocktail lounge.

"Here we are," Samantha said as they reached the door, and a wide-eyed Nelly followed her inside.

They were shown through the lounge and to their table, and Nelly sat down, looking out the window and down on the city, which roared with life outside.

"This is really nice," Nelly said, looking back up and around at the luxurious space. She hadn't noticed Samantha had ordered two cocktails and was taken by surprise when her drink was placed in front of her.

"So, this is going really fast. You're really affectionate," Nelly said, smiling in disbelief that she was sitting across from the beautiful woman.

"We can go slower if you like. I could have taken you to an average restaurant, had an average meal and conversation, but you don't seem average. And yes, I am you didn't seem to mind," Samantha said, taking a sip of her drink and letting her words sink in. Nelly raised her eyebrows in agreement.

"Fair point," Nelly said when she finally replied.

"So, what's your deal, then?" She added, making Samantha laugh.

"My deal?" Samantha questioned playfully.

"Yeah, like, what do you do for work and that sort of thing. Do you always pick up girls at the dog park?" Nelly teased, making Samantha laugh.

"I'm a HR manager, and no I don't, but I think we both know you picked me up baby girl," Samantha said watching how Nelly responded to the pet name, getting turned on when Nelly slightly blushed and swallowed before looking for her drink to take a sip.

"I'm 45, single. I like younger women. I live in an apartment overlooking the city, and I like pretty shiny things," Samantha added, somewhat boring Nelly, who sipped her drink.

"Now tell me something a little less superficial. Tell me about your first heartbreak," Nelly said, excited to see Samantha's reaction.

"You are such a cheeky girl," Samantha said, signaling the waitress and ordering a selection of tapas before looking at Nelly with the dominating glare she would have saved for a much later occasion.

"Tell me about yours first," Samantha ordered more than asked. Nelly thought about the statement before smirking and shaking her head no.

"I kinda asked you first," Nelly replied, causing Samantha to smile on the inside, although continuing to stare Nelly down. Samantha kicked off her heels under the table and placed her freshly pedicured feet on either side of Nelly's chair, taking her by surprise.

"You want to play that game, do you?" Samantha said, her voice becoming serious. She sensually moved her feet over Nelly's thighs and parted them. Nelly complied willingly but kept her eyes on Samantha, not sure what to make of the women sitting across from her. Samantha kept her feet on Nelly's chair, forcing her thighs apart as she raised an eyebrow at Nelly before gently stroking her over her panties. Nelly gasped and sat up straight, pulling away from Samantha, but Samantha's legs were long enough that Nelly couldn't actually get away from Samantha's touch. Nelly clenched her jaw while looking at Samantha with wide, surprised eyes before looking around the room. Biting her bottom lip, she rolled her hips forward, pushing herself against Samantha, who enjoyed watching Nelly crave more of her touch.

"Ok, I'll go first," Nelly said, a flush of pink covering her cheeks as she stumbled on her words.

"I was 19. Her name was Daniela. She was way too old to be fooling around with a teenager, and I was way too young to be trying to gain the affection of a woman. She was German. Her accent was so incredibly sexy. I really liked her, but I didn't know what the hell I was doing, and she thought I was only using her for a ride home. It took years to get over her. She was everything I thought I wanted in a partner. She was tall, dominant, affectionate, caring, stylish, and so sophisticated. But I was a kid and way too immature to be able to be with anyone, and it didn't get very far. We tried to have sex. It was so bad! She came in only wearing a towel wrapped around her hips one time. Her abs were breathtaking. She was in the army when I spent time with her. It was one of those tragic moments in life that I look back on and cringe. Like how could she have even entertained the idea of fucking with me?! I can't imagine being with a 19year old now, let alone when I will one day be her age. I kinda just threw myself at her. It was a complete trauma bond and response, which I've since corrected, sort of. But I'm glad now that it didn't work out, coz I wouldn't have had the incredible life I've had or be sitting here with you if it hadn't turned to shit for me at least. She probs never gave me a second thought, but it took me years to get over her," Nelly explained, taking Samantha aback by how open and forthcoming Nelly was about her first heartbreak.

"Wow," was all Samantha said as she took in the words Nelly had just poured out onto the table.

"Trauma bond and response?" Samantha asked, making Nelly giggle.

"Another time, yeah?" Nelly asked, her eyes telling Samantha that this wasn't something to press on.

"Sure," Samantha said, sipping her drink.

"So, you like older women then? I don't have the body of the woman you just mentioned," Samantha said, annoyed at herself for wanting validation. She knew she was attractive, but she hadn't seen her abs in years and was surprised that Nelly made her question her appearance.

"Yeah I do, I like how they make me feel, I don't know why I just always have. My tastes are diverse. You have things she didn't. Don't worry, Mama, you're good," Nelly said, winking at Samantha playfully.

That's the only problem with all this normalization of kink. Girls be calling you Mommy without actually knowing what they are saying, Samantha, said to herself, hoping that Nelly wasn't just being friendly but actually knew what she was referring to.

Chapter 2

Samantha and Nelly had stayed in the bar until closing, walking out onto the street in the early hours of the morning.

"I haven't been out this late in ages!" Nelly exclaimed, stumbling into the back of Samantha as she walked.

"Come here, angel," Samantha said, turning around and holding Nelly as her knees buckled.

"Oh my god, how embarrassing," Nelly giggled, snuggling into the older woman as they waited for a taxi. Samantha whistled one down, unknowingly turning Nelly on and helped her into the backseat.

"I don't want you to go," Nelly said, reaching for Samantha.

"Make sure she gets home safely," Samantha said to the driver before taking Nelly's hands in hers and kissing them.

"I'll see you soon, princess," Samantha said before pulling away from her and closing the door. They had exchanged numbers, and Samantha sent her a message almost immediately.

I have had the best time in a long time, thank you, darling, the message read before Nelly smiled and closed her eyes.

Nelly woke in the morning and turned over in bed before she opened her eyes. She loved that split second between sleep and being awake. She could feel the stillness of her mind, and it made her smile for the moment of pure peace. She heard her phone go off and looked to see she had a missed call from Wendy.

"Fuck!" Nelly moaned out in frustration. Wendy was Nelly's most recent ex, and although they had broken up several times, she was like the party drug Nelly couldn't seem to leave alone. Opening the voice message, she knew that it wouldn't be good and winced, ready to hear the attack.

"I need to come over to get a few of my things. We are done this time. When are you free?" Came the voice down the phone, and Nelly bit her lip looking at the time.

Like, now would be fine, Nelly replied via text message, seeing Wendy reply almost immediately.

Good, see you in an hour, came her answer, and Nelly groaned and threw her phone into her bed. Quickly, she got out of bed and raced around her small apartment, collecting Wendy's things, she didn't want this to take any longer than necessary. She and Wendy had met at a party years ago and had hit it off straight away. Wendy had felt like a safe space for Nelly, and they had moved in together shortly after becoming official. The problem was, Wendy liked to drink and became aggressive with Nelly. She had hit Nelly on more than one occasion, and it had taken Nelly all her youthful courage to leave Wendy, just to fall back into her life, time and time after that. Wendy always promised that she would get help, see somebody, sort it out, and it was good for a while, months at a time, just so long that Nelly would let her guard down and then Wendy would unravel all over again, each time becoming worse than the last. Nelly hoped that Wendy would just take her stuff and go, she didn't want a scene, not today.

"Hi," Nelly said as she opened the door to Wendy, standing on the other side.

"Hey," Wendy replied, looking better than Nelly had wished she did.

"Can I come in, hun?" Wendy asked, dipping her head to meet Nelly's eyes.

"Don't call me that," Nelly softly said as Wendy pushed past her and into the apartment.

"Everything is in that box. You can just take it and go," Nelly said, trying to maintain some kind of control over the situation.

"Or, I could grab a cup of coffee, and you can tell me how you have been?" Wendy offered. Nelly just shook her head. She couldn't believe how innocent and kind and gentle Wendy sounded. It was a far cry from the violent rage she dished out last time Nelly was in her presence.

"I just need you to go," Nelly replied, walking back over

to the door and opening it. Wendy eyed her angrily, not happy about being told no. She got up from the sofa, picked up the box, and sauntered toward Nelly, placing the box on her hip and reaching out, taking Nelly's jaw in her hand before Nelly could stop her.

"You'll never find anyone who loves you more than me, remember that this is what you wanted," Wendy cruelly said, aggressively letting Nelly's jaw go, her tight grip leaving red marks on Nelly's cheeks and tears in her eyes as she slammed the door shut. Nelly slid down the back of the door and cried into her knees as she held them to her chest and tried to calm herself. Reaching into her shorts pocket, she pulled out her phone and replied to Samantha's message.

Same here, I'd love to do it again sometime, typed Nelly before putting it back into her pocket and getting up, deciding that she needed a hot shower.

Nelly pulled her thin jacket tighter around her waist as she waited for Samantha outside her tall office building. She had half a mind to cancel their plans as she was looked up and down by the countless suits who passed her in the lobby.

"Hi sweetheart, sorry I'm a bit late. My last meeting ran overtime," Samantha said as she reached out to embrace Nelly, pausing when she saw the bruises on each side of Nelly's cheeks. She hadn't done as good a job at covering them up as she had thought, but Samantha didn't mention it and held onto her firmly.

"Ready to go?" Samantha eagerly asked, Nelly just silently nodding and trying to look confident. Samantha sensed the girl's distant behavior and held out her hand, her eyes warm and loving, and Nelly gave a half-smile and held her hand as they left the building.

Walking down the street, Samantha slowed her walk to match Nelly's shorter stride and affectionately rubbed Nelly's hand with her thumb. Her heartbeat racing as Nelly reached out to cuddle her arm as they walked. Stopping once they reached the pier, Samantha sat down on a bench and pulled Nelly close into her.

"Do you want to tell me about it, sweetheart?" Samantha whispered into Nelly's ear as her hand ran through Nelly's hair. Nelly thought for a moment before shaking her head, only snuggling further into Samantha, who kissed her forehead and held her as they watched the waves crash onto the sand. Samantha looked over the sand and watched as the seagulls danced in the sky, wondering what was going on in Nelly's mind that could take her so far away. The afternoon sun warmed her hair, and as Samantha sighed and ran her fingers through her hair, Nelly reached out and touched her thigh.

"I am trying to do something I don't usually do. I'm trying to wait, but you have no idea how sexy you are," she said, looking up at Samantha and getting lost in her eyes.

"Yeah, baby girl, you can't fuck the pain away. Not with me anyway," Samantha replied, reaching out and stroking Nelly's cheek.

"So, um. There is this ex I have, and she's a bit violent. She did this," Nelly said, showing Samantha the bruises on her face. Samantha frowned and felt her heart hurt with how Nelly's eyes swelled with tears.

"Shh, it's ok, sweetheart, come here," Samantha said, feeling more connected to this woman than she could have predicted.

"I just feel like such a loser. Like I thought I was stronger than this, you know?" Nelly asked, wondering if Samantha would up and run, wondering if this was all just too much leftover drama to start something new. Samantha was wondering the same thing, hoping that she wasn't getting into another project that would just up and leave when she had put her back together.

"Look," Samantha said, pulling away from Nelly slightly to turn and look at her.

"I think that maybe you need to take some time to sort this out for yourself. I don't mind helping you through it, but I don't want to be a bandaid for your broken heart," Samantha explained. Nelly just nodded her head.

"Well, she came and picked up the last of her stuff this morning so it is well and truly over," Nelly said, half laughing when Samantha tilted her head and looked at her unconvinced.

"Yeah, but these tears are fresh, honey. So it's not as over as you want it to be, not yet," Samantha said, reminding herself that Nelly might not even be the type of girl she needed.

There's a big difference between a damsel in distress and a baby girl, Samantha, reminded herself. Standing up and stretching before holding her hand out to Nelly, who all but jumped into her arms.

"Dinner?" Nelly suggested. Samantha had to think about it, but Nelly's warm body snuggling into hers got the better of her and she opened her coat to keep her extra warm as they began to walk back into town.

Chapter 3

"You look really nice," Nelly almost whispered as Samantha sat down by the window seat in an Italian restaurant. This was the sixth time they had met up over two weeks, but Samantha felt like she had known Nelly for months. She smiled, seeing the blush cover Nelly's cheeks and watching as she sat down.

"I thought you might like it," Samantha replied, looking down at her thick navy cable knit pullover. It made her breasts look even bigger than they were, which is why she had worn it. She subtly smiled to herself before looking back up at Nelly.

"I could just dive right into you," she said, refusing to hold back any longer. Nelly bit her bottom lip, her eyes sparkling.

"Well, we are in a public place, that would be highly inappropriate," she teased, causing Samantha to raise her eyebrows.

"What I would do to you would definitely cause a few heads to turn," Samantha replied, not missing a beat. Nelly could feel herself getting turned on and looked away to try and regain composure. Nelly wasn't sure how to move their relationship along. They had gone on coffee dates, been to the movies, and on a picnic, but every time Samantha got too close, Nelly would push her away. Samantha knew this too, and so they both sat in silence while they waited for their order to be ready.

"Do you want to come to mine after this?" Samantha asked suddenly. Nelly thought for a moment, a mix of lust and fear in her eyes.

"For, maybe hot chocolate?" Nelly said, trying to hint that she didn't think sex was a good idea tonight. Samantha nodded her head, understanding the younger woman's meaning, making Nelly smile.

"Yeah, ok then," Nelly said, leaning back and having her pizza placed down in front of her by the waitress.

"I should have just assumed," Nelly laughed as Samantha pressed the top button on the elevator.

"Well, it's just that the view is far nicer at the top," Samantha replied, leaning back against the elevator mirror and placing her hands on her hips, eyeing Nelly.

"Don't look at me like that," Nelly giggled, turning around and ignoring Samantha.

"Like what?" Samantha whispered into Nelly's ear as she wrapped her arms around Nelly's waist and pulled her body back into hers. Nelly felt her pussy contract immediately, and her breath quicken.

This is going to be harder than I thought, she thought

to herself as she felt Samantha's hands gently rub her sides.

"We are here," Samantha said, having seen that Nelly had closed her eyes to try and keep herself from turning around in Samantha's arms. Opening her eyes, Nelly saw the luxury penthouse suite in all its glory and was speechless.

"So, you aren't coming to mine anytime soon!" Nelly exclaimed as she followed Samantha into the kitchen, making her laugh.

"Drink?" Samantha asked Nelly, who just nodded plainly as her eyes took in the space. Samantha poured two glasses of chilled wine and led Nelly over to the sofa. Sitting down, Nelly sunk into the soft fabric and let out a contented sigh.

"This isn't hot chocolate," Nelly cheekily pointed out. Samantha ran her hand through her hair before resting her head on the back of the sofa.

"No, but there's plenty of time for that," she replied.

"You are certainly comfortable here," Nelly said, feeling mildly out of her comfort zone. Seeing this, Samantha leaned forward and took the glass from Nelly's hand.

"Let's see if we can make you just as comfortable," Samantha said, taking Nelly's hand and pulling her into her lap.

"Don't fight me, honey, let me love on you a little," Samantha said as she felt Nelly's body stay rigid and somewhat afraid. Samantha stroked Nelly's hair until she felt her body relax and snuggle into hers. Wrapping her arms around Nelly, Samantha fantasied about having this as a part of their bedtime routine and Nelly in cute little socks and dressed in a onesie. Her thoughts got interrupted by Nelly shifting and laying in the perfect position to nurse, making Samantha's heartbeat race.

"I think I am too tired to go home," Nelly said as she closed her eyes and turned into Samantha, who held her tight. Samantha bent her head and kissed Nelly's cheek as Nelly brought her hands up and placed them at her chest.

"Do you want to stay the night with me, sweetheart?" Samantha asked, brushing the hair out of Nelly's eyes as she nodded yes.

"Hold on then, honey, I'll take you to my room," Samantha said as she stood up, Nelly in her arms much to her surprise.

"I didn't think you were that strong," Nelly said, her eyes wide in disbelief.

"There are a few things you are yet to learn about me," Samantha replied before walking into her room, pulling back the sheets and placing Nelly in bed. Samantha crawled into bed next to her and held her gently, biting her bottom lip when Nelly put her thumb in her mouth in her sleep.

Nelly woke to the sound of silence. She turned her head to see that Samantha was lying on the other side of the bed, both their clothes still on from the night before. Getting up, Nelly tiptoed out of the room and into the living room. Holly was on the floor but was undistracted as she played with a toy. Nelly decided to try and find the bathroom and began walking through the apartment. She passed the huge artworks hanging elegantly on the wall and the media room with the big green pool table in the middle. She walked out onto a balcony, which led to a spa and sauna. Looking over the balcony rail, she watched as the world buzzed under her feet and sighed, surprised that she was in this place and feeling like an imposter. Nelly walked back into the apartment through a different door, finding herself in the type of room she had only seen in porn videos. Raising her eyebrows, she reached out to touch the black satin drapes and let her eyes roam, slightly overcome with what she was seeing. The thick black carpet felt soft underfoot, the large bed in the middle of the room looked inviting, but the flogging cross in the corner made Nelly shudder. The toy box in the corner of the room made her tilt head to the side in confusion. She began to lift her foot to step further into the room when she heard Samantha clearing her throat behind her, making her spin around and gasp in surprise.

"You need to ask to go in there, sweetie," Samantha lovingly explained. Nelly realized her mouth was opened and shut it quickly, trying to brush what she had seen off like it was nothing.

"Oh, sorry, I kinda got lost," she said, sidestepping Samantha and beginning to walk away, turning back slightly to see Samantha following behind her.

Nelly walked back inside and went to sit down on the living room sofa and collected her things in the type of rush that made Samantha uneasy.

"I better get going," Nelly said, unsure of how to be around Samantha now that she had seen her sex room.

"If that's what you want," Samantha lazily said, making herself a coffee. Nelly stopped packing her stuff into her leather handbag and turned to face Samantha.

"So when I asked you what your deal was, you didn't think to tell me that you were, are, some sort of sadistic dominatrix?" Nelly said, rather accusingly. Samantha tried to suppress a smirk before coming back over to Nelly, her red bra showing through her white satin dressing gown.

"Why would I have said that I was a sadistic dominatrix?" Samantha innocently asked as she sipped her coffee. Nelly just scoffed and stuffed her jacket into her bag.

"Um, hello, because you have a fucking sex dungeon in your house!" Nelly replied, pointing in the direction of the room with her whole hand and waiting for an answer.

"I have that room, yep, but I am no sadist. I'm a Mommy, but I still like to punish a girl," Samantha said, placing her hand on Nelly's thigh and affectionately squeezing it.

"The fuck does you being a Mum have to do with it?" Nelly asked in frustration, not understanding what Samantha was talking about.

"Um. So, no. I'm a Mommy Dom, darling. If I am going to have a sub, she has to identify as either a middle or a little. Not all the time, I am no charity, but like, a little more than 50% of the time," Samantha said, getting lost in how much of a baby girl she truly enjoyed having. Nelly just put her head in her hands and sighed.

"I've got to go," she suddenly said, getting up, only stopping as Samantha grabbed her wrist.

"Can we talk about this, baby? This is not how I wanted you to find out," Samantha asked, letting Nelly's wrist go as she pulled away.

"Not right now," Nelly said as she walked over to the elevator and impatiently waited for the doors to open. Walking toward hers, Nelly turned around, more fear in her eyes than Samantha would have liked to see.

"Don't come over," Nelly hesitantly asked, causing Samantha to stop in her tracks.

"You don't need to be afraid of me. You can say no without me forcing you, and you can get in that elevator without me locking you out," Samantha said as the doors opened, and Nelly hesitated, taking one step in and letting Samantha's words sink in.

"I'll text you later," Nelly said as she got into the

elevator, the doors closing slowly, Samantha's face disappearing and the decent causing Nelly to exhale like she had been holding her breath for years.

Chapter 4

Nelly didn't text. She didn't call, and she didn't message over social media. After a week of silence, Samantha was beginning to wonder how much longer Nelly needed, and if there was any point in reaching out herself.

Maybe I should just forget about her. She thought to herself as she entered her usual café after work.

"Hey, I haven't seen you around lately," the waitress said as she walked over to where Samantha was sitting. She was young, roughly the same age as Nelly, and Samantha wondered if the longing in her voice was directed towards her.

"Well, I've been a little busy. Have you missed me?" Samantha playfully teased, watching as the waitress tried to get her blushing cheeks under control.

"Um, so, the usual," Tammy, the waitress asked, pulling her hair to one side.

"No. Surprise me with something new," Samantha replied, enjoying the fluster she was causing the girl. Tammy left in a hurry, making Samantha chuckle to herself as she opened her paper just to close it again.

"Hi," Nelly said. Nelly had sat down just as Samantha opened her newspaper, causing Samantha's eyes to widen.

"Hi?" Samantha questioned, raising her eyebrows at Nelly.

"Yeah," Nelly said, unsure of why Samantha seemed guarded. Samantha looked at Nelly, her 'come save me' stare, giving off more energy than usual.

"Ok. How have you been?" Samantha asked, folding her newspaper down and surrendering to the situation.

"Fine. Sorry I didn't message or whatever. I just needed to get my head around the fact that you're like...you know," Nelly stammered. Samantha thought for a moment.

"Baby. If you can't handle this, that is totally ok. Don't stress about it," she said, enjoying Nelly's indignant look when told she couldn't handle the situation.

"Yeah, that's what I'm trying to tell you. That's why I wanted to do this in person. I think maybe I could, like it," Nelly said, annoyed that their dynamic wasn't as affectionate and loving as before.

"I don't want to have to force it on you, and I don't know if you'd be into it or just trying to please me," Samantha explained, making Nelly pout, her eyes filling with water. Samantha stood up and moved seats, sitting next to Nelly and bringing her in for a cuddle before pulling back to wipe her tears.

"Shh, it's ok, honey," Samantha said, not being able to help herself from smiling at Nelly.

"But what if I wanted to try?" Nelly said, looking up at

Samantha and giving her the biggest puppy dog eyes.

"Tell me what you think you want to try?" Samantha asked, seriously considering Nelly's offer.

"I want to be with you, like, be your girlfriend and then like with the sex stuff, try doing the stuff you like. I've just never done anything like this before, it's always been pretty basic," Nelly explained, half convincing Samantha that this could work. The waitress came back with a slice of Honey cake and a vanilla latte, giving Samantha a sad smile just as she walked away.

You need to stop flirting with everyone. Now you need to give the girl a generous tip, so she doesn't think you are an asshole, Samantha thought to herself as she passed Nelly the latte.

"Have a sip," Samantha said to Nelly, who obeyed her without question.

"It's pretty good, here," Nelly said before handing the glass to Samantha.

"I don't think diapers are for me," Nelly suddenly said, causing Samantha to choke on the warm liquid and start to laugh.

"So, you want to talk about this here, right now?" Samantha asked, her perfect eyebrows raised as she put the glass on the table.

"Well, yeah. We could whisper," Nelly said, mischievous eyes sparkling, making Samantha just roll hers.

"So I've done a bit of exploring online, and I think I'd sort of be more a middle than a baby coz like I don't really have any desire to play with baby toys and stuff," Nelly said reaching for the Honey cake, getting her hand swatted away.

"What does a relationship like that even look like," Nelly said as Samantha leaned back in her chair and watched Nelly's excited face.

"Depends. I have had relationships that were completely caregiver centered and ones that have had no element of kink at all, but the later isn't what I am looking for," Samantha explained.

"So, what are you looking for?" Nelly asked, taking a sip of the latte once more. Nelly wondered if she would look as glamorous as Samantha when she was her age. Her wavy hair that came down just under her breasts, her long eyelashes, and puffy lips. The stare that seemed to intimidate Nelly and turn her on at the same time made Nelly smirk.

"What happens in 25years when I am not exactly young anymore?" Nelly asked, making Samantha laugh.

"Let's just get through this conversation first, honey," Samantha laughed, taking a bite of her cake.

"It's like everything darling, it'll take time to figure out our rhythm, but I want to try with you too," Samantha said, letting her heart get the better of her. Nelly looked at the woman she believed was way out of her league, and her surprised eyes made Samantha laugh.

"Come on, little girl," she said, standing up, leaving a $10 tip and holding out her hand to Nelly, who took it eagerly as they left the café.

Nelly waited on Samantha's bed, wondering what was taking so long. Samantha had been in her room-sized wardrobe for the last ten minutes, and Nelly wondered what on earth could be taking so long when Samantha said she was only changing into something more comfortable.

"Sorry, honey," Samantha said as she came out of the double-doored room, making Nelly roll her eyes. Samantha wore her hair down, her pink sweatpants were tight on her ass, and the white singlet under her grey zipped up sport hoodie made Nelly blush.

"Well, now, I am over-dressed!" Nelly playfully complained, making Samantha smile.

"Shall we then?" Samantha said, taking Nelly's hand and twirling her around before she led her through the apartment and to the playroom. Feeling Nelly pull back on her hand, Samantha turned to her, coming over to kiss her on the top of her head.

"We aren't fucking tonight, baby girl, don't worry," Samantha said as Nelly cautiously looked into the room that was primarily designed for sex. Nelly looked up at Samantha, her puppy dog eyes aching to be able to trust the Amazonian goddess who stood in front of her.

"Ok," Nelly said, biting her lip and following Samantha into the room. Samantha sat Nelly down on the bed and went over to the free-standing cupboard by the far wall of the room and opened both doors.

"Want to come and find something you can relax in?" Samantha asked, as Nelly slowly walked over to where she was standing, cuddling into Samantha almost involuntarily as she looked.

"These are cute," Nelly softly said, slightly regaining her confidence as she flicked through the clothes. Taking out a pair of thigh-high pink stripy socks, Nelly smiled and kept looking, stopping when she saw a short pair of white shorts and a matching t-shirt with a kitten on the front. Looking back at Samantha, Nelly shyly smiled and bit her bottom lip before Samantha took the items and led Nelly back to the bed.

"Can I help you put them on, honey?" Samantha asked, sitting down on the bed and having Nelly standing in front of her, between her thighs, nodding shyly.

"Ok, come here," Samantha said as she reached out and took the front of Nelly's jeans in her hand and jerked her forward, making Nelly fall onto her lap, her hands on Samantha's thighs making her smirk. Samantha expertly unbuttoned Nelly's jeans and wriggled them off her hips, gently caressing Nelly's thighs, making her giggle somewhat nervously.

"It's ok, sweetheart. Mommy's got you," Samantha said,

Nelly, exhaling loudly, realizing she had been holding her breath. Samantha wondered how long it would take for Nelly to drop her guard and let the little girl within her to come out and feel safe, deciding that time would tell as she finished dressing her.

"There," Samantha said as she leaned back on her elbows, Nelly standing in front of her. Nelly looked down and ran her hands over the shirt and looked back, and smiled at Samantha.

"What now?" She innocently asked, Samantha pushing the thoughts of ripping the clothes off of Nelly to the side.

"We could snuggle on the couch, watch a movie?" Samantha suggested, seeing the wicked grin of Nelly's come back across her face.

"Only if I can pick," Nelly said, giving Samantha a cheeky look before turning and bolting out of the room. Samantha laughed as she followed Nelly to the living room and sat on the sofa as she watched Nelly look for how to turn on the tv.

"Looking for this?" Samantha teased as she held her phone up, Nelly tilting her head to the side in confusion.

"I control everything in this house with my phone," Samantha said, feeling smug as Nelly looked to the side and walked to the couch, snuggling into Samantha.

"So, it looks like I'll be picking the movie," Samantha whispered as she wrapped her arm around Nelly as she flicked through the possible options. Settling on a mild action rom-com about two spies, Samantha heard Nelly's tummy rumble.

"Hungry, baby girl?" Samantha asked, hoping that what was going to come next wouldn't cause Nelly to run away. Nelly nodded her head and watched as Samantha began to massage her breasts sensually.

"Um, what are you doing?" Nelly asked, already knowing the answer.

"Well, you could have some milk," Samantha suggested, taking Nelly aback slightly, causing her mouth to gape open, as Samantha confirmed what she had thought.

"You don't have to, you also don't have to try and stay within a particular 'age,' you can just enjoy what you enjoy, and maybe you'll enjoy this?" Samantha explained. Nelly began to blush as she fought with herself to give in to what she wanted to do but hating herself for feeling weird about it.

"I, um," Nelly stammered, watching Samantha unzip her hoodie slowly and lift her singlet.

"If you hate it, forget it. But come and try honey. Can Mommy take the lead?" Samantha asked, seeing Nelly struggle with her desires and her shame as she silently nodded, happy to have Samantha take control. Samantha lay Nelly over her lap and held her tightly, stroking her cheek with her thumb as her other hand positioned her nipple into Nelly's mouth. Squeezing her breast, Samantha watched as Nelly's eyes grew wide as she tasted her milk for the first time. Nelly could feel her heart wildly beating before something came over her, and she closed her eyes and relaxed into Samantha's arms and moaned contently.

"There you go, little one, let Mommy look after you," Samantha said as she patted Nelly's tummy gently as she watched the girl suckle. Nelly felt her head rush with a feeling she hadn't felt before. Something between ultimate safety and complete calmness, a set of feelings she wasn't used to feeling, her eyes beginning to fill with tears, and the pain she carried with her was soothed.

"You're safe, honey, Mommy's got you," Samantha whispered as she watched Nelly's blue eyes turn navy as she let the tears fall down her cheeks. Samantha held her, only stopping when Nelly tried to sit up and pulled Samantha's singlet back down.

"Are you full, sweetheart?" Samantha asked, kissing Nelly's furrowed forehead, Nelly only nodding as she snuggled into Samantha and watched the rest of the movie in silence.

Chapter 5

"Mommy," Nelly whispered the next morning. Samantha had let Nelly stay over, and she smiled as she saw Nelly's face close to hers with the morning sun coming in behind her.

"Good morning, sugar," Samantha sleepily replied, rolling over to check the time. Nelly jumped up on the bed and waited for Samantha to turn back around

"I made breakfast," Nelly said proudly, causing Samantha to look at her suspiciously.

"You made breakfast? I distinctively remember you telling me you couldn't cook," Samantha teased, grabbing Nelly and pulling her back under the covers and wrapping her up in her arms and legs. Nelly giggled as she struggled to get away, causing Samantha to get turned on as she rubbed her clit and nipples in her attempt to escape.

"Ok, ok, I bought it," Nelly giggled as she surrendered to Samantha, who had taken to gently patting her bottom.

"That's what I thought," Samantha said, letting Nelly turn around in her arms and lay on top of her, Nelly, snuggling into her breasts.

"But I put it on plates," came Nelly's muffled response

as Samantha pulled her singlet down and pressed Nelly's mouth onto her nipple, holding her willing head in position as she continued to pat Nelly's ass, smirking when she felt Nelly begin to grind on her thigh.

"That's what I expect, little darling," Samantha said, gripping onto Nelly firmer as she felt Nelly's thigh pressing into her wet mound.

"Oh, little one. You aren't ready for me just yet," Samantha teased as she playfully spanked Nelly's ass before pulling her head back by her ponytail, milk dripping from her lips and landing back on Samantha's breast.

"Come on, let me see what you have gotten up to," Samantha said, Nelly's whingeing eyes making her smirk.
Nelly had bought croissants, breakfast juices, and scrambled eggs and had set it out elegantly on the dining room table, Samantha nodding her head, impressed with the girl's efforts.

"Nice job, honey," Samantha said as she sat down and began to eat.

"I wanted to say thank you," Nelly said, sipping her juice. Samantha frowned, looking at Nelly with curiosity.

For what?" Samantha asked. Nelly laughed and looked at her, thinking she was joking.

"I've never been with somebody who is so, gentle and kind and lovely. I feel like you're more than I deserve," Nelly confessed. Samantha scoffed and shook her head.

"Oh, honey," she replied, reaching out and stroking

Nelly's cheek affectionately, before pushing her chair out and patting her lap. Nelly stood and moved to sit on Samantha's lap, cuddling her as she finished breakfast, enjoying how open with her body Samantha was and how much affection she so freely gave.

Nelly practically skipped into work on Monday morning, delighted with life for the first time she could remember. Samantha felt the same as she sat down in her big office chair, she smiled up at the ceiling and sighed in contented bliss. The phone rang, breaking Samantha's happy train of thought and answering it, she had to clear her throat to sound like the ballbusting manager her colleagues knew her to be. Nelly's job was a little less formal, as she pulled on her work uniform, she straightened her tie and rolled her eyes.

Time to sell some holidays, she thought to herself, noting the vast difference between who she was last Friday and who she was today. Nelly worked as a travel agent and was grateful she could keep her phone on her as she worked, sending Samantha dirty messages throughout the day.

You need to stop, I am about to go into a meeting, and my panties are already soaked you wicked little thing, Samantha messaged as she left her phone in her briefcase and headed into the meeting. Nelly just smiled as she too put her phone away, excited to see Samantha in a few hours. They had decided to meet up for dinner at a new Japanese restaurant that had been getting rave reviews online, and Nelly thought about how she was going to seduce Samantha that night.

"So, how was your day?" Samantha asked as Nelly sat down at the restaurant 5mins late. She had missed her train and had to catch a later one. She was grateful that Samantha didn't seem to care.

"Yeah, fine. The usual. Somebody booked a holiday in South Africa, which looks really exciting actually. They have booked one of those tours around an animal park where they are the ones in the cage so the animals can roam free. I really like that concept. Wild animals shouldn't be locked in cages," Nelly said, Samantha, enjoying the conversation and excitement in Nelly's voice.

"I agree. It is quite cruel," Samantha replied before ordering. They talked through the night, laughing and throwing back shots until they were asked to leave because the restaurant was closing for the night.

"Oh, sorry, come on, baby," Samantha said, getting up and walking to the counter to pay.

"I'll be outside," Nelly said, squeezing Samantha's hand affectionately as she pushed the door open and walked into the cold night air. Breathing in, Nelly smiled a genuine smile, feeling like all the stars had finally aligned.

"There you are," Samantha's voice cut through the air, Nelly turning around and half jumping into her arms,

Samantha opening her coat and wrapping it around Nelly.

"Come on, Mommy, let's go home," Nelly whispered as she kissed Samantha on the cheek.

"I want to see what's under that dress," she quickly added, blushing at her remark.

"Do you now?" Samantha replied, winking at Nelly, admiring how wide-eyed and innocent she looked. A taxi pulled up, and they quickly got in, eager to get home.

"You're not going to need this anymore," Samantha said, taking a baby wipe from her handbag and sensually wiping Nelly's crimson lipstick off her lips. Nelly was grateful the driver got all the green lights on the way to Samantha's apartment and practically jumped out of the car when he pulled up at her building. They walked in silence, through the lobby, both imagining what was about to unfold.

"Can I kiss you?" Nelly said the moment the elevator doors closed. Samantha eyed her hungrily.

"I would be offended if you didn't," she replied, reaching out and pulling Nelly into her, embracing her fully and almost leaving Nelly breathless. Nelly's lips met Samantha's, and as they passionately kissed, Samantha tenderly pawed over Nelly, finally able to touch her where she had wanted. The elevator doors opened, and Nelly took a step back, just to find Samantha step forward and envelop her once more, making her giggle.

"Wait. I need to catch my breath," Nelly laughed,

worried her asthma would begin to play up if she continued.

"I can't have you needing to rush to the emergency room," Samantha playfully said, slowly taking off her coat and letting I fall on the marble floor. Nelly watched as Samantha began to unzip the back of her dress and stood before Nelly in just her lingerie and heels.

"Fuck, I'm lucky," Nelly said in her girlish voice, making Samantha swoon. She pushed Nelly back down on the bed and kicked off her heels before lying next to her.

"Take off your shoes," Samantha instructed, watching as Nelly obeyed her command.

"And your jeans," Samantha continued, watching as Nelly wriggled to her get jeans off. Nelly went to take her panties off, stopping when Samantha placed her hand on top of hers.

"Not yet, your shirt," Samantha said, redirecting Nelly. She unbuttoned her silk blouse and lay in her lingerie next to Samantha, shivering as the air conditioning cooled her skin.

"Get under, baby girl. Mommy can't have you getting cold, can I?" Samantha said, making Nelly smile. Samantha turned on a slow melodied soundtrack and began running her hands over Nelly, kissing her gently as she snaked her way down and then back up Nelly's body.

"I usually wouldn't be so nervous. You just make me so nervous," Nelly whispered, unable to summon that cheeky and playful girl she was sometimes.

"That's ok honey, can I take the lead?" Samantha replied, Nelly, nodding her head and gasping as Samantha quickly turned her around and sat behind her. Samantha let her hand roam over Nelly's tummy, snaking them down until she slipped them under her panties, making Nelly push her head back against Samantha's large breasts and moan.

"You are such a wet little thing," Samantha said, her words fanning the fire that had built inside of Nelly for weeks now.

"Spread your legs for Mommy," Samantha instructed, Nelly following her commands. Nelly bit her bottom lip and moved her hips as she softly moaned while Samantha stroked her clit.

"You're already so swollen for me. This is what you wanted?" Samantha said as she slipped a finger into Nelly, who raised up on her hands, surprised by the intrusion. Samantha just wrapped her other arm around Nelly's waist and pulled her back down, making her take the finger inside of her as she wiggled it.

"Shh, just relax, little bunny. Mommy is going to treat you real nice," Samantha said, feeling Nelly's muscles begin to contract, sliding in another finger and working her clit at the same time.

"Mommy," Nelly whispered in a long breath, closing her eyes and slightly rolling into Samantha as she was fucked. Samantha pulled her bra down and pushed Nelly's mouth onto her nipple, smiling as Nelly instinctively began to suckle using both hands to lift Samantha's breast to her lips. Samantha pumped her fingers harder and faster inside of Nelly as she suckled, feeling her own juices begin to drip onto her panties. Nelly moaned into Samantha, only adding to her arousal, and as Nelly bucked her hips aggressively against Samantha's hand, she came hard. Nelly looked up at Samantha, and her eyes rolled to the back of her head as she closed her eyes and melted into Samantha's embrace. Samantha smiled, gently took her hand from the younger girl's pussy, and licked her fingers clean.

"Sweet little honey," she said, pulling down her panties but waiting for Nelly to come down from her orgasm. Samantha stroked her body, enveloping her as she made sleepy noises while she snuggled.

"I thought that might be the case," Nelly said as she opened her eyes again after feeling inside Samantha's panties. Samantha enjoyed keeping a neatly trimmed, thick bush, which Nelly explored as she touched Samantha's body. Nelly slid her fingers between Samantha's thick pussy lips, and just as she was about to enter, Samantha pulled her hand away, laughing when she saw the look of confusion on Nelly's face.

"I want it on your mouth, little one. Can Mommy sit on your pretty little face?" Samantha asked. Nelly nodded and pulled her long hair to one side. Samantha moved over Nelly's face and pulled her panties to the side, lowering gently onto

Nelly's lips. Nelly stuck her tongue out and made Samantha shudder as she was licked slowly.

"That's it, honey," Samantha moaned, subtly rocking her hips and grinding her pussy against Nelly's tongue.

"Suck Mommy's clit, baby," Samantha instructed, pleasure clear in her voice. Nelly obeyed, moving between teasing her pussy with her tongue and sucking her clit, gently at first, but then with more passion as Samantha's juices began to drip onto Nelly's tongue.

"Oh baby," Samantha moaned, grinding hard on Nelly's face as she came. Nelly wriggled under Samantha's thighs, making her smile as she took her time to get off the younger woman.

"Let's get you cleaned up, sweetness," Samantha said, wiping her cum off Nelly's lips before kissing her gently. Samantha noticed the tears forming just behind Nelly's eyes and paused.

"Did I hurt you, baby?" Samantha asked, concern in her voice. Nelly just shook her head and tried to wipe the tears away, getting up and quickly walking to the bathroom. Samantha followed her, stopping Nelly from shutting the door on her.

"Hey, come on, talk to me," Samantha said, sitting on the edge of the bath, watching as Nelly paced back and forth.

"I don't know what to say. I just feel all churned up inside, and I shouldn't because like you are awesome," Nelly blurted out, looking at Samantha fearfully, worried she would push her away.

"Tell me about sex with your ex," Samantha said, taking Nelly by surprise. She looked at Samantha, who just looked at her knowingly and waited.

"It was rough, really physical and aggressive, I guess," Nelly thoughtfully replied, looking at Samantha with confusion.

"And tell me about the sex we just had," Samantha instructed. Nelly came to sit next to her, resting her head on Samantha's shoulder.

"It wasn't like that. It was soft and gentle and passionate," Nelly said as she remembered how safe Samantha had made her feel.

"So, do you think that you might not know how to handle feeling safe and vulnerable at the same time, and that's why you're a bit freaked out?" Samantha said, leaning back to turn on the bath.

"Maybe," Nelly said, letting Samantha put her into the bath as the water warmed up. Samantha raised an eyebrow at Nelly, making her laugh and shake her head.

"You must think I'm so lame that I can't even figure myself out," Nelly said as Samantha poured in relaxation gel into the water before joining her.

"No, honey, I don't think you are lame. I think you just need Mommy's love, and that's exactly what you are going to get," Samantha replied, pulling Nelly into her arms and gently rocking her as she calmed down.

Chapter 6

Samantha drove Nelly home in the early hours of the morning, tucked her up in bed, and waited until she was asleep before she left, kissing her forehead before she closed her apartment door.

Oh, this girl, Samantha thought to herself as she smiled on the drive back to her apartment. Samantha had a bad track record of girls, never being able to keep a relationship for longer than a year or so, and she desperately wanted to keep Nelly. She couldn't wait until Friday when she would be able to hold Nelly once more, and Samantha drove to work for the next four days, craving to have her baby girl back in her arms.

"Sorry I'm late, meetings," Samantha said, rushing into the bar, kissing Nelly full on the lips as she sat down. Nelly just giggled from behind her glass of whiskey and rolled her eyes.

"I think that might be something I have to get used too, huh?" Nelly asked as Samantha looked at her apologetically.

"Maybe?" Samantha replied, hoping that it wouldn't be a big deal.

"Well, if you keep coming with gifts, I think I can handle that," Nelly teased as she looked at the design shopping bags Samantha had walked in with.

"Funny you mention that. It was exactly what I was trying to do," Samantha said, winking at Nelly and passing her a bag.

"If you don't like them, we can go and get you something else. I saw these on my lunch break and thought how sweet they might look on you," Samantha explained as Nelly took out the earring box and opened it, her eyes going wide as she opened the box and saw the pink diamond studs in a rose gold setting. Nelly looked up in shock, making Samantha laugh as she ordered a drink.

"Can I help you put them in?" Samantha asked as Nelly nodded, smiling as she took out her silver hoops.

"I have never had something like this before," Nelly said as she opened the camera on her phone and looked at her gift.

"I just couldn't go passed them," Samantha replied, sipping her cocktail and admiring Nelly.

"Thank you, Mommy," Nelly whispered in Samantha's ear as she affectionately hugged her before sitting back down and tucking her hair on one side behind her ear.

"So, it's the weekend. I kinda have a few ideas," Nelly said, taking the print out of her bag the word document she had constructed of all the adult baby things she liked the look of, taking Samantha by surprise.

"Really?" She questioned, somewhat impressed that Nelly had taken some initiative.

"Like, maybe not all at once, but yeah," Nelly said as she got up to stand next to Samantha, who wrapped her arm around Nelly's waist as they looked at the ideas together.

"I can work with this. Come on, baby girl," Samantha said, feeling her nipples begin to leak in anticipation. Nelly grabbed her backpack and coat and followed Samantha out of the bar.

"So, not as big as you thought you were, huh?" Samantha questioned as Nelly reached for the paci that Samantha held just out of her reach. Nelly was dressed in a short pair of denim shorts and a cropped white t-shirt, her abs on clear display, and a pink bow headband in her hair.

"Mommy," Nelly whined as she reached for the paci, Samantha giving in to her cute puppy dog eyes and pushing it into her mouth.

"Can we do that lego set together, Mommy?" Nelly asked, taking a bite of the Salmon Samantha had made for dinner.

"Yep, a little later. Mommy wants to watch the news first. Come and cuddle with me," Samatha said. Nelly got up from the table and took her plate over to the couch and sat on the floor between Samantha's thighs as Samantha played with her hair.

"This is really scary," Nelly said as they watched the segment about terrorists. Nelly got up and walked back to the kitchen and put her plate in the dishwasher before coming back and snuggling into Samantha. Nelly distracted herself by playing with Samantha's breasts, enjoying making her nipples hard and lazily nursing. Samantha absent-mindedly rocked Nelly and patted her thigh until the news ended. Laughing, Samantha looked down at Nelly, who had fallen asleep with her nipple in her mouth. Slightly moving, Nelly's eyes opened sleepily, and Samantha rolled her onto her back and pulled a fluffy blanket around Nelly, tucking it in as she went to shower and change into her pajamas.

"Mommy," Samantha heard from her bedroom, smiling when she saw Nelly at the door.

"Yes, little one?" Samantha asked as she pulled her soft robe around her and tightened it. Nelly reached her arms out to her, and Samantha wondered how she had gotten so lucky.

"Can we do lego now?" Nelly asked as Samatha looked at her expectantly.

"I think you are forgetting a very important word, young lady," Samantha said, seeing the mischief in Nelly's eyes.

"I don't think I am," Nelly replied, causing Samantha to laugh.

"Well now, I guess Mommy has to remind her little girl to use manners," Samantha said, taking Nelly's wrist in her hand and pulling her over her lap. Nelly was no match for Samantha, and she secured her hands behind her back and her legs down with one thigh.

"Where do you think you are going, little girl? Mommy has you now," Samantha teased, as she began to run her fingernails over Nelly's bare skin, giving her goosebumps. Samantha and Nelly had spoken at length about the type of punishments that they would both be comfortable with, and Samantha was excited to be able to test out one on Nelly.

"Oh, I'm not going to spank you, honey," Samantha said, causing Nelly to stop moving, her mind racing at what could come next. Samantha pulled Nelly's pants down before she spat into her hand and placed it against Nelly's pussy, spreading her lips quickly and rubbing her clit forcefully.

"Mommy is going to force orgasm after orgasm on you, sugar. You're going to be wrecked once I am done with you, and all you are going to be able to do is moan the word please until I am satisfied," Samantha said, using a stern voice Nelly hadn't heard before. Nelly hadn't thought the Samantha would try this punishment out of something she thought was only mild disobedience, but as Samantha rubbed her clit, she moved her hips in time to Samantha's touch.

"What are you doing, baby girl. Mommy hasn't said you could move," Samantha said, causing Nelly to moan as she tried to stay still, her pussy contracting with desire, her thighs flexing. Samantha fucked Nelly agonizingly slow, making Nelly groan in frustration for fifteen minutes before letting her cum, only to continue her onslaught, refusing to give her any recovery time.

"What do you need to say to make Mommy happy, baby girl?" Samantha asked.

"Please, Mommy," Nelly breathlessly said, dragging out the words as another orgasm washed over her body.

"That's right. From now until I tell you, they are the only words allowed to escape that pretty little mouth," Samantha said as she placed her hand in Nelly's hair, grabbing a fist full and pulling her head back as she fucked the girl lying over her lap.

"Please, Mommy," Nelly begged, involuntarily bucking her hips violently as she came again only to be continually fucked.

"Good girl," Samantha replied, leaving her clit alone and sticking two fingers into Nelly's wet pussy and hearing her gasp as she was filled. Samantha pumped her fingers in and out of Nelly until her forearm ached, causing the girl to rest limply over her thighs as cum poured from her pussy.

"Please, Mommy," Nelly wearily moaned, almost calling red just as Samantha pulled out of her and turned her around, so she was looking up at Samantha and getting squished into her breasts.

"Don't make Mommy have to teach you that lesson again," Samantha warned as she pinched Nelly's nipples through her shirt until she flinched.

"Yes, Mommy," Nelly said, her eyes glazed over and her

body exhausted.

"Good girl. Let's get you cleaned up," Samantha said, lifting Nelly in her arms and taking her to the bathroom to shower.

"And because you have behaved like such a baby not knowing how to say please, you can wear a diaper tonight to help you remember," Samantha said as she lay Nelly down on her bed.

"But I'm not that little, Mommy," Nelly whined as wriggled and fought Samantha, losing as Samantha successfully diapered her and pulled on her pajamas.

"I don't know about that, you look pretty little right about now," Samantha said, picking Nelly up and carrying her to the living room and put her down near the table where her lego box was and watched as she pouted.

"Don't complain about it, or I'll make you wet it too," Samantha warned, making Nelly's eyes go wide and look away.

"That's better. Now, can Mommy help you make this?" Samantha asked, pulling Nelly into her lap and brushing her hair from her eyes.

"Yes, please, Mommy," Nelly replied, the mischief in her voice, not escaping Samantha as she helped her open the box.

Chapter 7

"Baby girl, Mommy is home," Samantha called from the door of their new house. Samantha and Nelly had moved into an apartment just outside of the city together. It wasn't the luxury penthouse suite Samantha was used to, but it was more beautiful than any place Nelly had ever lived. Holly and Sasha, Nelly's golden retriever puppy who wasn't such a puppy anymore, got along, which made them all living together simple and easy.

"Hey, Mommy. I'm in here," Nelly yelled from the kitchen. Samantha rolled her eyes, wondering where 'in here' was as she hung up her bag on the wall hook and began uncuffing her cufflinks.

"Oh baby," Samantha said as she walked into the kitchen to find that Nelly had been busy, from the looks of things, for hours.

"I wanted to make you dinner, and dessert," she said proudly. Samantha rolled her sleeves up and looked around the kitchen.

"And you left Mommy with the washing up?" Samantha teased, grabbing Nelly and kissing her passionately before holding her in her arms as she looked over to the dining room table and saw the delicious spread Nelly had prepared.

"So we have carrot soup with thick-cut bread to start, roast duck and seasonal vegetables as main and for dessert," Nelly said, pausing and leaning over to the fridge to show Samantha the chocolate cake she had made.

"Mudcake!" she said proudly. Samantha kissed her cheek.

"You are so wonderful," she said as she walked over to the table and sat down.

"How was your day?" Nelly asked as they began to eat. Samantha rolled her eyes.

"Everyone there is a complete idiot, and I hate them all. But apart from that, it was fine. What did you get up too?" Samantha replied, noticing that Nelly had already fed the dogs.

"How long have you been home?" She added, wondering how Nelly could have had time to pull this off in the thirty-minute time difference between Nelly getting home and Samantha finishing work.

"Yeah, so, I kinda wanted to talk to you about that. I've changed jobs. It just wasn't working for me anymore, and I wanted something that is going to make me feel happy and not caged in," Nelly began to explain. Samantha wondered why Nelly hadn't talked to her about her feelings, but she stayed quiet. In the six months they had known each other, Samantha had grown to learn that Nelly liked to make a move before she announced it.

"I saw that the music store down the road from my bus stop was looking for admin staff. So I went in there yesterday afternoon and asked a few questions, and they said they would be happy to take me on and yeah. I signed the contract this morning. I went into work to give them my two weeks' notice, but the boss was so mad she made me take my holidays instead, so I was home by like ten and decided that I would make you this great dinner," Nelly said, making Samantha smile.

"Well, here's to you, my love," Samantha said, raising her glass of wine and toasting to Nelly.

"You're not mad?" Nelly asked. Samantha frowned.

"Why would I be mad? This is your life, baby girl. You can make any decision you want in it. Mommy is just here to help you when you need me, but you didn't need me for this. You put your big girl pants on, and I am so proud of you. I am especially proud that you cooked! I might have to get you in that kitchen a little more regularly," Samantha laughed.

"But I think dessert will have to wait, honey. I am so full, and I want to fix up your nails tonight. I can't have my pretty girl getting around town looking unloved, and that chipped color is driving me crazy. Mommy is going to have a shower, you clean up as much as you can, and I'll do your nails once I'm out, alright?" Samantha said, getting up from the table and walking over to Nelly, kissing her on her forehead before disappearing into the bathroom.

There was something about Samantha that made Nelly want to please her. It was unlike anything she had ever experienced in the past, and she smiled to herself when she finished putting away the dishes just as Samantha came out of the bathroom.

"Baby, I didn't expect you to get all of it done. Oh, you are such a good girl for Mommy," Samantha said as she fawned over Nelly, loving the way Nelly snuggled between her breasts.

"I was thinking. Maybe I could get black, please, Mommy?" Nelly asked as Samantha, and her sat down in the nook they had turned into a nail salon set-up. The nail salon where Samantha used to get her nails done had closed down, and she had been unable to find a studio she liked, so she had gone out and bought everything she needed to do their nails at home. She had even made Nelly watch hours upon hours of nail tutorials to make sure that she could do nails as well.

"Really? I was thinking more a sweet baby pink?" Samantha teased. Nelly just rolled her eyes and giggled.

"Mommy, I'm too big for baby pink," Nelly said, reaching for the black. Samantha took a moment to look at Nelly in her grungy little outfit and smiled.

"Well, you are allowed to be too big for baby pink, but you aren't allowed to get too big that you don't want these anymore," Samantha said, shaking her breasts in Nelly's face making her giggle before she began to do Nelly's nails.

"Do you think that we could go to the park on the weekend? I heard there is a really nice market that's held every Sunday. Maybe we could pick up some yummy food and have a picnic?" Nelly suggested as she watched Samantha.

"Yeah, we could. I was hoping to unpack a few more boxes, though, so it just depends on how much we get done, honey," Samantha replied as she concentrated.

"Ok," Nelly replied, just as Samantha finished up.

"There, all done, baby girl. Now, Mommy wants a little quiet time tonight. Do you want to do your sticker by number book or go online for a while?" Samantha asked. She and Nelly had decided that they needed to restrict Nelly's screen time after Samantha had woken up to Nelly still being online at 3 am when they had gone to bed at 10 pm the night before.

"Online!" Nelly half squealed, wrapping her arms around Samantha, who held her lovingly before letting her go.

"Alright, see you in a little while," Samantha said as Nelly bounded off into her own little space in the apartment. There was an outdoor space that came with their apartment, and Nelly had transformed it into something like a fairy garden. There were strung up fairy lights and bean bags and comfy blankets, and she settled in with a hot chocolate for a few hours of mind-numbing online entertainment. She had often wondered what Samantha was up to during her quiet times, even having snuck in a few times to look at her without her knowing. But she would always just do the same thing, sit in her chair by the fire and sip Scotch. It wasn't that she was a big drinker, but every now and then, she just wanted to be left alone. Nelly had been grateful when Samantha had told her that it wasn't personal; it was just something she needed to do to unwind from a day sometimes. Nelly had thought that maybe she was texting someone else, but Samantha had put that fear to rest by taking her lock off her phone and allowing Nelly to check her phone and emails whenever she felt the need. When Samantha had told her friends that Nelly checks her phone and emails, they had been concerned, saying how she should be allowed to have her privacy, but Samantha just laughed. What was so private that she was doing? Getting emails from the juice bar where she had a loyalty card telling her she can have a free birthday juice? Samantha had explained that Nelly needed more reassurance that she wasn't going to get hurt and that she was more than happy to give it to her.

"What are you up too, baby doll?" Samantha said as she sauntered outside to were Nelly was sitting. Nelly looked up just as Samantha came to sit down next to her and wrapped a blanket around herself.

"This is sobering. It is freezing out here!" Samantha said the alcohol she had felt pumping through her veins only moments ago by the nice warm fire slowly disappearing into memory.

"I haven't noticed," Nelly replied, looking at her fingers and noticing how blue they were.

"And that is why Mommy doesn't let you go online whenever you want," Samantha said, taking Nelly's phone and putting it in her pocket.

"How's everyone?" Samantha asked. Nelly didn't talk about her family very much, and her friends were the people she worked with.

"Fine. Nobody is doing anything particularly interesting. Although some people from my old job are thinking of going out tomorrow night and they've invited me. I said I'd see if we had any plans first," Nelly said, amusing Samantha.

"Imagine if you told them the truth, that you had to check with Mommy to see if you had been a good enough girl to go out," Samantha teased, making Nelly laugh.

"Yeah, baby girl, go. Do you need me to drop you off or pick you up?" Samantha asked, Nelly just shaking her head no.

"Ok then, well, I'll be here if you change your mind, ok, princess," Samantha added before standing back up and taking Nelly by the hand as they went inside.

"I don't know if I want to let you out of the house after all," Samantha said as she looked at Nelly walk into the living room. Samantha had decided to order take out Chinese for dinner and put her chopsticks down as she saw Nelly stand in from of her.

"You think I'm pretty, Mommy," Nelly asked, teasing Samantha by sitting down on her lap and wrapping her arms around Samantha's neck.

"Yes, I do," Samantha said, feeling her pussy tighten with desire. Samantha had bought Nelly a pair of pink heels, and she had teamed them with a sparkly silver dress that stopped just under her ass and dropped low between her breasts. Her hair had been straightened and pulled back with a sparkly silver clip, and her make up was natural yet alluring.

"I've got a little bit of time before I need to go, Mommy," Nelly whispered in Samantha's ear, running her hands through her hair and kissing her affectionately as she felt Samantha reposition her. Her hand falling in between Nelly's thighs, brushed her pussy, and her other hand supported her neck, and Nelly tilted her head back.

"Gets you every time, little one. Not such a big girl now,

are you? You're Mommy's little plaything," Samantha said, pulling Nelly's thong to the side and sliding her fingers up and down the girl's wet slit.

"Please, Mommy," Nelly begged, igniting the fire in Samantha's eyes. She continued to stroke the girl, who wriggled on her lap, desperate to be given release.

"You do know how to be a good girl for, Mommy, don't you?" Samantha asked as she pushed her two fingers into Nelly, rubbing her g-spot and making her begin to moan with her eyes closed.

"Tell Mommy, you like it," Samantha said as she felt Nelly dangerously close to orgasm. Nelly bit her bottom lip and began to play with her tits, moaning and moving her body on Samantha's lap.

"I like it, Mommy. I want it so bad, please, Mommy," Nelly begged.

"No, you're not there yet. Mommy is going to make you wait a little longer. I know your body now, baby girl, you can't trick, Mommy," Samantha teased, quickening her thrusts just enough to drive Nelly wild but not enough to give her release.

"Please, Mommy, let me cum, please," Nelly yelled as a banging came from the door. Samantha placed her hand over the girl's mouth as she took her over the edge, making her squirt and cover Samantha's hand in her pussy juices. The banging continued much to Samantha's amusement.

"Just a minute," Samantha yelled out, happy when the

banging stopped as she lifted up her girl and led her to the bathroom.

"Mommy," Nelly said in her groggy, afterglow making Samantha giggle.

"Baby girl, you've got a big night ahead of you, you can't fall asleep now," Samantha said as she cleaned Nelly up all the while Nelly only wanting to snuggle into Samantha's huge breasts.

"But Mommy," Nelly murmured, Samantha finally giving in and placing her nipple in Nelly's mouth.

"You can nurse when you bring your no doubt drunken ass home to Mommy, ok, baby girl?" Samantha said, fixing Nelly's hair before she took her nipple out of her mouth and pulled her singlet back up.

"I don't even want to go now," Nelly half whined as she walked to the door.

"You will once you get there. Have fun, little one. Remember to text Mommy if it's all too much," Samantha said as she playfully spanked Nelly's ass as she walked out of the door.

Samantha was right. Nelly did get in the mood the moment she had her first drink. The music was loud, her friends and her look glorious, and the dance floor had just enough people to make it fun, but not enough to make it crowded. As Nelly dance, she felt how the music took her away to a place she hadn't been in a long time, and she smiled to herself, thinking about how great her life had become.

It was a few hours off dawn when she reached into her purse to take out her phone. Her friends wanted to stay out later than she had thought they would, and after an hour of trying to convince one of them to come back with her so they could leave together, she had lucked out. Taking her phone out, she hoped that Samantha wouldn't be mad to get woken up.

"Hey," Nelly slurred, realizing just as she was going to say, Mommy, that she was in a public place.

"I was wondering when I would get this call," Samantha sleepily replied, somewhat glad Nelly had called.

"Yeah, so um, I thought I'd be home by now, but they don't want to come home, but I kinda really do, but I don't want to go by myself," Nelly began to ramble, getting cut off by Samantha.

"Send me your location and then stay there. Mommy is coming to get you, little girl," Samantha said, getting out of bed and grabbing a hoodie as she made her way to the door.

"You're the best," Nelly replied, before hanging up and sending Samantha her location.

"Oh, I know," Samantha said to herself as she whistled for the dogs to follow her.

"Nelly?" A familiar voice asked as Nelly opened her eyes and swayed against a brick wall.

"Oh fuck off," Nelly whispered to herself as Wendy's reflection was in her face as she waited for Samantha.

"Sweetheart, are you ok?" Wendy asked as she looked at Nelly. Nelly began to walk away from her, only to have her grab her upper arm and grip it firmly.

"Where do you think you're going?" Wendy asked, holding Nelly firmly in place.

"Let me go," Nelly said as she tried to pull away.

"Cute dress," Wendy said, letting Nelly's arm go. Nelly knew that Samantha would be there any moment, and she also knew that she had sent her location to Samantha. However, in her drunken state, she hadn't thought of the possibility of ringing Samantha and telling her what was going on and to meet her somewhere else.

"I heard you don't work at the travel agents anymore," Wendy said, standing next to Nelly, who had her arms crossed over her chest.

"What do you want?!" Nelly yelled, turning to face Wendy. Wendy got off the wall and placed an arm on either side of Nelly, pressed her body against hers, and pinned her there.

"I want you," Wendy said before kissing Nelly passionately, just as Samantha pulled up to see. Nelly bit Wendy's lip, causing her to pull away and reach out of hit her, just as Samantha grabbed her arm, which was in the air.

"I think you better get the fuck out of here," Samantha

said to Wendy, who looked angry and confused.

"So, this is who you replaced me with?! Really, I am way hotter than her!" Wendy yelled at Nelly, who sort comfort in Samantha's arms.

"She always ruins everything," Nelly murmured against Samantha, who led her back to the car.

"She's not hotter than you either, Mommy," Nelly said, the fear in her eyes that she would be rejected, not something Samantha had seen for many months all but broke her heart.

"I know she's not, sugar," Samantha said, winking at Nelly and locking the door before walking back to Wendy.

"If you ever come near her again," Samantha began to say before Wendy cut her off.

"You'll what?" Wendy replied. It was true that Wendy was younger and leaner than Samantha, her blonde hair shining in the moonlight.

"I'll fucking finish what I'm about to start," Samantha said as she dropped her fist into Wendy's cheek before she turned and walked back to the car.

"She won't bother you anymore, honey bun," Samantha said to Nelly as she drove them home.

"Apart from the end, did you have a good night? Your photos are cute," Samantha said calmly as Nelly clung onto her arm.

"Yeah, it was good. She kissed me, you know. Like I'll understand if you want to break up or something," Nelly said, looking up at Samantha with her sad puppy dog eyes.

"Baby, she didn't kiss you, she assaulted you. There is a big difference," Samantha replied, easing Nelly's mind that she would be left heartbroken.

"And no, Mommy doesn't want to break up with you or something, ok? So just get that thought right out of your head," Samantha said to Nelly, kissing her forehead.

"Don't you think you'll get in trouble for punching her?" Nelly asked as they pulled into their car space. Samantha smiled, there were a few things Nelly still didn't know about her, and one of those things was that her family were the type that really shouldn't be messed with.

"No, I think it'll be ok. I don't think she wants to have anything more to do with us," Samantha replied, walking Nelly into the house and getting her a glass of water.

"Shower and bed, Mommy?" Nelly asked sleepily.

"Come on, lovely girl," Samantha said, picking Nelly up as she began to fall asleep and took her into the bathroom. Samantha helped Nelly get undressed and quickly washed and blow-dried her hair before dressing her in a dino onesie and tucking her up in bed.

"I don't think my tummy can handle the feel of any more liquid, Mommy," Nelly said with her eyes closed when she felt Samantha's nipple pressing against her lip.

"Then don't suckle, but it's going in your mouth, honey. Close your eyes now, go to sleep, baby," Samantha said lovingly as Nelly obeyed her like the good girl Samantha had trained her to become.

Chapter 9

A knock came at the door the next morning, earlier than Samantha would have cared for.

"Shh, Mommy's got it," Samantha said as Nelly opened her eyes and blinked sleepily. Samantha got dressed in her best as the knocking became louder, causing Nelly to become curious.

"Mommy, I can get the door if you want?" Nelly asked as she saw Samantha put on her best coat and heels.

"Baby. You know the box that I told you never to open. If I ring you, I need you to open it and find the piece of paper with the name Joe on it and the phone number. I need you to ring that number and tell them, 'Samantha needs your help,' and then hang up. Don't wait for a response, don't say any pleasantries, alright?" Samantha said, causing Nelly no end of confusion. Samantha kissed Nelly and ran her fingers through her hair as she sighed and walked to the door, opening it to see that it wasn't who she thought it was at all. Samantha had assumed that Wendy had called the police and that they had come to charge her with assault. But it was just a girl scout wondering if she wanted to buy any cookies. Samantha laughed and handed the girl a ten-dollar bill before closing the door.

"You need to talk," Nelly said from behind the door, taking Samantha by surprise.

"That was some badass hustler shit you just said to me. Who is Joe? What the fuck is going on, Samantha?" Nelly said, causing Samantha to stop in her tracks and look at Nelly the way she hated being looked at. It meant she was going to be punished.

"Nelly. I am going to warn you one time," Samantha replied, somewhat understanding that Nelly had the right to have her questions answered. Nelly sighed, trying to figure out how to asked her questions and still be within the agreed-upon rules of their relationship.

"Mommy, I'm scared. All that stuff you just told me, it sounded like something from a gangster movie," Nelly said, sitting on the bed and watching Samantha undress.

"Well. My family, they know some good lawyers, can we keep it at that, honey? I don't have much to do with them for a reason, and I want to keep you out of their world," Samantha replied, causing Nelly to all but lose her shit in excitement. She got up and ran to the kitchen, took a notepad and pen from the bench, and ran back into the bedroom where Samantha was lying naked in bed under the covers.

Is your family in the mob?! Nelly wrote down in her scribbliest writing and passed it to Samantha. Samantha rolled her eyes and pulled Nelly under the covers with her.

What mob? Samantha wrote back before putting her hand over Nelly's mouth as she opened it to speak. Samantha looked Nelly dead in the eye until she calmed down.

"And that is all we are ever going to talk about it," Samantha said with a tone which told Nelly more than she needed to know.

"Ok, Mommy," Nelly replied, settling back into bed.

"That's right," Samantha said more to herself than to Nelly, who was already dreaming in Samantha's arms.

Samantha and Nelly fell into a predictable routine of 9-5 working hours, afternoon sport, and Thursday night shopping trips. They took the dogs on mountain hikes on the weekends, and Samantha began to introduce Nelly to her friends over Sunday brunches by the river. Life was easy, it was calm, it was happy, and for the first time in forever, Nelly wasn't trying to fight it. She embraced the glamorous lifestyle that she and Samantha were creating and loved every moment of it.

"Mommy's home, princess," Samantha called from the front door. It was Thursday, and Nelly was excited because there was a new pair of shoes she had been looking forward to buying all week.

"I'm just getting dressed, Mommy," Nelly called from the bedroom. Samantha kicked off her heels and grabbed a beer from the fridge before walking into the bedroom to find Nelly struggling with the zip at the back of her dress.

"Can I help?" Samantha asked, putting her beer down and zipping up Nelly's dress.

"Thanks, Mommy," Nelly said, kissing her affectionately. Turning around and smiling at Samantha, Nelly looked down at the dress she had bought last week.

"Yeah you're cute, and don't you know it," Samantha said as she eyed Nelly.

"I was hoping we could go to the mall a little earlier tonight, Mommy. There's this pair of sneakers I am really looking forward to buying," Nelly said, fixing the clip in her hair.

"Oh, about that. A friend of mine from college is in town and was wondering if we could meet up tonight for drinks? I know we sort of have a plan of what we do, but how about, if it's the only thing we are getting tonight, we get them on the way?" Samantha asked, watching as Nelly thought.

"Yeah, ok. Is what I'm wearing, ok?" She asked. Samantha's friends were always model beautiful with stories of jet setting lifestyles, and for some reason, no matter how friendly they were, Nelly always felt left out. Like she was watching a movie, that she was just a spectator to the conversation.

"You always look so gorgeous, baby girl, what you are wearing is fine," Samantha said before walking into the bathroom to get ready.

"Don't be nervous, she's really lovely," Samantha whispered to Nelly as they approached the bar.

"I'm not nervous," Nelly snapped back, proving Samantha's point.

"Mmmhmm," Samantha replied, before greeting the other woman. She was tall, red-haired with fair skin and green eyes that shone when they landed on Nelly.

"You must be Nelly, Samantha has told me so many wonderful things about you," the woman gushed.

"Nelly, this is Amanda, Amanda, Nelly," Samantha said, sitting down and signaling to the waitress.

"Let's get tequila, for old times sake," Samantha said, ordering three shots and three beers as chasers. Nelly smiled despite herself. She didn't really want to like Amanda, but she was so kind and gentle, taking Nelly's hand and sitting down next to her, almost ignoring Samantha, who just sipped her beer and relaxed.

"So Sammy tells me you two met at a dog park? And that you picked her up!?" Amanda asked, the surprise evident in her voice.

"Sammy," Nelly laughed. She rarely even called Samantha, Samantha, so to hear her with a nickname made her laugh.

"Yeah, I bet you are just used to calling her Mommy," Amanda said, Nelly, freezing instantly and going red.

"Oh, it's alright, hun. I'm a Mommy too. I know how it

works," Amanda said, trying to reassure Nelly, but her guard was going back up, and both Samantha and Amanda could see it.

"Come here, baby," Samantha said, knowing that Nelly needed to be closer to her than to Amanda.

"Shy?" Amanda asked as Samantha wrapped her arm around Nelly.

"She gets a little wary of new people. Some people have mistreated her," Samantha said, kissing Nelly's forehead. She passed Nelly her phone and smiled when she snuggled up to her as Nelly began playing games online.

"Cute, though," Amanda replied, Samantha just smiling before she directed the conversation in a different direction. The night dragged on with Nelly jumping in and out of the conversation, Samantha giving her money to go and buy a burger from another place in town, and Amanda slowly gaining Nelly's trust. Towards the end of the evening, Amanda suggested that they have chocolate cake, and it was Nelly's pleading eyes that won Samantha over in the end.

"How long are you in town for?" Nelly asked as they shared the slice of cake.

"Three nights. I'm a flight attendant, so I never stay in the same place for too long. I like it, but it means that my home life is always a bit of a mess," Amanda confessed, looking at Samantha.

"Yeah, but you could have from all over the world and

just keep them on a rotation," Nelly cheekily suggested, coping a look of Samantha and making Amanda laugh.

"You're trouble," she playfully said, making Nelly giggle.

"I must admit, I have done that a few times, but I am more ready to settle down now. I am jealous of you Sammy, you've got such a sweet, little girl, here," Amanda said, feeding Nelly the last bite of cake.

"And doesn't she know it," Samantha added, reaching out to thumb away the chocolate sauce from Nelly's bottom lip.

"Where are you staying? Do you want to hang out at ours?" Samantha said as she noticed the wait staff beginning to tidy the bar for closing.

"I can't tonight. But if you are free tomorrow night? We could start with drinks at yours?" Amanda suggested, Nelly, nodding her head before Samantha had even replied.

"I think that's a yes," Samantha laughed as they got up to leave.

"You're a tease, do you know that? Samantha said to Nelly on the way home. Nelly was busy looking at her new sneakers in their box and looked up at Samantha, not having heard what she said.

"Huh?" Nelly replied. Samantha looked down on her confused face and beamed.

"I said you're a little tease. Don't play games with

Amanda, she will think you are trying to seduce her, and she'll always take the bait," Samantha said as Nelly placed her hand on her thigh.

"Just like you did, Mommy?" Nelly teased, making Samantha laugh but roll her eyes.

"We haven't even spoken about adding people to the mix. Is that something you would be down for?" Samantha asked, Nelly's face becoming serious.

"I don't know, that seems like a lot. I think I would be down for it if you are. Maybe not sex, but defs some play with dynamic stuff," Nelly replied. Samantha hadn't realized that she was hoping that Nelly would say no sex and smiled to herself.

"I'm glad you said that. I don't feel comfortable sharing you sexually, but I can handle the power play stuff too. I'll let Amanda know that you might be in little space when she comes over tomorrow if that's cool?" Samantha asked. Nelly thought about it, before nodding.

"Maybe she can help me with my sticker by number picture?!" Nelly exclaimed as Samantha continued to drive them both home.

Chapter 10

"Why are you so stressed out, Mommy?" Nelly asked as she sat on the bed, watching Samantha get increasingly flustered.

"Because I hate everything that I own," Samantha said as she pulled off the shirt she had on and threw it angrily on the bed. Nelly wondered why she was so worried, she'd never seen Samantha loose control before, and it made her nervous. She got up and slowly made her way over to Samantha, looking at her before going to the cupboard and taking out a pair of tailored black jeans, matching heels, and a thin cashmere top, passing it shyly to Samantha.

"What about this?" Nelly asked, making Samantha calm down and see how she had unnerved Nelly.

"Thank you, baby," Samantha replied, pulling Nelly into her arms and kissing the top of her head, letting Nelly cuddle before she let her go.

"Amanda is used to me having a particular lifestyle and," Samantha began making Nelly blush.

"And this isn't good enough for her?" Nelly said, trying to figure out what Samantha was going to say.

"I'm not ashamed or embarrassed about our place,

honey. It's just that I don't want Amanda to look down at me. I have known her for decades, and she can be a bit of a show-off," Samantha tried to explain. Nelly just nodded her head. She could see that Amanda liked to have the world's attention.

"Well, if she is mean, Mommy, I'll just bite her," Nelly said, playfully biting into Samantha's arm.

"You will not!" Samantha replied, spanking Nelly's ass and making her run out of the room, giggling down the hall.

A knock came twenty minutes later from the door, and Nelly got up to get it.

"Let me," Samantha replied, eyeing Nelly to sit back down where she had been working on her artwork. Samantha usually let Nelly wear what her heart desired, but tonight Samantha had chosen her outfit. She and Nelly had fussed over the bow Samantha wanted in her hair. Nelly wanted to wear her skinny jeans and a metallic loose fitting singlet with her black faux fur and leather jacket, but Samantha had other ideas. So Nelly had ended up in her skinny jeans, baby pink hoodie and matching bow. Samantha had promised that if she was a good girl, then she would be allowed to wear her new sneakers and maybe the jacket, and that was the only reason why Nelly was trying so hard not to pout.

"Hello Amanda," Samantha greeted from the door as Amanda walked inside. Samantha took her coat and bag and hung them on one of the wall hooks before inviting her through to the living room.

"Hey cutie," Amanda said, standing behind Nelly, who bent her head back and looked up at her.

"Hi Amanda," Nelly said before going back to her art. Amanda smiled and looked around the apartment.

"Did you move in with her, Sammy?" Amanda asked as Samantha handed her a drink.

"No, we moved into it together," Nelly called from the living room, making Samantha smirk.

"She's very independent and didn't want me to just put her up in the penthouse," Samantha explained as they walked back into the living room and sat on the couch. The fireplace warmed the space, and the crackling of the fire mixed with the taste of whiskey felt peaceful.

"It's actually really lovely," Amanda said approvingly, unbeknownst to her easing Samantha's fears.

"What are you making there, Nelly?" Amanda asked, leaning forward and eyeing Nelly expecting a response.

"It's a tiger," Nelly replied, looking back at Samantha, wanting approval.

"It's very good," Amanda added, seeing the detail and care Nelly had taken. Nelly continued to work on her artwork before Samantha leaned down and pulled her up onto the couch and into her arms.

"What do we say when someone gives us a compliment, baby girl?" Samantha asked as Nelly leaned her body into

Samantha's but turned her head to face Amanda.

"Thank you," Nelly softly said before burying her face into Samantha's cleavage and sucking her thumb.

"She's feeling a little bit, little tonight," Samantha explained as Amanda watched somewhat longingly.

"Oh, I can see that," Amanda replied, reaching out and stroking Nelly's back affectionately.

"I need to finish getting ready, would you mind watching her for a moment," Samantha said as she kissed Nelly's forehead and placed her back on the floor.

"Not at all," Amanda said, the eagerness in her voice evident. Samantha winked at Nelly, who smirked back at her as she disappeared into their bedroom.

"Want to play a game?" Nelly asked, walking over to where she and Samantha kept a deck of cards.

"Like, poker?" Amanda teased, making Nelly laugh.

"I was thinking more like, snap," Nelly said, taking out the cards and passing them to Amanda. She shuffled them, dealt them out, and as they began to play, Amanda snapped the cards, Nelly's hand on top of hers a fraction too slow.

"You'll have to do better than that, baby girl," Amanda laughed as she took the cards, and they began to play once more. Samantha could hear the laughter coming from the living room as she finished her makeup and sprayed perfume. She and Nelly had decided that they would let Amanda in on the non-sexual side of the dynamic for the evening, and by all accounts, it seemed to be going well. She turned her head and looked out onto the scene, which played out in front of her and smiled, just as she heard Amanda's hand come down hard on Nelly's.

"Ouch!" Nelly squealed, Amanda's eyes going wide as she realized that she had brought her hand down far too hard on top of Nelly's.

"Oh, sweetie, I'm sorry, are you ok?" Amanda said as Nelly frowned and pouted, trying to be ok.

"You've got to be tough if you want to play with the big girls, honey," Samantha said, walking out and going to the fridge to get an icepack.

"I am tough," Nelly said, slightly insulted. Samantha walked over to where Nelly was sitting and picked her up. She sat her on her lap and rocked her gently as she wrapped the icepack around her hand. Amanda got up and poured herself and Samantha another drink before joining them on the couch.

"Maybe we should have stuck with coloring," Amanda said, surprised when Nelly reached for her. She looked at Samantha, who smiled kindly at her as she took Nelly in her arms and wrapped them around her. Amanda smelt like jasmine and something else that Nelly couldn't figure out, and she snuggled into the nook of Amanda's neck.

"Oh, I could just hold you forever," Amanda said as she melted into Nelly, Samantha reaching out and stroking Nelly's cheek.

"She is a sweetheart. That's for sure," Samantha replied, taking Nelly's paci and placing it in her mouth as she closed her eyes and relaxed into Amanda's embrace.

"We are going to be late for our reservation if we stay here, though," Samantha added, Nelly opening her eyes as her tummy rumbled.

"And I think, little miss, needs something to eat and soon!" Amanda laughed, rubbing Nelly's tummy before she could stop herself.

"But first," Nelly said, ripping her bow headband from her hair and messing her hair up so that it had that flowy effect she liked so much. Samantha laughed and got up to get her sneakers and jacket.

"I told her that she had to wear it before we left the house because she just looks so divine in it," Samantha explained, passing Nelly her things.

Nelly held both Samantha's and Amanda's hand on the way to the restaurant, only letting go once they walked inside.

"See, Mommy wasn't going to let you look out of place," Samantha whispered to Nelly as they sat down. Nelly held Samantha's hand under the table and squeezed it gently. It had been fun so far, and Nelly liked that Amanda never tried to overstep.

As the night went on, Samantha could see that Amanda had

taken a shine to Nelly, but in true Nelly style, once she knew that Amanda liked her, she had begun to pull away. Amanda had decided to let any thoughts she had of further play go and turned her attention to the waitress, causing Samantha and Nelly to laugh at the obvious flirting which occurred between the two of them. After dinner, Amanda excused her self and went outside, explaining that she needed to take the phone call, which had interrupted their evening. Samantha and Nelly turned toward each other and began talking while they waited for Amanda to return.

"Hey, yeah, I am here with both of them," Amanda said down the phone.

"No, I can tell you for certain that they don't have any idea," she added, answering the person on the other end of the line.

"Well, they don't live there anymore. So it won't be that difficult," Amanda said.

"Good," said Wendy, on the other line.

"What do you want me to do then?" Amanda replied. Wendy had stalked Samantha online after she convinced herself that Samantha had been the reason she couldn't get Nelly back. She had found Amanda in Samantha's friends' list and contacted her after learning that she had a large amount of gambling debt. Wendy had resolved herself to the plan that if she couldn't have Nelly, that she was going to take her for everything that she and Samantha had, and was going to rob them. Amanda had agreed to help her after Wendy had promised to clear the debt and that no harm would come to either Samantha and Nelly. Amanda knew that Samantha was wealthy and assumed that she would simply go out and buy everything new.

"All you have to do is send me their address, and keep them out for the next two hours," Wendy hissed down the phone.

"Fine," Amanda replied, ending the phone call and sending her their address. She inhaled sharply before nodding her head as she thought about where they could all go for the next two hours.

Chapter 11

"All good?" Samantha asked as Amanda sat back down. Nelly had gone to get the dessert menus.

"Yeah. Hey, why don't we do something a little unexpected and take Nelly to the movies tonight?" Amanda suggested, hoping that Samantha would agree to the idea.

"I don't know. It's already pretty late," Samantha replied, looking at the time on her phone.

"But I don't know when I will see you again. Come on, my treat," Amanda pressed just as Nelly sat back down.

"I like treats," she said, looking up at Samantha.

"Amanda wants to take you to the movies," Samantha said, smiling at the joy in Nelly's eyes as she looked from Amanda to Samantha.

"So, is it a yes from your Mommy then?" Amanda teased, looking at Samantha, who just rolled her eyes.

"Yeah. Let's skip dessert here and get treats when we are at the cinema," she said, paying for dinner before getting up. Nelly looked online for movie options as they walked the four blocks to the cinema, deciding on a thriller which surprised Samantha.

"You are going to be so scared I can just see you all over

me while I'm trying to watch it," she said, taking her phone from Nelly's hands.

"Well, if you don't want to cuddle her, I certainly will," Amanda teased, running her fingers through Nelly's hair.

They arrived at the cinema, ordered their tickets and snacks, and went inside. There was only one other couple that sat in the middle of the audience, so Samantha directed Nelly and Amanda to some seats in the back.

"This is so exciting," Nelly said, clapping her hands.

"Shh," came a whisper from both Samantha and Amanda, only making Nelly laugh. They sat down, Nelly in the middle, and it didn't take more than ten minutes before Nelly was snuggling into Samantha's side, the suspense almost too much for her to handle.

"It's ok, baby girl. Mommy has got you, this is all just make-believe," Samantha lovingly whispered as she put up the armrest so that Nelly could be even closer to her. Amanda sneakily looked at the time. Right now, she knew that Wendy would be in their apartment, watching as furniture was loaded into the removalist truck. She thought about the debt that she would be free from and tried to rid herself of the guilt of doing this to her friend.

It's just money, and Sammy has heaps of it, Amanda told herself for the hundredth time as the movie reached its climax. Nelly jumped and burried her face into Samantha's side, Samantha wrapping her arm around the girl and patting her affectionately for the rest of the film.

"So I might have made a mistake," Nelly giggled as they walked home. Nelly refused to let go of Samantha's hand and held on firmly whenever they passed something which reminded her of the movie they had just seen.

"You're quiet," Samantha said to Amanda. Amanda just smiled at her.

"I am more tired than I thought I would be," she lied. The truth was that she was being eaten up inside by the betrayal she had done to her friend. They said goodnight, Amanda holding onto Samantha for a longer time than necessary before going their separate ways.

"Until the next, ten years or so," Samantha called as they walked away, causing Amanda to laugh and wave back at her before turning around and phoning Wendy.

"They are on their way home now, if you aren't already gone, you need to go now," Amanda said, the knot in her stomach becoming physically painful.

"Good job. I got everything I wanted. The money is in your account. Don't contact me again," Wendy replied, hanging up the phone and driving out of Samantha's and Nelly's street just as she saw them turn the corner. Amanda sighed and checked her account. Sure enough, Wendy had stayed true to her word and put a little extra on top for her troubles. Amanda rolled her eyes, surprised in herself that she could be so easily manipulated.

"What the fuck," Samantha said as she opened their apartment door. She walked in slowly, taking out her pistol from her purse. She heard Holly and Sasha barking from the courtyard and frowned at what she was seeing.

"Jesus, Samantha," Nelly said as she saw Samantha draw her gun, finally understanding why once she too walked inside.

"Baby. Stay behind me," Samantha said as she slowly walked around the apartment. The place was bare. Nothing was messed up, nothing was broken, but it was bare—the paintings on the walls, the furniture, the rugs were all gone. The crockery and cutlery were all still in the kitchen, but the alcohol had been stripped from the bar. Samantha walked into their bedroom and saw that the bed was gone, along with all of their clothes, sports gear, jewelry, and shoes. Their perfumes, hair products, and technical gear was also gone, and Nelly cried when she saw that her bunny, which she slept with, was also missing.

"Mommy," Nelly said as she looked up at Samantha with tears running down her face.

"It's going to be alright, baby girl. Mommy is going to make this alright," Samantha said as she put her gun away, deeming that there was no threat, that there was nothing at all.

"What are we going to do?" Nelly asked as they sat on

the floor in the middle of the living room. Samantha was grateful they had left the fridge, as she took a can of coke out for herself and Nelly.

"We just have to buy it all again, honey. Which is going to be fun, I mean, you are always saying you want to go on a shopping spree," Samantha replied, trying to find the positive in the situation.

"We will have to do something with the dogs. Maybe Val from next door can look after them for a week or so," Samantha suggested, Nelly, nodding her head in agreement.

"Where will we sleep?" Nelly asked, crawling into Samantha's lap.

"We will go to a hotel tonight, maybe for the next few weeks, depending on how long the bed takes to arrive. I'm going to call in sick for the rest of the week. I think you should too. If you tell them what has happened, I think they will be understanding," Samantha said as she got up and took Nelly's hand in hers.

"Thanks, Mommy," Nelly said, causing Samantha to look down at her in confusion.

"For looking after me," Nelly explained, making Samantha laugh.

"I don't think I've done a very good job at looking after you, baby girl. Look at the mess we are in right now. I've never been robbed in my life! I feel like I've failed you," Samantha said before she unlocked the courtyard and put the dogs on their leads. Samantha shook her head in disbelief before grabbing her phone and walking out the door.

Val had agreed to look after the dogs saying that she would love the company and before they knew it, Samantha and Nelly were walking down the street and towards a five-star hotel.

"You haven't, though, Mommy. Maybe we should reconsider moving into a more, safer neighborhood after all, though," Nelly said, feeling as though it was her fault because she had been the one who had wanted to make sure she could pay for half the rent. Samantha had said she could just move in with her, but Nelly was too independent just to be kept, she wanted Samantha to know she could hold her own.

"How about we just agree that this sucks, that it is neither of our faults and while we are looking for a completely new interior, we also look for a new apartment?" Samantha suggested as they neared a hotel.

"Agreed," Nelly replied, hoping that she could go to sleep at last.

Chapter 12

Samantha and Nelly opened the door to their hotel room, turned off the lights, and fell into bed, not waking until mid-morning.

"Hey, sweetie," Samantha said as Nelly pulled a face.

"Yeah, I think a shower and teeth clean is in order as well," Samantha laughed as they both got up.

"I still can't believe it. I think we should get some clothes first because we only have what we wore last night," Nelly said as she stripped and got into the shower. Turning the water on and washing her hair and body as Samantha watched. It was going to be their first-year anniversary in three weeks, and she had planned to take Nelly to Paris, something which would definitely have to wait.

"I think we should just get the basics of everything first. I don't want it to take too long to get stuff. We need to get back on our feet," Samantha said, undressing and pushing Nelly against the wall.

"You missed a spot," Samantha seductively said as she rubbed between Nelly's thighs and over her pussy.

"No, that's always the first place I do," Nelly replied, winking at Samantha, who laughed. Nelly wrapped her arms around Samantha's shoulders as she was finger fucked, moaning into Samantha's shoulder as she was brought close to an orgasm.

"That's enough," Samantha suddenly said, pulling out of Nelly, who whined, wanting release.

"That is so mean!" Nelly said, spanking Samantha's ass, gaining her attention once more.

"Don't hit Mommy," Samantha said, clear warning in her tone, which Nelly thought about if she wanted to listen to or ignore. Deciding it was best to listen, Nelly got out of the shower and back into her clothes. Samantha soon joined her, and they wrote a list of all the clothes they would need to buy.

"Mommy. I can't afford to get all this stuff. And I know you'll say that you can buy it for me, but I feel bad about you getting it. Especially since I know your version of basic and mine are very different," Nelly said as they walked down the street.

"Honey. It's Mommy's job to look after you. You don't need to feel bad about that. If it makes you feel better, you can tell me what stores you want us to go into? I know you like a few second-hand stores, and I'm happy to get you something there. I just want to make sure you have everything you need, alright?" Samantha said as they walked into a big department store. Samantha took Nelly to the lingerie section first, and Nelly walked around and found different things she liked, and it didn't take her very long to have a full selection. Samantha, on the other hand, took so long as she wanted to try everything on that she had told Nelly to take a copy of the list and go around the store to try and find other things she needed. What she didn't tell Nelly was that she was going to use that time to arrange a few things. The first being a new place to live.

She rang her cousin, who owned the company she first rented the penthouse from and asked him if there was any property that would be fitting. Delighting in the fact that he said there was a newly built apartment in the heart of the city that had river and park views. Wasting no time at all once he had sent her the photos, she told him to fill her out an application and send it to them.

The benefits of family, she thought to herself as she exited the change room.

"Oh, hey, I found like most things on this list," Nelly said as she walked over to Samantha, who put the pieces she had just tried on, on the counter.

"Can you ring these up with whatever she's getting, please," Samantha kindly said before leading Nelly away.

"What do you think of this?" Samantha asked as she showed Nelly the photos making her sigh.

"I'm just going to have to get used to you looking after me, aren't I?" Nelly asked, causing Samantha's pussy to tingle at her final surrender.

"Yes, you are, sweetie. And about time too," Samantha

replied, kissing Nelly on the top of her head.

"It's really beautiful, I'm not going to ask how you manage to afford it," Nelly said as she walked into the winter coat section.

"Good girl," Samantha answered, patting Nelly's ass affectionately before disappearing into another section of the store.

They emerged hours later after having lunch and had their purchases sent to the hotel. Nelly was exhausted and had become somewhat bratty as she and Samantha rested in the hotel room.

"Mommy wants a rest, baby girl," Samantha said when she took the television remote off Nelly and turned the tv off.

"But Mommy," Nelly whined as she coped a look from Samantha.

"Oh, you'd better not," Samantha warned. Nelly just huffed, rolled her eyes, and crossed her arms.

"I don't think I'm the only one who needs a nap," Samantha said, taking off her clothes and walking over to Nelly in her lingerie.

"I don't need a nap," Nelly huffed, annoyed that she only moments before yawned.

"Oh, I see," Samantha replied, making Nelly more annoyed that she wasn't taking the bait.

"Well, come here anyway, miss I don't need a nap,"

Samantha said, pulling Nelly to her nipple and spanking her ass hard when she tried to refuse.

"Don't be a bad girl for Mommy, baby," Samantha calmly said as she continued to spank Nelly until she stopped fussing and began to suckle.

"Good girl," Samantha cooed, cracking her neck from side to side and pulling her hair to one side. Nelly frowned as she obeyed Samantha, making Samantha laugh and begin to rub over Nelly's jeans.

"I think these need to come off," Samantha said, unzipping Nelly's jeans and helping her wriggle out of them. Nelly continued to nurse as Samantha slipped her hand in Nelly's panties and stroked her softly.

"Such a good girl for Mommy," Samantha said, gently beginning to finger fuck Nelly who moaned against the thick nipple in her mouth.

"Mommy," Nelly slowly moaned.

"I shouldn't hear little girls who have Mommy's nipple in their mouths," Samantha said, repositioning her nipple in Nelly's mouth. Samantha continued to take her, stroking her g-spot as Nelly wriggled in her arms, desperate to be allowed to orgasm. Samantha held Nelly's mouth to her breast as she filled her with a third finger, stretching Nelly's pussy and making her cry out in pleasure and pain.

"Breath through it, honey. You're safe with Mommy," Samantha lovingly whispered as she took the girl as her heart desired. Nelly tried to pull back as the orgasm flooded her senses, but her body fell limp in Samantha's arms, her nipple being lazily played within Nelly's mouth.

"Mommy," Nelly said as Samantha took her off one breast just to put her on the second.

"Are you still going to try and tell Mommy lies about you not needing a nap?" Samantha asked, fully aware that Nelly always needed a nap after sex. Nelly just slowly shook her head and closed her eyes as Samantha squeezed milk into her mouth, forcing her to continue to suckle.

"I'm not finished with you yet," Samantha said as she reached into her handbag and took out the new strapon she had bought without Nelly seeing. Lying Nelly on the bed, Samantha secured the belt to her hips and stroked the dildo predatorily as she looked at Nelly's tired body on the bed.

"You are so perfect," Samantha said as she grabbed Nelly's ankles and pulled her towards the tip of the dildo. Samantha rubbed it with lube before moving behind Nelly and pushing the tip into Nelly's pussy, making her put her ass up much to Samantha's delight.

"Good girl, you'll take this fucking like Mommy's little slut, won't you baby girl?" Samantha said as she slowly pushed herself inside of Nelly's wet pussy. Moaning, Samantha held her hips in position as she completely buried her dildo inside of Nelly, who gasped at how filled she was.

"You know how to make it stop," Samantha said before

she began to take Nelly from behind rhythmically. Nelly bit her bottom lip and twerked for Samantha as she was fucked, making Samantha reach around and rub her clit. The weight of Samantha's breasts on her back made Nelly moan as she felt herself enveloped by the older woman as she aggressively fucked her.

"That's it," Samantha said in a low, aroused voice as she felt Nelly's pussy juices squirt out around the dildo and onto her thighs. With a few final thrusts, Samantha pulled out of Nelly and watched as she collapsed in a heap on the bed. Bringing her knees to her chest, Nelly breathed through the after the shock of the multiple orgasms Samantha had just given her. Samantha took the strapon off and walked into the bathroom, cursing her period from stopping Nelly from fucking her as well.

"Here, baby," Samantha said as she walked back to where Nelly was still lying. She scooped Nelly up in her arms, and carried her to the shower, washed her down, and then took her to the other bed in the hotel suite.

"Mommy got you something special, little one," Samantha said, taking out a light pink onesie and gently dressing Nelly, happy that she didn't have to fight her.

"There, Mommy's perfect little girl," Samantha cooed as Nelly snuggled into her side and began to fall asleep.

Chapter 13

"Mommy?" Nelly softly said as she woke up a few hours later. Samantha had rested as well but had also spent a considerable amount of time online looking at and buying furniture for the next apartment.

"Just out here, baby girl," Samantha called out from the balcony. Nelly walked to the door and looked at Samantha.

"You look like you are in your element, Mommy," Nelly said, observing the bottle of champagne and room service that Samantha had set up.

"Well, Mommy never likes to work on an empty stomach," Samantha replied, laughing.

"Come here and sit on my lap," she quickly added as she saw Nelly begin to walk away. Nelly turned back around and made her way outside, resting her head on Samantha's shoulder as she looked on the new laptop screen at the luxurious furniture collection displayed.

"Have you left anything for me to decide on, Mommy?" Nelly asked as Samantha showed her all the items she had purchased.

"Of course. You are going to pick out the most important elements, the decorations," Samantha said, making

Nelly laugh.

"Thank goodness!" She teased and began to scroll through sites looking for bath towels and bedding.

"Mommy," Nelly whined as she felt Samantha's fingers begin to open the bottom of her onesie.

"Shh," Samantha replied as she groped Nelly, pushing her forward so her elbows were on the glass table and her back curved in.

"You look so sexy," Samantha whispered as Nelly felt her move the strap on in her pants.

"Are you packing?" Nelly laughed, turning her head to face Samantha just to have Samantha grab her messy ponytail and direct her head to face forward.

"Yep," Samantha replied as she pulled it from her pants and positioned Nelly over the top.

"Sit," Samantha commanded, hearing Nelly gasp and moan as she sat on Samantha's lap, her dildo entering her slowly. But Samantha wasn't interested in waiting and bucked her hips up, filling Nelly and guided her back down so that she was secured on top of her.

"Mommy, it's too big," Nelly moaned, feeling Samantha begin to bounce her on her lap.

"No, it's not," Samantha replied, reaching around to rub Nelly's clit, feeling her take it more easily as she was stimulated.

"See?" Samantha said smugly as Nelly curved her back

even more in an attempt to have the tip hit her g-spot.

"Bounce for Mommy," Samantha commanded and held onto Nelly's hips, enjoying the feeling of her ass grinding down on her lap.

"Mommy, no," Nelly said as Samantha placed her thumb in Nelly's mouth, pulling her body back and fucking her less deeply.

"Don't say no to Mommy, kitten," Samantha plainly said as she denied Nelly an orgasm. Samantha could feel Nelly begin to give in, which always made her body come from the slightest of touches, so she held her in place, getting turned on by Nelly's futile attempts to maintain stimulation and pulled out of the girl.

"Get on your knees," Samantha said as she moved forward on the chair. Nelly obeyed and opened her mouth, knowing what Samantha wanted.

"Good girl," she cooed as she slid down Nelly's throat until her eyes watered. Keeping herself inside her mouth, Samantha stroked Nelly's head lovingly.

"Swallow," Samantha commanded, ramming Nelly's throat when she took too long.

"Don't make Mommy wait," Samantha warned before slowly face fucking Nelly. Samantha knew that Nelly's knees would hurt, but as she stood up and continued to force her dildo down Nelly's throat, the sight turned her on too much. She began to rub her clit and pinch her nipples, her head rolling back as her hips pounded into Nelly's mouth.

Just one, Samantha thought to herself as she felt her orgasm building.

"Put your arms behind your back and look up at me," Samantha instructed, moaning as Nelly followed her orders and looked beautifully submissive.

"Yes," Samantha slowly moaned as she felt her pussy flood and finally took her dildo from Nelly's lips. Nelly put her hands on her thighs and waited patiently, her knees sore and red.

"Thank you, baby girl," Samantha said, reaching out and lifting Nelly up, catching her when her legs gave way.

"Mommy's got you. I'm not going to let anything bad happen to you," Samantha said as she led Nelly inside. She took off the strapon and looked through the shopping bags for some cream, finding it and also finding a magazine for Nelly.

"Here, sugar," Samantha said as she passed Nelly the magazine before rubbing her knees with the soothing cream.

"Does that feel nice?" Samantha said Nelly's cheeky sparkle in her eye, telling her that she was feeling better already.

"No," Nelly said plainly.

"No?" Questioned Samantha playfully, looking at Nelly shake her head. Samantha put the cream away and went to sit beside Nelly on the bed.

"What do you need then, sweetie," Samantha asked,

sweeping Nelly's hair from her face.

"I need a cookie," Nelly replied in her little voice, making Samantha laugh.

"A cookie?" She questioned, eyeing her playfully.

"And a chocolate shake?" Samantha added, making Nelly's eyes go wide with excitement.

"Yes, please, Mommy!" Nelly replied quickly.

"Come on then. We better drop into Val's and check on the dogs while we are out," Samantha suggested as they began to get ready to leave.

Chapter 14

It was five days before Samantha and Nelly were able to move into their new apartment. Samantha had organized the furniture delivery people to turn up to the new house and unpack everything and another company to place it beautifully in the house. She had taken Nelly down to the park with the dogs, and they had spent the whole day out while their once empty apartment was transformed into the grand vision they had designed together.

"I hope that is the last adventure we have for a while," Nelly said as they walked the dogs up the street and around the corner to a 24-hour diner. Samantha tied the dogs to the table leg, and Nelly went inside and took two menus before returning outside and sitting down.

"I think it will be. I'm sure that Amanda had something to do with it. It was just too much of a coincidence," Samantha said, looking over the menu and picking out blueberry pancakes. They watched as the sun went down and the stars came out, Samantha getting a phone call to say that the apartment was ready.

"Wonderful, thank you," came her reply. Nelly had gotten used to Samantha taking care of things, and she sipped her coffee as Samantha finished the conversation. She thought back to when they had first met and smiled to herself, half proud that she had been somebody that someone like Samantha would be interested in. Nelly was a different woman than the girl who Samantha had first met, and she wondered how long her youthful looks would last before Samantha wanted to find somebody new and younger and more, princess, in distress like.

"Ready to go?" Samantha said, interrupting Nelly's thoughts.

"What? Yeah, sorry I was just thinking," Nelly said, getting up and taking Sasha's lead in her hand.

"You know, we have our anniversary coming up. I was thinking it might be nice to do something for it," Nelly said as they walked to their new home. Samantha wrapped her arm around Nelly and looked down at her and smiled.

"I was thinking the same. But maybe we could do something locally? I think having some calm after this storm might be in order," Samantha replied, Nelly, nodding in agreement.

"So, maybe we could stay in town and go to the ABDL convention that weekend?" Nelly suggested, hoping that Samantha would agree. Nelly had seen an advertisement in one of the online communities she was a member of and had been eager to go.

"Really?" Samantha said, imagining seeing countless

babies and all sorts of stuff she wasn't interested in.

"Please, Mommy," Nelly begged, turning to walk backward but facing Samantha.

"We might find something new or cool or something," Nelly said, Samantha, smiling at her lovingly as she led her out of the way of oncoming people.

"We don't have to go for the whole time, but just like, a day or so and see what's there," Nelly continued, stopping at the corner and waiting for the traffic to slow.

"Alright. But we are going to go to that new restaurant, the one that serves lobster as well," Samantha said, making Nelly laugh.

"That's hardly a hard compromise to make," Nelly smirked.

Samantha held Nelly's hand as they walked into their new home, and they both sighed in happiness, looking around the space.

"You did alright, Mommy," Nelly said, playfully nudging Samantha. Nelly's eyes sparkled as she looked at the home, which looked like it came from the pages of a luxury home magazine.

"Yes, I did," Samantha said, feeling rather impressed with herself.

"This will do nicely. You know, maybe having our stuff stolen turned out to be the best thing for us," Samantha said, confusing Nelly.

"How do you mean?" Nelly asked as Samantha led her into one of the spare rooms.

"Mommy," Nelly whispered in surprise as Samantha pushed her into a room that had been set up as a room just for her. Nelly looked at Samantha in disbelief.

"Surprise, baby girl," Samantha said as she sat down on the day bed that was set up against the wall.

"How did you organize this without me knowing?!" Nelly exclaimed as she looked over her new things. There was a skateboard rack with three boards already lying in the spaces and a bookshelf with fashion books as well as a craft table by the window. There was a shelf with a selection of fluffy bunnies from her favorite brand and a new laptop on a wooden desk.

"Well, you sleep a lot, honey. So I just did everything when you were snuggled up next to me," Samantha said as Nelly opened the cupboard and saw the collection of house clothes and onesies.

"Mommy," Nelly said, tilting her head and rolling her eyes.

"What? Don't even pretend that you don't need your paci sometimes," Samantha said as she rubbed her nipples.

"But not tonight?" Nelly asked knowingly, coming over to Samantha, who wrapped her arms around her and held her tight.

"No, not tonight," Samantha agreed, rubbing her breasts against Nelly and kissing her on the top of her head and enjoying how the girl felt in her arms.

"But first, let's try out that new bath, little one," Samantha said, gently standing up and pushing Nelly backward.

"Can we use the spa features, please, Mommy?" Nelly asked, but Samantha was already shaking her head no.

"Not tonight. I want to get clean and get into bed. Mommy is tired, baby girl," Samantha explained, happy that Nelly accepted her answer and didn't push the issue.

"You can have your bath toys though, honey," Samantha suggested as they entered the huge room, and Nelly stripped, telling the house to play music and dancing around the bathroom for Samantha.

"Easy, little girl," Samantha said as Nelly slipped off her t-shirt, and Samantha caught her in her arms.

"Thanks, Mommy," Nelly giggle as she got into the bath and began to splash around happily.

"You're little tonight," Samantha said as she got in behind Nelly, delighted that they both fit very comfortably. Samantha washed Nelly's body, lathering her up in body wash and rinsing her off gently as Nelly played with the soapsuds. Samantha bathed herself quickly before getting out of the bath and leaving Nelly to play while she dried herself and got into her short pajama shorts and matching singlet. Nelly loved it when Samantha wore this type of thing to bed because it hugged her curves, and she could also see her nipples poking through the material.

"Out you come, little girl," Samantha said as she took Nelly's hands and helped her stand up. Nelly shivered as the cold night air hit her body, and Samantha wrapped her in a thick fluffy pink towel to dry her off.

"I think you'd better go to your room, baby girl. Mommy is going to diaper you tonight," Samantha said as Nelly quietly and sleepily walked into her room and lay on the floor. Samantha took a diaper down from the box on top of the cupboard as well as some powder and began to diaper Nelly, who quietly sucked on the corner of the towel.

"See, I knew you'd need Mommy tonight," Samantha said as Nelly reached up to grab on Samantha's big breasts with hung in front of Nelly. Samantha chose a black onesie with pink thigh high socks and helped Nelly to her feet, just for her to drop back down to her knees and lift up her arms.

"Oh, Mommy's little one," Samantha cooed as she bent down to pick Nelly up and carried her into their bedroom. Tucking Nelly in, Samantha lay next to her and watched as Nelly began to suckle from her without any instruction.

"Mommy's special girl," Samantha said as she closed her eyes and let Nelly have all of her.

Chapter 15

"I know you couldn't think of nothing worse, but I am really happy we are going to this," Nelly said in the car on the way to the ABDL convention two weeks later. It was true, Samantha could think of many more places she would like to go to rather than this, but it was important to Nelly, and she could hardly say no to the girl.

"It's not that I hate the idea, I just only like you. So I don't care what all these other people do," Samantha replied. Truth be told, she was worried that other Mommies wouldn't think she was a very good one, or that Nelly wasn't a real little or middle because she didn't subscribe to many of the stereotypical elements of the kink. But she wasn't about to let Nelly know of her fears when she knew they were just silly insecurities.

"We are here," Samantha said, trying to sound enthused. Nelly looked at all the people and bit her bottom lip.

"Maybe this was a bad idea," she said, looking at Samantha. Samantha frowned and looked at Nelly, wondering why she would think that.

"Like, I don't really have that whole vibe going, you know?" Nelly said, making Samantha laugh.

"I might feel the same way about myself. Let's just go in and have a look around, and if it's not for us, then we can leave, and if there's something you want to look at, then we can stay, alright. No pressure, honey," Samantha said, unbuckling Nelly's seat belt.

"Thanks, Mommy," Nelly said, getting out of the car.

"Maybe I can call you Mommy in here without people wondering what the deal is?" Nelly asked as they walked into the convention and stopped in their tracks. They looked at each other and smirked, knowing that they would probably stay for longer than they had initially thought.

"Yeah, I have a feeling you can," Samantha said as a man dressed in full ADBL attire casually walked passed them. They spent time strolling through the differing setups. There were cartoonists and stuffed toy displays and paci's that could be personally designed and decorated. Samantha took her blazer off and held it over her shoulder as they walked from vendor to vendor, Nelly's eyes and subtle smile, telling Samantha more than her words. Samantha ran her hand through her hair, closing her eyes and shaking her head as Nelly turned to look at her, captivated. Samantha opened her eyes to find more than just Nelly's eyes on her, and it made her smirk that she could still catch the gaze of strangers. Nelly didn't miss a beat either, and walked back over to Samantha, took her hand and walked with her towards the next display.

"Oh, is somebody jealous?" Samantha teased, causing

Nelly to roll her eyes.

"As if," said Nelly, far too defensively to fool Samantha, who just laughed and twirled her as they walked.

"What time was that event you wanted to go to, baby?" Samantha asked as she saw a large group of people making their way to the entrance of the convention.

"Oh yeah. I was going to go with some people to make a stuffie," Nelly said, pulling out her phone to check the time as Samantha checked her watch.

"Oh. I got a message. I think that's them," Nelly said, tilting her head to the group, following as she replied to the message. Samantha thought it was adorable that Nelly was nervous and shy as she approached the group.

"Hey, are you guys heading off to make stuffies, or am I in the wrong place?" Nelly said, surprised that she was feeling so confident and shy at the same time.

"Hey, yeah, that's us. I'm Joshy," a man said, waving at Nelly, making her smile and look back at Samantha.

"I'm Nelly," Nelly said, shrugging her shoulder and letting her hair fall around her face as she felt Samantha come up behind her.

"See you later, baby," she said, kissing Nelly's cheek and putting her headband in her hair before winking at her and walking back into the convention, she had seen some stickers that she knew Nelly would love and wanted to buy her a few things before she got back.

Bye, Mommy, Nelly text as she walked down the street with the new group of people.

Were you too shy to say that in front of your new friends? Samantha replied, knowing that it would make Nelly blush.

Maybe, Nelly replied, making Samantha laugh as she looked at the different emojis Nelly had added to the end of her message. Samantha just smirked as she put her phone away and went to the various vendor stalls. She knew that she spoilt Nelly, some other Mommies had told her so on the online community she was a member of, but she didn't care. She liked that she was in a position to spoil her baby, and Nelly was such a great partner in all aspects of their relationship that Samantha didn't mind treating her to special things when she saw them. Although Nelly leaned more to a middle, she still loved stickers and wearing a diaper sometimes, so Samantha bought her a pack of diapers with cute animal faces peeking out as well as a matching snapback of a husky puppy.

She is going to look so cute in this, Samantha excitedly thought as she paid the vendor before looking around the rest of the convention.

Nelly ended up making a pastel fuzzy bunny, which Samantha laughed at the moment she saw it.

"Baby girl, what on earth is that?" She asked, making

Nelly laugh in shock.

"It is my bunny," Nelly giggled as she was wrapped up in Samantha's arms. Samantha kissed the top of Nelly's head and felt Nelly snuggle into her.

"Come on, little one. Let's go back home," Samantha said as Nelly followed her to the car.

Samantha was happy that they lived in the same city as the convention as she drove down the street, seeing how busy the hotels were. People were everywhere, and just the general bustling atmosphere of the city made her wonder how hard it would be for Nelly to get to sleep that night.

"Baby?" Samantha asked, placing her hand on Nelly's thigh and turning her head to look at her. Smiling, Samantha saw Nelly cuddling her new stuffie and thought it best to continue to let her sleep.

Turns out, it won't be very hard at all, Samantha thought to herself as she felt Nelly turn and cuddle onto Samantha's arm, which was still in Nelly's lap.

"Shh, we are nearly home, princess," Samantha said as she continued to drive her happy, sleepy baby girl home.

Mommy Saves the Day

An MDLG themed story of Mommy Dom Carol, who was looking for a cheeky ABDL girl...little did she know her world was about to be turned upside down by little Ivy

Tina Moore

Chapter 1

Ivy didn't care about other people. She didn't have the luxury of feeling the emotions that went with being one of those 'helpful' people. After growing up in the system, she had changed her name the moment she turned 18. She considered it her birthday gift to herself, a kind of rebirth if you like. She had done other things as well. Like cut and dye her hair, from long and blonde to should length and jet black, the way her heartfelt. She left the house where she had only just been placed in and jumped on the first bus out of town. She didn't really know what she was going to do, all she knew was that no one cared about her, so she didn't have to care about anyone but herself.

"Wake up, kid, you have to get off now," a man said, gently shaking Ivy awake. She grabbed her ripped backpack and walked off the bus, stopping and sitting down on the seats at the terminal and watched the bus drive off.

Well, you're here now. The place you said you'd always get to. I mean, this was always the plan, even if you have no idea what you are going to do next, she thought to herself as she sat there. She hadn't thought of a plan besides, get out of town, and as she checked her phone, she wasn't surprised that nobody had called her for her birthday.

Why would you even bother checking? You know that they don't give a shit about you. They never have, you were always just a paycheck to them. But you don't have to think about that anymore. You know what the plan is. You know how you're going to get everything that you have ever dreamed about. So it's time to put all that shit to the side and decide that you are going to have a good life regardless of the shitty start you've had, she thought to herself as she got up and walked out of the bus terminal and into her new life.

Carol cracked her neck and thanked a higher source that is was Friday. She was a nurse at a plastic surgeon practice and loved the regular working hours. After years of shift work, the most alluring aspect of the job was that she could maintain a 'standard' work-life balance. Carol was older than the young nurses she worked with and enjoyed their youthful and playful personalities. They had taken to calling her Mama, something that she both enjoyed and found somewhat frustrating. The problem Carol had with it was that she was a Mommy Dom, not that any of those girls would be able to tell. She didn't overly dominate them, even when she had to correct their behavior, she never told them what to do in a demeaning way, but she did care for them. She would make cakes for birthdays and organize staff dinners and events. She shared with them recipes and had even helped one of the girls move house when she got kicked out by her boyfriend.

"Hey, Mama, can you help me word this ad. It needs to be put in the job-seeking section of the website, and I don't really know what to say," one of the girls asked Carol as they were eating lunch.

"Sure. How about this afternoon when it's a little quieter?" Carol replied, enjoying how the girl's tight work uniform hugged her slim figure.

"Thanks, Mama, sounds perfect," the girl excitedly said as she got up, placing a hand on Carol's shoulder as she walked back into the building. Carol could feel herself slipping into her Mommy space, and she tightened her calves and loudly exhaled as she fought herself back out of that space.

Not right now, you can go home and think about her all you want, but that's not what she is after, and you can't manipulate her into a situation that you want, but she doesn't, but you can sure think about her, Carol said to herself as she finished her lunch.

And that is exactly what she did. Carol lay down on her bed after a warm shower and ran her hands over her body, imagining that it was her young co-worker, timidly touching her for the first time.

"Like this?" She imagined the slender brunette almost whispering as Carol guided her closer to her pussy.

"Yes, baby. Be a good girl and stick out your tongue for

Mommy," Carol imagined herself replying as she thought of how she would hold the girl's face in her hands and rub her wet pussy over the girl's mouth, feeling her hot tongue against her clit.

"Fuck me," Carol angrily moaned out loud as she opened her eyes and groaned in frustration. She got up and began putting on her lingerie, annoyed that her daydream was better than her reality. She decided that she needed to go for a walk, so putting on her activewear, Carol headed out into the Friday afternoon sun.

Ivy had spent the first three nights in the big new city in a motel. She had worked two jobs since she had turned 15 and had managed to save enough money to last her a few months, but she knew that she needed to find a job and fast. Having spent the day handing out resumes to diners and gas stations, Ivy had ended up in a coffee shop, drinking a white chocolate latte and taking small bites of a choc chip cookie.

This is what life could be like. Going to work, even though I don't have a job yet, and then coming to cool cafes and enjoying all these things you've only ever seen in magazines, she thought to herself as she watched the people walk by and wondered what kind of lives they led. She had always enjoyed doing this. She had thought it was because she was learning how to behave in the world; it wasn't like her foster families were ever interested in helping her make sense of the world. Ivy reached down for her backpack at the same time as Carol walked past her, causing Carol's knee to run straight into Ivy's head.

"Oh darling, I am so sorry, are you alright?!" Carol said as Ivy gasped in pain, placing her hand over her head and biting her bo. Ivy frowned and ground her teeth. She knew that she shouldn't tell this woman to go to hell though that was what her first thought was.

"Yeah, I'm fine," Ivy said, looking at Carol dead in the eye and almost having to catch her breath. Never in her 18 years had she been near somebody with the warm, loving energy that she felt from the woman in front of her, and it pierced the numbing condition Ivy had cloaked around herself.

"Are you sure?" Carol questioned, slightly frowning as Ivy tried to get up, only to become dizzy and fall back into her seat. It felt all too much for Ivy, who noticed the world begin to spin as she looked up at Carol, who reached out to touch the large bump which was forming on Ivy's forehead.

"Should we call an ambulance?" A waitress asked. That was the last thing Ivy heard before her whole world turned black.

Chapter 2

"Hey there," Carol said to Ivy, who looked around, frightened at the unfamiliar surroundings.

"It's ok, honey, you're in the hospital. You passed out in the café. We looked into your purse. Ivy, is it?" Carol said as Ivy sat up, wincing.

"Yeah," Ivy replied, frowning as she saw the strange woman again. A nurse walked into the room and handed Ivy her discharge papers, placing them on the bedside before giving Ivy a fake smile and walking out. Ivy hated women like that nurse who always seemed to look down on her because she can from trash.

"I wish you hadn't of called an ambulance. I kinda can't afford any of this," Ivy said timidly, embarrassed and beginning to blush. She felt a knot in her stomach begin to form as she thought about how she was going to get out of this situation. She knew that she wasn't in a position to run, her head still hurt way too much, but she also knew that even with all her savings, she wouldn't be able to pay for these medical bills. Ivy just looked up at Carol, who was smiling at Ivy in a way that Ivy couldn't understand. She hadn't seen the expression that was on Carol's face directed toward her before, and it made her uncomfortable because she didn't know how to respond.

"Sweetheart, I am the one who put you in here. So, of course, I've already taken care of the bill. I can't begin to tell you how sorry I am. Your family must be worried sick about you, is there someone I can call for you?" Carol said, making Ivy suspicious and wary. In her 18 years of experience, when people did kind things for her, they always wanted something in return, but as if reading her mind, Carol smiled.

"You don't owe me a thing, Ivy. It was just the right thing to do. I had no idea how hard my knees where," Carol said, causing Ivy to giggle despite herself.
Ivy filled in the paperwork and made her way to the front of the hospital.

"Can I offer you a ride home?" Carol asked, seeing Ivy looking confused as she tried to orientate herself.

"Um, no, it's cool I can manage. You've been more than amazing. Thanks for everything," Ivy said, hailing a taxi that just drove past her. It was late, far later than Ivy liked being out, and the cold night air made her shiver.

"Come on, there'll be no cabs here for a while yet," Carol said, smiling warmly. Ivy hated herself for feeling so drawn to this woman, but she rolled her eyes and followed Carol toward her car.

"Seatbelts," Carol said once Ivy was sitting in her luxury SUV. It was the type of car that Ivy had only seen in magazines.

No wonder she could afford my medical bills, this bitch is rich as fuck, Ivy thought to herself as she put on her seatbelt.

"So, where is home, honey?" Carol asked, turning the heating up as she saw Ivy thin arms covered in goosebumps.

"Um. So I'm staying in a motel at the moment. It's the Lucky Star. Do you know it? I can find it on my phone," Ivy said, biting her bottom lip and quickly finding it for Carol.

"You're a little young to be on your own, aren't you?" Carol asked as she drove toward the motel.

"I'm the oldest I've ever been," Ivy smugly replied, causing Carol to laugh. Ivy found it strange that Carol didn't seem phased by her hostile, sarcastic remarks and smiled to herself, enjoying that Carol wasn't offended by her snarkiness. Ivy had a tendency to push people away when they got too close, and she liked that Carol didn't seem phased by her attempts to push her away. If Ivy was being honest, she didn't really want Carol to go. She just wasn't sure if she could trust her.

"Well, I can't dispute that. But not many 18-year-olds stay in a motel on the outskirts of town, do they?" Carol replied, causing Ivy to lift her knees to her chest.

"Guess not," Ivy replied, putting her knees back down when Carol gently patted them.

"Sorry," Ivy said, turning to look out the window. Carol

looked at the rough diamond sitting in her passenger seat. Ivy's black hair was tied up in a half bun, her skinny black jeans had rips in the knees, and her baggy t-shirt with the sleeves folded up made her heart swell. Her chipped crimson nail polish and worn out black leather combat boots added to her look, and Carol wondered how long it would be before Ivy was on the streets.

She is just a picture of cuteness that's for sure. A little bit on the young side, I couldn't even take her to a bar. But look at those sad little eyes, Carol thought, wishing she could find a way to keep Ivy.

"Do you want to get something to eat, or whatever?" Ivy asked suddenly, turning to face Carol. The look on the older woman's face made Ivy feel safe, an unusual feeling for her, and made her beg to a higher being that Carol didn't say no.

"That would be nice. Where are you thinking? What do you like?" Carol asked, laughing at the face Ivy pulled.

"What do I like? Um, food?" Ivy replied as Carol pulled into a diner a few minutes from the motel. Ivy had never been one to be a picky eater, mostly because she never really knew when her next meal was coming and secondly because even if she knew, the options were slim.

"So here would be fine?" Carol asked as Ivy raised her eyebrows and nodded. Carol pulled into the diner parking lot and looked around. It wasn't the sort of place she would choose if it was her choice, and she tried to look relaxed about leaving her SUV out in the open, deciding that she needed to make sure they got a window seat so that she could make sure that her SUV wasn't stolen.

"Ok," Carol said more to herself than to Ivy as she got out of the car and walked inside.

"Just, try not to give me concussion this time, yeah?" Ivy teased as they sat down.

"I will do my best," Carol replied, making Ivy laugh. Carol didn't want to feel herself entering Mommy space but as she sat in the booth opposite Ivy in all her youthful glory, it was hard not to.

"I'll take the pancakes, a chocolate shake, the cheeseburger and fries, and a soda. Thanks," Ivy said, ignoring the expression on Carol's face.

"What?" Ivy asked when Carol ordered the fish and salad.

"Nothing, it's not my place to judge," Carol replied, only causing Ivy to become more annoyed.

"Hey, what's your name anyway?" Ivy asked, realizing that she didn't know the name of the woman sitting in front of her.

"Oh, sorry. I'm Carol," she replied, extending her hand playfully. Ivy took it and felt something like electricity pulse through her veins, holding onto Carol's hand for longer than necessary.

"And to answer your question from before. I left the

home I was last put in. That's why I am out here alone," Ivy said, watching the cars drive passed the diner.

"Were you in foster care?" Carol gently asked, not wanting to upset Ivy, who just nodded her head.

"And this. This is because I sort of only eat once a day," Ivy added after her order was placed in front of her.

"Why once a day?" Carol asked as Ivy began to devour her pancakes.

"Because. I have a food budget of about $12 a day for food, and there's no fridge in the motel," Ivy explained, surprised that Carol could get so much information out of her so easily.

"Are you working?" Carol asked as she ate her fish. Ivy just shook her head.

"My whole plan was to move here, find a job and save up for a place to rent," Ivy said, looking at Carol, who just smiled back at her.

"I think it's very brave and stoic what you are doing, sweetheart," Carol said, making Ivy just smile and scoff at her compliment.

"Yeah, well. I didn't want to end up being just another fucking loser, did I?" Ivy said, enjoying the shock on Carol's face.

"Language, young lady!" Carol playful said, making Ivy smile like a naughty girl getting into trouble. She had to admit. There was something about Carol, which she liked even if she didn't know how to describe the feeling.

"Would you take my number? So that if you need somebody for, I don't know, anything you have someone in this crazy city to call? I'm sure you don't need anyone, you're clearly able to look after yourself, but it might be nice to have a friend here," Carol said, offering Ivy her business card. Ivy looked at Carol for a moment, unsure whether to take the card or not.

"You don't have to ring if you don't want to. But I would feel better knowing that you aren't alone here. Would you take it for me?" Carol said, Ivy tentatively reaching out to take her card.

"The motel is only a block away from here. I can walk it. Thanks for everything," Ivy said as Carol walked to her car.

"Honey, the only people who are out this late, are hookers, and girls that pimps want to turn into hookers. I'm not letting them get their hands on you. Get in the car," Carol said, making Ivy laugh at how her voice made her sound more dominant.

"Fine," Ivy said. She bit her lip as Carol leaned into the car and buckled her into the seat. Ivy knew that her eyes were giving her away, but she couldn't help it. As much as she tried to hide it, Carol turned her on. She wasn't sure if it was her whole, I'll protect you from the world thing, or the fact that Ivy hadn't felt seen in her whole life, but whatever it was, it was working. Carol noticed Ivy involuntarily spread her thighs, and her breathing became shallow as Carol closed in the distance between then. She felt her own clit begin to tingle with desire and fought herself not to reach behind Ivy's head and kiss her passionately. Carol stepped back and licked her lips before pulling her hair to one side and walked to the driver's side.

"Plus, I like having you around, you're fun with your moody little attitude," Carol laughed as she drove out of the parking lot.

Carol had dropped Ivy home as she had promised, but when Ivy lingered at the door, Carol offered if she wanted her to come inside. Carol had all but swooned when Ivy timidly nodded her head. Ivy knew she was a lesbian, but she had never allowed herself to try anything, but there was something about Carol that made her feel as though she wasn't in control of herself anymore.

"I um, guess I should have kept it a little tidier," Ivy said, blushing as she collected her things and placed them in the corner on a chair. Looking around the room, uncertainty in her eyes, Carol sat down on the edge of the bed and patted for Ivy to join her.

"I've never done this. Like any of this," Ivy nervously said, Carol, reaching out and running her fingers through Ivy's hair.

"Yeah, I sort of figured," Carol loving replied. They sat in silence, Carol wondering if this was a good idea after all. Ivy hesitantly reached out and put her hand on Carol's thigh.

"Can I kiss you?" Ivy asked so quietly that Carol almost didn't hear it. Smiling warmly, Carol nodded and took the lead. Placing a hand on either side of Ivy's face and bringing her lips down on the younger girl's lips, gently at first, then more passionately as she felt Ivy gain confidence. Ivy moaned as she pushed against Carol's mouth, her body turning hot before she pulled away, panting.

"It's ok. We don't have to do anymore, honey," Carol said, reading the look in Ivy's eyes. The fire, the fear, the desire, and the caution. Ivy just stood up in front of Carol, her thighs straddling Carol's as she slowly took her t-shirt off, revealing her thin frame, her slightly protruding ribs and perky b-cup breasts in a black lace bra.

"You are so beautiful, baby," Carol breathlessly said, getting caught off guard by how angelic Ivy looked. Running her hands over Ivy's body, Ivy wrapped her arms around Carol's neck and melted into her. Feeling Carol's heavy, soft breasts against her tummy, Ivy grinded on her lap, making soft sounds as she continued to give in to desire.

"I want to feel you," Ivy softly said as she began to pull on Carol's clothes, making her laugh.

"Just wait a moment, sugar. Let's get under the covers. You're getting cold," Carol said, using Ivy's cool skin as an excuse to hide her body. Although she was not ashamed of her figure, she didn't want to turn Ivy off by her body. Ivy stood up, peeled back the covers and giggled as Carol pushed her into bed and onto her back.

"Hey," Ivy said, in a little voice, half surprising herself. She hadn't remembered a time she had felt this happy or free and safe as Carol scooped her up in her arms and kissed her.

"Hey, honey," Carol lovingly said in her Mommy voice. Ivy snuggled into her as she stroked her back and grabbed the waistband on her jeans, pulling her up, higher on her ass.

"I think these need to come off," Carol whispered, making Ivy laugh.

"What about this?" Ivy replied, pulling on Carol's shirt.

"Well, it's only fair," Carol replied, letting Ivy take it off. Carol watched Ivy's eyes as she took everything in, enjoying how her timid touch made goosebumps over her body. Ivy stroked the top of Carol's breasts, enjoying how soft and warm her skin was before wriggling up to kiss her once again. Ivy felt Carol wrap her arms around her and rolled Ivy over to have her laying on top of her.

"I um," Ivy said as she pinned Carol down by her shoulders.

"It's ok, sweetie, we don't have too," Carol replied, reading Ivy's eyes and allowing herself to be dominated, knowing that Ivy needed to feel empowered and in control.

"It's not you, it's just, um," Ivy started to explain as Carol began to shake her head, stopping Ivy from continuing.

"It's just that you wanted to, and now you don't. And it's

that simple honey, and anyone who can't handle that needs to take a good hard look at why they have such high rape traits," Carol replied, watching as Ivy sucked her own thumb and lay down on top of Carol.

"You don't need to apologize, beautiful," Carol continued as she felt Ivy snuggle into her cleavage. Ivy thought back to all the times she had told someone no, and they hadn't listened. It made her heart hurt and tears well up in her eyes.

Why didn't they care as much as Carol does, Ivy thought to herself as she felt Carol begin to stroke her back and gently pat her bottom as she fell asleep.

Chapter 3

"Morning girls," Carol beamed Monday morning. Gabi and Hope, some of the girls' Carol worked with looked up, suspicion written all over their faces.

"You're overly happy today, Mama. Do we even want to know what you got up to on the weekend?!" Hope giggled as Carol put her things away.

"No. And even if you did want to know, I don't kiss and tell," Carol teased as she got on with her day, leaving the girls full of curiosity.

"Hey, I hope it is ok that I called," Ivy softly said down the phone. Carol had told her that her lunch break was usually around one in the afternoon, and as Carol had her lunch, she felt herself enter her Mommy space as she listened to Ivy's sweet voice.

"Not at all, darling," Carol replied, instantly feeling her pussy tighten with desire.

"Ok, great," Ivy said, unsure of what else to say, but wanting to hear Carol's voice.

"How are you?" Carol said, filling the space that began to fill between them. Ivy had heard back from the diner where she and Carol had first spent time together.

"Good. I got a job, at that diner we went to," Ivy replied, pride in her voice that her plan was coming to fruition.

"Well done, baby!" Carol exclaimed, delighted for Ivy.

"I hope you aren't working the late shifts though," Carol quickly added, thinking of all the unsavory remarks Ivy was no doubt about to hear.

"Well, I have a few of them. But that's fine, I need the money, and they give you a free drink with every shift," Ivy replied happily. Carol looked around to see that Gabi and Hope were both watching her with amusement in their eyes, and Carol rolled her eyes at them, making them giggle.

"We should do something to celebrate. Are you free tonight?" Carol asked. Ivy had never had anyone celebrate her achievements before, and it made her feel wonderful.

"Um, yeah I am actually, I start next week. So, I'm all yours," Ivy replied, a hint of seduction in her voice, making Carol swoon.

"Great. I'll pick you up at seven, and I'll keep where we are going a surprise, but I think you'll like it," Carol said, giving Ivy knots of excitement and anticipation in her stomach. Hanging up the phone, Ivy looked at the clothing options she still had available and frowned.

I really need to do some washing, she thought, opening her purse to find a few dollars' worth of coins. Checking the time, she rushed out the door, knowing that she wanted to make sure her body was perfectly shaven and her make up flawless for her date tonight.

"Who was that?" Gabi asked as Carol passed them.

"My date," Carol said rather impressed that Ivy seemed to enjoy her company as much as she did hers.

"How young is this one?" Hope teased. It was common knowledge that Carol liked younger women, and the girls she worked with had often joked about it with her. Carol didn't mind; in fact, it turned her on. She had gone hoe countless times and fucked herself thinking of how she would put them over her knee and spank them until they weren't giggling anymore, or filling their mouths with her nipple and dressing them in sweet little onesies.

"She's a baby, that's for sure," Carol replied, amused that her response had multiple meanings.

"Knock knock," Carol said as she leaned against the opened door to Ivy's motel room.

"Hey," Ivy happily said, turning around and making Carol's heart swell as she looked into Ivy's big green eyes.

"Hi, sweetie," Carol said, walking into the room and taking the girl in her arms.

"Mm, you smell divine," Carol said, nuzzling into Ivy's neck and making her giggle.

"It's just body spray," Ivy replied, pushing Carol away and grabbing her purse. Carol held out her hand dramatically, making Ivy look at her with those big innocent eyes as she took Carol's hand, and they walked to the car.

"So, where are we going?" Ivy asked, her tight black dress hugging her body was draped in a black denim jacket, and Carol noticed that she was once again wearing her combat boots. Her hair was shaken out, and the layers made her look particularly street cool.

"Well, I noticed how much you liked burgers. So I am taking you to an all you can eat burger place where you can design your own burgers. It will probably make me put on five kilos, but it'll be worth it to see what type of creations you come up with," Carol said, laughing at her joke as Ivy rolled her eyes.

"You are lovely, Carol. And your body is really nice," Ivy said, surprising Carol as she felt her hand on her thigh.

"Really nice?" Carol teased, making Ivy bite her bottom lip.

"Yeah, it feels safe. Like a Mommy or whatever," Ivy replied, beginning to blush. Carol noticed that whenever Ivy spoke from her heart, she would finish the sentence with the word whatever to try and create some emotional distance.

It must have been so rough for you, little girl, Carol thought to herself thinking, having involuntarily placed her hand on top of Ivy's.

"Well, there's plenty of time for that later. Right now, let's get this little tummy filled," Carol said, pulling into the restaurant and tickling Ivy as they walked inside.

"Ok, this is amazing!" Ivy exclaimed, looking around at the three leveled building and the huge buffets on each level. Carol directed her to a secluded table and sat next to Ivy.

"I like that you sat there, it makes it feel less like an interview or whatever," Ivy said as Carol put her arm around her.

"Can I do this?" Carol asked, Ivy, pulling away from her slightly.

"Yeah. It makes me feel a bit weird though," Ivy replied, as Carol nodded and took her arm away.

"But I like it," Ivy quickly added, taking Carol's arm and wrapping it back around her, making Carol laugh.

"Alright," she said, squeezing Ivy firmly.

After 2 hours at the restaurant, Ivy was finally full.

"I have no idea where all that food goes!" Carol teased. She thought it was cute that Ivy had a full little tummy, happy that she was able to give the girl what she wanted.

"This was great. I don't think I will move for a month, but so worth it," Ivy replied, resting into Carol. Carol noticed how Ivy's eyes began to look over her, and she laughed.

"I don't think I can tonight, honey. I'm not like you, if I eat a big meal, that's me done for the night," Carol explained.

"But you could watch me and tell me what to do," Ivy seductively whispered into Carol's ear, making her pussy instantly tingle.

"Careful what you wish for young lady," Carol said, patting Ivy's thigh predatorily.

"Come on, let's get out of here," Ivy said, kissing Carol on the cheek. Carol felt such a strong urge to tell Ivy that she was a Mommy Dom, but she was afraid that Ivy would freak out and end their time together, so she decided that she would try to put it into the game Ivy wanted to play. Carol began to drive out of the lot as she saw Ivy start to tear at her cuticles.

"Pull your dress up," Carol instructed, taking Ivy by surprise. Ivy looked up at Carol and, without breaking eye contact, slowly lifted the hem of her dress high enough that Carol could see her pink lace panties through her tights.

"Spread your thighs for me," Carol continued, her voice becoming hoarse with desire. Ivy slowly obeyed, pushing herself forward and feeling her clit begin to throb.

"Like this?" Ivy replied, pushing her pussy out and arching her back.

"Just like that," Carol replied, reaching down to stroke her over her tights. Feeling the heat coming from Ivy's sex, Carol pulled on her tights, and in one quick motion, her hand was in Ivy's panties. Feeling Ivy's wetness, Carol tenderly stroked Ivy's slit, pushing her pussy lips apart and teasing her hole.

"Such a sweet little thing," Carol purred, having to remind herself that she was driving and to stay focused.

"Play with your titties for me," Carol instructed, feeling her own clit begin to pulse and swell as she watched Ivy follow her commands. Carol pulled on Ivy's puffy pussy lips allowing her juices to coat her fingers before Carol flicked her wrist and was inside of Ivy before her body knew what was happening.

"Oh my god," Ivy gasped, sitting up quickly as she felt Carol's fingers inside of her.

"Just tell me red if you want me to stop, alright?" Carol lovingly said as she began to wriggle her fingers inside of Ivy. They pulled into the motel car park, and Carol turned off the engine.

"Kiss me," Carol instructed, smiling into the kiss as she felt Ivy's tongue against hers as she unbuckled her seat belt. Carol continued to finger fuck Ivy, reaching over and pushing her chair back and climbing on top of her. She liked that Ivy still had her seat belt on. It made Carol feel even more dominating as she saw Ivy's restricted body.

"Stick your tongue out for me," Carol said breathlessly as she unbuttoned her blouse with her other hand, her body lying gently on top of Ivy's.

"Suck my nipple," Carol instructed, moaning loudly in pure delight as she felt Ivy suckle on her desperately.

"Yes, baby girl," Carol groaned as she fucked her slowly. Carol didn't want Ivy over the edge just yet, and she kept her a writhing mess under her as she pleasured her.

"Say, I like it, Mommy," Carol moaned involuntarily,

Ivy almost freezing underneath her. Ivy pushed Carol's heavy breast from her lips.

"Mommy, I like it," came the words Carol longed to hear, putting her breast back in Ivy's mouth and fucking her harder.

"That's it, baby girl," Carol moaned as she felt Ivy's pussy relax and her eyes roll to the back of her head.

Why do I like this? What the fuck?! Ivy yelled to herself, but any other thoughts where fucked from her mind as Carol took her over the edge, making her squirt for the first time. Ivy looked up at Carol, who bent her head to kiss her on the tip of her nose, frowning as she saw Ivy's eyes begin to swell.

"Honey, what is it?" Carol lovingly asked. Getting off Ivy, Carol moved back to her seat as Ivy wiped the tears from her eyes.

"Nothing. Sorry," Ivy replied, getting out the car and walking toward her door.

"Hey, it's not nothing. Talk to me, honey," Carol said, getting out and following Ivy into her room. Ivy was sitting on the bed as Carol walked in and shut the door. Ivy looked up at her as tears streamed down her face.

She is a beautiful crier, Carol thought, sitting next to Ivy and putting her hand on the girl's thigh.

"Baby girl?" Carol questioned as Ivy got up and began to pace around the small room.

"I don't know. I don't know why I am crying or what I'm

doing, and this all just feels like so much," Ivy said, beginning to hyperventilate. Carol got up and walked over to her, took her hand, and led her back to the bed. Carol positioned Ivy, so she was being cradled, and as Ivy pushed her away, Carol just held on tighter.

"Just wait, sweetheart. I'm not going to hurt you. You're safe with me. Let me soothe that hurt in your heart, darling," Carol affectionately said, gently rocking Ivy in her arms, feeling the girl relax but maintain her furrowed expression.

"I don't know how to handle all this," Ivy whispered as Carol thumbed away her endless tears rolling down her face.

"I know, honey. Is it because I'm so loving?" Carol asked, making Ivy bite her bottom lip.

"Maybe," Ivy replied, turning into Carol and burying her face into the older woman's cleavage.

"Why did you want me to, you know, call you Mommy?" Ivy shyly said, her words muffled against Carol's shirt. Carol felt a knot begin to tighten in her stomach, hoping that this wasn't the night she would lose Ivy. Carol took a deep breath and exhaled slowly, Ivy sensing there was something to this story and getting up to sit next to Carol.

"So, have you heard of BDSM before?" Carol asked Ivy, who just rolled her eyes, making Carol laugh.

"Like everyone has," Ivy replied, happy with herself that she knew what it was.

"Well, there are different types of expressing those core

elements and values of BDSM, in particular, D and s. One of those ways is for the Dom to express themselves in a more nurturing and almost maternal if you like, method of dominating their submissive. Then, in turn, the submissive enjoys that type of domination, where they are looked after and cared for as though they are younger than they biologically are," Carol said, trying to explain MDLG as best she could, laughing as Ivy tilted her head as she listened.

"Ok, so it's like a lot less whips and orgasm denial and more, like what?" Ivy replied, Carol, finding it endearing that Ivy wanted to share all her knowledge.

"Well, like everything in BDSM, both parties need to agree on how their relationship will be. But for me, I like it when the submissive calls me Mommy. And I like calling my sub pet names like baby girl, little one, and just generally sweet names that a Mommy would call her baby. I like looking after my girl, but I enjoy that to be from a more maternal slant than anything else," Carol said, realizing that she had never had to explain MDLG to someone before. Usually, she wouldn't bother getting involved with a girl who didn't identify as an AB, but she couldn't pull herself from Ivy, no matter how hard she had tried.

"Ok. So, wow, that's kinda interesting, I guess," Ivy said, trying to find a place to process that information.

"So, what stuff would you do then?" Ivy questioned, getting up and walking over to where her water bottle sat.

"Honestly, it would depend on what was agreed upon. Usually, people who enjoy this kink enjoy doing things called 'little things.' It depends on how they feel. They might feel like they want to be cared for like a baby, and then they want their food to be cut up and to play with soft toys and have naps, for example. But then on the other end, you have what is called 'middles' who are a lot more independent because they feel like they want to be cared for still but also have a lot more desire to be independent. If you want, I can send you some really good content to explain it more," Carol explained, Ivy finding the conversation interesting.

"So, it's like, a lifestyle thing or a sex thing?" She asked, coming to sit back down next to Carol.

"It could be one or the other, or it could be both. It just depends on the type of dynamic between the two people," Carol said, watching as Ivy took in all the new information.

"Cool," Ivy suddenly said, shrugging her shoulders, making Carol laugh.

"Cool?" She questioned, wanting a little more insight into what Ivy was thinking.

"Yeah, so like, you're a Mommy Dom, so what?" Ivy said, crossing her legs and looking up at Ivy.

"Right, and for this to continue then, you'd have to enjoy being my little or middle, I'm not really fussed which one, I adore both," Carol said, watching the penny drop for Ivy.

"Oh. Ok, I don't know what you'd want me to do," Ivy replied, making Carol laugh.

"How about this. You take a week or so and spend some time researching the kink and see if it's something that resonates with you. If it doesn't, that is totally fine. You'll never lose me as a friend, but we shouldn't continue to see each other in this capacity because it wouldn't be fair on either of us," Carol explained, sweeping Ivy's hair out of her eyes.

"Yeah, there's nothing worse than not meshing with someone," Ivy replied, kissing Carol on the cheek.

"Ok, get out. I have to search the hell out of this stuff," Ivy playfully said, pushing Carol off the bed.

"Alright, alright!" Carol exclaimed, giving in and getting up. She turned around and found Ivy on her knees on the bed, reaching out for a hug at which Carol rolled her eyes.

"You kick me out, then want cuddles? Such a baby," Carol playfully said as she held onto Ivy before kissing her goodnight.

Chapter 4

Ivy didn't sleep for two nights after Carol left. Between working at the diner and researching everything she could on ABDL and MDLG, she didn't have time for anything else, least of all sleep. Carol had messaged her a few links to different websites, but the thank you messages was all she had heard of Ivy. Carol was wondering by the third week of silence what Ivy was up to and decided to give her a call, frowning when she didn't pick up.

Damn, I might have scared her off. That was the last thing I wanted to do. Maybe I should call her and see if she's free for dinner or something, Carol thought to herself as she sipped wine at a bar with her work colleagues.

"Your turn!" Hope exclaimed as Carol felt her thigh being shaken and looked around at the girls' faces in front of her, their expectant and expressive faces telling her that she must have missed something.

"Sorry I was somewhere else. What?" Carol said, making the girls' laugh.

"Oh, we know, you've been somewhere else all week!" Gabi exclaimed, making Carol roll her eyes.

"So, the question was, where have you had public sex?"

Hope questioned, sipping her drink and smirking. Carol had slept with Hope when she first came to the practice. It was nothing particularly noteworthy and very vanilla, but Hope had clearly enjoyed her time. Carol raised an eyebrow.

Why don't you tell them, honey? Carol said to herself as she stared Hope down, making her blush and quickly look away.

"In the back seat of my car, in a parking lot at the beach at midnight," Carol replied, with wicked satisfaction that Hope excused herself to go to the bathroom. Gabi just laughed and clapped her hands as Carol chuckled to herself.

"Oh, you girls. I have had a lovely time, but I must go," Carol said as soon as Hope returned.

"But you've only had one drink!" Gabi said, enjoying how Carol looked at her and put her back in her place.

"I'll see you two on Monday. Try not to break too many hearts between now and then," Carol said, standing up and putting her coat on, winking at them before she left the bar. Walking down the street, Carol took her phone out, dialing Ivy's number but deciding not to call her and put her phone back into her coat pocket in frustration.

Fuck it, Carol thought hailing a taxi and deciding to go to Ivy's motel room.

Ivy had worked a double shift, and she wearily dragged her feet down the street. She knew what she wanted to do the moment she got home, have a bath, and snuggle into her blankets. Tonight was going to be her last night in the motel as she had successfully acquired a small unit to rent closer to town. She turned the corner of the last block she had to walk and thought about how nice it would be to have a fluffy onesie to wear to bed. Biting her lip and wondering how long it would take her to afford half of the little things she had decided she needed. Ivy had decided that she definitely had some of the interests of a little and had experimented with getting into little space, realizing that is was considerably harder to do without Carol around. But she also wanted to explore it without Carol around because she was embarrassed about the thought of being in that space and doing the things she wanted to do with Carol watching her. So she had decided to just hide from Carol, which had been working well until she looked up to see Carol out the front of her motel room.

"Hi," Carol said as she saw Ivy stop walking and stand half frozen. Ivy looked around, unable to hide any longer.

"Hey," she replied, fumbling in her backpack for her keys. Carol watched, wanting to have this conversation but also not wanting to make Ivy run.

"I haven't heard from you," Carol said as Ivy stood in the doorway. Ivy just shrugged her shoulders, looking up at Carol and raised her eyebrows in the bratty way that Carol loved.

"Ok," Carol decisively said, walking into the motel room

and pushing Ivy aside before sitting on the edge of the bed.

"Hey, you can't just barge in here," Ivy complained, Carol just shrugging her shoulders and gave Ivy the same look she was just graced with.

"Fuck, what do you want from me?" Ivy angrily replied, annoyed that she couldn't understand the feelings she was feeling.

"I want you to try to tell me what's going on," Carol lovingly said, disarming Ivy and making her less angry and combative.

"I don't know the words," Ivy softly said as she felt her heart soften and begin to hurt. Ivy had gotten used to being on her own. She had gotten somewhat comfortable with having no one to rely on, and she had made peace with the fact that no one cared about her. And then Carol had come along and changed all of that, and it was just too much for her to feel. Too different, too loving and too kind.

"I've never had somebody care. I don't know what it's meant to feel like. When you are nice to me, it like, hurts," Ivy tried to explain, Carol nodding her head and wincing as she imagined how much pain Ivy must continuously feel. Carol took her coat off, deciding that she wasn't going anywhere tonight.

"Baby," she said affectionately and reached out her hand to Ivy. Ivy looked at her with hesitant eyes, wanting to be embraced but also wanting to feel the familiar feeling of neglect.

"You smell good, Mommy," Ivy mumbled into Carol's neck, making Carol gasp and hold onto Ivy firmer, not wanting to let you go.

"I've missed you," Ivy confessed, looking up at Carol and hoping that the older woman would never leave her.

"I know darling, I've missed you too," Carol said, kissing Ivy on the forehead and rocking her in her arms. They stayed like that, Carol nurturing Ivy as the night dragged on. Carol had underestimated how invested she had become in Ivy and felt herself going into Mommy space quickly and more deeply than she had experienced. It wasn't the frenzied obsession she had experienced during their first dates. It was something deeper, something calm and powerful, a feeling of primal protection and lust and desire that caused a gleam of passion to reflect in her eyes. Ivy noticed the change and rolled out of Carol's embrace, standing up in front of her.

"Can I show you something?" Ivy asked, Carol, smiling at her lovingly, the warmth in her eyes pulling Ivy into her little space, making her giggle. Ivy looked at Carol with a disarming look, Carol hadn't seen too frequently, and she sighed in contented bliss as she felt the world turn in slow motion.

"Of course, honey," Carol replied, watching as Ivy crouched down next to the bed and took out a box, opening the lid and stepping back. Carol looked at Ivy, who began to blush as Carol peered inside. She raised an eyebrow as she saw the contents, before smiling up at Ivy.

"Well, you have been busy," Carol said, patting her lap, delighted that Ivy walked over to her without thinking about it and sat on her lap as they looked into the box together.

"I researched," Ivy proudly said as she reached in and took out a pink paci.

"Mm, I see that," Carol replied, taking it from Ivy's hand and teasing her mouth open with it. Carol felt her heart pounding as Ivy rested her head back on Carol's shoulder as she sucked her paci, playing with Carol's long hair as she snuggled.

"What else do you have in here, sweetheart?" Carol asked, taking out a diaper and watching as Ivy's eyes grew wide, and she snapped out of little space, taking the paci from her lips.

"Um, I haven't tried that yet," Ivy said, her adult voice filled with the usual fear Carol had become accustomed too.

"And we don't have to, baby," Carol said, easing Ivy's fears.

"Ok, cool," Ivy said, the silence between her and Carol almost deafening.

"So, would you interested in putting that back in your little mouth and letting me get you out of these work clothes?" Carol asked, wanting her sweet little girl back in her arms. Ivy thought for a moment before biting her lip and putting her paci back in, Carol's encouraging smile easing her nerves.

"Have you eaten, baby?" Carol asked as she slowly undressed Ivy, seeing her protruding ribs. Carol frowned, noticing that Ivy was skinnier than usual. Ivy just shook her head and laughed when Carol rolled her eyes.

"I can just make a sandwich," Ivy said, lifting her legs up so Carol could take off her ripped skinny jeans.

"Hmm, let me do it while you shower," Carol said, holding Ivy lovingly before she walked back out to the table Ivy had been using as a kitchen bench.

I need to get her out of here, Carol thought as she made Ivy a peanut butter sandwich. Ivy walked out of the shower, naked and wrapped her arms around Carol, taking a bite of the sandwich.

"Get a plate, you little monster," Carol laughed.

"I don't have any plates," Ivy quickly replied, giggling as Carol rolled her eyes and grabbed the diaper in one hand, and she held onto Ivy's waist with the other. Carol raised a questioning eyebrow at Ivy, who just swallowed a mouthful of sandwich in a gulp before nodding her head slowly.

"Lay up on the bed for Mommy," Carol loving instructed, Ivy, feeling her cheeks flush pink.

"It's ok, baby. Mommy needs to get you ready for bed," Carol said, stroking Ivy's forehead until she relaxed.

"We can stop whenever you want, baby," Carol whispered as she kissed Ivy's cheek and stayed pressing her body into Ivy's as she wrapped her arms around Carol's neck. Slowly releasing her, Ivy opened her mouth and let Carol put her paci into her mouth. Carol slid the diaper under Ivy's bottom and tenderly ran her fingers over the girl's body before fastening the diaper to her waist. Seeing the slight embarrassment creep back into Ivy's eyes, Carol quickly pulled on Ivy's pajama bottoms and a baggy t-shirt, as Ivy grabbed at her.

"Alright, alright, baby, do you want to cuddle with Mommy?" Carol laughed as Ivy became slightly frantic in her need to be snuggled into Carol's deep cleavage. Nodding, Ivy curled up into Carol, her sleepy eyes making Carol turn the lights off in the room and feeling Ivy's breathing become slow, kissed her baby girl goodnight.

Chapter 5

"I've heard some people get really non-verbal when they are in little space," Ivy said the moment Carol opened her eyes the next morning. Blinking, Carol looked around the room and let herself adjust to being awake.

"Pardon?" Carol sleepily asked, wondering how late it was, the sun was streaming through the windows, and she guessed that it was no wonder that Ivy never slept in with how bright the room became.

"Some littles become non-verbal when they are in little space," Ivy repeated as though she had just discovered something nobody else knew.

"Yes. What is your point, baby?" Carol said, sitting up and watching as Ivy's eyes lit up.

"I think I am one of those. Because last night when I was sleepy and deep in little space, I didn't want to talk," Ivy explained, feeling empowered as she understood something about herself for the first time. Carol smiled and pulled her into her arms.

"Well, that would definitely explain your little grabby hands, baby girl," Carol said playfully, covering Ivy's face in kisses.

"So, you do have work today?" Carol asked, watching Ivy play with her breasts.

"Nope, I am moving into my new place today!" Ivy exclaimed, Carol, tilting her head in curiosity.

"Really? Where are you moving to?" Carol asked, putting her bra on much to Ivy's disappointment.

"It's like ten minutes' walk to the middle of town," Ivy replied, sitting up on the bed and feeling the diaper crinkle into her, reminding her that she was wearing one. Carol noticed the shock on her face, unsure of which space to be in as the new day dawned.

"Well, that sounds like you have a lot of big girl things to do. Do you want Mommy to take your diaper off so you can put your big girl panties on, darling?" Carol asked, Ivy, pulling her usual thinking face before nodding her head.

"Say, yes, please, Mommy," Carol lovingly prompted, enjoying gently training her baby girl.

"Yes, please, Mommy," Ivy repeated, looking down and touching the front of her diaper. Carol liked that Ivy was so sweet and unguarded when she was in little space and wondered if she would get to the stage where she was comfortable wetting her diaper.

"Ok, lay down for Mommy," Carol said, moving so she was crouching down next to Ivy. Ivy let Carol put her paci in her mouth as she took the diaper off and pulled on Ivy's panties. Ivy wriggling playfully as Carol's hair tickled her tummy.

"Oh, you are just too precious," Carol said, sitting back and looking at her sweet girl.

"So, like what are we?" Ivy asked, resting on her elbows, her paci in her hand.

"What would you like to be? Do you want this to be labeled?" Carol asked, excited that Ivy wanted to commit to her.

"Yeah, like, are we together or just like, I don't know, fucking around?" Ivy asked, trying to explain her thinking, making Carol laugh as she playfully spanked Ivy's ass.

"Hey!" Ivy exclaimed, nuzzling into Carol as she wrapped her arms around her.

"You're funny. We are not fucking around. I would like this to continue, do you want me to ask you if you want to be my girlfriend?" Carol asked, amused that she was having this conversation. Usually, when she was with a girl, she never used terms like girlfriend, but as she eased Ivy into the kink, she felt it wouldn't go astray to make connections that Ivy understood.

"Yep," Ivy simply replied. Carol stood up and put her blouse back on. Ivy's eyes never leaving her.

"Do you want to be my girlfriend, Ivy?" Carol asked, pulling her trousers on and watching Ivy's eyes light up.

"Yes, very much so," Ivy replied, getting on her knees from the bed and cuddling Carol's waist, snuggling into her and feeling safe for the first time in a long time.

"Well, good. And you're happy to keep learning about MDLG? You aren't going to lose me if you don't," Carol asked, not wanting to have Ivy be with her but not enjoy the kink.

"Mommy," Ivy said, giving Carol a playful look.

"You might have introduced me to the whole thing, but I'm the one who learned that I liked it," Ivy said, putting all of Carol's fears aside. Ivy reached for Carol's blouse, and slowly unbuttoned the buttons Carol had just done up.

"What do you think you're doing?" Carol asked as Ivy pulled it off and threw it on the bed.

"What does it look like I'm doing," Ivy said, pulling her top off and moving closer to Carol. Carol smirked and grabbed Ivy's hair, turning her around and pushing her down until she was on all fours on the bed. Carol gripped Ivy's hips in her hands and pushed against her ass making her giggle.

"Mommy," Ivy half whined, turning Carol on as she dry humped Ivy's ass.

"You know, little girls who tease Mommy, always get themselves in far deeper than they thought they would," Carol said, reaching around and pushing her hand into Ivy's jeans, cupping her panty covered pussy. Ivy gasped and arched her back as she felt Carol pull her panties to the side and push her head down.

"You're lucky I don't have my strap on here, or this little pussy would be destroyed," Carol said as she began to fuck Ivy at a pace she wanted. Ivy moaned and gripped the sheets, her back muscles flexing and straining as she let Carol pound into her.

"Mommy, I," Ivy started to beg just as she tightened her pussy muscles and relaxed, feeling her cunt flood and her hips drop. Carol wasn't finished and lay on top of Ivy as she continued to take her, loving how the girl was panting and moaning as another orgasm shook her little body.

"Sure a good girl," Carol cooed as she pulled out from Ivy and cuddled her affectionately. Ivy just sucked her thumb and snuggled into Carol, beaming up at her.

"Don't you have any furniture?" Carol asked Ivy as they took her backpack and travel bag into the new place. Ivy was busy walking around the space, in heaven that this was all hers.

"Um, no," Ivy replied. She planned to just sleep on the floor until she could afford a bed and take it from there.

"So no fridge, no washing machine or dryer, no bed or cupboard," Carol said, looking at Ivy and smiling at how impressed Ivy looked.

"Yep. But it's got a really soft carpet and a modern kitchen and bathroom, and I can actually afford it!" Ivy replied, warming Carol's heart.

"Ok, princess. Come on. Mommy is about to get her Mommy on," Carol said, watching as Ivy tilted her head to the side, trying to understand what Carol meant. Happily skipping over to where she was standing, Ivy held Carol's extended hand and walked out the door.

"Where are we going?" Ivy asked, her stomach rumbling making Carol laugh.

"First, we are getting breakfast, then I am buying you furniture for your new place," Carol explained, confusing Ivy.

"Why?" Ivy asked, surprised that Carol would suggest such a big gesture.

"What do you mean, why?! You haven't got a bed, darling," Carol said, pointing out the obvious, not making Ivy any less confused.

"But you don't need to do any of that stuff. Maybe breakfast. But you don't need to buy me other things," Ivy explained, Carol rolling her eyes as they stopped at a trendy breakfast bar.

"Baby girl. Mommy isn't just your girlfriend, and this isn't an equal thing for me, where we only do things that we can both afford or do. This is a; I look after you to the absolute best of my ability and capacity, sort of thing. Like what a sugar Mommy would do, but I don't expect you to fuck me in return. I know you are a big independent girl who doesn't need anyone, but Mommy wants to look after you. I want to make sure you have a big comfy bed to sleep in, that you have a fridge to put all your snacks in and help you make a nice home so that when Mommy isn't with you, I know you are in a safe space with everything you could need. Maybe also a few things you want," Carol explained, enjoying watching Ivy take in all the information.

"So, like, somebody I can count on all the time?" Ivy softly asked, having the painful feeling in her heart as the fear that Carol might end up leaving her racked her mind. Carol nodded, wiping the tear that escaped Ivy's eyes and kissing the tip of her nose.

"But what if you go?" Ivy whispered. Carol got out of her SUV and walked around to Ivy's side, opening the door and unbuckling her seatbelt.

"If I ever was to go, it would be because it would be best for both of us. And I wouldn't just abandon you, baby girl. I would make sure you were alright and taken care of and supported. Mommy wouldn't just up and go and not tell you why alright? So you don't need to worry yourself with that thought because I have no intention of leaving you," Carol said, holding onto Ivy and gently pulling her from her seat until she was standing up.

"Ok," Ivy said, wiping her tears away and nodding her head, deciding to believe Carol.

"Good," Carol replied, taking Ivy's hand and walking into the restaurant with Ivy's hand firmly holding hers.

"Tell me what you like," Carol said as they walked into the furniture store. Carol made Ivy write a list of all the things she needed and thought it was sweet that Ivy was surprised with the items Carol insisted on buying her.

"I really don't think I need shoe racks," Ivy laughed as Carol put two into the trolley.

"Where are you planning on storing your shoes then?" Carol asked, an eyebrow raised.

"Like, on the floor," Ivy said, shrugging her shoulder, Carol nodding to herself, satisfied that Ivy needed them after her response. Ivy just laughed and followed Carol around the store.

They picked out a bed, a cupboard, and a fridge, Ivy putting in pink bunny bed linen and making Carol smirk.

"Such a baby girl," she whispered as she also put in plain white and navy sets.

"For when you don't feel little. It's important to honor all the sides of yourself," Carol explained as Ivy started to take them out of the trolley, just to think for a moment and put them back down.

"Makes sense. It's really easy to get sucked into that place and never want to leave. But I guess sometimes I'll have to, huh?" Ivy asked, putting in pillows and fluffy blankets.

"Exactly," Carol replied, adding bath towels to the trolley. They ended up also buying a two-seater sofa, a coffee table, tv cabinet, two rugs, a tv, microwave, crockery, cooking utensils, cutlery, and a house plant. Ivy had won the battle of the washing machine as she said she would rather use a laundromat because it is fun. Carol seriously doubted how much fun waiting for laundry would be, but as Ivy was adamant she liked to use them, Carol made Ivy agree to tell her when going wasn't fun anymore and that she would get her one for her place then. They had decided to get everything delivered that afternoon, and as Carol drove Ivy to an ice-cream parlor, Ivy's head was spinning.

"I'm so grateful. I'm so surprised, I'm so like, wow," Ivy said, her mind racing with what had just happened. Never in her life had anyone ever bought her something, and then this amazingly beautiful woman not only wanted to be in her life, but she also was totally fine with spending thousands of dollars on her just to make sure she had cool stuff.

"Are you happy?" Carol asked, already knowing the answer. Ivy just looked at her with wide, surprised eyes and nodded yes.

"So happy, Mommy," Ivy said, holding Carol's hand as she drove.

Chapter 6

"How will you get to work, baby girl?" Carol asked as she woke up in Ivy's new bed Sunday morning. Carol had made sure that Ivy was settled into her new place, but had secretly not been able to bear the thought of leaving her alone. She wanted to be in Mommy space with Ivy for as long as she could, and Ivy never seemed to mind.

"I'm catching the bus, but I am working the late shift, so we have until 4," Ivy replied from the bathroom. She had woken up early and gone to have a shower.

"I don't know how I feel about you working the night shift," Carol said, walking into the bathroom as Ivy dried herself.

"Why? Are you scared something might happen to me?" Ivy teased, Carol grabbing her wrist and pulling her into her.

"Maybe," Carol replied, swaying with Ivy making her giggle.

"Well, don't be. Hardly anyone comes into the diner past midnight anyway. Plus, the pay is a little better working night shifts," Ivy replied, making Carol raise an eyebrow.

"Are you busy today? Do you want to do something?" Ivy asked Carol, escaping her grip and running into the bedroom. Carol lay on the bed as she watched Ivy dress. She pulled on her signature black skinny jeans and baggy band t-shirt and tied her hair up in a messy ponytail.

"What?" Ivy asked as she saw the subtle smile spread over Carol's lips.

"You are just so perfect," Carol replied, making Ivy blush.

"Yes, let's do some grocery shopping," Carol replied, making Ivy roll her eyes.

"Mommy, that's so boring," Ivy whined, making Carol laugh. Usually, she had a no whining policy, but she and Ivy hadn't talked about rules or punishments, and Carol was hoping to keep that conversation for a later time. She was worried that Ivy would be triggered and emotionally withdraw from her if the topic of punishments came up, and Carol didn't want that to happen.

"I know it is, but we can make it fun. Is your food budget still meal by meal? Maybe we need to start thinking about having a weekly food budget instead so that you always have food around and don't have to worry about being hungry," Carol suggested.

"Oh, I'm never worried when I'm hungry," Ivy playfully teased.

"You are such a cheeky girl," Carol replied, taking Ivy's hand and heading out the door.

"What is the point of this stuff?" Ivy asked as Carol put in tinned tomatoes into the trolley.

"Because I am going to teach you how to cook so that you don't keep buying sugary cereals and think that it is an appropriate snack," Carol replied, making Ivy laugh.

"But it has a nice crunch to it," Ivy replied, getting a playful spank on her ass. Carol bought the ingredients to make simple dishes like Bolognese, carbonara, and bacon and egg pie. Ivy tried to sneak in as much junk food as she could get away with, adding cakes and soda to the trolley just for Carol to take most of it out again.

"Choose three trash foods, and that is it, young lady," Carol said, holding Ivy's chin in her hand and making her look up at her until she blushed. Ivy hadn't heard Carol's strict Mommy voice before, and it made her excited, slightly turned on, but also aware that she didn't want to piss Carol off. Ivy chose a packet of chips, a bag of gummy bears, and a tub of ice-cream in no time at all, coming to the register and taking out her purse.

"It's ok, baby," Carol softly said, Ivy's eyes going wide.

"What do you mean?" She whispered back as the lady scanned the groceries.

"Let me set you up, you can buy them for yourself next time," Carol replied, paying the lady and walking out of the store, Ivy numbly following behind her.

"Why are you doing all this nice stuff for me?" Ivy asked

on the way back to her apartment. Carol placed her hand on Ivy's thigh and rubbed it affectionately.

"Because I want to, if I'm selfish, it makes me feel good to look after you. You deserve somebody who can treat you right, and I want that person to be me. This is what I meant when I said that I view my role in the relationship as the person to take care of you. I don't expect you to take care of me like this, because that isn't what a baby is meant to do; it's Mommy's job. I expect different things from you," Carol replied, Ivy, listening attentively.

"Like what?" Ivy asked, her little voice escaping her, making her laugh.

"I expect that you are loyal to me," Carol began to say, making Ivy laugh.

"That's kinda like the most basic rule of being in a monogamous relationship," she said, making Carol smile. She didn't like being interrupted, but she would let that one slide.

"I expect you to be honest with me. If we do something that you are uncomfortable with, I expect that you tell me straight away. I will push a little bit on your limits, but if you ever feel that it's too much, you need to tell me. It's not tough to push way past what you are comfortable with, even if it's not a physical thing, emotion and psychological boundaries need to be respected by you and by me. And most of the time, I will be able to read who you feel, but you still need to tell me, alright," Carol explained. Ivy listened as she watched Carol pull up at her apartment.

"Yeah, that all makes sense," Ivy said, taking two shopping bags in her hands and walking inside.

"That all sounds really heavy and serious," Ivy said as she began to put the groceries away. Carol placed her hands on Ivy's shoulders and turned her around.

"It is," she replied, smiling down at Ivy, putting her at ease.

"What else? I know that can't be it. I've read things online about rules and stuff," Ivy said, taking out a bottle of water and sitting on the sofa, Carol coming to join her.

"Oh, have you now?" She teased, pulling Ivy into her arms, making her snuggle into her chest.

"Yep," Ivy said, closing her eyes as she listened to Carol's heartbeat.

"I don't want to give you so much to think about just yet. Let's start with you calling me Mommy. Not when you are in front of your friends or at work, but every other time," Carol said as Ivy sipped the water.

"And, how would you feel about wearing a diaper to bed and letting me pick out your pajamas?" Carol asked Ivy as she kissed the top of her head.

"Ok, Mommy," Ivy said, nuzzling into Carol. The warmth of her body made Ivy sleepy, and Carol checked the time to make sure she wouldn't be late for work.

"Come on, little girl. No time for naps on Mommy right

now. You need to get ready for work," Carol said, gently pulling Ivy off her chest.

"But, Mommy," Ivy softly whined, her grabby hands reaching out for Carol.

"How about this. Mommy will pick you up in the morning before I go to woke and make sure you get home safely and all cleaned up and tucked into bed?" Carol suggested. Looking into Ivy's yearning gaze, she knew that she and Ivy would need to find a way to have a compatible work schedules.

She needs me, Carol thought as Ivy put her thumb in her mouth and nodded her head.

"Alright. Come on, let me get you ready for work then," Carol said, taking Ivy's thumb from her lips and replacing it with her paci. Carol walked over to Ivy's new cupboard, took out her uniform and lingerie, and returned to the bed. Taking Ivy's arms, she undressed her until she was lying naked on the bed. Carol admired the girl's youthful body, feeling her pussy begin to tingle and moisten.

"You are so beautiful," Carol said as she stroked Ivy's body from her collar bone to her clit, making Ivy squirm and giggle.

"Mommy," Ivy said playfully and jumped into Carol's loving arms. Ivy loved the feeling of Carol's arm completely enclosing her body, and she snuggled into the nook of Carol's neck as she closed her eyes once more. Feeling her body become heavy, Carol stood up and let Ivy gently fall on the bed, smiling at her warmly when she opened her eyes.

"Give Mommy your paci baby girl. You don't need that anymore," Carol said, as Ivy obeyed her.

"Such a good girl," Carol added as she began to dress Ivy in her work uniform. Carol had chosen Ivy's black lace panties and matching bra and had to restrain herself from rubbing over Ivy's nipples with her thumbs as she saw them become hard. Ivy noticed her cheeky sparkle in her eye, not going unnoticed by Carol.

"Do you like how it looks, Mommy?" Ivy teased, getting to her knees and rubbing her hands over her perky breasts. Carol just glared at Ivy before turning around to take her uniform in her hands. She raised an eyebrow as she held it out to Ivy, who had begun to rub herself through her panties.

"Ivy," Carol warned, the stern tone in her voice making Ivy giggle as she continued to tease Carol. Carol sat down on the bed and watched as Ivy performed for her, never changing her expression and enjoying how Ivy upped her teasing to try and get Carol to crack. She pulled her panties down and sucked her finger before sliding it up and down her slit, causing Carol to clench her cunt tightly as it began to throb once more.

If I had a cock, it would be rock hard right now, Carol thought as she shifted and pulled Ivy towards her until the girl was straddling Carol's soft thigh. Carol held Ivy's hips down and pushed her thigh up, pressing her panties into her pussy and making her gasp.

"Mommy, I'm going to be late," Ivy giggled as she tried to push Carol away.

"Oh, you think you can tease Mommy and just get away with it?" Came Carol's throaty reply. Ivy half froze, her wide eyes of surprise turning Carol on as she began to rock Ivy's hips back and forth, hardening the girl's clit.

"Mommy," Ivy gasped as she placed both her hands on Carol's shoulders, biting her bottom lip and moaning as she was taken.

"There's a good girl," Carol moaned when she felt Ivy's hips move to their own accord. Carol unzipped her jeans and put her hand in her pants, enjoying watching Ivy get herself off in front of her. Carol held onto Ivy with one hand on her back as she rubbed her clit with the other. She tilted her head back as she felt her orgasm building inside of her and closed her eyes, and she lifted her thigh once more to have Ivy's pussy closer to hers.

"Tell Mommy when you are close, little bunny," Carol said as she felt her pussy explode, her squirting cunt soaking her panties and the crotch of her jeans. She watched as Ivy continued to jerk her pussy against Carol's thigh, desperate but not able to cum. Carol thought for a moment before quickly flipping Ivy onto her back, pushing her hand away, and began rubbing her. Carol pinned Ivy's hands above her head with one hand and pushed her nipple into Ivy's mouth before going back to rubbing the girl's clit. Carol loved the sound and feeling of Ivy moaning against her breast and fucked her harder. She could see that Ivy couldn't cum with just her clit being stimulated and gently pushed a finger into Ivy's pussy, causing her to groan in pleasure and buck her hips.

"This is what you want, baby girl? Mommy inside of you, getting you off with her tit in your mouth. Mommy's dirty, little girl," Carol said, causing Ivy to be taken to a place she had never explored before. Carol eased another finger into Ivy and began fucking her harder, knocking her clit with her knuckles at every push. Feeling Ivy's pussy begin to tighten, Carol fucked her faster, curling her fingers inside Ivy and hitting her g-spot. She wrapped her arm around Ivy's head as she lowered her body onto the girl's as she fucked her with a predatory passion, as Ivy screamed and shook violently, falling silent after her orgasm racked her body. Carol felt Ivy's juices coat her fingers and enjoyed how her cunt dripped as Carol took her fingers out of the girl. Ivy lay on the bed, breathing heavily, as though she had just sprinted up a hill, and Carol replaced her breast with Ivy's paci. She wiped her down with a wet wipe and continued to dress her until she was in her uniform, still laying on the bed.

"Mommy," Ivy softly said, the need in her eyes matched by her little voice.

"Mommy's here, baby. I'm not going anywhere," Carol

replied, wrapping Ivy in her arms and rocking her gently.

Chapter 7

Carol had pinned a teddy bear pin to Ivy's uniform and watched as she practically skipped inside to start her shift. Carol had ended up driving Ivy to work because she had missed her bus. Deciding that she would get Chinese take-out, Carol drove to her favorite restaurant, picked up her order, and drove home.

Oh, it is going to get really lonely here the longer I am with her, Carol said to herself as she sat down on the couch and checked her phone. She had been hoping that Ivy had messaged her, but after seeing the blank screen, settled in for a night of movie streaming before the workweek began.

Mommy, I miss you. Ivy's message woke Carol up. Looking around the dark living room, the only light coming from the tv screen, Carol fumbled around the couch looking for her phone. Smiling as she saw the message from Ivy, she looked at the time. It was only half an hour earlier than she was planning on getting up, so deciding to have a shower and get dressed, Carol made her way to the bathroom. She stripped off and threw her clothes in the wash basket before running the warm water. Feeling horny, Carol got out of the shower and went to her top drawer, taking out her dildo and walking back into the shower, she lifted one leg onto the lower nook. Designed originally for shampoo and conditioner, but having become a personal favorite for scratching an itch. Carol pushed the soft silicone cock into her pussy in one slow motion, sighing in relief as she felt the dildo fill her, pressing on her hilt. She moaned as she quickly fucked herself, thinking of Ivy sitting in front of her, watching as she pleased herself.

"Do you like watching Mommy?" Carol said out loud, thinking of Ivy's eyes sparkling up at her. Pumping the dildo in and out of her cunt, Carol enjoyed feeling like a dirty older woman as she imagined sticking the dildo into Ivy's mouth and making her lick and suck her juices off as her eyes watered. Cumming hard, Carol pulled the cock from her cunt and let her juices flow, moaning, putting it back in, and bringing herself to a second orgasm before she cleaned herself and got out of the shower.

That should do it, she thought as she dried herself, imagining that Ivy wouldn't be in the mood after her shift. Carol dressed in her work uniform, wrapping her coat around her curvaceous body and running her fingers through her wavy hair, deciding to wear it down until she got to work.

I'm in the parking lot, baby girl, was the message she gave Ivy as she waited for her. She was five minutes late, and Carol thought that was unusual. Carol played a game on her phone as she waited. Ten minutes passed and then 15 minutes, making Carol slightly agitated. Ivy knew that Carol still had to make it to her work on time. Deciding to go in and drag her girl away, Carol locked her SUV and went inside.

"Hey, is Ivy still here?" She asked another waitress who just nodded and pointed to out the back.

"Thanks," Carol said, surprised the waitress was so forthcoming with the information. Carol walked toward the back, feeling her stomach tighten as she heard loud yelling coming from behind a door. Turning the door handle, Carol walked in to see Ivy sitting on an office chair, her boss sitting on the edge of the desk, pulling on his cock.

"Hey, what the fuck, you can't be here. Fuck off!" The man aggressively said, putting his dick away. Ivy turned around to see Carol standing behind her, Ivy's mascara stained cheeks was all she needed to know.

"Carol, I," Ivy began to say, stopping as Carol held out her hand and glaring at the man.

"Let's go," was all Carol said as Ivy scrambled to collect her things. Carol fought the urge to punch the man in the face. Her main concern was getting her baby girl out of the situation.

"I'm sorry I called you Carol, I'm sorry that all happened," Ivy began to say as Carol drove towards her apartment.

"Baby girl, it's ok. You can call me Carol when there are other people around, remember?" Carol lovingly said as she watched Ivy break down in tears.

"Almost home, little one," Carol gently said as she pulled into Ivy's street, parking out the front and ushering her inside, locking the door behind her.

"How much time do you have?" Ivy asked, wiping her tears. Carol smiled at her kindly.

"As much time as you need. I messaged the girls and told them I'd be in later," Carol replied, Ivy, giving her a sideward smile.

"Let's get you out of these clothes," Carol said, causing Ivy to flinch as she reached out to touch her upper arm.

"Hey, little one, Mommy isn't going to hurt you," Carol said, opening her arms and waiting for Ivy to walk into them cautiously.

"There's my good girl," Carol said as she walked Ivy to the bathroom, stripping her clothes off.

"He said that he would give me a raise if I sucked his cock," Ivy softly, suddenly said as Carol turned on the shower and began to lather her body in shower gel.

"Oh, baby girl. He is a pig. I'm sorry that he put you in that situation. Why didn't you just get up and walk away?" Carol asked, watching as Ivy took over.

"I don't know, it kinda all happened so fast. He knew I was a lesbian; it was just like, too much for my mind to respond to. I felt frozen," Ivy replied, getting out of the shower and being wrapped in a towel before Carol took her to her bedroom.

"Good thing, Mommy, came barging in," Carol said, taking out a thick diaper and fluffy pink onesie.

"Yeah, you're good at barging into places," Ivy replied, giggling and feeling herself begin to relax. Her hands were reaching out and grabbing for Carol.

"Shh, baby girl, Mommy is here," Carol said, replying to Ivy's clinginess. Ivy sucked on the paci Carol put in her mouth and lay still as Carol diapered her, making her diaper particularly thick with an extra, double thickness pad before fastening the tabs and dressing Ivy in the onesie.

"Mommy's little bunny," Carol lovingly said Ivy touched the front of her diaper, wondering why Carol had made it so thick. Her thighs were forced to stay slightly apart, and Carol picked her up and placed her on her hip, surprising Ivy.

"Yeah, Mommy still has a few tricks up her sleeve, baby girl," Carol said, impressed with herself as she pulled back the sheets on Ivy's bed and lay her gently down. Carol lay next to Ivy as she snuggled into her chest, getting gentle pats on her padded bottom until she was almost asleep.

"Mommy wants you to stay like that until I come back and change you when my day is over. I don't want you going back to that diner. Mommy will support you until you find a new job. But that place is out of bounds now, alright sugar?" Carol whispered to Ivy as Ivy nodded her head before falling asleep.

"See you soon, little girl," Carol said as she kissed Ivy on the forehead and left for work, messaging Ivy the new rules about the diner before she started to drive.

After she woke up in the late afternoon, Ivy happily stayed in little space. She watched some cartoons, followed the Bolognese recipe that Carol had written down for her, and ate a late lunch while coloring in.

I wish every day could be like this, Ivy thought as she pulled on her fluffy black socks before walking to the kitchen and taking out a packet of popcorn. She messaged Carol several times, happy that Carol always replied quickly, and before she knew it, it was 5:30, and Carol was on her way back to her.

Carol raced back to Ivy the moment her shift evened and noticed the strange way Ivy was behaving the moment she walked into her apartment.

"Baby, what are you doing?" She said, putting her bag down and going to the fridge to take out a beer.

"I have to go to the bathroom, Mommy, but you said to stay like this," Ivy replied, making Carol laugh. She eyed Ivy and decided that she was going to see how far she could be pushed.

"Well, then go, baby girl. You can still go without taking that off," Carol replied, patting the spot on the couch next to her.

"It hurts too much to sit, Mommy," Ivy said. Carol took a long drink before putting her beer down and getting down on the floor, pulling Ivy down with her.

"Sit in front of me, baby girl," Carol lovingly said, falling into Mommy space as though a switch was flicked on in her mind. She pulled Ivy's hips back into her and wrapped her legs around Ivy's, pulling them open. Carol placed her hand over the mound of Ivy's pussy and pressed into her, her other hand pressing on her bladder.

"Mommy," Ivy said, beginning to squirm, fighting Carol as not to wet her diaper.

"Wet your diaper for Mommy, baby girl. It will feel so much better," Carol whispered, enjoying how Ivy's head moving from side to side made her breasts shake.

"I can't Mommy," Ivy whispered back, Carol seeing the blush of red beginning to cover Ivy's face.

"Such a good girl. Come on, little one. Mommy is right here, try for Mommy, baby," Carol encouraged, feeling Ivy's diaper becoming warm but stopping when Ivy gasped and sat up straight, pushing against Carol.

"Where are you trying to go, baby? Mommy has you in her arms," Carol gently teased, pressing on Ivy's bladder firmer and feeling her surrendered to her request and wetting her diaper.

"There there, Mommy's got you," Carol said as Ivy

began to cry.

"You don't like being a wet girl, do you, baby?" Carol said as Ivy bit her bottom lip and shook her head.

"Well, Mommy can fix that. Lay down," Carol instructed Ivy, following her command immediately. Ivy looked up at Carol with the puppy dog eyes, which always melted Carol's heart. Carol had learned that Ivy gave her those eyes when she was deep in her little space, wanting to be looked after, wanting to be safe, and have somebody to trust and knowing that she was that person for Ivy made her heart swell.

"Bottom up," Carol instructed, gently tapping Ivy's thighs, smiling down at her when she obeyed. Carol took Ivy's diaper away, wiped her clean, and slid another diaper underneath her. Ivy didn't feel like talking; she felt sad. Sad that somebody had tried to take advantage of her, sad that she thought she would have probably done it if she didn't have Carol. Carol had made it perfectly clear that Ivy wasn't to be with anyone but her, and even though the thought of sucking her bosses dick grossed her out, she knew in her heart that even three months ago, with the carrot of extra money being on the table, she would have done it.

"What are you thinking about, little one," Carol asked. Ivy looked up at her suddenly and shrugged her shoulders.

"I just feel like being quiet tonight, Mommy," she softly said. Carol guessed that Ivy's withdrawn behavior was because of the situation she had walked in on, and she frowned.

"Baby girl. Mommy needs you to tell me what is going on so I can help you," Carol said as she clipped Ivy's onesie back up and lifted her into her arms. Ivy just rested her head on Carol's chest and sucked her thumb. She couldn't find the words to describe what she felt, so she just closed her eyes and felt her heart feel heavy.

"I just feel sad, Mommy," Ivy replied softly, and Carol knew not to try and push her for anything else.

"Alright, baby girl. Can Mommy take the lead tonight, then?" Carol asked. She hated that she would have to leave Ivy alone in her apartment eventually and thought about racing home to pack an overnight bag. Ivy felt the same way and sighed heavily.

"Mommy, I don't want you to go," she said, tugging on Carol's woolly sweater.

"I don't want to go either, baby girl," Carol whispered back.

"How about I fix you up something for dinner, and you come to my house for a few nights?" Carol suggested. Ivy apartment was 20minutes from Carol's, and it made more sense for Ivy to go to her apartment as Carol's work was only 10minutes from her home. Ivy held her tummy and looked up at Carol, wishing she could be the happy girl she knew Carol loved.

"I don't really feel like eating, Mommy," she said as she shrugged her shoulders. Carol looked at Ivy and saw just how little she was feeling tonight and smiled.

"Then you can just have a bottle. Come on, darling, let's pack you a bag. You can come and see where Mommy lives," Carol said as Ivy nodded her head.

Carol had packed all of Ivy's clothes, granted there weren't many adult clothes to choose from, but her collections of onesies were also packed.

"Mommy has diapers at her house, so you don't need to pack yours, baby," Carol said when Ivy handed her a pink diaper.

"But do you have pink ones?" Ivy said, before putting her paci in her mouth. Carol smirked, kissed Ivy on the cheek, and packed the pink diapers.

"I think that is it, honey. Mommy has a special surprise for you in the car," Carol said, looking over the apartment one last time before closing the door. She had pulled a pair of baggy jeans over the top of Ivy's onesie and was happy to see how padded her bottom looked. This was one of those things which put Carol into Mommy space, and she liked that Ivy seemed to enjoy it just as much.

"Mommy, what is that?" Ivy asked as she saw the adult car seat when Carol opened the back door. Carol's SUV had the darkest legal tint, which meant that no one would be able to see Ivy in the back from outside of the car.

"It's for you, to make sure that you are safe when we go

driving," Carol said, patting Ivy's bottom to indicate that she needed to get in the car. Ivy obeyed and climbed into the back, sitting down in her car seat and letting Carol pull the restraints over her chest and buckle her up.

"There, you aren't going to get away from me, little miss," Carol said as she stroked Ivy's cheeks with her thumbs either side of her face and kissing her on her forehead before closing the door. Ivy felt her diaper push into her as the SUV roared into life and began driving toward Carol's house.

"Are you alright back there, honey," Carol said, looking in the rear-vision mirror and saw Ivy playing with her bunny.

"Yeah, Mommy," Ivy replied, enjoying how little, safe, and protected she felt. Carol smirked, seeing Ivy bounce her bunny over the side of the car as she tilted her head from side to side as she played. Carol felt her heart swell and wondered how lucky she was that Ivy was hers. She imagined forcing a vibrator into Ivy's diaper and locking her in place, making her take it as she drove around the city, her little girl a horny mess in the back, and the thought made her juices run.

Chapter 8

Ivy had fallen asleep in the back seat, and Carol smiled as she watched the young girl sucking on her paci and having her head tiled against one side of the car seat.

"Shh, it's just Mommy, baby girl," Carol said as Ivy woke up startled. Seeing Carol's loving face, Ivy resettled and let Carol carry her into her apartment. It was late, and Carol was happy there was no one about as she fumbled with the keys, Ivy's bag on her shoulder and her baby girl in her arms. Carol walked inside, locked the door, and sighed in contented bliss. This is what she had always wanted—a baby girl who was as enthralled by her as she was with her little one. Somebody who would let her experience and experiment all her deepest Mommy desires, and as Carol dropped Ivy's bag by the side of the bed, feeling her diaper become wet made her smile in satisfaction.

"What a good girl you are," Carol said to a sleeping Ivy, laying her down on the floor and beginning to change her wet diaper.

"Such a beautiful little girl," Carol added as she cleaned Ivy, powdered her, and put a fresh diaper on the girl's thin frame. Carol noticed that Ivy's ribs protruded less obviously, and she felt content that she was looking after her baby girl very well. Ivy opened her eyes to find Carol putting a new onesie on her and looked around the unfamiliar apartment, her eyes going wide.

"It's alright, little girl. You are in Mommy's house," Carol said, catching Ivy's eye and putting her at ease. Carol hadn't seen Ivy this little before, and she liked that Ivy was so comfortable that she could slip this deep into the space.

"I'm hungry now, Mommy," Ivy softly said, as she felt Carol rub over her diaper covered pussy affectionately.

"I thought you might be. Mommy is going to make a bottle for you. Crawl behind me, little one. I want you to sit on Mommy's couch," Carol instructed, happy when Ivy sleepily obeyed. Carol made up a chocolate protein shake and walked over to where Ivy was sitting cross-legged on the couch.

"Come here," Carol instructed, cradling Ivy in her arms and pushing the nipple of the bottle between her lips.

"Such a good girl," Carol cooed as she watched Ivy hungrily drink. Carol liked that Ivy snuggling into her breast as she drank, making her nipples hard and wishing that she had milk of her own for Ivy.

"In the morning, I want to buy you a few new outfits and accessories, alright, baby?" Carol said, Ivy, nodding her head happily. She loved that Carol always wanted to make sure she had the best of everything. Ivy closed her eyes as she felt her tummy filling up and shook her head to dislodge the bottle from her lips.

"Don't fuss little one," Carol said, trying to put the bottle back into her mouth, but Ivy continued to push it away.

"Are you finished, little girl?" Carol asked, trying not to become angry with Ivy. Ivy just nodded her head, and Carol smiled at the slight swelling of Ivy's tummy, patting it gently.

"I'm full, Mommy," Ivy said in the little voice, which always made Carol melt.

"Well, alright, then. But you need to tell Mommy when you have had enough. You almost got yourself a spanking because I thought you were being bratty," Carol explained, Ivy's eyes going wide.

"Yes, that's right. Mommy was almost about to turn you over and make that little bottom red," Carol said, turning Ivy over and playfully spanking her, making her giggle and squirm about on Carol's lap. Carol pinned Ivy to her thighs, making Ivy groan as the pressure of her full tummy was pushed down and made her have the hiccups.

"Oh, little one. Did Mommy play too rough?" Carol teased, Ivy hiccupping again. Ivy nodded, and Carol pulled her onto her lap and patted her back as she rocked her gently.

Carol reluctantly left Ivy in the house Tuesday morning. After a night of holding onto her little girl, Carol felt that nothing could ruin her mood. She had left Ivy with a list of things to do so she didn't get bored and had set her phone up with the apartment's Wi-Fi. Getting messages all day from Ivy, Carol couldn't believe how wonderful her life had become. It was noticeable to the other girls' at work who benefitted from Carol's fantastic mood.

"I bought everyone donuts," Carol cheerily said as she walked into the staff lounge.

"Oh, yes," Gabi said, jumping up and down excitedly.

"You know. I don't care who she is. This girl is good for all of us!" Hope said with a mouthful of strawberry iced donuts.

"Yeah, she goes alright," Carol said, remembering how sweet Ivy looked in the dino onesie Carol had dressed her in that morning.

"Actually. We haven't filled that receptionist position yet, have we?" Carol asked the girls who just shook their heads.

"Right. Well, I think I know just the girl," Carol said, winking at them and leaving the room.

"Do you think she's is going to give the job to her girlfriend?" Gabi asked Hope, who was busy getting another donut.

"I don't care, as long as she keeps bringing us treats, I don't care who she hires," Hope replied.

"Baby girl," Carol called as she walked into the apartment. She put her bag down and walked through the house until she found Ivy coloring in by the window. The breeze was making Ivy's hair catch the wind, making her look magnificent. Carol noticed that she had changed into the adult clothes Carol had permitted her to wear if she felt like going for a walk.

"Mommy!" Ivy exclaimed, looking up, squashing any doubt in Carol's mind as to which headspace Ivy was experiencing.

"Hey there, little one," Carol replied, coming to sit down next to Ivy and feeling her climb into her lap.

"Mommy's little angel," Carol said, wrapping Ivy in her arms and rocking her as she watched Ivy continue to color.

"I have a question for you, and you can say no, alright, baby girl," Carol said, making Ivy stop and turn her head to look at Carol, her big waiting eyes melting Carol's heart.

"How would you feel about coming to work with Mommy?" Carol asked, Ivy, tilting her head to the side and thinking.

"What do you mean?" Ivy said, putting her crayon down.

"Well. We need a receptionist. And I was wondering if you wanted to give that a go? Mommy would be the one to train you as it is a small private practice, but I think you would really like it there. Plus, then you could write it on your resume, and it would give you some experience?" Carol suggested Ivy thought about it for a moment, shrugging her shoulders and feeling shy.

"Yeah, I guess. Would I fit in?" Ivy asked, making Carol's smile widen.

"Yeah, baby girl, you would fit in. We couldn't be too wrapped up in each other, even though the other girls know you are mine. They don't know that I am into this lifestyle, so any Mommy, baby dynamic would be off the table. But it would only be for when we are work. Once you get in the car, you'd be my little girl again," Carol explained, Ivy considering the offer.

"I didn't think I was ever going to be good enough to be a receptionist, Mommy," she said, making Carol laugh. She hadn't thought so highly of the job before. Not that she treated people differently based on their occupation, but she was amused at how highly Ivy clearly viewed it.

"Baby girl, you're going to be amazing! So, tomorrow you'll come with Mommy to work. I should maybe tell you. The girls call me Mama at work," Carol said, Ivy's head snapping back around to look at her dead in the eye.

"No, it's not like that. They don't mean it like the way you do. It's just that I am the oldest one there, and I am constantly helping them sort their shit out. So, when you hear them, you don't need to be jealous. You can call me Mama at work if you'd like, but you might need to pretend that you didn't know. Or you can call me Carol. It doesn't bother me either way. Alright?" Carol explained, half stumbling over her words, making Ivy laugh.

"Did you sort that out for yourself?" Ivy said, feeling less little and her usually adult sarcastic self once more. Carol noticed and raised an eyebrow, amused when Ivy wasn't put back in her place.

"Oh, so this is how you thank Mommy? You being a little smart ass?" Carol said, standing up and making Ivy fall off her lap, forcing her to stand up as well. Carol grabbed her wrist and walked quickly into her bedroom, shutting the door behind Ivy and pinning her against it. Carol had a cross, connected to the back of her door, and she cuffed Ivy's wrists above her head, and her ankles spread wide, locking her in place.

"I haven't had to punish you so far, I was wondering when this would happen," Carol said, making Ivy laugh.

"Oh, you won't be laughing in a moment, young lady," Carol said, kissing Ivy's forehead and slapping her panty covered pussy at the same time making her gasp.

"That's right," Carol said, rubbing Ivy's pussy, feeling her panties becoming wet with her juices.

"Such a ready little girl. Always horny for Mommy, aren't you?" Carol breathed into Ivy's ear, making her shiver and pull against the restraints.

"Where do you think you are going, little girl?" Carol teased as she slapped Ivy again, making her moan in pain and pleasure as Carol rubbed her sensually once more.

"Mommy," Ivy moaned, pushing her pussy out against Carol's hand only to be spanked again.

"Why are you moving like a little whore? Mommy doesn't want to fuck a whore tonight. Mommy wants her little princess," Carol said, pushing Ivy back and going to get a gag.

"I don't want to hear your complaints," she said, pushing the pacifier gag into Ivy's resisting mouth and strapping it in place.

"There. This might teach you to wear more than panties and a t-shirt around the house," Carol said, pinching Ivy's nipples and making her moan against the gag.

"Mommy can't hear you sugar," Carol said, taking Ivy's chin in her hand before shaking her head and letting her go. Taking a pair of nipple clamps from the drawer, Carol carefully put them on Ivy's hard nipples, over her t-shirt, concerned that she didn't want to push Ivy too much, but wanting to do exactly what she wanted with the girl. Carol could feel her pussy moisten, the slick juices making her full pussy lips wet. Taking her pants off, Carol also loosed her blouse, exposing her large breasts, cocooned in her emerald lace bra.

"Oh, I know you like the look of this," Carol said as she rubbed her breasts sensually in front of Ivy. Ivy watched, her eyes growing wide and becoming mesmerized by the woman in front of her. Carol felt her heart soften, making her smile and shake her head as she forgot for a minute that she was meant to be punishing Ivy.

"That's enough of that," Carol said, making her breasts bounce one final time before taking out her riding crop, instantly making Ivy strain against the cuffs.

"Baby girl, Mommy isn't going to hurt you more than you can handle," Carol said, seeing the fear in Ivy's eyes. Although the idea of flogging was Ivy's, Carol was acutely aware that Ivy had been beaten by one of the foster parents she had had over the years. The look in Ivy's eyes told Carol that maybe even though she had said she was down for it, she might not be ready. Running the crop over Ivy's body, she saw Ivy fight back the tears, her fight to be freed, slowly ending, and Carol decided that she wasn't going to push Ivy on this tonight.

"Mommy's got you, baby girl," Carol said, throwing the crop on the floor and holding Ivy until her rigid body relaxed into Carol's loving arms. Ivy's breathing was shallow and frightened. Carol uncuffed Ivy's wrists, feeling her fling them around Carol's neck as she pulled herself closer to the woman who held her firmly.

"Mommy's here," Carol whispered.

"I'm sorry I was a smart ass," Ivy said as the tears rolled down her cheeks. Carol untied Ivy's ankles and went back to holding onto Ivy.

"And sorry I just cussed," Ivy added, realizing that she had broken another rule.

"Shh, little Ivy. Mommy can forgive that tonight," Carol

said as she bought Ivy to the bathroom.

"Have a shower for Mommy," Carol said, turning the water on. She wanted Ivy to have some control over herself, and she sat down on the floor as she watched Ivy shower.

"I think I want to go and try the job, Mommy," Ivy said as she lathered her body with shower gel.

"I think that would be a good idea," Carol replied. Ivy got out of the shower and dried herself.

"I want to try it again," she softly said to Carol, who raised an eyebrow.

"Try what?" Carol said, patting the bed and waiting for Ivy to lay down on it. Carol began to diaper Ivy, giving her the bunny she loved so much to cuddle.

"I want to try the riding crop again. But maybe not when I'm tied up," Ivy said, piquing Carol's concern.

"Why do you want to try?" Carol asked, pulling on a yellow fluffy diaper cover, Ivy's thigh-high white sockies, and putting a tight white t-shirt on her baby girl.

"You look like a cute little duckie," Carol said, cuddling Ivy.

"I want to try it because I think you like it, and I want you to be able to do things you like," Ivy replied, melting Carol's heart.

"That's so sweet, baby girl. But Mommy doesn't like it when you don't," Carol explained. Ivy frowned.

"But maybe I just didn't like it that way. Maybe I like it

a different way?" Ivy replied, running out of the room and going to get the crop. Carol wondered if this was a good idea. The last thing she wanted to do was trigger Ivy, but her mind relaxed when Ivy came running back into the room.

"Here," Ivy said, handing Carol the riding crop. Carol took it in her hands and immediately felt herself respond to it. She loved how it made her feel in control, if not somewhat cruel and sadistic.

"Maybe if I cuddle into you," Ivy suggested, Carol, opening her arms to the girl and enjoying the mix of primal desire and tender love she was experiencing.

"Suck your thumb, baby girl," Carol said in the low voice she always got when she was wildly aroused. Ivy obeyed, and Carol watched as Ivy's eyes grew wide like they always did when she was in little space. Carol replaced Ivy's thumb with her breast and moaned as the girl began to suckle eagerly.

"Good girl," Carol slowly said as she pulled her hair to one side and lightly patted Ivy's thigh with the crop. Ivy wriggled in her arms, only adding to Carol's enjoyment, and she brought the crop down harder into Ivy's soft skin, causing her to make high pitched squeals.

"This was a good idea, you clever little girl," Carol said, kissing Ivy's forehead. Carol continued to gently mark Ivy's skin until it was red and hot, having to restrain herself from belting Ivy the way her pussy so desired.

In time, Carol said to herself as she watched Ivy

painfully flinch.

"You are doing so good, baby girl. Come to Mommy's other side," Carol encouraged as she nursed Ivy in her other arm as her other hand began to claim Ivy's other thigh as her own.

"Mommy," Ivy said, wincing as she gasped and tried to pull away from Carol.

"It hurts," she added, making Carol moan in pleasure but stop herself from continuing.

"Oh, baby girl! You have been such a good girl for Mommy!" Carol said, putting the crop down and running lotion over Ivy's thighs. Ivy bashfully smiled.

"I wanted to be good for you. I liked it like that more than the first way," Ivy said, filling Carol with pride.

"I'm so proud of you for coming up with this idea," she said as she patted Ivy's padded bottom.

"Come on. Come to the living room so Mommy can make us dinner, and you can play until then, alright, baby?" Carol said, picking Ivy up and carrying her out of the room.

Chapter 9

"What if they don't like me?!" Ivy nervously questioned on the way to work. Carol rolled her eyes. This was the seventh time they had had this decision that morning.

"Baby. What has Mommy said?" Carol answered, placing her hand under Ivy's skirt and rubbing her clit through her panties. Carol had made Ivy sit in the front passenger seat today to try and make her feel more grown-up.

"Mommy!" Ivy exclaimed, trying in vain to push Carol's hand away.

"This is Mommy's little pussy, and if I want to rub it, I'm going to damn well rub it. Now answer my question," Carol replied, enjoying how Ivy submitted and pushed her hips out to make it easier for Carol to play.

"That they will like me because they aren't bitches and that if anyone does something mean they have to answer to you," Ivy moaned as Carol slipped a finger into the entrance of Ivy's pussy.

"You are lucky we don't have time. Or I would pull over and make you take it before work, young lady," Carol said, causing Ivy's head to spin with desire. Pulling out of her quickly and kissing her cheek, Carol stopped the car.

"We are here, little one. From now on, call me Carol, is that understood Ivy?" Carol firmly said, Ivy, just nodding her head.

"Ok, here goes," Carol said, opening her door and waiting for Ivy to join her before locking the SUV and walking toward the building. Carol was nervous. She hadn't realized that just how young Ivy looked until she saw her reflection in the glass doors of the practice. She wondered if the girls would make fun of her or Ivy if they would give her a hard time or not, and she begged the universe that Hope wouldn't be cruel to her little girl.

"Hi, you must be Ivy?" Gabi said as they walked into the staff lounge.

"Yeah, hi," Ivy confidently replied.

"Pretty sweet that your girlfriend could hook you up with a job," Hope said as she turned around. Ivy just raised an eyebrow at her.

"She's good like that," Ivy replied, matching Hope's aggressive attitude and never breaking eye contact until Hope looked away.

Oh gosh, Carol thought to herself as she put her handbag away.

"So, this is where you can put your things. And we close the practice at 1 for lunch. It's an hour, and on Wednesdays, we go to the sushi place around the corner," Hope said, deciding that it was better to be friends than enemies.

"Ok cool," Ivy replied, smiling at her warmly.

I should have known she would be fine. She's been fighting all her life. She was always going to be fine, Carol said to herself, smiling to herself and shaking her head as she walked with Ivy to the front desk.

"You fucked Hope, didn't you, Carol?" Ivy said as she sat down at the office chair, turning on the computer. Carol raised her eyebrows and bit her bottom lip, trying to hold back a smile but failing.

"I knew it! No one is that bitchy straight off the bat unless they are jealous!" Ivy quietly exclaimed, shocking Carol to hear her name from Ivy's lips.

"It was years ago, and it was only once. And I am going to have a really hard time letting you speak to me like I'm not your Mommy," Carol said, whispering the last part of her sentence, making Ivy beam.

"Don't push it," Carol warned, and she sat down next to Ivy and began teaching her the computer systems the practice used.

"Don't even think about it," Carol said as Ivy collapsed on the couch after the workday. Ivy's head hurt with all the information Carol had poured into it, and all she wanted to do was have a nap.

"I'm thinking about it," Ivy moaned into the couch cushions. It had only been a few days since Ivy's ex-boss exposed himself to her, and yet it felt like months ago. That's what Ivy had noticed the most when it came to Carol, time moved so slowly, and yet so fast at the same time.

"Well, maybe you should think about this instead," Carol said, walking into the living room, stroking her thick strap on dildo. She and Ivy had looked at it together online, but Ivy didn't know that Carol had actually bought it. Gasping, Ivy rolled onto her back and looked up at Carol.

"Open wide," Carol said, enjoying how Ivy obeyed so willingly.

"Make it wet, Mommy is going to fuck my frustration away, and you're little body is what I'm going to use to do it," Carol said, making Ivy giggle.

"Was it hard for you today, Mommy? To hear me laugh with the other girls and call you Carol," Ivy teased, getting her nipple pinched until she yelped.

"Oh little girl, you asked for it," Carol replied, pulling Ivy's pants down quickly and parting her pussy lips, pressing the tip of the toy against her entrance.

"Little princess, it looks too big to fit," Carol playfully said, pinching Ivy's nipples again.

"Mommy can help with that," Carol teased, pouring lube over the toy and letting it drip down to Ivy's asshole, making her squirm.

"You can't get away from me, little one. Mommy is going to take you how I want to," Carol groaned as she pushed harder against Ivy, moaning in pleasure as Ivy's pussy was stretched open by the thick intruder.

"Such a tight little girl," Carol said, watching Ivy, making sure she didn't push her too far. Carol began to fuck her, rocking her hips back and forth, keeping the rhythm constant as Ivy became accustomed to the sensation.

"You like it, don't you, little girl?" Carol questioned, feeling Ivy's muscle relax and take her more easily.

"Yes, Mommy. Oh, Mommy, I love it," Ivy replied, bucking her hips and giving Carol all the encouragement she needed. She pinned Ivy's hips down and drilled her, turning her sweet girl into a moaning mess as she pounded the young girl's pussy.

"You aren't allowed to cum, little girl," Carol said, making Ivy's eyes pop open and moan in agony.

"But Mommy," Ivy complained, feeling dangerously close to orgasm. Carol put a pacifier in Ivy's mouth and placed her hand on her throat.

"Mommy said no," Carol replied, feeling Ivy try to hold back an orgasm but failing like Carol had hoped she would. Continuing to fuck her, Carol could feel Ivy's juices drip around the dildo with every thrust.

"Such a dirty little girl," Carol moaned as her own orgasm flooded her being making her shiver and her nipples got hard as the frustration of the day was fucked away. She continued to use Ivy as her second, third, and the fourth orgasm took over her, finally pulling out as she panted heavily. She placed her hand over Ivy's used pussy and felt Ivy curl into her arms.

"You are leaking, beautiful," Carol said, feeling Ivy's juices coating her hand. Carol got up and took off the strap on, stripped herself and Ivy naked, and took them both to the shower.

Chapter 10

Ivy spent the rest of the week learning all about the programming systems, interacting with clients, and navigating the staff lounge. She and Hope had made peace, and Hope had even invited Ivy out for drinks with her and Gabi after work on Friday.

"I don't know if I should go, Mommy," Ivy said Thursday night. Carol had made Ivy a bubble bath and was busy washing her hair. She had made it especially lovely tonight by dimming the lights. Ivy's eyes became sensitive at night, and she loved that Carol remembered.

"What are you scared about, baby?" Carol replied, rinsing Ivy's hair. Ivy picked up some bubbles and blew them into the air.

"What if they are mean and just wanted to get me away from you so that you can't tell them to stop?" Ivy explained, making Carol's heart melt.

"You are such a sweet little girl underneath all that makeup and eyeliner," Carol said, wiping Ivy's face clean.

"But what if, Mommy?" Ivy said instantly. Carol held Ivy's face in both her hands and looked her dead in the eye.

"Has Mommy ever let you down?" Carol asked. Ivy

pretended to think, making Carol scoff.

"No, Mommy," Ivy giggly replied.

"Right, so if you feel that it isn't going the way, you want it to or thought it would. What are you going to do?" Carol asked.

"Call Mommy," Ivy replied before standing up in the tub.

"Good girl," Carol replied, taking a towel down from the rack and drying Ivy's body.

"Mommy, guess what?" Ivy replied as Carol began to diaper her.

"What, darling?" Carol said, holding up two onesie options and letting Ivy choose.

"It's my birthday next week," Ivy said, pointing at the blue on with the puppy on the front. Carol smiled and looked at Ivy with nothing but love in her eyes.

"Well, Mommy will have to give you a special day then, won't I?" Carol replied, watching as Ivy stood and followed her into the living room.

"I've never had something special for my birthday before," Ivy said as Carol took the nuggets out of the oven and into Ivy's bowl. She added a little container of sauce to the bowl and placed it into Ivy's lap. Carol went back to the kitchen and took her plate of seafood paella and came to sit next to Ivy.

"What do you want to do for your birthday, then, little

girl? I think we should do something little, and something grown-up," Carol suggested making Ivy clap her hands.

"Yes, please, Mommy," Ivy replied, snuggling into Carol.

"Eat your nuggies, baby girl. We can look online tonight to see where you want to go," Carol said, feeding Ivy a nugget and watching as she cuddled up to her while they watched the news.

"I think he is really hot!" Gabi exclaimed Friday night at the loud Bowling Alley. Ivy felt embarrassed that they couldn't go out clubbing because she was underage but thought it was really lovely that the girls' didn't seem to care. Carol had dropped Ivy off and given her strict instructions that she was to call her if things went downhill. Ivy loved that about Carol; she was always so supportive and loving.

"Well, his bowling sucks," Ivy said, replying to Gabi, making Hope laugh.

"I don't think it's his bowling that she is impressed with," Hope said before dramatically eating a chip. The guy that they were loudly talking about heard them and walked over, winking at Gabi before taking a bowling ball from their section.

"Oh, that's all I needed," Gabi playfully said before going over to talk to him, leaving Hope and Ivy alone.

"Well, we can't even play without her, and it's her turn!"

Ivy exclaimed, taking a sip of her soda.

"Yeah, whatever, we will just wait for her. So tell me, did you grow up around here?" Hope asked. Ivy had been hoping that she wouldn't have to keep retelling her story; it made her cringe.

"No, I'm from out of town. I moved here this year," Ivy replied, watching Gabi flirt with the boy.

"And, you and Carol met how?" Hope asked, making Ivy's head turn back to her.

"At a café," Ivy replied, not wanting to give away too much information.

"You know. Carol and I fucked once. But I guess she likes younger girls, so it didn't work out," Hope said. Ivy just nodded her head.

"Yeah, I don't really care what you guys did," Ivy said, watching the lights at the bowling alley flicker and shine.

"Are you worried that as you get older, Carol will leave you for a younger girl?" Hope pressed. Ivy felt herself getting angry. Of course, she had thought of that. She didn't need Hope to bring it up as well.

"Hope, get fucked," Ivy said, standing up and heading towards the entrance. Hope stayed sitting in the booth, somewhat impressed with herself that she had made Ivy crack so easily.

Ivy walked out onto the street. She wasn't sure where she was going, but she just needed to keep walking. She took out her phone, deciding that she would ring Carol when she got to wherever she was going. Passing the bars, she wished she could go in, passing the type of restaurants that Carol loved and across the street to a pizza joint. She kept walking, passed a cupcake store which sold marvelous creations, and found herself in a trendy looking diner downtown.

"Hi, what can I get you?" The curvy Latina woman behind the counter asked. Ivy just shrugged her shoulders looked around for a menu.

"Here, sweetie," the woman said, handing her a menu and pouring her an espresso.

"Thanks, Ma'am," Ivy sadly replied, making the woman laugh.

"Oh, honey, call me Nancy," Nancy replied, making Ivy smile faintly.

"Ok, Nancy," she replied. Satisfied, Nancy walked to the other end of the counter and began talking to other customers. Ivy liked the woman's warm smile and loving eyes and made her Miss Carol. Taking out her phone, she saw that Carol was ringing her.

"Hey," Ivy said down the phone. She looked around, half expecting Carol to be somewhere looking at her.

"Baby, what happened? Hope messaged me saying that you stormed out?" Carol questioned. Ivy liked that there was concern and not anger in her voice.

"You were meant to ring Mommy if something was

wrong," she added. Ivy bit her bottom lip and tilted her head as Nancy place a slice of pie down in front of her.

"I didn't order this?" Ivy questioned, unsure as to why Nancy had done that.

"I know, but trust me, you're going to like it," Nancy replied, winking at Ivy before disappearing once again.

"I know I was meant to ring. I was just so angry I didn't want to ring you when I was that mad. I just needed to walk. I'm in some diner downtown. It's actually really nice. If I send you my location, could you come and get me, please?" Ivy asked. Carol understood why Ivy hadn't called and nodded her head as she listened to the story.

"Of course, baby girl. It's getting late. I don't want you move from that spot, alright?" Carol instructed Ivy, taking a bite of the pie and raising her eyebrows.

"Ok," Ivy replied, making Carol laugh.

"What are you missing, my love?" Carol asked. Ivy gave a sideward smile before biting her bottom lip.

"Ok, Mommy," Ivy whispered, making Carol smirk.

"There's my good girl. Sit tight. Mommy is on her way," Carol replied, hanging up the phone.

"So, what do you think?" Nancy said as she poured Ivy a hot chocolate. Ivy smiled at her. She had that same loving eyes that Carol did, and it made her wonder if she had them because she was a Mommy as well or if it was just because that was her face.

"Pretty good," Ivy replied, making Nancy laugh.

"Pretty good?!" She exclaimed faining pretend disbelief. Ivy giggled and took a sip of the hot chocolate.

"This, however, is really good," Ivy said, taking another sip.

"Well, it's the secret ingredient that makes it soo good," Nancy said as she saw Ivy's big puppy dog eyes and smiled.

"What is it?" Ivy asked, feeling her anger go away, and her guard go down. Nancy put two marshmallows into the mug before raising an eyebrow at Ivy.

"Well, if I told you, it wouldn't be a secret anymore," Nancy said, winking at her and smiling at Carol, who came to sit next to Ivy. Gasping, Ivy wrapped her arms around Carol and held her tight.

"I see you've been busy," Carol laughed as she saw the selection of treats in front of Ivy.

"I had time," Ivy replied, letting Carol go and sitting up.

"So, tell me what happened," Carol said, taking a bite of the pie and moaning in appreciation.

"Have you tried this?!" Carol asked, taking another bite.

"See that, that is the correct response," Nancy laughed as she walked passed.

"Yeah, I have, it's good," Ivy replied, Carol, pausing and looking at her as though she had lost her mind.

"Good?! It's a lot better than good," Carol said, deciding that she was going to finish the pie herself.

"So?" Carol pressed, wanting to know how Ivy had ended up downtown.

"So, everything was going fine. In fact, it was really fun. But then Gabi went off to flirt with some guy, and Hope started asking me all these questions. I answered most of them, but then she bought up that you guys and messed around and that you only like young girls and that when I get too old, you'll probs dump me for a younger girl. So I told her to fuck off," Ivy said before picking up her hot chocolate and holding it in both hands as she drank.

"Right. I'm not going to dump you because you get older. For goodness sake, that is the creepiest thing I have ever heard. It makes me sound like a pervert!" Carol exclaimed, shaking her head.

"Yeah, but like, it just made me so mad. Coz I had thought that maybe that would happen and when she said it I just like, got really angry," Ivy tried to explain. Carol placed her hand on her chest, and looked at Ivy, slightly hurt that she would have those thoughts.

"Oh, baby girl," Carol said, wrapping her arms around Ivy.

"Mommy is never going to leave you," she whispered in Ivy's ear, causing Ivy to snuggle into the crook of Carol's neck, a few tears escaping.

"Alright?" Carol questioned, watching as Ivy nodded her head and fought the urge to suck her thumb.

"Maybe we need to get you into a sport or something to find some better friends. I don't think I want those girls' hanging around you when I am not there," Carol said, standing up and kissing Ivy on the top of her head before going to pay.

Chapter 11

Carol took Ivy home, Ivy falling asleep in the car within minutes.

"Come on, baby girl," Carol said as she gently woke Ivy up and held her hand as they walked inside.

"Mommy, can we plan my birthday now?" Ivy asked, Carol, smiling down at her.

"Not tonight, I want you ready for bed, and then you are going to nurse until you fall asleep," Carol said, helping Ivy take off her clothes and running a shower for her.

"Ok, Mommy," Ivy said, getting up the warm water and quickly showering.

Carol dressed Ivy in a black diaper cover and a loose white shirt, setting her up in the living room on a blanket on the floor as Carol changed into her pajamas.

"I thought you might like this," Carol said, only coming back into the room wearing long pajama pants and rubbing her full breasts. Sitting on the couch, Carol patted the spot next to her and smiled as Ivy crawled over to her.

"Up you come," Carol said as she lifted Ivy onto her lap and sighed in content bliss as she felt Ivy begin to nurse.

"Such a good girl for Mommy," Carol said, patting Ivy's padded bottom as she rocked her.

"You are perfect, little Ivy. You will always be Mommy's beautiful little girl. No matter how old you are," Carol whispered as Ivy looked up at her with her big eyes and long lashes.

"Shh, close your eyes, honey. Time to sleep," Carol said, placing her hand over Ivy's eyes and stroking her forehead, feeling Ivy suckle slower until only her lips were pursed against Carol's nipple.

"Mommy? Can we do it now?!" Ivy asked as sitting at the end of the bed, waiting for Carol to wake up.

"I fear how many more times I will have to tell you no if we don't just do it now!" Carol laughed, opening her arms and having Ivy snuggle into them.

"So I've had a few thoughts," Ivy said, taking out of her phone and showing Carol her image boards.

"You have been busy! When have you had time for all this?" Carol laughed. Ivy just rolled her eyes.

"It doesn't take that much time, Mommy," Ivy said, scrolling through the images.

"You want to hike up a mountain and have a picnic at the top? That's cute. I can get you a cute little hiking outfit!" Carol said, imagining how irresistible Ivy would look. Ivy just rolled her eyes.

"I think you might be too tired once we get to the top, Mommy," Ivy said, worried that Carol wouldn't be able to keep up.

"Don't let this fool you, Mommy is both stronger and fitter than you," Carol said, winking at Ivy and making her blush. Carol just smirked.

"We need to go present shopping. You're going to have a budget. I think $200 for little things and $400 for big girl things because big girl things are more expensive," Carol said, explaining herself when she saw Ivy open her mouth to speak, assuming that it was to protest the amounts.

"I wasn't about to complain! I was about to say that it doesn't need to be that much!" Ivy said, enjoying how Carol just shrugged her shoulders.

"Well, it is, so there enjoy," Carol laughed, causing Ivy to cover her in kisses.

"If I had known I'd get this reaction, I'd buy your affection more often," Carol laughed as she felt Ivy's hand slip into her pants.

"I'm not your whore. You can't pay me to fuck you," Ivy sensually whispered, making Carol chuckle.

"That's some very grown-up language for someone wearing a diaper," Carol said, pulling Ivy onto her thigh.

"Then," Ivy said, quickly taking it off, along with her shirt.

"Better?" Ivy teased feel Carol take back control and roll

her onto her back.

"Now it is," Carol said, placing her hand on Ivy's pussy and making quick work of turning her into a moaning mess.

"That was not my plan," Ivy moaned as she felt Carol begin to kiss her neck.

"It happens," Carol laughed as she pushed her fingers into Ivy and took her over the edge.

"Oh, you make it too easy for Mommy," Carol said as she replaced her hand with her thigh and pressed Ivy's clit into it, refusing to let her come down from one orgasm as another one built within her.

"You're so mean," Ivy said, trying in vain to overpower Carol.

"I told you Mommy was stronger than you little girl," Carol whispered as she wrapped Ivy in her arms and continued to hump her.

"Mommy," Ivy said, pushing Carol away as she came over Carol's thigh, gripping into the older woman's skin and leaving red marks on her as she felt herself moisten her thigh.

"Well, I know how you can thank Mommy," Carol said, ripping the bed sheets off her and Ivy and kicking off her pajama pants. Carol toyed with her cunt, pulling her lips wide and pushing Ivy's head down.

"Get busy, little one," Carol said, holding Ivy's head to her cunt and rubbing it over her face, moaning as she felt Ivy's tongue taste her pussy juices. Ivy loved how Carol tasted and lapped at her cunt, causing Carol to moan and play with her breasts as she flooded Ivy's mouth.

"You were horny today, Mommy," Ivy giggled as she wiped her mouth on the bedsheets before coming up and cuddling with Carol.

"Yeah, I was actually," Carol chuckled to herself, surprised at how quickly she came.

That afternoon, Carol and Ivy went to the mall in search of Ivy's gifts. Ivy liked that they went together, and when the stores were only a few hours till closing. She didn't want to go during the peak shopping times because large numbers of people made her feel uneasy. Ivy loved that Carol never made a fuss about the few things Ivy really needed from her, and as they walked through the mall, a large fluffy pink blanket caught Ivy's eye.

"Oh, this is so nice!" Ivy said, running her fingers over it. Carol smiled and looked around the store. She had to admit. Ivy did have good taste in linen and soft furnishings.

"I think I need this," Ivy said, the store assistant coming over to help her.

"It's your birthday. You can get anything you want, honey," Carol said. Ivy also bought a pair of fluffy pajama shorts, and she smirked at Carol when she said she needed to get a bigger size.

"For my diaper," Ivy whispered, Carol, smirking and

enjoying what a sweet girl she had to call her own. They went from store to store, looking at everything from activewear to technology, custom-designed stuffies, and animated backpacks. After hours of searching and buying, Ivy was finally ready to go home.

"This was so much fun, Mommy!" Ivy exclaimed as Carol put her into her car seat. They had carked around the block from the mall so that Carol could put Ivy in it today.

"I'm glad you had such a good day, baby girl. You can't have your presents until your birthday though. And if you complain, I'll return all of them," Carol said, seeing what Ivy was about to ask.

"Ok, Mommy," Ivy said, reaching for her paci and blankie.

"There's my good girl," Carol cooed before she closed the door and walked around to the driver's seat.

Ivy could hardly wait the two days until her birthday. She was so excited at how her life had turned out and so delighted that Carol was her girlfriend and Mommy and as she lay in bed next to Carol on the last night as an 18-year-old, she thought of all the times where she wanted more than anything to give up and just accept defeat. As she looked over and snuggled into Carol, she was so happy that she kept going and kept believing that she could create a beautiful life for herself.

"Happy Birthday, baby girl," Carol whispered in her ear.

Ivy blinked her eyes open and looked around.

"Mommy," Ivy happily said. Carol kissed her forehead and felt her diaper.

"Let's get you changed, little one. What type of day do you want today? Your big girl one or your baby girl one?" Carol asked. They had decided to celebrate Ivy's birthday over two days. Each day dedicated to one of her main headspaces.

"Baby girl, one!" Ivy said as she flung her arms in the air.

"I had a feeling you would pick that one," Carol laughed as she placed Ivy on the floor and changed her.
Dressing her in a fresh diaper, a pair of black denim overalls with a light pink t-shirt underneath, and black ankle socks, Carol sat her up at the kitchen bench.

"Alright, let's have a yummy fruit platter for breakfast, and then you can open your presents," Carol said as Ivy clapped her hands. Carol had cut up melon in the shape of stars, strawberries dipped in chocolate, and there was also a range of other berries. Ivy's eyes went wide.

"Mommy, this is delicious!" Ivy said, finishing her breakfast quickly.

"Easy there, tiger. You're going to get a sore tummy if you eat that fast," Carol said, pulling Ivy's plate away from her and giving her a warning look.

"Sorry, Mommy, I just want to open my presents!" Ivy exclaimed.

"You won't be able to open them because you'll feel sick and need a nap if you keep that up," Carol said, giving Ivy her plate back and watching as she tried to eat slowly.

"Oh, this is just too painful. Down you get," Carol laughed, letting Ivy walk over to the collection of presents on the coffee table. Carol had set up balloons and streamers over the table, and Ivy played with the balloons until Carol came over and pulled her into her lap and took the first present down.

"Do you want Mommy to help you, or can you do it by yourself, little one?" Carol asked, placing the colorfully wrapped box in Ivy's lap.

"I can do it, Mommy," Ivy replied, resting her head back on Carol's shoulder as she ripped the packaging off. Although Ivy knew what she was getting, it didn't stop her from being excited and giggling as she saw the wooden train set she unwrapped.

"We can set it up in the living room if you like, honey," Carol said, Ivy, nodding her head as she reached for another gift. Slowly, Ivy unwrapped everything, the colorful paper surrounding them as she opened the last gift, her pink fluffy blanket.

"Mommy, this is the best birthday I have ever had," Ivy said, cuddling into Carol with her blankie in her arms.

"I'm glad you have liked it so far, baby girl," Carol said as she kissed Ivy all over her face.

"But it's not over yet, little one," Carol said, causing Ivy to look at her in confusion.

"What do you mean?" Ivy asked, reaching for her custom-designed bear and sparkly pink ball.

"Well, I thought it might be nice for you to have a little play with all your new toys, and then we will have a nap, and after we can out for ice-cream and come back for your cake. And you can decide what we have for dinner as well," Carol said, watching as Ivy tried to comprehend her words.

"Mommy," Ivy said, bursting into tears. Carol had wondered when this would happen. Ivy had cried when she was overwhelmed with happiness on more than one occasion.

"It's alright, little one. Mommy's got you. This is what good girls get for their birthday, and you are the best girl in the world," Carol loving said, letting Ivy cry in her arms until she began to calm down.

"Are you alright little one?" Carol asked as Ivy nodded her head and wiped her tears away.

"And we haven't even got to tomorrow yet!" Carol said, making Ivy laugh.

"Maybe we can wait for a day or two, Mommy?" Ivy said, Carol, kissing the top of her head and agreeing with the look in her eyes.

"So, you have a little play now, baby girl. Mommy is going to tidy all this up, and then we can have lunchies, a nap, and then go out in the afternoon," Carol said as Ivy began to build up her train set.

Chapter 12

Ivy woke up early the next morning and tiptoed out into the kitchen and sat up at the table, ready to make her creation. She used all the glitters that she had and giggled as she watched her picture come to life, even getting glitter on her face.

"I made it for you, Mommy," Ivy proudly said as she held up the glittery picture for Carol to see. Carol smiled at her as she walked down the corridor and wrapped her dressing gown around her waist.

"Let me see," Carol sleepily said as she sat on the couch and let Ivy snuggle in next to her.

"It's Mommy and Ivy at the store picking out presents," Ivy said, pointing to the glittery figures. Carol kissed the top of Ivy's head and looked at the picture.

"I love this," Carol softly said, a tear rolling down her cheek, confusing Ivy.

"Then why are you crying, Mommy?" She asked, taking the picture out of Carol's hands and frowning curiously at her.

"This is the first picture I've ever been given. I guess I wasn't expecting it get to me so much," Carol replied, wiping her eyes.

"So, does that mean you like it?" Ivy playfully said as she looked up at Carol, making her laugh.

"Yes, it does. And I have just decided that you need a lot more craft supplies to make even more," Carol said, taking the picture and putting it on the fridge.

"But not today," Ivy replied, hoping that her day of big girl things wasn't off the table.

"No," Carol said, spinning on the spot, a wicked gleam in her eye.

"Definitely not today," Carol said, eyeing Ivy up and down.

"I see that you are already dressed," Carol said. Although Ivy had gotten into little space easily to make Carol the picture, she had dressed in her adult clothes while Carol was sleeping. Her black jeans, white sneakers, and grey hoodie still made her look like a little girl with her messy ponytail and black denim jacket.

"Nothing gets passed you. So, Carol, what have you got planned for today?" Ivy said, enjoying the few times she was permitted to call Carol by her first name. Carol raised an eyebrow, finding it harder to adjust but loving her flirtatious naughty girl all the same.

"Get your ass off the bench," Carol said, slapping Ivy's thighs and making her sit on a bench stool instead.

"See, I'm still Mommy," Carol teased, taking Ivy's chin in her hand and shaking her head, making her giggle.

"Maybe," Ivy replied, taking out her phone and posting a selfie.

"You need to hurry up and eat something because we have a few things to pick up before lunch," Carol said, wanting to get out of the house as soon as possible.

"I thought you were going to make my breakfast?" Ivy asked, making Carol laugh.

"Oh no, big girl, Mommy is gone until tonight. Get yourself something before you starve," Carol playfully replied, winking at Ivy before taking her coffee and disappearing out of sight. Ivy rolled her eyes and went to the cupboard, taking out a bowl, spoon, cereal, and milk. Munching on her breakfast loudly, Ivy followed Carol as she fluttered around the kitchen, living room, and bedroom.

"You're going to get a tummy ache if you don't sit down," Carol said, putting in her earrings as Ivy put her sunglasses on her head with one hand, her spoon in her mouth and her cereal almost spilling.

"Yes, Mommy," Ivy said, ignoring her suggestion but enjoying how it felt to be able to do whatever she wanted and to have Carol's loving care still.

"Fine, get sick, see if I care," Carol said, putting her scarf on and slapping Ivy's ass.

"You care," Ivy whispered as she sat in Carol's lap and finished her breakfast. Loving how it felt to have Carol wrap her loving arms around her as she ate, Ivy melted into the embrace and felt herself becoming content in a blissful state she was slowly getting used to.

"Mommy?" Ivy asked, wanting Carol's attention.

"Yes, baby girl," Carol replied, stroking Ivy's arms.

"Can I wear a diaper on my big girl day?" Ivy asked, making Carol smile.

"Of course, little one," Carol replied, secretly loving that Ivy still wanted little things when she was about to go out and buy a diamond necklace.

"You're just, Mommy's little girl, aren't you?" Carol asked as she took the bowl away from Ivy and turned her into her, holding her lovingly, and Ivy looked up and into her eyes and nodded.

Carol had dressed Ivy in a pair of denim jeans and a tight white t-shirt that showed her tummy, a pink bow in her hair, and a pair of street sneakers.

"You look cute," Carol said as Ivy twirled for her before sitting on the bed and watching Carol get dressed.

"Mommy, not that one," Ivy said as Carol took out a pullover.

"What's wrong with this one?" Carol said, looking at the cream-colored pullover. Ivy just gigged and got up, taking down her favorite pullover that Carol owned.

"Oh, I see," Carol said as Ivy held it up to her. Ivy smirked and sat back down, looking at Carol suggestively.

"Don't look at me like that unless you want trouble, young lady. I am not about to have us be late for your first surprise of the day," Carol warned as Ivy lay back on the bed and spread her thighs. Carol walked over to Ivy and slowly dressed herself before patting between Ivy's thighs.

"Anyway, baby girls don't get fucked," Carol said, making Ivy pout.

"But, Mommy, I am so horny, please?" Ivy begged amusing Carol, who shook her head no.

"And don't even think about it," Carol said as Ivy tried to put her hand down her pants. Carol grabbed Ivy's wrist and pulled her to her feet.

"Is Mommy going to have to punish you, little girl?" Carol asked as Ivy squirmed to get away from her.

"No," Ivy pouted, standing still and snuggling into Carol before sucking her thumb.

"Maybe if you're a good girl for me, I'll let you show me how badly you want it," Carol said, patting Ivy on the bottom before leading her towards the car.

Carol had a day full of cafes and shopping planned, and as she unbuckled Ivy from her car seat, she could tell that Ivy was fidgety.

"What is it, baby?" Carol asked as they held hands and walked into a jewelry store.

"What if people can tell I am wearing a diaper?" Ivy

whispered as she looked at the rings in the cabinet.

"They can't, don't worry, baby. I wouldn't do that to you," Carol said as she double-checked. It was true, the diaper she had put Ivy in today was thin, and her loose jeans made it impossible to tell what she had on underneath. They looked through the store, Ivy finally deciding on a ring she liked before they continued through the mall. Ivy didn't know what it was, but something was hurting her heart. It wasn't a feeling she had felt for a long time, and as she walked with Carol through the stores, she felt herself becoming more and more dissociated. She smiled and talked to Carol like nothing was wrong, but knew that something was going on, even if she couldn't put her finger on it.

Eventually, Carol was buckling Ivy back up in her car seat and kissed her on the cheek before going into the driver's side and driving back home. Ivy wondered if Carol could tell that she was faking it, almost like she was watching someone else's life, and not being able to feel any of the feelings she thought she should.

You've just gone on a huge shopping spree. You should be happy. No one has ever treated you this good, what's the matter with you? Ivy thought to herself. She looked out the window and wished that she could disappear. She felt sick like a knot was forming in her tummy that she couldn't seem to unravel.

"Baby?" Carol said, breaking Ivy's train of thought. Ivy

looked up to notice that they were in the driveway, Carol looking at Ivy inquisitively, clearly having asked her a question.

"Huh?" Ivy replied, Carol, getting out of the car and walking around to open her door.

"Baby girl, what's wrong?" Carol said, unbuckling Ivy's seat belt.

"I don't know," Ivy whispered in response, making Carol smile understandably.

"It's alright, baby. I know that maybe today was a bit much," Carol said as she picked up the handful of bags and took Ivy's hand in her other hand. Ivy just nodded her head and began to cry.

"Shh. It's alright, baby girl, Mommy's here," Carol said as she took Ivy inside. She dropped the bags by the door and took Ivy to the couch, sitting down and letting her snuggle up next to her.

"Mommy's sweet girl," Carol said as Ivy grabbed at her softly.

I bet she is overwhelmed because last time she had a birthday, she was running away from home. She's probably never had somebody treat her so well, and I guess it was all a bit too much for her, Carol thought to herself as she felt Ivy's breathing be shallow and fast.

"Do you know what you need to feel better, baby girl?" Carol asked, watching as Ivy shook her head no.

"How about a hot bath and a nap?" Carol suggested. Ivy just shrugged her shoulders. She wasn't sure what she needed or wanted. All she knew was that she didn't want to feel like this anymore.

"Mommy," Ivy softly said, reaching for Carol, who scooped her up and carried her to the bathroom.

"Down you go," Carol said, lowering Ivy to the floor and beginning to undress her.

"Such a beautiful little girl," Carol said, putting a paci in Ivy's mouth. Carol began to undress Ivy. She dimmed the lights and put on a soft melodied soundtrack before continuing to take Ivy's clothes off.

"I'm sorry, Mommy. I don't know why I feel like this," Ivy softly said as tears rolled down her cheeks.

"Oh, sweetie, it's ok. Sometimes the world just gets a bit too much," Carol said, understanding that Ivy wasn't being bratty or ungrateful. She was simply triggered by the feeling of being loved at this level because it was so different from what her whole life had been like. Even though they had been together for a year, Carol knew that Ivy would probably have many more moments like this as their relationship progressed and deepened.

"Ok, let's get you into this water," Carol whispered, taking Ivy's hand and leading her into tub and watching as she brought her knees up to her chest.

"Do you want to lay on your tummy, that way the water

is all over you?" Carol suggested, Ivy, moving her body under Carol's direction.

"Thanks for looking after me, Mommy," Ivy whispered, smiling for the first time in hours and feeling her body come back into balance.

"That's what I'm here for baby girl. To make sure that you are looked after and that nothing bad happens to you," Carol replied, sitting down next to the tub as Ivy brought her face to rest on Carol's thighs, wetting her jeans.

"It's ok, baby," Carol lovingly said as Ivy looked up, worry in her eyes that Carol would be angry with her.
Carol gently poured warm water down Ivy's back, giving her shivers and making her giggle.

"There's my happy girl," Carol loving remarked as she saw the sparkle start to come back to Ivy's eyes. Ivy reached her arms up, Carol having to think twice before taking her shirt off.

"Do you need Mommy cuddles, little one?" Carol said, undressing, and stepping into the tub. Ivy nodded as she watched Carol sit down and started to snuggle into her once she was under the water.

"I don't ever want you to leave me, Mommy," Ivy said as she nestled her head into Carol's neck.

"Oh, baby girl. Mommy is never leaving you," Carol replied and kissing down Ivy's collar bone and making her giggle.

"Don't Mommy," Ivy whined, encouraging Carol.

"Or what baby girl," Carol teased, hoping that Ivy was in the mood for more than cuddles.

"Or I'm gonna get all tingling," Ivy replied, blushing and trying to push Carol away.

"Maybe that's what I want," Carol said, grabbing Ivy's wrists and pulling her back toward her and wrapping her arms around her.

"I'm glad that you feel better, baby," Carol said as Ivy straddled her thighs and felt the water on her clit as her thighs were spread, opening her pussy and causing her hips to react.

"Can somebody feel the warmth of the water on their pussy baby," Carol said, intuitively knowing what was happening. Ivy bit her bottom lip and nodded her head. Carol smirked and decided that she wanted Ivy horny and unsatisfied tonight. She had only just got Ivy back to feel happy. She didn't want her to become overwhelmed again.

"Let's get you, dry baby girl," Carol said, getting out of the water before drying herself and then Ivy.

"I want you," Ivy said, making Carol laugh, feeling Ivy's hands begin to touch her body.

"I can see that. But you know what baby girl, not tonight. Tonight I want you all wrapped up in a blankie and snuggling next to Mommy. Alright, little one?" Carol said, taking Ivy's wrist in her hand and leading her to the bedroom. Ivy, who was clearly disappointed by Carol's plans, just nodded her head, not wanting to be bratty for her Mommy.

"There's my good girl," Carol said, beginning to diaper Ivy and put her in a light blue onesie. Carol watched as Ivy got comfy in bed as she pulled on her pajamas and got into bed with Ivy.

"Mommy's snuggly little girl," Carol cooed, pulling the blankets around the both of them and tucking Ivy into bed.

"Mommy?" Ivy softly whined, tugging on Carol's t-shirt. Carol smiled down at Ivy.

"Do you want to use your big girl words, baby?" Carol asked, beginning to pull her shirt up. Ivy just shook her head, making Carol smile at her lovingly before settling her as she nursed.

"Beautiful girl," Carol said, watching Ivy be little in her arms, enjoying the feeling of being the person Ivy needed the most.

Mommy's Always Here

An MDLG and ABDL story about meeting the perfect person at the wrong time and how the love of a Mommy can help heal all wounds

Tina Moore

Chapter 1

There was no explaining how Leila felt. She was numb. The swirling world around her seemed so full of life, so happy, so content that it almost made her sick. Leila had just broken up with her Mommy after spending six years together. It was mutual, that's what Leila kept telling herself, but deep down she knew that it wasn't. Leila had put on weight over the last two years, and that was something Donna couldn't look past. Leila hated herself for it, but what she hated, even more, was that she didn't have the control or discipline to stop herself. It's not as though she ate particularly unhealthy foods, but with her new job and moving to a new city, her exercise routine had gone out of the window. What was more was that Leila was about to celebrate her 36th birthday.

Who, in their right mind, would want an overweight, 36-year-old as their baby? I will never find someone who will want me. I'm not what other women look for. I'm not what they want, Leila thought as she took the train to her new apartment. She had moved out of the home she and Donna had bought together and moved into a small, one-bedroom apartment just outside of town. Leila looked around the train and sighed.

How could she have been so cruel? I never even did anything to deserve that treatment, Leila asked herself, catching her reflection in the window of the train as it went through a tunnel. Looking away out of disgust, Leila tried to fight back her tears.

Idiot. You're a fucking idiot. She called herself as she stood up and made her way to the door, ready to get out. There was the usual hustle and bustle of the impatient people as she disembarked and felt the push come behind her, knocking her to the floor. People swarmed around her, but not to help, simply to get to where they needed to be. Leila looked up, sighing and resting her hands on her knees as she looked around.

I'm invisible, no one is ever going to notice me, and I mean, why should they, I'm nothing, she sadly thought, picking up her bag and putting it back on her shoulder before standing up and walking out of the station.

Leila walked down the street, looking over her hands and taking off the ring Donna had given her as a present.

"I won't be needing this anymore," Leila said out loud. She was just about to put it in the bin when she saw a young homeless woman and decided that she would have better use for the ring than the bin.

"Here," Leila said to the girl wrapped in rags. The girl looked up at her in shock. Something about her sparkly eyes made Leila catch her breath, and as the girl gingerly accepted the ring, Leila smiled despite herself.

"I can't take this," the girl said, standing up and pushing the ring back into Leila's hands. Leila frowned and watched the woman scurry down the street.

"Wait, stop," Leila said, catching her breath as she turned the corner to follow the woman just to be stopped by three police officers. Leila froze, her heart pounding, and her cheeks flushed red. She saw the homeless woman behind them, taking off her rags and letting her hair out. Leila wasn't sure if it was the run or the beauty of the woman, which kept her cheeks burning red, but as the woman walked back over to her, the answer was clear. The woman was tall, athletic, and in her late 20's from what Leila could tell. She had shoulder-length blonde hair and eyes that seemed so warm and loving.

"This is why I couldn't accept your ring," the woman said, her voice deep and smoldering.

"I see," Leila said, blushing with embarrassment.

"You're sweet. But, you might have messed up what we were doing if you had kept insisting," the woman explained, making Leila roll her eyes and nod.

"This is just the perfect end to the kind of day I've had. Sorry," Leila said before smiling once more and turning to walk away.

"Wait," the woman said, thinking for a moment before jogging after Leila.

"I'm Avery, but everyone calls me Avs," Avery said,

extending her hand and waiting for Leila to shake it.

"I'm Leila," Leila replied, enjoying how Avery's hand seemed to make hers look small.

"What are you doing later? Like nowish?" Avery asked, taking Leila by surprise.

"I was thinking, drinks, and dinner, maybe?" Avery said, making Leila laugh in surprise.

"Um, yeah, sure," Leila said, shaking her head, surprised that the beautiful fit cop wanted to hang out with her.

"Sweet. Just give me like five minutes," Avery said, winking at Leila before running back to her colleagues.

"So, do you live around here? I guess you don't come from around here, you're voice to refined," Avery said, making Leila laugh.

"I've been called a lot of things, never once refined though," Leila replied as they walked. It was just on dusk, and the lights of the city started flickering on. This was Leila's favorite time of day when the transition between day and night made the city glow.

"I'm not from around here, no. I moved here recently. After a break-up," Leila said. She was nervous that Avery might want to stop it right there and then, she didn't seem to be the person who enjoyed being a rebound.

"No, I get it. I moved precincts when I broke up with my

ex. That was like, seven months ago now. We were only together for two years, but it was a really intense two years. She taught me a whole lot of stuff I had no idea about, but we just weren't what the other person needed," Avery said, indicating that they should go into the bar which was coming up.

"After you," Avery said, holding the door open for Leila. Leila walked into the bar and smirked.

"I had half thought you'd take me into a cop bar," Leila laughed, Avery, fainting shock.

"I'm not like that," she said, leading Leila to a table towards that back of the bar. A waitress came over and took their drink order, and as she disappeared, Leila got up to take her coat off.

"So, what do you do for work?" Avery asked as Leila sat back down.

"I'm a journalist," Leila proudly said, blushing when she heard herself.

"Oh my gosh, I sound like a kid who is saying they came first in a race," she said, putting her head in her hands and laughing. Avery just looked at her and smiled lovingly.

"I thought it was cute," she said, half to herself as she sipped the Scotch, which was put down before her by the waitress.

"So, that's what I do. I work for an independent paper, and the hours are really long. That's why my ex and I broke up.

We just drifted apart," Leila explained.

"How long ago was that?" Avery asked, getting the waitresses attention.

"3 months ago. We have a house together which we are selling at the moment," Leila replied, stopping as the waitress stood next to her.

"Can I order for you?" Avery asked, hoping Leila would say yes. It had been a while since she had ordered for anyone, and Leila seemed to need some taking care of.

"If you'd like," Leila replied, the delight evident on Avery's face.

"We will take the pork belly, grilled vegetables, and the mushroom and chicken gnocchi. And another round of drinks," Avery said, somewhat impressing Leila.

"I was actually going to get the gnocchi," Leila happily said, biting her bottom lip before she remembered that she was on a date.

"You don't have to pretend to be someone else. I think it's sweet that you got excited like that," Avery said, leaning forward and taking Leila's hand in hers and stroking the back of it with her thumb. Leila could feel her eyes glaze over, which meant that she was dangerously close to slipping into little space. She leaned back and caught her breath, cleared her throat, and looked around the room.

"So, is this where you bring all your dates?" Leila teased, making Avery laugh.

"Yeah, it is actually," Avery replied, shocking Leila before Avery smirked and shook her head.

"I'm joking. No, I heard that this place has an outstanding chef, and well, I like to eat good food so, I thought why not take a beautiful woman out on a date here," Avery answered, making Leila roll her eyes. The last thing she thought of herself was that she was beautiful. She almost cringed at the compliment but tried not to show that she disagreed, failing to do so.

"No? Ok, you tell me who you are then," Avery said, leaning back and folding her arms across her chest. Leila just looked around the room.

"I'm surprised we are talking with such depth," she confessed, surprised that Avery was sitting across from her, let alone wanting to know about how she saw herself.

"I don't care for small talk. I like to get into it with people, really learn who they are," Avery said, the softer side coming out once more. Leila finished her first drink just as the second round was placed on the table.

"I guess I used to be pretty. I was never as fit as you, but I also wasn't this goddamn fat," Leila said, looking down and wishing her thighs didn't touch.

"I think I would describe myself as a homebody who would rather hide from the world than be a part of it," Leila replied, more honestly than she had ever intended to be.

"Wow," Avery replied, surprised at how much Leila

hated herself.

"You have been hanging around the wrong people if that's what you think about yourself," she quickly added.

"Well, I didn't think I should lie to a cop," Leila tried to joke, raising her eyebrow and looking around when Avery's face remained blank.

"Alright, you convinced me. I'll be your girlfriend," Avery suddenly said, causing Leila to choke on her drink.

"Pardon?" She asked, her eyes popping out of her head. Avery just winked at her before smiling that wicked grin.

"You are kind and gentle and compassionate, not to mention beautiful, and if you can't see that, I can't let you out of my sight. It wouldn't be right of me to let you continue to go through life hating it and yourself so much. So, I'll be your girlfriend," Avery said, pleased with herself and confident in her picking up ability.

"I don't think that's a very good reason to be with someone. I don't need you to rescue me," Leila said, somewhat annoyed that Avery had chosen her.

"I am not rescuing you," Avery replied, dragging out the word rescuing to prove a point.

"What I am doing, if you'll let me is going to show you what you are really worth. And if, after four months, you and I haven't clicked, then I will happily let you go on your way and be in your life in whatever capacity you want me in. But come on, give me a chance to give you a great time," Avery said, making Leila speechless. Leila's mouth was gaped open, but she shut it slowly as she shrugged her shoulders.

"What do I have to lose?" She said out loud, making Avery laugh as they began to have dinner.

Chapter 2

"You really do think you are God's gift to women, don't you?" Leila teased the following weekend. She and Avery had gone shopping together for outfits, which they were going to wear that night when they went out together. Avery had tried on a short red dress and was dramatically flipping her hair as she modeled it for Leila.

"Oh, I don't think it, darling, Mama knows," Avery said, winking at Leila and making her speechless for the umpteenth time that day. Leila turned and walked away as she felt her cheeks blush red, hoping that Avery missed it.

"Have you found something that you like, honey?" Avery asked, following Leila back out onto the floor.

"This isn't really my kind of store," Leila softly said, concerned that there would be nothing to fit her and feeling self-conscious.

"Can I take the lead?" Avery said, holding Leila's face in her hands. Leila looked away, shrugged her shoulders, but quickly looked back when Avery kissed the tip of her nose and melted her with her killer stare.

"Good, ok, come with me," Avery said, taking Leila's hand and began taking her around the store. Avery picked up several dresses that made Leila roll her eyes but continued to let Avery have her fun.

"None of these will look any good on me," Leila complained as Avery pushed her into a changing cubicle.

"Have you tried them on yet? Do you know that for sure, or are you just having a little tantrum because you are nervous about being in here?" Avery said, making Leila shake her head and look at herself in the mirror. She turned around, so she didn't have to see herself and undressed. Taking down the first emerald green sparkly dress, Leila turned back around and was surprised at what she saw. The dress, something that she would have never picked up in a million years, actually looked good on her.

"By the deadly silence, I'm going to take a wild guess and say that it looks nice?" Avery smugly called out, gasping as Leila opened the door. Leila was still in shock as she showed Avery the dress. The neckline showed off her full, plump breasts, their top curve looking like something from a porn magazine, the fitted waist tucked-in elegantly, and the calf to mid-thigh split showed off enough of Leila's thigh without making her feel self-conscious.

"My my, what a beautiful girl you are," Avery remarked, taking in the sight before her.

"How did you know this would look like this?!" Leila questioned, surprise and shock still evident in her voice.

"I mean, I thought it would suit you, even I couldn't

predict that you would be this radiant!" Avery happily replied.

"Do you want to try on the others?" Avery asked, interested in seeing Leila in more stunning outfits. Leila tried on the other five dresses, each time being as surprised. They all made her look divine. They didn't hide the fact that she was heavier; they just complimented her. That's what Leila loved about Avery. She never made her feel like she needed to change who she was, Avery just wanted Leila to be the best version of herself that she could be in the moment.

"I can't get all of them," Leila said, holding the dresses in her arms.

"Why not?" Avery asked, frowning at her in confusion.

"Um, have you seen these price tags?" Leila laughed, putting three of the dresses back, just for Avery to pick them back up again.

"Yes. Who said anything about you buying them? I'm the one who suggested this. I'm the one who pays. Anyway, baby, I can't, in good faith, knowing how beautiful you looked in these dresses, let you leave without all of them," Avery said, adding them to the collection of outfits she had waiting for her behind the counter.

"I don't know what to say," Leila said, shocked that someone would so freely spend a couple of thousand dollars on dresses for her. Avery turned around and brought Leila in close, holding her until she felt Leila relax in her arms.

"You don't have to say anything, baby. I like doing this

for you," Avery replied before turning back around and paying the woman behind the counter.

"So, I still can't believe that you did that," Leila said, happily holding onto her bags and swinging her arms. She felt different. She felt confident and secure and secretly loved the way the passers-by were looking at her designer shopping bags.

Even if this is fake confidence, gosh, it feels nice compared to the feeling of nothing I usually have, Leila thought to herself, acutely aware that the confidence stemming from an egotistical perspective wasn't the most authentic confidence to behold.

"Sweetie, this is what I am saying. Look at you, you look happy, you look free, you look like you can take on the world. If that isn't rewarding for me, I don't know what is," Avery replied, smiling and biting her bottom lip when Leila involuntarily reached out to hold her hand. Realizing what she had done, Leila freaked and tried to pull away, only to be caught by Avery's tight grip.

"Oh no, you don't. I've got you now," Avery playfully said, winking at Leila in the way, which always made Leila get butterflies in her tummy.

"Pick me up at 8?" Leila asked as they stopped outside her building. Avery wrapped her arms around Leila and stroked her hair affectionately.

"You got it, sweet thing," Avery replied before playfully slapping Leila on the ass and watching her walk into her building.

Avery then turned and walked back up the street, across the road and into a café where she sat down, ordering a coffee and watched as the people walked passed the window. She had some time to kill before she needed to go home and get ready for her date and wasn't interested in just sitting at home watching television until then. She had hoped that by now, she could bring it up with Leila.

Just take your time; you've got ages before the deadline. She might be into it. She seems like somebody who could be into it. I mean, look how cute she is, I could totally imagine her being my baby, Avery said to herself as she sipped her coffee. Avery's ex had introduced her to the MDLG world, helping her to realize her Mommy side. Avery had been so surprised the first time her ex had shown her what the kink was all about that it made her laugh. She had assumed it was the stereotypical BDSM but just getting called Mommy instead of Mistress. How wrong she had been. The problem with her ex was that she never seemed satisfied with Avery's domination. She didn't follow the rules, she challenged Avery at every turn, and nothing was ever good enough for her. At first, Avery thought it was just part of who she was as a little, but she soon grew tired of only experiencing the punishing side of their dynamic. Avery wanted more. She wanted the sweet, needy Mommy's girls that she read about. She wanted cute dates together to parks and to get pictures drawn just for her. She knew that she had to break up with her ex when she realized that she could never be the little Avery wanted and that she could never be the type of Mommy her ex needed. She just wasn't that controlling, and that's what she wanted.

"Anything else, Ma'am?" The waitress asked, interrupting Avery's thoughts. Avery looked up, somewhat startled.

"Oh, no thanks, just the check," Avery replied, checking the time and deciding that she should head home if she was going to make it on time to pick up Leila.

Leila had spent the afternoon watching cartoons. It wasn't the most productive use of her time, but if she was going to have a big night with adult drinks, adult clothes, adult conversation, she knew that she needed some little time. Usually, the weekends were when she had the most little time as the few hours she managed to get during the Monday to Friday grind was just that, only a few hours. But there was no way she was going to turn down a night with her stunning new girlfriend, even if the way they got together was the most unconventional pick up she had ever experienced. So, coming into her apartment, Leila had put her new dresses neatly in the cupboard, taken a shower, and changed into something more comfortable. Her kitten diaper and pink onesie, her hair in a messy ponytail, and her white paci. She had set herself up in front of the tv and turned on her favorite cartoons, snuggling into the pillows and blankies, imagining that it was Avery she was snuggling into.

I wonder if she'll think I'm weird, probs. I even think I'm weird, so she will as well. I wish I could be comfortable within myself, what if she finds out I want her like this, Leila thought, trying to wipe the thought from her mind. The last thing she wanted to do was push Avery away. She would usually never date somebody out of the scene, but Avery just had something that Leila loved being around. Leila couldn't put her finger on it. Avery was warm, loving, authoritarian, and tender. It made Leila ache. She was just the type of woman that Donna had been when they first got together. The thought of Donna made Leila's stomach churn. The cruel things she had said to Leila as their relationship ended haunted her. That she was ugly, too old to be a baby, that she should try to lose the weight because no one wants a big baby, that one cut her up the most. Leila shook her head as she tried to fight back the tears and buried her face in the pillows as she felt her heartbreak all over again.

"Why was she so mean?" Leila cried out loud. She sat back up and checked the time, it was 6 pm, and she knew that she should get ready so that Avery didn't walk in on her little space, but she just couldn't move. The hurt she felt inside her weighed so heavy that she closed her eyes and drifted off to sleep.

A loud knocking came from the door, startling Leila awake. It was pitch black in the room as she blinked sleepily and looked around the space.

"Leila?" Avery called from behind the door, making Leila's stomach knot.

"Oh my god," Leila said as she jumped up, turned a light on and looked around the room.

"Um, just a minute," Leila yelled out, ripping the onesie and diaper off, running into her bedroom and putting on some house clothes before racing back out to answer the door.

"Hey," Leila said, panting and pulling down her shirt. Avery looked at Leila's face and tilted her head.

"Hi," Avery replied, smirking and running her fingers through Leila's hair.

"You ready?" Avery questioned, causing Leila to snap into life and looked down at her outfit.

"Um, yeah, I am so sorry, I fell asleep," Leila said, walking backward and allowing Avery to walk inside. Avery was wearing the tight black dress with the back cut out, which she had bought earlier that day and her makeup was stunning, Leila could tell that she had taken a long time to get ready.

"Do you have kids?" Avery asked as she sat down on the couch and crossed her legs seductively. Leila looked around the living room where the cartoons were still playing. The blankies and her pacifier were still on the couch.

"Um, no, my niece was here," Leila lied, she didn't have a niece. Avery raised an eyebrow before picking up the pacifier.

"This doesn't look like a kids," she said, walking over to Leila, who froze and burned red.

"It's ok," Avery softly and affectionately said as she pushed the paci into Leila's mouth and held it there with her fingers. Leila looked into Avery's eyes fearfully, worried what she would think.

"I had my suspicions," Avery said, taking Leila's hand and gently leading her back to the couch, sitting down and positioning Leila in the nursing position. Avery wrapped her arms around Leila and stroked her cheek with her thumb.

"You had suspicions?" Leila asked, taking out her paci and slightly relaxing into Avery.

"Yeah," Avery replied, looking down on Leila lovingly.

"But I'm older than you?" Leila asked, making Avery frown.

"And? You're not older than me all the time," Avery said, winking at Leila, who giggled despite herself.

"And, I'm bigger than you," Leila said, feeling all her insecurities coming out into the open. Avery tilted her head, finally understanding the source of Leila's fears.

"Honey. Does that bother you?" Avery asked, worried that her own athletic build would be a deal-breaker.

"Doesn't it bother you? You are so beautiful, why would you want a fat baby?" Leila asked, tears forming behind her eyes. Avery gasped and shook her head.

"No, it doesn't bother me that you are who you are. Is that how you view yourself?" Avery replied, making Leila burst out crying.

"Hey, shh, it's ok," Avery cooed, soothing her.

"That's what my ex said I was," Leila said through her tears. Avery frown and sat Leila up, turning her so that she was looking her in the eye.

"Leila. Your ex sounds like a piece of shit. If she wasn't happy with you, taking it out on how you look is the weakest, most horrible thing to do, and quite frankly, she didn't deserve how amazing you are. I know we have only known each other for a week, but you are so special, and if she was too stupid to understand that, then she is just an idiot," Avery said, making Leila laugh.

"It doesn't bother me that you are older than me, and I find your body beautiful. Life is a journey, and if someone isn't willing to go on that journey with you, then they don't deserve you. I would think you were amazing if you were 50kg heavier, and I would think you were amazing if you were 15kg lighter. You're value and validity isn't determined by how much you weigh or how old you are, baby girl," Avery said, making Leila cry all over again.

"Oh honey, come here," Avery said, opening her arms

and wrapping them around Leila.

"That is the nicest thing anyone has ever said to me," Leila confessed, snuggling into the crook of Avery's neck and feeling the sting of a thousand cuts ease for the first time.

"Oh, I'm sorry, I made your dress wet," Leila said, seeing that her tears had soaked a section of Avery's dress.

"You make my panties wet too," Avery said, never missing a beat and making Leila laugh.

"Really?" Leila asked, wiping her tears. Avery kissed both her cheeks before getting up.

"Really," she replied, going to the fridge.

"What do you want to drink, sweetheart? Milk, or wine? I am down for both," Avery asked, holding up the two bottles. Leila thought for a moment before smiling.

"Wine. I don't want my new dresses to go to waste," Leila replied, getting up to go and get ready.

Chapter 3

"Good morning, sleepyhead," Avery said, rolling over and brushing the hair out of Leila's face. Opening her eyes, Leila stretched and yawned before smiling at Avery.

"Hey," she softly said, her voice hoarse from the cocktails and cigarettes she had the night before.

"Hungover?" Avery asked, feeling her head begin to throb. They had both been excited to find out their kink preferences and had painted the town red, only returning back to Leila's apartment as the morning sun rose over the horizon.

"Oh, yes," Leila laughed, touching her forehead and frowning.

"Ok, we need coffee, a decent fry up, and sunglasses," Avery said, getting up and slowly making her way to the shower, turning it on and stripping. Leila followed her to the bathroom door, peeping her head around the door.

"You can come in," Avery happily said. Leila cautiously walked in, looking at Avery's fitness model body as the water trickled down her abs.

"Come and join me," Avery seductively said, making Leila blush as she was caught staring.

"Ok," Leila said, timidly taking her pajamas off and

covering up her body as she got into the shower.

"How am I supposed to make sure you are clean if you are trying to hide from me?" Avery loving asked as she gently took Leila's hands away, making her blush.

"You are beautiful, Leila," Avery said, holding her face in her hands and making her look at her. Leila looked to the side, her face still in Avery's hands as Avery kissed her lips, taking her by surprise.

"I'm sorry, I thought it would be ok. We kissed last night," Avery said, letting Leila go.

"Yeah, sorry, it is. I just was surprised, I had sort of thought maybe you were only kissing me because you were drunk," Leila confessed making Avery roll her eyes.

"No, I kissed you because I wanted to. Because I find you gorgeous," Avery said, taking the bottle of shower gel in her hands and squirting it over her body before beginning to rub it in.

"Can I," Leila said, reaching out to touch Avery but stopping herself and making Avery smile.

"Yeah," Avery replied, taking Leila's hands and rubbing them over her body. She didn't need to guide Leila for very long as she took over and began rubbing her muscles and tight body passionately.

"Oh my god, your body is amazing," Leila said as she let her fingers go dangerously close to Avery's clit. Avery just bit her bottom lip and raised her eyebrow.

"What do you think you are doing?" Avery teased, making Leila giggle.

"Depends what am I allowed to do," Leila replied, surprised at how confident she now felt. Avery leaned against the shower wall, took Leila by the wrist, and washed her hand clean of any shower gel before placing it against her pussy, pushing Leila's fingers passed her slit, opening up her pussy lips.

"I'll let you do that," Avery whispered, Leila, enjoying the feel of Avery's body. Gently, running her fingers up and down Avery's pussy, pressing into her cunt, watching as Avery shook her head.

"Not today," Avery replied, Leila, wanting a reason but accepting the boundary and going back to stroking her.

"Tell me where I can touch you," Avery said, gasping as Leila began to tease her clit.

"Wherever you want," Leila said, shrugging her shoulder, half worried that Avery wouldn't want to touch her at all.

"Well then," Avery said, taking Leila's hand from her cunt and turning her around so that she was facing the wall. Avery took Leila's hands and put them high up against the wall making her giggle.

"You're not meant to laugh when I frisk you," Avery playfully said, beginning to massage down Leila's body sensually. Leila hadn't been touch like this in years and felt her head spin as she felt Avery snake her hands over her shoulders and breasts, coming around to the back of her and kissing down to her ass.

"My god, you are divine," Avery mumbled to herself as she grabbed Leila's ass in both hands and grinded against her, feeling her clit harden. Leila felt hers do the same and gasped as she felt Avery's kisses going further over her ass. Turning her around, Avery was kneeling before her, raised an eyebrow, and gently patted Leila's thigh.

"Leg up, baby girl," Avery said, watching as Leila put her foot on the edge of the shower ledge.

"Just tell me to stop if you don't want this anymore," Avery said as she stuck her tongue out and slowly licked Leila's slit, making her shiver and her nipples harden.

"Oh, I knew you would be a sweet girl," Avery said, burying her face between Leila's thighs and eating her out passionately. Leila gasped and moaned, feeling Avery's tongue inside of her, making her wonder how she could get it so deep.

"Play with your tits for me," Avery said, coming up for air, just to dive back in, Leila obeying her instruction immediately. Leila pushed herself onto Avery's face, moaning as the water sprinkled their bodies.

"Fuck," Leila said, almost swearing she could feel Avery smile as she continued to suck her clit and curl her fingers inside of her, only easing off to allow her tongue to take over. Leila shuddered and buckled over, grabbing Avery's head and pressing it against her as she felt the earth-shattering orgasm rage through her body. Avery tapped the side of Leila's thigh, causing her to let her head go and she came up, gasping for air.

"Fuck me that was hot," Avery said, Leila, sliding down the wall and making Avery smile and join her.

"I loved that little bit of suffocation play you had going at the end. I didn't know I was into that," Avery said, wiping her chin and letting the water pour over her face, slicking her hair back.

"I didn't mean it, it was just so good I didn't want it to end," Leila quietly said, making Avery laugh.

"I'm glad you liked it. The first time can sometimes be really awkward," Avery replied, seeing Leila's face and shaking her head.

"No, that was not awkward," Avery said, cracking her neck before getting up, reaching out her hand to Leila.

"I've just eaten, but you need breakfast," Avery said, Leila, taking her hand and standing up.

"Cringe," Leila said, making Avery laugh and gently spank her ass as she walked out of the shower first.

"I'll just get the salad," Leila said as she folded the menu back up and took a sip from her glass of water. Avery looked over her menu, Leila's sad face telling her all that she needed to know.

"Do you want a salad? Because that face is not the face

of someone happy about their selection," Avery said.

"I just think I should get it," Leila said, shrugging her shoulder.

"Ok, forget about what you think you should or shouldn't get. What would you want to get if you could have anything off the menu?" Avery asked, Leila, opening up the menu once more and looking over the choices.

"A burger and fries with a chocolate shake," Leila said in almost no time at all.

"Right, then baby, that's what you should get," Avery said, reaching out and holding Leila's hand.

"But, it's not the most healthy choice," Leila said, looking around at the other patrons.

"People look at me like I shouldn't be eating that sort of stuff when they see me," Leila said, looking into her lap. Avery got up and moved so that she was sitting next to her and wrapped her arm around her.

"And if anybody looks at you like you shouldn't be doing exactly what you want, I'm going to have words with them," Avery said, taking Leila's head and resting it on her shoulder.

"I'm not going to let anyone hurt you, sweet girl," Avery said, making Leila's heart swell.

"I really like you," Leila whispered, feeling Avery's body against hers.

"I really like you too," Avery replied, winking at Leila.

Chapter 4

Avery was a dream come true. She was kind, considerate, and never seemed to push Leila too far out of her comfort zone, but just enough that she started to feel brave again. It showed in her work too. Her articles had taken on a flare she had thought she had lost, even her skin seemed to glow.

"It's all thanks to you, you know," Leila said over late lunch. Avery was tired. Leila could see by the sleepy smile that she gave her as she read Leila's latest article.

"Well, I can't take all the credit," Avery replied. Avery had scratched up knuckles from a bar fight she had been called to last night, Leila only seeing her now, the first time in three days.

"It looks like they are getting infected," Leila said, frowning as she looked at Avery's hands.

"They'll be fine," Avery said, playfully rolling her eyes at Leila.

"Come on, come back home with me and let me dress them properly. Let me look after you," Leila said, standing up and waiting for Avery to join her.

"Shouldn't it be the other way around?" Avery said, slowly standing and walking over to join her.

"Not all the time," Leila said, her smile warming Avery's heart.

Leila opened the door to her apartment, the afternoon sun making the crystals on her television cabinet glisten and shine.

"Sit down," Leila said, going over to her medicine box and took out the supplies.

"Want a drink?" Leila asked, making Avery laugh.

"It's 3 in the afternoon," Avery replied Leila, coming to the couch with her medicine box and beginning to lay out everything she needed.

"Yes, and?" Leila questioned, making Avery laugh.

"No, I don't, but when you've been such a good girl and looked after Mommy, how about I reward you?" Avery said, causing Leila's head to tilt.

"Reward?" Leila asked, wanting to know more details. Avery just sat back and held her hand out to Leila, who began disinfecting the cuts.

"Ouch," Avery plainly said, trying not to flinch.

"Sorry," Leila replied, wrapping Avery's hands in bandages and sitting back.

"You know how we went dress shopping, and it was enjoyable, to say the least?" Avery asked, reminding Leila of the first time she had trusted Avery.

"Yeah," Leila cautiously replied, not sure where Avery was talking the conversation.

"Well, I wonder if you would want to go, little shopping?" Avery asked, Leila, rolling her eyes.

"Of course, I would!" Leila exclaimed, clapping her hands.

"Great. I was actually nervous that you might say no," Avery confessed, making Leila laugh.

"Um, why?" Leila questioned. It was very rare that Leila saw Avery nervous, but she liked it. It made her feel special, that Avery was just as afraid to lose her as she was Avery.

"I don't know. Everyone is different, and I kinda assumed you'd love it, but at the same time, you make me nervous. I don't want you to think I am trying to buy your affection or love or whatever," Avery said, making Leila laugh.

"I don't, don't worry," Leila replied, snuggling into Avery and closing her eyes as she felt Avery's arms close around her.

"I could just fall asleep right here," Leila softly said, feeling Avery kiss her forehead.

"But then we couldn't go shopping," Avery said.

"Oh, you mean right now?" Leila replied, sitting up and looking at Avery.

"Yeah. There's an event tonight, and I know there will be a few vendors. We could always go online, but when there is an opportunity to feel and try on the product, I like to take that opportunity," Avery explained. Leila smiled at her before silently standing up and taking the medicine box back to the kitchen.

"What is it?" Avery asked, seeing something in Leila's face that she couldn't figure out.

"Nothing. It's just, I didn't know it could feel this nice," Leila said, feeling tears well in her eyes. She liked that Avery didn't try to comfort her and let her feel her feelings instead of trying to make everything ok.

"Are you alright with it feeling this good?" Avery asked. Leila thought about the question shaking her head and shrugging her shoulders.

"I want to be," she said, making it sound more like a question than a statement of conviction.

"But?" Avery asked, giving Leila time to understand her own thoughts.

"But I'm not, and it might be like this for a while, and I want to be transparent with you because I don't want you to think I'm awful or ungrateful because I'm not. I just, it hurts every time you are so nice to me because, for the longest time, I was told that I didn't deserve nice things or for nice things to happen to me. I guess at some point, I started to believe that was true as well, and it'll just take a minute for that to undo," Leila explained, looking plainly at Avery once she finished talking. Avery stood in front of her and slowly nodded her head.

"You don't scare me," she whispered before winking and taking Leila's hand in hers.

"I'm glad," Leila replied, grabbing her keys and walking out the door.

Avery and Leila caught a taxi to the event, arriving an hour after it had started.

"Do you think it's a problem?" Leila nervously asked, making Avery smile.

"It's not a sit-down dinner. Nobody cares when or actually if we even show up, so yes, it is totally fine," Avery replied, making Leila laugh. They walked into the bar, and Avery loved that Leila immediately held her hand.

"Oh, do all the cute things make my baby girl feel little," Avery whispered in Leila's ear. She knew that there was no need for discretion, but she enjoyed turning Leila into the shy little girl she had come to love.

"Mommy," Leila whined, turning red. Avery loved that about Leila. She triggered so easily.

The event was held in a large conference hall in the middle of the city. Avery had been to many of the events held in this room, and she knew the view over the park was breathtaking. Tonight, however, the blinds pulled down on the windows and for a good reason. This event, while not particularly exclusive, still attracted all manner of clientele from all industries, and discretion was more than welcomed. As they moved around the room, they saw a large area set up for play, including a ball pit and painting station. Diaper, onesie, and pacifier vendors were set up along the far wall, and a QandA stage was set up in the middle of the room.

"This is really cool. How did you know about this?" Leila asked, looking around the room, smiling widely.

"Mommy's just clever," Avery replied, taking Leila's hand and leading her over to the multiple onesie vendors.

"What about this one?" Avery asked, Leila, looking at her like she had lost her mind.

"Alright," Avery laughed, putting the space-themed onesie down.

"This is more what I am going for," Leila said, holding up the cute black and white ghost onesie.

"Oh, wow, I can imagine you in this!" Avery exclaimed, taking it from Leila's hands and looking for more styles with a similar flare.

After half an hour, Avery held a bag full of onesies in one hand and Leila's hand in the other, getting slightly pulled as they made their way to the painting wall.

"You can do one painting baby girl, but then we have to go home," Avery said, causing Leila to take as long as she could get away with to make her creation. Clocking onto Leila's sneaky ways after 20minutes, Avery told Leila that she would have to finish the painting at home, causing Leila to give her puppy dog eyes and pout.

"Don't give me that, Mommy was clear," Avery said, Leila, realizing that it was better to be a good girl than a brat, and stood up reluctantly, pleasing Avery. There was something in the way that Leila submitted that drove Avery wild. It was more than just her following an instruction. It was her willingness to be inconvenienced for Avery's desires. Avery knew that she could push Leila to do whatever it was that she wanted, and her need to directed turned Avery on unlike anything she had ever experienced.

Is it that? Or is it the power and responsibility that comes with it? Avery thought as she looked over to Leila, who was happily walking next to her. Deciding that it didn't matter what the reason was, that the feeling was reward enough, Avery stopped walking and turned Leila into her.

"I love you," Avery suddenly said to Leila, who froze. She hadn't heard those words, said with such conviction in years, and the sound made her mind spin.

"Why?" Leila softly asked, looking down and kicking the sidewalk. Avery let her eyes smile as she reached out to slowly lift Leila's chin to make her look at her dead in the eye.

"What's not to love?" Avery replied, making Leila's eyes glaze over, and her mouth gape open in surprise.

"I know that sometimes you don't feel loveable. But I love you, and nothing that you are about to say or do will change that," Avery said, making Leila laugh despite herself and shake her head.

"You don't have to say it back. I just wanted you to know where I was at," Avery said, as they began to walk down the street once more. Leila was glad that Avery didn't want a reply because she didn't have one. It had been so long since Leila had felt the type of feelings that Avery seemed to reach so easily, it felt almost too good to be true, and the fear that it could all go away stopped Leila from diving as deeply as Avery. Conflicted, Leila kissed Avery goodnight and closed her door, looking around her apartment and going straight to the kitchen and pouring herself a drink. She took out her phone and looked through the photos she had taken with Avery, hating herself for not being able to give Avery the easy, happy relationship she wished she could.

Why does it have to be so hard for you?! Leila felt her heart cry out as she had a shower, the hot water pouring over her body, and her alcohol-filled veins making her head spin. Deciding to sit down on the shower floor, she put her head in her hands and began to cry. It wasn't that Avery had said that she loved her; it was the pain that Donna didn't. It wasn't that Avery had bought her things, it was that Leila wanted it to be Donna who did. It wasn't about Avery at all. It was about Donna. It was that Avery was everything Donna wasn't, and it was that Leila wanted it to be Donna. Shaking her head, wondering why she still grieved for that soulless, cruel woman, Leila stood up and put her face to the showerhead and let the water wash her tears away.

Maybe I don't know that I am allowed to be happy or something, Leila thought, deciding that drinking in the shower was a terrible idea and that she needed to see a therapist before she ruined everything with Avery.

Chapter 5

Leila had found a therapist online who had a practice close to where she lived and thought that she might as well give it a go.

What do I have to lose? Leila thought to herself as she crossed the road and picked up a take away coffee before continuing down the street. She walked up the concrete stairs, opened the glass door, and walked inside the small foyer, the receptionist greeting her warmly.

"Hey there," she said, smiling at Leila.

"Hi, I have an appointment with Christina Clarke," Leila replied, putting her hands in her pockets.

"Leila? Great, go right in," the receptionist said, and she pointed to the hallway. Leila gave her one of those, smiles that are more like pushing your lips together and walked down the hall.

"Hi, Leila?" Christina warmly said, stopping Leila in her tracks. Leila had seen this woman before. At the event her and Avery had been too only a few nights ago, this woman was one of the guests on the QandA panel. The woman didn't seem to recognize her, though, but it would become apparent soon enough that they shared similar interests.

"Yeah, hi," Leila said, sitting on the chair Christina

directed her to. Due to Christina had been one of the guest speakers on the QandA, Leila already knew that she was a Mommy, but she incorporated a fair bit of extreme S and M into her and her subs sex lives. It wasn't something Leila was particularly into, but she appreciated the diversity of the speakers of that night.

"So, what brings you here?" Christina asked, crossing her legs and waiting for Leila. Leila sipped her coffee, looked to the side, and sighed.

"I think I'm addicted to pain. Like the emotional kind, and it doesn't feel good," Leila said, Christina, nodding and writing on her tablet.

"What makes you say that?" She questioned. Leila was glad she was allowed to elaborate.

"I'm dating this girl. She is amazing, everything that anybody could want, gives me the freedom to be myself, speaks my love language, is gorgeous, but I feel conflicted about her love. Like, I want to reject it, but I have no reason to," Leila said Christina listening.

"Have you felt this way in other relationships?" Christina asked, Leila, biting her bottom lip.

"No, my last relationship was for six years, she was older than I was, she changed when I wasn't what she wanted anymore and made me feel like shit," Leila said, happy that she didn't feel the need to cry.

"If she made you feel like shit, and this new woman you

are with doesn't, I wonder if you still feel like shit. Maybe you don't feel like you deserve to be loved by this new woman because you haven't healed from your past relationship," Christina said, offering Leila a thought she hadn't contemplated before.

"Yeah, maybe," Leila said, sighing.

"Well, how do I get over my ex? Why am I still feeling this way when she was so cruel?" Leila asked. Christina nodded her head.

"Sometimes, when people treat us in alignment with how we feel about ourselves, the desire to be reminded of that is strong. Tell me something you would never do, something really out there," Christina said, Leila, thinking hard, trying to take in her words.

"I'd never want to go skydiving," Leila finally said.

"Ok. So now imagine that you are with somebody who is an adrenaline junkie and goes skydiving with their mates, has a whole network of friends from skydiving, and constantly reminds you that you should try it. They could be beautiful, funny, speak your love language and be the best person in the world, but they go against one of your big values, which in this case could be safety. You see, when somebody displays behaviors that are against who and what we think we are, we reject them, and those who are in alignment with us, and we accept them. So, if you think you are nothing, and somebody treats you like you are something, do you see how that is in conflict? So what we need to do, is get you seeing yourself in a better light because you know it's not right to be treated like trash," Christina said, causing Leila to burst into tears. For the first time in her life, she had an explanation as to why she allowed people to be horrible to her, and a lifetime of bullying experiences came crashing down on her.

"Here," Christina said, offering her a box of tissues.

"It's totally normal to cry, that's why you come here, to heal yourself. It takes guts. You should be really proud of yourself," Christina said, making Leila cry harder.

The way home was a blur, mostly because Leila still had tears in her eyes, which refused to leave, but she was also filled with new thoughts and feelings. She was surprised that one session could have that effect on her, but she was most surprised as to why it had taken her so long.

"It was so great. She really got me and knew what to say," Leila said to Avery on the phone that night. Avery was working but had taken five minutes to check in on Leila.

"I'm so happy for you, honey," Avery replied. She was a big advocate for seeking help for any and all parts of life.

"I told you it was like going to the gym but for your mind," Avery said, making Leila laugh.

"I guess Mommy is always right," Leila laughed, snuggling into bed.

"Not all the time, but mostly. So, are you seeing her

again?" Avery asked, hoping that Leila had booked another appointment.

"Yeah, I'm going to see her weekly," Leila replied, making Avery smile.

"Good girl," Avery said, looking around. She was leaning against a street light waiting for her partner to collect their dinner order.

"Well, Mommy has to go now, baby girl. Are we still on for tomorrow?" Avery said, seeing him walk out of the store.

"Yes, I'm really looking forward to it, Mommy," Leila replied, snuggling into the shirt Avery had left behind. She had deliberately bought a large shirt to wear to bed so that she could spray it with her perfume and leave it for Leila to find. She wanted Leila to be able to wear it around the house if she wished, and the thought of that made Avery smile.

"What are you wearing?" Avery suddenly asked, her partner raising his eyebrows and giving her a smile before sitting back in the car.

"Your shirt Mommy," Leila happily said, throwing her arms in the air as she said it, wishing that Avery was there with her to cuddle her at that moment.

"Good girl," Avery replied, before hanging up the phone.

"Don't look at me like that, you'd asked the same question if anyone wanted you around for long enough," Avery said, teasing her partner before driving back out onto the road.

"Is it too much?" Leila asked. Avery turned around to see her baby girl standing in front of her. Leila was wearing a diaper, her new ghost onesie, and her hair out. Avery found herself speechless for the first time.

"No, you look, amazing," Avery breathlessly said, making Leila smile and look down at her feet. Finding that she believed Avery for the smallest moments, she smiled again, happy that she was beginning to change her thoughts about herself. Not the surface layer thoughts, but those deep subconscious ones.

"But you need some sockies, baby girl," Avery said, taking Leila's hand and walking her back into the bedroom and sitting her on the bed.

"I think the pink ones are going to go really nicely," Avery said, taking them out of the cupboard and walking back over to Leila.

"No, Mommy," Leila said, kicking her feet so that Avery couldn't get them on her feet.

"Oi. Don't test me, little one," Avery sternly said, grabbing Leila's chin in her hand and making her look Avery in the eye.

"But I don't want those Mommy," Leila said, pouting.

"I think somebody needs Mommy to teach them a lesson," Avery said, putting the socks on the bed and swiftly turning Leila onto her tummy.

"Stay," Avery commanded. She thought back to the types of punishments that Leila said would be ok and decided to combine two of them.

"Do you know what happens to naughty girls?" Avery asked, planning out her punishment as she traced her fingertips over Leila's skin.

"Answer me," she angrily said, raising her voice and bringing both hands down on Leila's ass, making her squirm.

"No Mommy, what happens," Leila said, feeling the sting through her diaper, surprising her.

"They don't just get punished, they get corrected," Avery explained, grabbing Leila's thighs and squeezing them until she heard Leila gasp in pain.

"So, Mommy is going to remind you to be a good girl. And I don't think you're going to forget this for a very, very long time," Avery said, whispering the second half of the sentence. Leila shivered. She could tell that Avery was enjoying this, and as she was rolled onto her back, she knew that Avery meant business.

"I don't think you understand how much it hurts Mommy when you are rude," Avery said as she got on top of Leila and straddled her, holding her down with one hand between her breasts and one on the leather strap. She spoke slowly as she flogged Leila's thighs time after time.

"Mommy," Leila gasped, surprised at how strong Avery was.

"Try again. The only thing I want to hear from that pretty little mouth is, I'm sorry, Mommy," Avery said as she switched hands and began flogging Leila's other exposed thigh making her squirm.

"Oh, you think this is debatable? Do you think we are having a negotiation, baby doll?" Avery said as she moved her hand onto Leila's neck.

"No, Mommy," Leila said, seeing that she was making Avery angry.

"Now, you are deliberately ignoring Mommy?" Avery said, dropping the strap and slapping Leila across the face.

"I'm sorry, Mommy," Leila loudly said, Avery, smirking.

"There we go, that's better," Avery said, slapping Leila two more times.

"Next time, don't make me ask twice," Avery said, getting off Leila and grabbing her wrist, pulling her down the hall and bending her over the back of the couch.

"Spread your fucking legs," Avery growled, waiting for Leila to obey her instruction.

"I told you that you'd remember this," Avery said, taking a vibrating dildo and lubing it before pulling Leila's diaper aside and pushing it into her ass.

"Oh, baby girl, did you think Mommy was going to put it in your pussy?" Avery teased, watching as Leila's body reacted.

"Let me feel those nipples," Avery said, reaching around

Leila and rubbing her nipples, pinching them and enjoying how hard they were.

"Don't worry, your pussy isn't going to be ignored," Avery said, taking a thicker vibrator and pushing it into Leila, who whimpered and bent her head forward. Avery knew that she was close to her psychological limit and decided to soften the punishment to extend the time Leila could take it for.

"Put your hands behind your head, baby girl," Avery loving whispered into Leila's ear, running her fingertips over her body and giving her goosebumps.

"I'm sorry, Mommy," Leila said, tears running down her cheeks as Avery turned her around.

"I know you are, baby girl. But Mommy isn't done with you yet," Avery said, fastening a strap on to her waist and sitting on a chair.

"Get on your knees," Avery affectionately said, beckoning Leila with a finger, her other hand rubbing the cock between her thighs.

"Open wide baby girl," Avery said, pushing her hips forward and wrapping her hand through Leila's hair and pushing her cock into Leila's mouth, watching as she began to jerk her head up and down.

"That's it," Avery said. She had always thought it fascinating how this turned her on. It was such a simple act, but for some reason, it made her clit throb and her pussy drip.

"Get up," Avery said, pulling Leila off her only to pull

out the vibrator in Leila's pussy and replace it with her cock, making Leila sit on her lap, facing her.

"Bounce for Mommy, let me see those titties shake," Avery said. She could see that she was pushing Leila, but she smiled at her as Leila rode her, seeing Leila want to please her.

"Such a good girl. You were so good taking your punishment, you can cum when you want baby girl, Mommy wants to treat her little one," Avery said, seeing the change in Leila's face, knowing that her punishment was over and gasped as she felt Leila push her back as she fucked herself on top of Avery.

"That's it, take what you want, get what you need little one," Avery said as she felt Leila tense up and shudder as she came, holding her as she came down and crashed into sub drop.

"Mommy's got you," Avery reassuring said over and over, and she gently took her cock from Leila's body and took it off. She took out the vibrator from her ass and repositioned the diaper and onesie comfortably on Leila.

"Mommy," Leila whined, reaching out for Avery, who came to the couch and laid on top of her.

"Mommy's here. Mommy's protecting you," Avery gently said, as Leila grabbed at her like a cat flexing its paws on a carpet.

"I feel weird," Leila said, holding onto Avery.

"I know you do, and it's ok to feel this. You've never felt

this way after a punishment before?” Avery asked, kissing all over Leila's face and making her smile.

"No, never," Leila said, shaking her head. Avery brushed the hair out of her eyes and got off Leila, sitting up and watching as Leila also sat up.

"It can happen, it's called sub drop. It's like when you crash after a scene. It's totally normal. You don't have to think so much into it. There's nothing wrong with you because you feel a little down. What is something you think might make you feel better?" Avery said. Leila wasn't sure what she wanted to do. She felt as though she just wanted to escape.

"Could we just go for a drive and listen to music?" Leila asked as she wiped a tear away from her eye.

"Yeah, baby girl, come on," Avery replied, taking Leila's hand and leading her into the bedroom to get changed.

Chapter 6

They drove around the city for what felt like forever. Leila rested her head against the window and listened to her playlist while Avery drove and gently stroked her thigh.

"Have you ever wanted just to run away from all of this?" Leila asked, looking out the window at the concrete jungle.

"Have you spoken to your therapist about how you feel as well?" Avery asked, turning into a side street and parking the car. She took off hers and Leila's seatbelts and turned to face Leila.

"No, not really. We just talk about how I feel about myself," Leila replied. Avery saw the look on Leila's face and knew that if Leila decided to run away and out of this city, that she wouldn't be able to catch up with her. It wasn't as easy for Avery to leave the city, and she hoped that she could somehow make Leila want to stay.

"I don't know what to tell you," Avery said, sighing and reaching her hand out to Leila.

"I don't either. I want to feel happy, but I just can't seem to. And I don't know if that's because of me, my past or the way I deal with stuff. It just seems too easy for everyone else but me," Leila said, putting her seat down and looking up the car ceiling. Avery did the same, and as they lay looking up at the ceiling, they held hands, both seeming to know that the journey they were both on was about to change.

Leila put the last of her things in the trunk of her car, Avery watching as she leaned against the brick wall of the apartment building. They had spent the last few days together, Leila deciding that she needed to get out of the city and clear her head. Avery wishing that she could stop her, but knowing that it would be selfish as this is what Leila needed and wanted. They had had one last Mommy and little interaction, and Avery tried to fight back her tears as Leila closed the trunk and turned around.

"Jesus," Avery said, shaking her head, looking up at the perfect blue sky and wiping her tears.

"I'm sorry, Avery. I wish that this could have been different," Leila said, unsure if she was allowed to hold Avery, Avery reaching out and pulling her into her and holding her like she would die if she let go.

"I know," Avery whispered, crying silent tears as she pushed Leila away and crossed her arms across her chest, nodding her head.

"You better go, baby girl," Avery said, looking into her arms and feeling her heartbreak.

"I'll message you when I know where I am going," Leila

said, getting into the car and driving away.

"Fuck," Avery said to herself as she turned and walked away, feeling her heart being ripped out and left on that sidewalk.

Avery went to the store and bought three bottles of bourbon on her way home. Calling in sick for her shift, she threw her phone against the wall, shattering the screen. She stripped down to her lingerie and opened the first bottle, drinking from it and playing music on the loudest level on her headphones. Sitting on the couch, drinking, crying, throwing the pillows against the wall was how she spent the rest of her day.

Fuck this shit, she thought to herself, halfway through her second bottle. She was somewhat surprised that she was still conscious, although she wondered how much of the night she would remember by the morning. Taking a shower, she put on the first thing she could find and headed out.

As she walked down the street, she wasn't sure what she was feeling, or even if she was feeling at all, she just needed to walk.

This is fucked, absolutely fucking fucked, she thought. Deciding to walk through a park to try and calm her mind, Avery thought back over the woman she had been in relationships with in the past. She didn't remember a woman getting under her skin like this before. She felt as though something had been taken from her, something that she had to willingly let go of because if she didn't, she would only be hurting Leila more, and that was something she couldn't imagine doing. She sat down on a park bench, the feeling of emptiness in her heart seeming to seep to the other parts of her, and as she lay down on the bench, she curled her legs up to her chest and closed her eyes.

"Hi, can I check-in for three nights please," Leila said to the receptionist of the motel. After getting the room key, Leila drove to the room, opened the door, and dropped her bag. It was nothing special, but it would do just fine until she figured out where she was going. Leila took a shower, put on her pajamas, and lay on the bed. Taking out her phone, she messaged Avery, delighted when Avery called her almost immediately.

"Hey baby," Avery said. Leila could tell that she had been drinking but could still hear the pain in her voice.

"Hi. So I'm in a motel-like 7 hours out of the city. I think I might keep driving in a few days and stop at a small country town another 8 hours from here," Leila said, snuggling into Avery's shirt. Leila heard Avery sniff and then sigh.

"Ok. I am really happy that you are doing this, it's important that you find who you really are and stuff," Avery said, sitting up on the bench and wiping her tears.

"Are you drunk?" Leila said, half laughing, making Avery laugh.

"Yeah, I am. I'm dealing with this in probably the most useless way, but hey. Don't judge me please," Avery said, worried that Leila would think she was pathetic.

"No! No judgment at all, Mommy," Leila said, making Avery burst into tears as she heard her say, Mommy.

"Sorry, maybe I shouldn't call you that anymore?" Leila asked, not wanting to make this any harder on Avery than it clearly already was for her.

"No, I kinda like it. You can still call me Mommy," Avery replied, making Leila bite her bottom lip.

"But, baby girl, Mommy has to go and get home. I've just realized how dark it is," Avery said, sobering up enough to realize that she had put herself in a dangerous situation.

"Are you out?" Leila asked, wondering if Avery was with another girl.

"Yeah, I went for a walk. I needed some air," Avery replied, making Leila smile and rollover.

"Ok, goodnight then," Avery said, holding her breath and beginning to walk out of the park.

"Night, Mommy," Leila said, Avery quickly ending the phone call and bursting back into tears as she left the park.

Chapter 7

The hangover that greeted Avery when she woke the next day was unlike anything she had experienced, and as she raced for the bathroom, she knew that she had ruined bourbon for herself forever.

"Goddamn it," Avery said out loud between being sick. When she did finally empty the contents of her stomach, she took a shower and headed out to get breakfast. She put her headphones on and walked down the street, angrily looking at every pretty face which passed her. Avery had the type of look which made other gay women instantly interested, and for the first time in her life, she cursed herself for being so alluring. She didn't want them looking at her. She wanted Leila. Leila with her beautiful face and soft lips. Her baby girl with the body of a goddess, her soft and creamy skin always warm to touch. Avery rolled her eyes to herself as she thought about Leila as she crossed the road and walked into a café. The smell of burned toast hit her instantly, and she sat down at the closest free table. Ordering a black coffee and a full breakfast, Avery sighed as she opened her phone, deciding that she needed to buy a new one.

Maybe having a giant tantrum wasn't the smartest

thing to do, she thought to herself, reflecting on last night's decisions, making herself laugh despite herself. She reached for the sugar packets and taking one out, ripped it open with her teeth before pouring it into her coffee and stirring. She wanted to message Leila, wanted to tell her that she was coming with her, that she was giving up her life in the city and that they would be together once again but decided to leave her phone in her pocket.

That would be the most selfish thing you could do, you know that she needs time and space to figure some stuff out, Avery thought as she looked at a happy couple passing her table, giggling intimately with each other.

Well, this just sucks, she thought, sighing and wondering how fast this day could pass.

Leila had spent her time sitting in her motel room thinking. She made tea after tea and thought. Thought about all the things Donna had done and said to her, thought about what her therapist had told her, and thought about Avery.

She was like my knight in shining armor, but I guess I need to save myself, Leila thought to herself as she made her fifth tea for the morning. It wasn't like Leila to cut and run, she wished that she had done this to Donna and not to Avery, but as she thought more and more about it, she was glad that she did it nonetheless.

"It wasn't that Avery was bad, but she gave me so many

experiences that I wasn't ready for. I wasn't ready for the intense love and passion she gave me," Leila said out loud. Somehow, hearing her own thoughts made it easier to comprehend what her head was doing.

"So, a little bit of separation will be good, because I can have a moment to learn to love myself first and then when I go back to Avery, if she has me back, then I won't be freaked out every time she does something nice," Leila said, continuing to think out loud. She sighed and opened the door of the motel room. She was meant to check out today, but she wasn't sure if she even wanted to go on.

"I don't think I have to go that far just to be ok with being liked," Leila said to the birds who were jumping around in the gutter. She finished her tea and went inside, grabbed her bags, and put them in the car. Sitting in the parking lot and deciding what to do, either turn around and go back home or continue and see what other personal revelations she could discover. She thought about Avery, the perfect woman that she chanced upon at an imperfect time.

"Typical," Leila thought as she rolled her eyes to herself and turned on the ignition. Driving out of the lot, she hit the road, turning on a playlist Avery made her and began driving the 8 hours to the next town.

"Hi, I'm glad I could reach you," Leila said, calling Avery. It was the middle of the night, but Leila knew Avery would be awake.

"Of course, how's it all going?" Avery replied. She got up from where she was sitting and walked outside, the night air hitting her like a slap in the face.

"Pretty good. I have almost reached that town. I'm about an hour away from the border. I think I'll stay there for a week and then decided what I'm doing next. If I stay there or if I come back," Leila said, Avery just nodded her head silently.

"You sound happier," Avery finally said, making Leila smile.

"I am actually. I even ate a burger in public today," Leila said.

"Wow, solid progress!" Avery laughed, happy that Leila was beginning to feel comfortable in her own skin. Silence fell between the two of them, the empty feeling in Avery's stomach, making her sigh.

"I miss you," Avery said, wishing there had been some way she could have kept Leila with her.

"I miss you too, I still sleep with your shirt," Leila said, hoping that it would make Avery understand how deeply she still felt about her.

"Do you? That's really cute, send me a photo if you've got time. I'd love to see," Avery replied, imaging Leila lying in bed with her shirt on.

"If you're lucky," Leila teased, making Avery laugh.

"I have to go, babe. Thanks for calling me," Avery said,

wishing that she was at home so she could burst into tears.

"Ok, talk to you soon," Leila replied, hanging up the phone and closing her eyes shut, trying not to let the tears escape her eyes.

Chapter 8

The weeks passed painfully slowly, Leila deciding that she would stay in town for a while and finding a furnished studio apartment. Avery went through the motions of work, house jobs, and sleep. She had been tasked with a new partner, a rookie straight out of the academy, and she felt like those grumpy old guys who had trained her.

"Hey, hey, what's up," Bec joyfully said when she saw Avery waiting by the car. They were to patrol in the car today, and Avery had to get Bec acquainted with the streets.

"Nothing, get in," Avery plainly said, annoyed by how bubbly the girl was.

"You got up on the wrong side of the bed today," Bec muttered as she sat down, Avery just looked at her before rolling her eyes and driving onto the road. All she wanted to do was drive to Leila, not have this rookie with the enthusiasm of a puppy coming for a ride-along.

"So, what sort of stuff are you into?" Bec asked, looking out the window.

"None of your fucking business," Avery replied, smiling, feeling somewhat satisfied that she seemed to crush Bec's spirt.

"Geez, you're a hardass," Bec sighed, shaking her head.

"My girlfriend and I are on a weird thing where she has gone to find herself," Avery said, deciding that if she was going to have to spend the day with this kid, then she might as well try to be friendly.

"Rough, no wonder you are so grumpy," Bec replied, making Avery scoff.

"Hey. So, what about you?" Avery asked. She wished that she hadn't the moment she saw Bec's eyes light up and then proceeded to tell Avery every little thing about herself. Where she went to school, where she worked before becoming a police officer, how she and her boyfriend wanted to buy a dog.

Well, this was a mistake, Avery thought to herself as she looked at the time wishing Bec would shut up.

"How was your day?" Avery asked Leila, ringing her the moment she got home from work.

"Fine. I think that I'll come back in about a week or so. I've had a lot of time to think, and I feel like, if you are keen, then I would like to be with you again," Leila said, holding her breath. Avery didn't know what to say. This is what she had been waiting for for over a month, and now that Leila was finally saying the words she wanted to hear, she felt numb.

"Will I still be enough for you?" Avery asked, feeling worried that Leila would want something she couldn't give her.

"Mommy, you were always enough," Leila said, making Avery burst into tears.

"Oh my god, baby," Avery said, wiping them away and pacing around her apartment.

"Avery?" Leila asked, unsure of how Avery was feeling.

"Yeah, it's ok, I'm fine. I'm more than fine. I thought that you wouldn't want to be with me when you came back, even if you were coming back," Avery said, making Leila realize for the first time how hard it had been on Avery.

"I am so sorry. I didn't realize that this was hurting you so much," Leila said, wishing she could get in the car right now and drive until she reached Avery.

"I didn't want you to know. I wanted you to have the time you needed to sort out all the stuff you wanted to sort out, and then, well, I didn't really have a plan after that. Making sure you had the time to clear your head and stuff was my only priority," Avery said, making Leila beam.

"You really are the best person I have ever known, let alone been with. I'll take two days to get back home, but I'm ok now. Mommy? I'm coming home," Leila said, hanging up the phone and smiling up at the ceiling. She didn't hurt anymore. She could still identify the hurt, but when she thought about the things which haunted her, they didn't cause her the unwavering pain and heartache they had in the past.

"I got one thing right," Leila said, putting on Avery's

shirt and falling asleep.

Avery felt like a madwoman as she raced around to all of the shops she knew Leila loved. Picking up flowers, chocolates, a necklace, and books, Avery knew that she didn't have much time left before Leila got back into town. They had arranged to meet at Avery's apartment, Avery said that Leila could sleep there until she found a place of her own, but was secretly hoping that she would never want to leave. Avery went to the liquor store and bought Leila's favorite wine and then dropped into the donut shop and bought a dozen glazed donuts before returning home. She washed her sheets, vacuumed the place and cleaned the bathroom, putting the flowers in a vase, and placing the rest of Leila's gifts out on the coffee table. Now all she had to do was wait. She was sure Leila would arrive at around 2 in the afternoon, and she checked her phone countless times, waiting to get a phone call to say that Leila was outside. The buzzer on Avery's apartment had been broken for so long that everyone living in the building had gotten used to their friends ringing before being let up.

At 2:30, there was still no word from Leila, and Avery was feeling anxious.

What if something happened to her? What if her phone was stolen or her car flipped, or she was in an accident? Avery thought, making herself feel sick just as she heard her phone ring.

"Hi," Avery quickly said, answering the phone almost immediately, sounding desperate but making Leila laugh.

"Hey, I'm out front," Leila replied casually, Avery racing to the door and buzzing her up. Avery hung up, knowing that the reception cut out when people used the elevator and opened her front door. She walked to the elevator door, decided against it, and quickly ran back to her apartment so that Leila wouldn't see her. Avery heard Leila's footsteps as she walked down the corridor towards the apartment and waited in the doorway.

"Welcome home," Avery said, laughing and opening her arms to Leila, walking toward her and wrapping her arms around her in a tight embrace. Leila smelled the sultry notes of Avery's perfume and relaxed into the embrace, her heart missing the woman more than she had let herself believe.

"Gosh, it feels good to be back," Leila sighed, resting her head on Avery's shoulder.

"Come on, let's get you inside. You must be exhausted after such a long drive," Avery said, taking Leila's bags and walking into the apartment, closing the door behind her, and putting them down.

"I got you a few homecoming gifts," Avery said, making Leila look at her curiously.

"You didn't need to, but I will never turn a gift down," Leila said, causing Avery to notice the change in how Leila received her presents.

The old Leila would have felt undeserving of anything. I like this new version. She is more self-assured, Avery thought to herself as she led Leila to the living room and sat down on the couch.

"Wow, you have really outdone yourself, haven't you!" Leila exclaimed, making Avery laugh.

"I wasn't sure what to get you, so I got you, everything," Avery replied, accepting a donut Leila offered her.

"Yummy," Leila said, her little voice escaping and making Avery melt.

"I've missed you, baby girl. I'm so proud of you for going out into the world on your own for a while and figuring yourself out. But I'm really happy you came back to me," Avery admitted, Leila, moving closer to her to snuggle into her side.

"Same. It was weird at first, but I needed it to feel like the real me again. It didn't feel right not being around you, though," Leila replied, smiling at Avery and wondering how long it would take them to get back into their Mommy and little dynamic. Avery took another donut, Leila leaning forward and taking a bite.

"I know you only bought 12, so there'd be enough for you too," Leila giggled, making Avery feel playful.

"Maybe I did," Avery said, picking up another one and walking to the kitchen to grab a bottle of water. She thought for a moment before picking up Leila's sippy cup and holding it up, raising a questioning eyebrow. She didn't want to push

Leila back into something she wasn't ready for, but she also wanted her baby girl back, relieved when Leila nodded yes.

"So, you want to just jump straight back in?" Leila giggled as Avery came back to sit down next to her.

"If that's something you want as well? I don't want to push you," Avery said. Leila smirked and pushed Avery backward.

"Like that?" Leila cheekily said as Avery sat back up, taken by surprise.

"I'm going to let you have that, but never again, little one," Avery said, pointing a finger to Leila, who yawned and checked her watch.

"It's only early afternoon, and I am exhausted," Leila said, resting her head on the back of the couch and closing her eyes.

"Well, if you feel like you want a little TLC, can Mommy give you a bath and get you ready for an early night?" Avery said, feeling that nervous knot tie back up in her stomach. She thought it was funny how Leila made her so self-conscious. Usually, she had the game of a stud, but something about this girl made her question herself more than any other girl ever had.

"I'd really like that," Leila replied, happily accepting the pacifier Avery put in her mouth before leading her to the bathroom.

"Gosh, Mommy is happy you are home with me, little

one," Avery said as she began to undress Leila. She ran the bathwater and added bubbles, helping Leila into the tub before sitting on the floor next to her and watching as she played.

"Mommy's missed your little giggles," Avery said, resting her head on the side of the bath and happily smiling.

"Sorry, Mommy," Leila replied, reaching out to touch Avery's cheek. Avery kissed Leila's hand.

"Don't be, I'm just so happy you are happy and safe and feeling good," Avery replied. Reaching into the tub and beginning to wash Leila's back.

"You know something, Mommy," Leila said, taking her pacifier out of her mouth.

"No, what honey," Avery replied, gently taking the washcloth and washing Leila's face.

"I didn't wear a diaper the whole time, I only wanted you to diaper me, and if you couldn't then I didn't want to wear one," Leila said. Avery wasn't sure how to take the information, but she was happy that it clearly meant something to Leila.

"Well, good thing Mommy is here now, I can't have my little girl not diapered for bedtime!" Avery playfully exclaimed, taking Leila's hand and standing her up before rinsing her off.

"I still have all your stuff in my closet. I had hoped you'd come back to me," Avery said, drying Leila off and putting her hair in a ponytail.

"Cutie," Avery said, enjoying how gorgeous Leila looked

before taking her hand and leading her to the bedroom. Leila sat on Avery's bed and crossed her legs, giggling when Avery pushed her backward.

"Lie down, baby girl," Avery lovingly instructed, making Leila smile as she enjoyed entering little space for the first time in over a month.

Chapter 9

"Such a beautiful girl," Avery said, putting on a pink singlet and kissing Leila's forehead.

"Are you a hungry baby girl, or did all those donuts Mommy get you make you full?" Avery said, laying next to Leila and letting her cuddle into her close. She had missed how physically needy Leila was, and she loved it.

"I'm full Mommy, I had a sandwich on my way home too," Leila said, closing her eyes.

"Alright. What jammies should Mommy wear tonight?" Avery said, knowing full well the ones that Leila was going to choose.

"The fluffy gray ones, Mommy," Leila cheerfully answered. These were the most snuggly pair of jammies Avery had, and whenever she wore them, Leila would cuddle up beside her.

"I thought so," Avery said, putting them on. Avery had half anticipated that she and Leila would have sex, so she had showered shortly before Leila had arrived. Coming into bed next to Leila, she wondered if Leila would want to suck on her nipple like she had seen in a video from her favorite website. The fear of rejection from Leila was strong, and Avery bit her lip, 95% sure that Leila would like it, but nervous all the same.

"Hey, baby," Avery hesitantly asked, causing Leila to look up at her with curious eyes.

"Yeah, Mommy?" Leila questioned, seeing that there was something that Avery clearly didn't feel confident discussing. Avery took out her phone and showed Leila a screenshot of the image of a couple, the little nursing in the arms of her Mommy. Leila didn't know what to say. She wasn't sure what Avery was trying to tell her.

"Do you like how it looks?" Avery asked, Leila, blushing and looking away.

"Yes," she softly said, feeling vulnerable and somewhat embarrassed.

"Do you want to try it with Mommy?" Avery asked, Leila's little side smile telling her all she needed to know.

"I don't have milk, but I still think it could be nice," Avery said, positioning Leila into place. Avery's breasts were a generous C-cup and were smaller than any girls' Leila had dated, including her own. She had nursed on Donna's breasts when they first got together, but it had slowly become less and less as the years went on.

Leila shook her head, wanting to get the image of Donna out of her mind and smile at herself, delighted that the feelings of rejection and hurt were able to be processed so quickly.

"Open that pretty mouth," Avery said, running her finger across Leila's lips and watching as she closed her mouth around Avery's nipple, sucking instinctively, causing Avery to moan involuntarily.

"Oh my, good girl," Avery moaned, catching her breath as she felt herself thrown into depths of Mommy space she hadn't experienced before. Her eyes glazed over, and when she refocused, she felt like a different version of herself, and she loved it. Rocking Leila in her arms, Avery held her breast to Leila's lips, falling in love with how her mouth looked around her nipple and loved seeing how Leila's pupils dilated in pleasure.

"You like this too, hey baby girl?" Avery asked, Leila, nodding her head as she gently but hungrily sucked.

"I think that needs to become a part of the nightly routine," Avery said the following morning. Leila had fallen asleep with Avery's nipple in her mouth, Avery, with her arms wrapped around Leila's body. They had stayed like that until the morning when Leila had woken up first and had tiptoed to the living room. She sat on the couch and played on her phone. She didn't want to wake Avery up with the backlight of her game, but it hadn't taken Avery long to feel that Leila wasn't there.

"Same," Leila said, looking up from her game but quickly looking back down. Avery smiled, seeing Leila's thumbs working on overdrive to win the level she was on. Avery turned toward the coffee machine to see that Leila had already made her a latte and taking an apple from the fridge, Avery went to sit down next to Leila.

"After that level, put your phone away," Avery said, wanting her baby girl back.

"Ok, Mommy," Leila happily said, tapping so aggressively that Avery thought she might break her phone screen.

"Yes!" Leila exclaimed, putting her phone on the coffee table and turning to face Avery, who was looking at her in amusement.

"Why are you looking at me like that?" Leila asked, crossing her arms in playful defiance.

"Mommy can look at you any way I want," Avery replied, putting her latte down.

"I want to go over a few things with you like what you are going to do with your job, and I want a clearer understanding of what you want from me as your Mommy and girlfriend," Avery said, watching Leila's reaction.

"Alright," Leila said, looking down at herself and then looking back up at Avery.

"Yeah, fair point," Avery said, laughing and taking Leila's hand, leading her back into the bedroom.

"I love that if we were to have this discussion a few months ago, I simply wouldn't have been able to say what I want," Leila said as she undressed and put on a pair of off-cut denim shorts and a baggy long sleeve shirt. She put her hair in a cute messy ponytail and sat with Avery on the bed.

"Yeah, I know. I think it was so good of you to go out on your own and sort some stuff out. It was good for me too, I learned some stuff about myself and the different things I like," Avery said, bringing her knees up to her chest.

"Oh yeah? Like what, Mommy?" Leila sensually asked as she reached out and teased Avery's slit through her panties.

"Ha, like that little girls need to keep their hands to themselves," Avery replied, slapping Leila's hand away, although getting wet.

"Ok, but like on a serious note. Tell me some stuff," Avery said, giving Leila a look of warning.

"Alright. I really loved sucking on your nipples last night, which was perfect for me. I think that I'm going to have a hard time wetting my diaper, but I want to try it and get comfortable with it if that's something you wouldn't hate. I don't really want stuffies, I want more like, mentally stimulating stuff like blocks and models I can build, but I still want my bunny to sleep with. I think that I like onesies more than a shirt and diaper cover, and the only other thing that I really want is for my hair to be stroked when we cuddle," Leila said, surprising herself by how open and honest she was being. Avery smiled at her as she wrote down a few things, not wanting to forget or leave out anything that Leila had said.

"I like that I can train you in something," Avery replied once she was finished writing.

"What about you?" Leila asked.

"I want to do things like pick you up from places, maybe work, or if you go out, I want to stay up and pick you up. Not in a creepy stalker way, but a, looking after you kind of way. If you'd like, I'd also want to end up moving in together, either here or we find a new place together. Apart from those things, I love everything we do, maybe have a routine for when I am working days and nights could be good as well, though," Avery replied.

"Sounds good to me. So," Leila said. It was a Saturday, and Avery had the day off.

"So?" Avery questioned, wondering what Leila was going to say.

"So, I know you have the day off. Wanna do something?" Leila asked, shyly smiling, hoping Avery wasn't sick and tired of her yet.

"I can't think of anything I would rather do more than hang out with you," Avery replied, making Leila clap her hands.

"So, maybe we could get dressed and go somewhere fun, like the beach or something?" Leila asked. Avery thought for a moment before answering.

"Could we make it a Mommy baby day? Or do you want to be a big girl?" Avery asked, making Leila giggle and blush.

"Mommy and baby day," she replied, delighting Avery.

"Well. Let's get you breakfast and then dressed. I know

a few spots along the coastline that have some secluded spots, which will be perfect for you to play," Avery said, going to the kitchen.

"What are you hungry for?" Avery asked, fully prepared to cook up a storm.

"That apple looked really good, actually Mommy," Leila said, making Avery tilt her head to the side.

"Just because I want an apple doesn't mean that I am trying to change my body, Mommy. I'm actually happy with myself for the first time in years, and I want to have an apple just because I like how they taste. And they crunch and I like that too," Leila explained. Avery was happy. She never wanted Leila to be anything but herself.

"Alright. Do you want Mommy to cut it up for you?" Avery asked, watching as Leila nodded her head before she got up to go and get out of her adult clothes.

I've been in so many head spaces this morning. I am genuinely surprised I am keeping up! Leila thought to herself, giggling as she felt Avery's hands on her back.

"And what are you doing, little miss?" Avery said, placing the plate of apple slices down on the bedside table.

"I'm getting dressed," Leila said, giggling and running to the cupboard.

"We both know you are too little to dress yourself," Avery replied, taking a diaper down from the shelf, a pair of overalls and a pink shirt.

"Mommy, it's the day time!" Leila squealed, rolling around on the bed.

"Oh, I know that, but it's too hot to go to the beach right now. So now Mommy is going to diaper you, and you are going to wet it before we go anywhere. Don't worry. Mommy will get you all cleaned up before we go," Avery said, seeing the shock on Leila's face.

"Such a cute little thing," Avery said, grabbing Leila's ankles and pulling her down the bed and onto her back. Leila's surprised face made Avery smile.

"Didn't you think Mommy was so strong? You're my little girl, of course, Mommy can move you how I want to," Avery said, flexing her large biceps, making Leila giggle and blush.

"Ok, bottoms up," Avery said, tapping Leila on her thighs and waiting for her to lift up as Avery slid a diaper underneath her.

"First, some powder to make you all soft, we don't want to get rashies now do we," Avery said, Leila, shaking her head no. Avery rubbed the powder over Leila's body, making her giggle before she pulled the tabs firmly, fastening the diaper to Leila's waist. Leila closed her eyes and sighed in contented bliss. There was something so beautifully triggering in the way Avery touched her, and this simple act had thrown Leila into little space in only the way Avery knew how to do.

"Sit up for Mommy," Avery said, waiting for Leila to

follow her instruction.

"Arms up," Avery said, pulling the t-shirt over Leila's head and pulling her arms through. Avery then helped Leila put her overalls on and made her giggle as she put her hair in a messy ponytail.

"My beautiful girl," Avery said. She bit her bottom lip for a moment before going back to the cupboard and taking out a pink bow hair tie, wrapping it around the one already in Leila's hair.

"Now you're finished," Avery said, ticking Leila all over and making her giggle.

"Mommy, don't I might," Leila said, stopping herself as she lay back and used her feet to try and keep Avery off her.

"You'll what sweet girl? Wet your diaper, that's kinda the point," Avery said, winking at her and making Leila blush.

"But right now?" Leila asked, the worried look on her face making Avery's heart melt.

"No, it doesn't have to be right now, just sometime today when you feel ok about it. Then Mommy will get you all nice and clean, and we can go to the beach," Avery explained. Leila thought for a moment.

"But straight away? You'll make sure I'm clean straight away?" Leila nervously asked, Avery just nodding her head.

"I know you don't like to be a dirty baby girl. Mommy isn't going to let you be, don't worry," Avery said, wondering if keeping Leila in her wet diaper for five minutes could be used as a future punishment.

"Ok," Leila said, satisfied that she had an understanding of the situation and got off the bed.

"Can we go play now, please, Mommy?" Leila asked, her ponytail tilting to one side as she asked the question.

"Of course, baby girl. Mommy wants to see you crawl though," Avery instructed, watching as Leila obediently got onto her hands and knees and began to crawl.

"But what about bunny?" Leila suddenly said, stopping and almost getting run into by Avery.

"You mean, this bunny?" Avery said, holding out Leila's stuffie, making her giggle.

"Mommy knows everything," Leila happily said as she continued to crawl into the living room.

"Mommy knows a few things," Avery said, enjoying that Leila thought she was the most knowledgeable person in the world. When Leila reached the living room, she crawled over to the coffee table to took out the coloring in book and colors Avery had bought for her.

"Mommy is going to make a light snack, you need to finish eating your apple slices, and then you can have a bottle," Avery said, watching Leila from the kitchen.

"Mommy, do you think I need to look different," Leila said, taking Avery by surprise.

"No, what makes you say that," Avery said, stopping what she was doing and coming over to sit down next to Leila on the floor. She knew that Leila felt self-conscious about her weight, and it made her feel sad that she wasn't happy within herself 100% of the time.

"My 20year high school reunion is coming up in 6months, and it's all I can think about. I want to go, but I don't feel good about myself all the time yet. I get moments where I do, but I want those moments to be longer," Leila said, biting her bottom lip and blushing.

"What is it about yourself that you want to change? It's ok and healthy to evolve and adapt, but only if it is for the right reasons," Avery replied.

"I want to look more like this," Leila said, taking her phone out of her front pocket in her overalls and showing Avery a photo of a curvy model.

"I think that if I just lost a little extra weight, that would make me feel more like me. I also want to change my hair and get my eyelashes tinted. I kind of want to start taking care of my appearance a bit more. Like, the old me is in the past, and I want to make a new me. When we went out the first time, and I was all done up, I liked that, and I want to look like that a lot more," Leila said, shrugging her shoulders.

She's thought about this, Avery thought to herself as she looked at the woman in front of her, smiled, and reached out her hand to stroke her cheek.

"Alright, well, what do you want to start with?" Avery asked. She was constantly being surprised by Leila and liked that she was always on some sort of improvement journey.

"I think the easiest stuff to do first would be like getting my hair done and eyelashes tinted. I want to buy some new make-up and try some new looks. I think maybe I should get a personal trainer too. I just want to feel like my body can do what I want it to do," Leila replied, bringing her knees up to her chest.

"That makes sense," Avery replied, nodding in agreement.

"That was a very grown-up conversation for someone wearing a diaper," Avery quickly added, winking at Leila and getting up to go back into the kitchen.

Chapter 10

Leila took what felt like forever to eat the apple slices, Avery coming to sit on the couch and watch her color in, having to tell her every once in a while to eat a slice.

"I am Mommy!" Leila giggled as she picked up the last slice. Avery went on her phone and looked up award-winning hairstylists in the area. She had decided she could probably also enhance her appearance and try a new salon. Avery made two appointments online.

"Finally," Avery joked, making Leila giggle and bounce while she sat the way she always did when she was happy.

"Chocolate or vanilla baby?" Avery called from the kitchen, holding up two different protein powders. Leila tilted her head as she thought before pointing to the vanilla one before going back to her coloring in. Avery made up the shake, put it in a bottle, and can back to the couch, patting her lap and waiting for Leila to lay in her arms.

"Mommy's sweet girl," Avery cooed as Leila drank. Avery knew that before long, Leila would make her diaper wet, although she was almost sure Leila was trying to hold it.

"You know, good girls' who wet their diaper sometimes get treats," Avery said, making Leila's eyes sparkle from behind the bottle. Leila knew that Avery knew that she needed to go to the bathroom. Leila also knew that Avery knew she was trying to hold it.

"What sort of treats," Leila asked, pushing Avery's hand away, just for Avery to push the nipple of the bottle back into Leila's mouth.

"Shh, Mommy shouldn't hear girls who have a bottle in their mouths," Avery instructed. Leila stopped drinking, worried that if she continued, she would wet herself involuntarily. Avery smirked at her before raising an eyebrow and squeezing the bottle, causing the milky drink to fill her mouth.

"Don't be a bad girl little Leila or Mommy will have to spank you, and you will still have to make your diaper wet," Avery explained, Leila moaning in frustration, understanding that there was no way out of this. Leila finished her bottle, and Avery patted the front of her diaper, making her blush.

"Come on, Mommy knows you are desperate to go," Avery said, enjoying the embarrassment she was causing Leila but aware that Leila couldn't be pushed too much further.

"You play down on the floor with your toys while Mommy tidies the kitchen. And when I come back, you'd better have been a good girl," Avery instructed, making Leila nervous and shy. She watched as Leila got down on the floor and began playing with her bunny. Avery took her time, emptying the dishwasher and packing away the food into the fridge and cupboard before coming back down to Leila. She wanted to allow her to go in her own time.

Coming back down to the floor, Avery pulled Leila into her lap and placed her hand on the front of her diaper, turning Leila around enough that she could see the frown on Avery's face.

"Mommy, I can't," Leila whined, in a vain attempt to sway Avery's mind on the matter.

"Hmm, I don't think that's the case," Avery plainly said as she pressed her hand against Leila's bladder, making her gasp.

"You can fight Mommy, or you can do what Mommy wants. But let me make myself very clear, if you fight Mommy, there will be consequences, and they'll really hurt," Avery whispered in Leila's ear, continuing to press into her.

"But Mommy," Leila said, biting her lip and beginning to cry.

"Don't try that baby girl. It won't work," Avery said, smirking as Leila stopped almost immediately, somewhat put out that Avery knew all her tricks.

"That's what I thought. Now come on, Mommy is here, and you can be a good girl for me," Avery said, redirecting Leila's mind to the command she had yet to obey. Leila shifted in Avery's arm, causing Avery to hold onto her firmly.

"You're about to be spanked, do you know that?" Avery said, grabbing Leila's breasts with both hands and squeezing them tightly. Leila pushed against Avery, trying to get away, only to be placed over Avery's thigh in one swift motion. Leila could feel herself almost give in as Avery's other thigh locked her in place, and her strong arm came crashing down on Leila's ass.

"Mommy!" Leila whined, trying to turn her head to look at Avery.

"Did Mommy say you could look at me? What was Mommy's instruction, Leila?" Avery sternly asked, bringing another blow onto Leila's ass.

"To wet my diaper," Leila said, feeling the sting of Avery's spanking.

"And did you listen to Mommy?" Avery asked, making Leila mad that she already knew the answer.

"No," Leila whined, copping another spank.

"No, what?" Avery growled.

"No, Mommy," Leila answered, Avery, stopping for a moment to rub between Leila's thighs.

"Are you going to be a good girl now?" Avery asked, squeezing her thighs tightly around Leila and keeping her hand in place as she waited for Leila's response.

"But Mommy," Leila said, Avery, letting go and getting up, taking Leila by the wrist and leading her into the bedroom.

"You asked me what this was for last night," Avery said, referring to the bolt in the wall with the O ring attached to it. Leila looked at her waiting for what was inevitably coming next.

"It's for when you're naughty and need time to think about your actions," Avery said, taking a rope and tying Leila's wrists together before threading the rope through the ring and pulling down, forcing Leila's arms to stretch above her head. With Leila's body elongated, Avery kicked her ankles apart, tying her thighs in a way that forced them apart.

"Mommy," Leila moaned, feeling her clit harden.

"Now, you want to be my sweet, obedient girl?" Avery mocked, kissing Leila on the cheek as she lubed a vibrator and unclipped the straps on Leila's overalls.

"We could be at the beach right now, but you wanted to test Mommy. Silly girl that is never a good idea," Avery said, pulling the overalls down until Leila's diaper was exposed. Pulling the front out, Avery slipped the thick vibrating dildo between Leila's puffy pussy lips, angling the tip, so it was on her clit, also simulating her to wet herself.

"You can stay like that until I get what I want. But just know, that for every five minutes that I don't get my way, I'm adding another toy to you," Avery said, pulling on Leila's nipples before walking out the door and closing it behind her, leaving Leila in the darkened room alone. Avery sighed as she walked back to the living room and began tidying away Leila's toys. She liked that Leila was so stubborn, it made training her all the more fun. Leila, on the other hand, was having a hard time and was surprised that she didn't want to give into Avery's commands as obediently as she had done in the past.

"So, let's see," Avery said, feeling Leila's diaper, shrugging her shoulders when she felt that it was dry.

"You really want to see what Mommy can do, don't you, baby?" Avery asked, pushing a paci gag in Leila's mouth when she tried to reply.

"No, I didn't really want to hear your answer," Avery said, fastening the gag in place before taking out a butt plug and lubing it up slowly.

"Yeah, you know where this is going, don't you," Avery said, watching as Leila tried to pull her thighs together, making Avery laugh.

"Nice try sweetheart," Avery whispered, pulling the back of Leila's diaper out and slipping her hand against Leila's ass. Avery grabbed her ass cheeks and forced them open before she pushed the butt plug into Leila, making Leila gasp and moan as Avery pushed it in place.

"I thought that maybe I would be finished by now, but I can see you still have that look of defiance in your eye," Avery said, taking the nipple clamps and dangling them in front of Leila's face.

"Oh, what's this?" Avery said, seeing that Leila wet her diaper. Leila pushed herself out toward Avery, willing to follow her command so that she wouldn't have to suffer the pain of the clamps, making Avery laugh.

"I'll start with these next time, I think," Avery said, discovering what Leila hated most of all. She cupped Leila's face in her hands, rubbed her cheeks with her thumbs, and kissed her nose.

"See, it wasn't so bad was it," Avery said, forcing herself to stay true to her promise that she would clean Leila up straight away.

"I have half a mind to keep you here as a lesson not to make me have to wait so long for you to obey me. But Mommy isn't a liar, so I'll clean you up right now. But if you make me wait this long again, I'll make you wait for the same time you made me. Fair?" Avery said, delighting in the shock and fear in Leila's eyes and the nodding of her head as a shiver ran through her body.

"Good," Avery replied, untying Leila but keeping the gag in, laughing when Leila pawed at it.

"Oh no, you can keep that in. I like you quiet," Avery said, Leila, looking away sheepishly, knowing that she didn't want to undergo another punishment. Avery took off the diaper, vibrator, and butt plug and took Leila's hand, leading her into the bathroom.

"Arms up," Avery said as she lifted Leila's shirt off, unclipping her bra and throwing it on the floor before lightly patting her ass, directing her into the shower.

"Mommy is going to join you," Avery said, stripping down quickly and turning the water on, letting Leila stand in the corner until she found the right temperature.

"We are going to wash our hair as well, and if you are a

good girl, when we are done here, you can take that out," Avery said, pulling Leila's hair out and beginning to wash her body. Avery slid her hands over Leila's curves, kissing down her body and making her nipples hard.

"And here I thought you were a sweet innocent little girl," Avery whispered as she let her hand slip between Leila's thighs, smirking as Leila spread her legs and let Avery stroke her clit. Avery loved that Leila couldn't reply, watching as her body told her all she needed to hear.

"Yes, that's right, sway those hips for Mommy," Avery coaxed, watching as Leila tried to gain a stronger touch from Avery. Pushing her against the wall, Avery stroked further along Leila's lips and pushed passed the folds of her pussy, feeling her wetness at her entrance.

"If you scream, Mommy will slap your face. Do you understand me?" Avery sternly said, watching as Leila nodded her head, her eyes suddenly going wide as Avery quickly pushed into her cunt, filling her pussy with two fingers and beginning to curl them inside of her.

"Uh uh, Mommy said no," Avery reminded Leila as she stifled her squeal, turning it into a low groan of pleasure.

"You are so lucky to have a Mommy who knows how to treat her princess," Avery whispered in Leila's ear as she held her tight and fingered her pussy, making quick work of bringing on an orgasm. Leila bent her head forward, her body shaking and her thighs almost giving way as Avery made her cum within minutes. Slowly her rhythm, Avery took a step back, ungagged Leila, and smiled as she saw her girlfriend catch her breath.

"You're going to need a lie down after the mind games I just put you through," Avery said, smirking as she looked at Leila's mentally exhausted face.

"Come on, baby girl," Avery said, taking Leila's hand and drying her off before letting her crawl into bed naked.

"I just want Mommy," Leila whined, reaching out for Avery, who was busy getting dressed in her bikini, putting house clothes on over the top before coming to rest next to Leila.

"Mommy's here," Avery said as Leila buried her face into Avery's neck and breathed in deeply. Avery wrapped her arms around Leila, enjoying how lucky she felt to have her all to herself and closed her eyes.

I'll just lay here for a moment, Avery thought, feeling herself begin to fall asleep but unable to wake herself back up.

Chapter 11

"Wake up sleeping beauty," Avery said an hour later. Leila had fallen asleep in her arms and was sucking her thumb in her sleep.

"Mommy," Leila sleepily said as she slowly woke up.

"We need to wake up, or we won't make it to the beach, and we won't be able to get to sleep tonight," Avery explained, causing Leila's eyes to go wide.

"The beach!" Leila exclaimed, making Avery laugh.

"Yes, come on. I'm ready," Avery said, gently rolling Leila out of her arms and getting up.

"I can't go in the water, I don't have a swimsuit here," Leila said, putting on a pair of shorts and a flowy top. Avery raised her eyebrows and took out a bag from under her bed.

"Maybe you didn't think you had a swimsuit, but I have one," Avery said, passing Leila that bag, her confused face making Avery laugh.

"You got me, swimmers?" Leila asked, Avery, nodding her head.

"So, you had this beach trip planned all along!" Leila squealed, taking out the swimmers and being pleasantly surprised at the choice Avery had made.

"These are cute," Leila said as she looked at the colorful striped one piece with the plunging neckline.

"Try them on, and if you hate them, then we can return them," Avery said as Leila undressed and put the swimmers on.

"They are actually really great, Mommy," Leila replied, looking herself over in the mirror. She wasn't sure how Avery did it, but she knew the perfect way to dress her so that her best features were highlighted, and the parts of herself she wanted to change where hidden.

"I love them," Leila softly said, turning around and looking at Avery.

"Are you alright?" Avery said, tilting her head to look at Leila.

"Yeah, you are just really amazing," Leila quietly confessed, causing Avery's arms to be wrapped around her in a big bear hug.

"You are really amazing," Avery said, kissing Leila on the tip of her nose and winking at her.

"Come on, get dress, I'll wait for you in the car," Avery said playfully as she half skipped out the door.

Avery and Leila held hands as they walked down the secluded path to the beach, enjoying the feeling of the sand between their toes. There was still two hours before sunset, and the water was warm after a day of the hot sun burning down on it.

"Are you going to come in?" Avery asked Leila as she stripped her clothes off. Leila took the time to admire her girlfriend's body. Avery's athletic form, highlighted by the afternoon sun, reminded Leila of the fitness models she had begun following on social media.

"Yeah, in a minute," Leila said, checking to see if anyone else was nearby. Avery caught on to what Leila was doing and came to sit in front of her.

"You are gorgeous, and you are valid, and you are mine, so I will protect you, all of you, your grown-up self, and you're little self, all of you. Ok?" Avery said, looking Leila in the eye and making her bashfully smile and nod her head.

"Ok," Leila said, giving in to Avery's words. She got up and undressed, nervously looked out along the shoreline, and smiled as she saw Avery's hand extended out to her.

Just take the leap, Leila said to herself, taking Avery's hand and walking down to the water.

Leila couldn't remember the last time she had been at the beach, let alone in the water, and as she tasted the saltiness of the ocean, a new sense of freedom washed over her body. Dipping her head under the water, Leila felt as the waves tumbled over her body, coming up for air and flipping her hair back. Running her hands through her wet hair, she caught Avery looking lustfully at her.

"Like what you see, Mommy?" Leila teased, watching as Avery swam up close to her.

"Yeah, I really do," Avery said, feeling Leila's body under the water, making her laugh.

"What were you doing for all that time you were away?" Avery suddenly asked, taking Leila by surprise.

"I just kind of isolated myself for a few weeks and let my mind stop trying to distract myself from all the shit I was trying to distract it with," Leila honestly replied.

"What did you do?" Leila asked. Leila ducked under the water as a wave came crashing into them, making Avery laugh as she got tumbled around in the water. Coming up for air, Avery wiped the water from her eyes and looked back toward the shoreline.

"I drank mostly. Was a bit of a jerk to a new woman at work and just generally felt miserable and sorry myself," Avery replied, making Leila frown.

"I'm so sorry," she said, causing Avery to shake her head.

"Don't be. Mommy's crappy coping skills is her problem. I'm happy you got what you needed out of it. I'm even happier you wanted to come back to me afterward," Avery explained, making Leila laugh as she began to head back toward the sand.

"What is it?" Avery said when Leila suddenly stopped swimming.

"I just want to stay here a little longer," Leila replied. She knew she wasn't meant to lie, so she decided just to withhold a part of the whole truth. But Avery knew her better than that.

"And why don't you want to go back in yet?" Avery asked, not satisfied with getting a half-truth. Leila looked to where another couple was putting their things down and bit her bottom lip.

"I know that woman," Leila said, the fear in her voice making Avery frown.

"An ex?" Avery asked, her Mommy space flooding her being. She felt the protectiveness flowing through her veins. She loved this feeling as it always made her feel as though she had superhuman strength.

"The ex," Leila said, emphasizing the word the. From what Leila had told Avery, Avery knew her ex Donna was a real piece of work.

"Ok. Hold Mommy's hand, and do not speak to her, alright. Do not look at her. Look at Mommy because when we get out of this water, I am going to be talking to you, and you know how much I hate it when you don't look at me when I am speaking," Avery instructed. Leila was happy that she was taking the lead with this and not making Leila do it alone.

"Thanks, Mommy," Leila said, grateful that Avery was so protective.

"What you want to do when we get home," Avery said the moment they stepped onto the shore. Donna was to the left of Leila, meaning when she was looking at Avery, she couldn't see Donna at all. Avery, on the other hand, could see both Leila and Donna and was glad because when Donna began to walk towards Leila, Avery could switch spots with her.

"Look at the ground, baby girl," Avery said. Usually, she didn't care to have her baby following such orders as she felt it was more for subs than littles, but in this case, she was going to make an exception.

"You have no business here, fuck off," Avery said before Donna could open her mouth to speak, leaving her speechless and putting a huge smirk on Leila's face.

"Get your things and let's go," Avery calmly said, holding Leila's hand and walking to the car, leaving Donna to stand dumbfounded behind them.

"Mommy," Leila giggled, still looking at the ground. Avery happily smirked that she could protect her little girl.

"You can look up now, honey," Avery said when they were in the car and driving home.

"Oh my god, that was so good!" Leila squealed, clapping her hands and making Avery laugh.

"Sometimes the best thing to do is leave it up to Mommy," Avery said, holding onto Leila's hand and turning on the radio as they drove home.

Chapter 12

They drove home in silence, just listening to the radio. Leila looked out the window, thinking of how far she had come, happy to be under Avery's care.

"We're home, sweetheart," Avery said, unsure if Leila was asleep or not.

"I know, Mommy," Leila softly replied, turning to face Avery as she took her seatbelt off.

"My sleepy girl," Avery said, reaching out and stroking Leila's cheek affectionately. She knew the emotional toll of seeing Donna would weigh heavily on Leila, even if it were a successful encounter. Avery also knew that Leila would be in a fragile state of mind, and she wondered if that would make it easier or harder for her to get into little space, potentially wetting her diaper once more.

"I'm not very hungry, Mommy," Leila said, walking into the apartment. Avery opened the door, and Leila dropped her bag before going to the couch and sitting down.

"No, you don't, come on," Avery said, holding her hand out to Leila. Leila rolled her eyes at Avery before submitting to her wishes and standing back up, taking her hand and going to the bathroom.

"I know you might not be hungry, but you still need to have a shower and get all the sea salt off that little body," Avery said, stripping Leila naked and running the shower. Avery liked that Leila wasn't trying to fight her and was sleepy, allowing Avery to take charge.

"You can get into some nice jammies, have a bottle and cuddle with Mommy in bed, baby girl," Avery said, making Leila close her eyes and smile as Avery washed her body. Not wasting any time, Avery quickly washed Leila, running the warm water over her body to rinse her clean and turned the water off.

"Go and stand over there and wait for Mommy," Avery said, pointing to the towel she had put down on the floor before disappearing into the bedroom. Leila knew what was coming, a diaper and onesie, and she waited with her towel wrapped around her for Avery to return.

"Here, lay down," Avery said, opening up another towel and placing it over the floor so that Leila wouldn't get cold. Leila obeyed, laying on the fluffy pink towel and felt Avery begin to diaper her.

"I know it was a warm day, but the news said it was going to get cold tonight, so you need to keep your sockies on," Avery said, pulling the onesie over Leila's head and putting on her socks.

"Ok, Mommy," Leila sleepily replied. Avery smirked.

She must be really tired if she isn't going to fight me on the socks, she thought to herself, knowing how much Leila hated wearing socks to bed. Avery led Leila to the bedroom, feeling Leila slowly dragged her feet behind her.

"Come on, sleepyhead," Avery said, turning back to see Leila sucking her thumb. She pushed Leila into bed, watching her snuggle into the bed sheets immediately and close her eyes.

"Mommy will be back shortly," Avery said, guessing that Leila would be asleep before she came back.

Avery walked into the kitchen and prepared a bottle for Leila. She warmed the milk and put a scoop of vanilla protein powder in the shaker before shaking it up, then pouring it into a baby bottle. Avery knew that she would be awake for a long time yet, so she didn't bother making herself anything to eat. Walking back into the room, she watched as Leila stirred, and Avery climbed into bed with her and pulled her into her arms, cradling her.

"It's just Mommy," Avery whispered, pushing the bottle into Leila's mouth, feeling her resist. Leila scrunched up her face, before rolling into Avery and began to drink.

"Good girl," Avery said, gently rocking Leila as she drank. Avery thought about what Leila had said about wanting to become the best version of herself and wondered how she could help.

I don't think I should train her. She might feel embarrassed she can't do something and try to push herself and hurt herself. Maybe I should get her a personal trainer, someone really lovely and kind, that doesn't show off their body so much. I don't think she'd like that, Avery thought.

But then again, maybe group fitness would be good. That way she can meet some new people, maybe make some friends and then have people to bounce ideas about different exercises and nutrition off? Avery questioned, slightly overwhelmed by the choices. The last thing she wanted was to suggest something and have Leila think that Avery didn't like her body or that she was in some way flawed or ugly. Leila stirred, causing Avery to be shaken from her thoughts and look down to see Leila's big eyes staring back at her.

"Baby girl?" Avery questioned, seeing the startled look in Leila's eyes.

"Mommy, I," Leila began to say, before biting her bottom lip and looking down toward her diaper.

"Oh sweetie, that's ok, Mommy will clean you up," Avery reassuring said. She placed the bottle down and rolled back the bedsheets.

"I don't like it, Mommy," Leila whined, making Avery smile.

"I know, that's why Mommy is changing you straight away," Avery replied, putting Leila's pacifier in her mouth and began to change her diaper. Leila shut her eyes tight, hating the feeling of being so exposed and patiently waited until Avery had a clean, dry diaper fastened to her body.

"There, all done, sweet girl," Avery said, letting Leila snuggle into her once more.

"Night night angel," Avery said, feeling Leila grab at her breast. Avery took her shirt and bra off, holding her breast to Leila's mouth and sighing when she felt Leila begin to suck on her nipple as she fell back asleep.

Chapter 13

"How serious are you about wanting to get into fitness baby, because I saw a great deal online if you're still interested," Avery called from the kitchen bench a week later. Leila had stayed at Avery's apartment since she had returned, and the two had slowly developed a comfortable dynamic, and smooth routine.

"Pretty serious," Leila replied, looking up from her laptop. She had begun to write for a very influential blog and was typing furiously to meet a deadline.

"What's the deal?" She added, putting her laptop top lid down slightly and giving Avery her full attention.

"10 group sessions for $100. They train just down the road at the park on the corner," Avery said, grabbing Leila's curiosity.

"That's cheap," Leila said, thinking about how it would feel to be able to move more freely and feel more confident in herself.

"When does the offer begin?" Leila asked, standing up from the chair, stretching and coming over to Avery, who sipped her second espresso.

"Next week," Avery said, making Leila smile.

"Well, we better go shopping then. I'll need some activewear," Leila smirked, happy to feel in control of her life. Avery playfully slapped her ass, and Leila turned around with the gleam in her eye that Avery had hoped to elicit.

"We can't," Avery said, enjoying the smirk Leila gave when she was told she couldn't have something. Leila always took that as a challenge to work for something harder.

"You'll miss your deadline," Avery continued, pushing her chair in and grabbing Leila by her neck, pulling her in close.

"You better be fast then," Leila replied, feeling Avery's hands on her hips and turning her around, bending her over the kitchen table and pulling her sweat pants off.

"Yes," Avery hissed, grabbing at Leila's ample ass and thighs, relishing how soft and smooth they were. Leila tried to turn around, but Avery placed her strong arm down on Leila's back, holding her in place as she reached around and began to tease Leila's clit through her panties.

"Someone's wet," Avery whispered, making Leila shiver as she was touched. Avery continued to slowly stroke Leila, feeling how her clit slowly grew into a swollen nub before she pushed her fingers into Leila's mouth, making her suck them.

"Get them wet, baby girl. Mommy wants them wet," Avery slowly said, keeping Leila in place by pushing her down with her hips. Leila obeyed, moaning as she felt herself being taken by Avery.

"Spread your legs for me," Avery instructed, causing a tremor of pleasure to run through Leila's body. Obediently, Leila spread her thighs, feelings Avery pull her panties to the side and placed her wet fingers over Leila's clit, rubbing softly. Avery breathed heavily, reaching into her pants and pulling out the strap on cock she was packing. Pushing it between Leila's pussy lips, parting them roughly, Avery pulled back and spat on it before sliding it back, feeling Leila press back on her. Avery grabbed Leila's hair, pushed the tip of the strap on into her, and waited for Leila's pussy to fully open up to her.

"Mommy loves how tight you are little one," Avery moaned as she gently pulled Leila back down on top of her. Avery was now laying on the floor with Leila sitting on top of her, taking the long fake cock up her cunt.

"That's it. Grind that pussy on Mommy," Avery said, feeling Leila begin to twerk on her lap. Avery could feel her own juices begin to flow as Leila worked herself toward an orgasm, moaning and bouncing on Avery. Avery reached for a vibrating butt plug and lubed it while Leila tried desperately to make herself cum. In one quick motion, Avery stuffed the butt plug into Leila's ass, feeling her clit tingle as she heard Leila groan as the unexpected intruder began to vibrate inside of her. Leila grabbed Avery's shins as she came, Avery slapping her ass hard with both hands.

"Did I say you could stop?" Avery growled, curious to see how much Leila could take.

"No, sorry, Mommy," Leila replied, beginning to twerk once again. Avery turned the butt plug up, causing Leila's pussy to drip over Avery's lap, just the way she liked.

"No, that's right, I didn't," Avery replied, slapping Leila's ass once more.

"Faster," Avery added, looking around Leila's back and enjoying watching her tits bounce as she worked herself toward another orgasm. Avery couldn't decide if she wanted Leila to have the satisfaction or not as she watched her. The way her back arched, pushed her full breasts out, her hair swept to one side and her lip red from the way she bit it made Avery mesmerized.

I don't even know who is using who at this point, Avery thought to herself in amusement as she watched Leila come hard for the second time.

"Stop," Avery suddenly commanded, impressed that Leila frozen mild twerk. Avery watched how Leila's juices dripped down the shaft and onto the harness. Slowly pushing up, Avery filled Leila once again, sitting up and wrapping her arms around the woman.

"Mommy's little slut," Avery whispered in Leila's ear, holding her tight as she bent her legs and stood up, impressed with herself for being able to hold onto Leila as she did so. Avery gently put Leila's feet back down on the floor, pulled out of her in one quick motion, and smirked as Leila's juices squirted onto the floor.

"You know, a mean Mommy might make you lick that up," Avery said, remembering a video she watched a few days ago, deciding that she wasn't going to make Leila do that by the look in her eye.

"But I'm not that mean," Avery said, undoing the harness and winking at Leila before they headed to the shower.

"So, what sort of thing were you thinking?" Avery said two hours later, as they walked through the doors of a big sports department store. Leila had thought this would be fun, like the shopping they did when they found dresses, but as she looked around, she felt out of her depth.

"I guess I was just looking for something like this," she quietly said, looking around wide-eyed and showing Avery the photos she had screen-shotted. Avery looked through the photos and smiled.

"This is some cool stuff, baby," she encouragingly said. Leila gave her a small smile and was glad when Avery took her hand and began to take the lead.

"I don't really know what I am meant to be looking for or like, where even to start," Leila timidly said, melting Avery's heart.

"I know, honey, that's why I am here," Avery replied, stroking Leila's cheeks with her thumbs, making her face go red.

"Avery," Leila half hissed, worried that someone might see them. Avery just giggled and began to flick through the clothing racks and found items that were as close to the ones which Leila had shown her.

"What about this?" Avery suggested seeing a shirt she thought Leila might like. Leila just nodded her head, feeling more confident now that she could see her outfits coming together.

"So, we have three pairs of tights, five shirts, some socks, and now we need some sports bras and shoes," Avery said, ticking things off the list she had created.

"Thanks for this," Leila said, taking Avery's hand and looking at her with the vulnerable eyes, which always melted Avery's heart.

"Baby girl, I wouldn't be anywhere else. You need me, I'm there," Avery replied, kissing the top of Leila's head.

"And maybe, a few caps," Leila said, picking up a cap and putting it on, causing Avery to raise an eyebrow.

"Mommy likes," Avery said, making Leila blush as they head to the sports bra section.

"I don't think any of these will fit me," Leila said, a worried look on her face.

"It's not about the size, baby. It's about the fit. You have to find the fit that suits you best you worry about the size after that," Avery explained, making Leila smile. They tried on several bras, finally finding the fit which Leila felt the most comfortable in and put three of them into their shopping cart.

"I had no idea that it could be so, fun," Leila said, surprised at how enjoyable the experience had turned out to be. The staff were friendly and helpful, no one looked at her like she didn't belong and what was best of all, there were so many options for her to choose from.

"So, shoes?" Leila questioned, looking around to find Avery already holding up a pair of shoes.

"These are cool," Avery said, showing Leila the blue and yellow pair, making Leila laugh.

"I was thinking of something a little more subtle," Leila laughed, picking up a pair of gray and pink Nike Metcon 5's. Avery raised her eyebrows, impressed with Leila's choice before getting the sales assistant's attention.

"Nice. I want a pair," Avery said, seeing them on Leila, who laughed.

"These are so cool," Leila said in her little voice the moment the assistant was gone. Avery agreed and put them into the shopping cart, before heading toward the register.

"It's a good thing that the class is so cheap because the sports gear cost a small fortune," Leila said as they drove home.

"Yeah, but now that you have everything you need unless you do a big shop like that again, you'll only pick up a few things at a time from now on," Avery replied as she watched Leila look at her new shoes. Avery smiled. She loved that she could help Leila become the person she wanted to become.

"So. When is the reunion?" Avery asked, wanting to know how much time they still had.

"Like six months away. I think that gives me enough time to get myself sorted. I don't want to change too much. I like how I look for the most part. I just want to feel more energetic and be a bit healthier. I don't want abs or muscular thighs, no offense," Leila laughed, realizing that she was describing Avery.

"Oh yeah, none taken," Avery laughed.

"No, it's fine. I know you want to look like the curvy models online. I'm just happy that you like my body," Avery said, realizing for the first time that she was slightly body conscious when it came to Leila's approval.

Everyone is insecure sometimes, Avery thought to herself, reminding herself of the self-help phrase she had read earlier in the day.

"Yeah, I think that is more who I am," Leila said, Avery, smiling at they pulled into the driveway.

"Ok. I have more work to do than I first thought," Leila panted, walking into the apartment. Avery was sitting on the couch watching a movie on her laptop and smiled as she saw Leila stumble into the kitchen and take out a bottle of water.

"So, good?" Avery asked, pausing the movie and closing

the lid.

"So good, but oh my goodness. So like, these girls can do so much stuff. They are machines!" Leila said, enjoying the afterglow of the session as the endorphins flooded her body.

"And I just feel all. I don't even know, happy?" Leila asked, making Avery laugh.

"Those are called endorphins, and you get that hormone released when you work out. This is good, baby! I'm so happy you liked it," Avery explained, getting up and sitting next to Leila on the bench stools.

"Yeah. It was really cool. Everyone is super nice, and I learned a lot already," Leila said before kicking her shoes off and sighing.

"Now I feel tired," she said, looking thoughtful as she felt the strange now emotions for the first time.

"Do you need Mommy to look after you?" Avery asked, hoping that she would say yes. Leila just nodded her head but giggled as Avery jumped up and grabbed her hand.

"Shower and naps," Avery said, Leila happily following behind.

"Ok, Mommy," Leila replied, yawning and closing her eyes as she walked.

***

"You look beautiful," Avery said six months later on the

night of Leila's reunion. Leila had been to the hair salon and had also had her makeup professionally done. She had taken one of the dresses Avery had bought for her on their first date to the seamstress to be taken in. As the red sequined dress glittered under the lights, Leila buckled her heels and looked up at Avery.

"Well, a little bit of thanks goes to you," Leila said, winking at Avery, who beamed.

"I am really proud of you," Avery said, tearing up and making Leila laugh.

"Why?" Leila asked, standing up, her heels making her taller than Avery for the first time.

"Because. You did it. You were in such a shitty place when we first met, and you did what you needed to do to become the person you needed to become. I would have loved you forever, but it was never about me, it was about you, and you looked at your life and who you wanted to become, and you made changes until you got there. Now you have a successful online presence, people follow your fitness tips, and you are an advocate for what a strong, healthy, and empowered woman can look like. Plus, you've got these great tits," Avery said, making the conversation slightly light by grabbing Leila's breasts and motorboating them, making Leila laugh.

"But on a serious note, I am really proud of you. You make me want to be a better person, somebody who is more aligned with who I truly am, and not somebody who just reacts to the world around them," Avery said, pulling a long rectangle box from her back pocket.

"So, in light of all your success, I wanted to give you something which hopefully shows you how inspired and grateful I am to have you in my life," Avery said, placing the box in Leila's hands.

"It's a good thing this makeup is waterproof," Leila said, before opening the box and gasping. Her eyes were dazzled by the diamond bracelet, clearly over 2carats, and set in white gold.

"Mommy," Leila said softly, looking at the beautiful bracelet.

"Do you like it?" Avery said, watching Leila's face.

"Yes. Of course I love it!" Leila exclaimed, smiling widely at Avery, who took it out of the box and fastened it to Leila's wrist.

"Turn it on its side," Avery said, wanting to show Leila the engraving.

"Mommy's always here," Leila read out loud, having to fan her eyes as they began to water.

"I love you," Leila said, kissing Avery on the mouth and feeling her heart pound deeply.

"I love you too, darling," Avery said, delighted with her life, the beautiful woman standing before her.

Mommy's Pretty Girl

Mommy makes everything better. That's what Meg learned as she entered an MDLG relationship with Anna who made all her ABDL dreams come true

Tina Moore

Chapter 1

Anna hated the flight back home. The busy crowds, the airport security, the way she always seemed to set the body scanners off made her cringe even thinking about it. Anna was the CEO of a successful lighting franchise specializing in high-end lighting fixtures. As part of her job, she would routinely travel abroad to inspect the manufacturing processes, explore different materials, and generally make sure everything was running smoothly. But over the 15years of being the CEO, Anna had increasingly developed a strong disliking to the travel side of her job. After going through a divorce, watching her parents pass on, and her dog getting on in years, Anna wanted to trade her high-flying career, for something a little more grounding. She would often fantasize about sitting in a bay window of a cozy white cottage, overlooking a garden filled with colorful flowers. The next part of her fantasy always thrilled her. The thought that a young, sweet girl would be there, needing her, craving her attention. She only let herself think of the things she would do to the girl, how she would control her with such loving care, late at night when she would slide her hand between her thighs, and imagine it was the girl's hand touching her and not her own.

A smirk came over Anna's face as she looked around the waiting gate, watching at a group of girls in their mid 20's. Anna always loved how these types of young, vibrant, and boisterous girls never seemed to dress for the weather or the occasion. This group was one of the same. In the middle of winter, not one of them had a coat which would keep the cold out, their short skirts showed the bare skin of their long toned legs, their backpacks slung over one shoulder, and the jackets that they did have were open, showing off tight t-shirts with trendy logos. One, in particular, caught Anna's attention. The quiet one at the back of the group, talking on her phone and looking rather distressed. She was dressed slightly different to the others, with her fluffy baby pink sweater matching her style-faded black skirt, her black combat boots with the laces undone, and her gray backpack made Anna instantly wet. Anna shifted in her seat, rubbing her thighs together discreetly, smiling at herself as she felt her clit beginning to throb.

Oh, the things I would do to you little girl, Anna thought to herself as the girl bent down to put something into her backpack before standing back up and flicking her hair almost in slow motion. The light, catching her blonde hair as she began to walk quickly, trying to catch up with her friends who were now sitting at the café across from the waiting gate. Anna checked her watch, seeing that it was ten minutes to boarding and decided she wanted closer proximity to the blonde, so getting up, she put her expensive, designer handbag on her arm and sauntered over to the café. Anna was amused at the looks she got, wondering if the people looking at her were thinking the same thoughts she was thinking about the blonde. Although nearing 46 years old, Anna had maintained an active lifestyle. What was more was that she had never been short of looking after herself, and her polished and refined body complimented her flawless and sophisticated style. After living in France for several years, Anna had learned that style is quite different from fashion. As Anna crossed the corridor and walked into the café, she flicked her wavy chocolate brown locks and began to take off her long, deep emerald green coat and drape it over her arm. Anna's eyes searched for the girl, delighting in the sight of the blonde sitting in the corner of the café. She was still busy on her phone as her friends talked around her. No, not talking, they were in the midst of a conversation which had deemed that shouting was the more appropriate form of communication. This time, she was messaging feverously, and as Anna ordered a coffee, she knew just how she would get the blonde's attention.

"Any sugar, Ma'am?" The boy behind the counter asked, making Anna smile.

"No thanks," Anna replied, amused that the boy blushed before looking away. Anna's dark pink satin blouse gaped just enough to expose her ample cleavage, and she imagined the boy jerking himself off to her image the moment he got home. She took her coffee, turned around, and rechecked her watch, enjoying how the diamonds within it glistened under the lights.

"Excuse me," Anna said, walking over to the group of girls, and waiting for them to go quiet and give her their attention. She liked the looks they gave her, unsure if she was about to tell them to be quiet or if she was just a sweet, mature lady needing something else. The tension, extended by Anna smiling at them as though she didn't want to rip their clothes off right there and then.

"May I trouble you for the sugar?" Anna asked, watching as they relaxed and laughed before trying to reach for the sugar, only to be beaten in holding it.

"Here," the blonde said, Anna, trying to keep her eyes from undressing the girl as she held out the sugar to Anna without looking up from her phone.

"Thank you," Anna said, deliberately touching the girl's hand as she took the jar, causing the girl to look up at her, double-taking and beginning to blush. Anna smiled at her knowingly, before taking the jar and walking back to where her handbag was claiming an entire table.

"Dude, you are so red!" Anna heard one of the girl's tease, making the others laugh along.

"What?! She's hot!" Anna heard the blonde say, enjoying the moments she had just stolen. Anna contently sighed as she sipped her coffee and waited for her seat number to be called over the speaker. She closed her eyes and imagined taking the beautiful blonde home, pushing her down onto the bed and strapon fucking her until she squealed.

You're Mommy's little girl, aren't you? Anna imagined whispering into her ear as she rammed her hard, holding herself inside of the young girl as she waited for a reply.

Yes, Mommy, Anna imagined her whimpering, feeling Anna taking her power away and knowing that she was only there out of the kindness and love of Anna's heart.

And what does Mommy's good little girl do, baby? Anna thought, thinking how she would pull out of the girl just to push the tip into her asshole and hold it there as she panted and tried to respond.

Whatever Mommy wants, Anna imagined, playing the scene out and feeling her panties moisten.

Yes, there's a good girl, Anna thought herself groaning as she slowly pushed herself into the girl's ass and feeling her surrender underneath her.

Fuck, Anna suddenly thought, opening her eyes and feeling her cunt contract as she subtly shifted positions and realized that having these types of fantasizes in public may not be the best idea.

Chapter 2

"Now boarding seats M-R," the announcer called over the system. Anna stood up and made her way out of the café. Much to her delight, she heard the sounds of the girl's laughter and general joyfulness behind her. Passing the attendant her ticket, Anna passed through the tunnel and moved down the ramp. She sighed, wishing that she had booked the upgrade when she had the chance. The thought of being stuck sitting next to somebody suddenly made Anna more agitated than she had first thought it would. With the company policy deeming that she could have the upgrade or keep the money on the business account for essential situations like dinners and an additional spending allowance. This trip Anna had decided to use the extra money on a shopping trip, but as the plane began to fill, she could think of nothing better than sipping champagne in her quiet pod.

"Hey," Anna heard, turning her head back toward the aisle to see the blonde standing in front of her.

"Hello," Anna replied, trying not to look as excited as she felt. The blonde reached up, putting her backpack in the overhead locker, her sweater riding up, and Anna seeing her exposed tummy, the faint lines of her abs making Anna want to reach out and touch her. Waiting to see that the girl had put her things away, Anna got up from her seat and made room for the girl to sit in her allocated spot by the window.

"I'm Meg," the blonde said, making Anna smirk.

"Sweet name. I'm Anna," Anna replied, seeing Meg nod her head before putting her headphones on and looking out the window. Anna sat back in her seat, delighted that she didn't book the upgrade and hoping that the last seat in her row would remain empty. With one seat between herself and Meg, Anna knew that there was plenty of space to relax and enjoy the flight, even if most of the flight would be in darkness. Anna always took the night flight because she didn't want to waste the day time traveling, but she suspected that Meg had taken it because it also happened to be the cheapest flight. The air hostess ran through the safety procedures. Anna was amused the Meg didn't feel the need to listen to them and continued to stare out the window. The plane jerked forward, and Anna knew that she had 13 hours to get what she wanted, which was Meg's unwavering desire to be her baby girl.

They spent the first hour in silence. Anna spent her time flicking through her magazine and Meg with her headphones on. Dinner came and went, Meg hardly touching her food and Anna taking out the snacks that she had bought, uninspired by the selection of airplane dinners on offer. It wasn't until the lights went out that Meg took her headphones off and began to look around for the inflight blanket.

"Damn," Meg softly said, assuming that Anna was asleep. Anna turned her body to face Meg, who looked at her apologetically.

"Sorry, I didn't mean to wake you," Meg said, Anna, reaching out to touch her forearm.

"You didn't wake me, sweetie. What is it?" Anna asked, Meg's head tilt and wide eyes making her smile.

"Um, I can't find my blanket," Meg said, shaking off the feeling the older woman was giving her. Anna took her hand off the girl and began to help her look.

"I think they only gave us one," Anna said, looking back to see if there was a hostess readily available. Turning back to Meg when there was no one in sight, Anna took her blanket off and draped it over the girl.

"Here, have mine, I'll get a new one," Anna said, placing her hand on the girl's cheek affectionately when Meg began to protest, quieting her immediately.

"I insist," Anna said, getting up and walking down the aisle. Meg smiled to herself and wrapped the blanket around her body, enjoying how Anna's body had made it warm. Meg closed her eyes and sighed as the smell of Anna's perfume soothed her, making her want the older woman's affection directed toward her once more.

My god she smells good, Meg thought to herself, placing one arm underneath the blanket and tentatively stroking herself between her thighs for just long enough to take the edge off before Anna reappeared.

"Did you get one?" Meg asked, watching as Anna unwrapped, not one but two new blankets.

"I got two. I thought maybe we might need an extra one. Who knows," Anna replied, smirking at Meg.

"Cool," Meg replied as Anna sat back down, watching as Meg stirred, trying to find a comfortable spot.

"Maybe we should put these armrests up?" Anna suggested, Meg, nodding her head in agreeance, her Bambi eyes turning Anna on the more she looked into them.

"And take it in turns stretching out," Meg added, hoping that Anna would agree. Anna thought for a moment, trying to keep her thoughts off, ripping Meg's clothes off.

"Good idea," Anna said, kicking off her heels and undoing another one of her blouse buttons, enjoying how Meg tried to hide the fact that she was gazing upon the older woman's full cleavage.

"You go first," Anna said, enjoying how Meg began to blush and try to get into a comfortable position.

"Ok. Thanks," Meg slowly replied as her eyes lingered on Anna's full breasts, which were now on display. She curled herself up into the fetal position and took up the space of her seat and the middle seat, which had luckily remained empty. Anna looked down at the girl's shivering body and placed the spare blanket over the top of her, causing Meg to look up.

"Thanks," Meg softly said before smiling at Anna and turning her head back to try and fall asleep. Anna knew that she would get no rest as the girl's head slightly touched her thigh, more so when Meg had fallen asleep. Anna smiled to herself.

If this is the closest thing I get to her touching me, it will do, Anna thought to herself, looking down at the beautifully innocent girl resting against her thigh. She felt her nipples harden, her pussy moisten and knew that she was dropping into Mommy space. Yet it was when Meg stirred, whined softly in her sleep, and placed her head in Anna's lap that Anna knew that this baby girl needed her.

What a sweet little kitten, Anna thought to herself as she tossed up whether or not to begin to stroke the girl's hair. Deciding against it, Anna let the girl continue to sleep, her thumb coming up and starting to be sucked, driving Anna almost over the edge.

Oh, what the fuck, Anna thought in agony as she watched Meg. Anna lifted herself off the seat slightly, waking Meg up and making her sit up, startled that she had entered her little space in her sleep.

"Oh my god, I am so sorry, I," Meg began to say, getting up off of Anna.

"Shh, it's ok, come on," Anna cooed, as she pushed Meg back down onto her lap, and started to stroke her hair.

"Is it ok if I do this, sweetie?" Anna asked Meg, nodding

her head but keeping her body rigid, embarrassed, and unsure how to feel.

"It's totally fine, honey. I don't mind at all. In fact, I quite like it," Anna said, smiling as she felt Meg's body begin to relax. Anna reached down and took Meg's hand in hers, bringing her thumb back up to her mouth, Meg parting her lips and starting to suck her thumb again.

"There you go," Anna cooed as she felt Meg fully relax as she closed her eyes and fell back asleep.

What a precious little girl, Anna thought as she stroked Meg's soft blonde hair.

A perfect little baby, she added, sweeping the baby hairs out of Meg's face.

Chapter 3

Meg slept for the better part of three hours, tossing and turning and melting Anna's heart.

Oh my, Anna thought as Meg rolled onto her other side, pressing her face close against Anna's stomach. Anna let her left arm sit on the side of Meg's ass, petting her gently as she slept, her other hand holding Meg's head in place, not wanting it to roll back and off her lap.

If only you were mine, Anna thought, imagining putting Meg in all sorts of cute outfits, giving her baths, and having cuddle time be a nightly occurrence. Just as she was thinking how sweet Meg's pink sweater was, Meg blinked her eyes open.

"Hey," Meg said, taking her thumb out of her mouth and rubbing her eyes but continuing to lay in Anna's lap comfortably.

"Hi honey," Anna replied, stroking Meg's cheek with her thumb and smiling as Meg suddenly opened her arms and wrapped them around Anna's waist.

"Thanks for letting me cuddle," Meg said, Anna, only just making out the words as Meg buried her face in the older woman's lap. Anna was sure that Meg would be able to feel the heat of desire coming from her body, but decided that it was better to allow Meg to feel it, rather than pretend that she didn't turn her on.

"It's my pleasure. But it's the middle of the night now, you need to go back to sleep, or you'll have a hard time in the morning," Anna said, making Meg laugh.

"I'm going to have a hard time regardless," Meg said, the annoyance in her voice evident.

"Oh? Why is that?" Anna asked, wanting to know more. Meg sat up, much to Anna's disappointment, but she watched as the girl took out her phone. Meg flicked through the photos, stopping when she found the one she wanted.

"This is my boyfriend, was my boyfriend. And this used to be my best friend. They have been sleeping together, and I just found out," Meg explained, her face full of anger and hurt.

"That's awful, I am so sorry," Anna said, reaching out and wrapping her arm around Meg. Meg just snuggled in, happily surprised that the hot older woman was so affectionate.

"Yeah, and what is worse is that I found out while I was away, and when I confronted him about it, he got so mad and threw all my stuff out onto the curb. Who knows what is left there by the time I get back home," Meg said, burying her face into the side of Anna's generous breast. Anna held her, not saying a word, but comforting Meg all the same.

"He sounds like a real piece of work," Anna said when

she finally spoke.

"Yeah," Meg replied, sniffling and wiping her tears away.

"In hindsight, I probably should have kept quiet about it until I got all my stuff out, but I was just so mad," Meg thoughtfully said, thinking out loud.

"Well, you're young, you learn those things with experience and over time," Anna said, thinking back to her messy divorce, before smiling down at Meg.

"I bet you've never been in such a fucked up situation," Meg said, feeling sorry for herself.

"Language, young lady," Anna said, enjoying the small laugh she elicited from Meg as she raised an eyebrow at her.

"And yes, I have. Lucky for me, we were already married, and he was rich. So I got half his shit, and the day it was finally all over, I was able to start living the life I had always wanted to live," Anna said, remembering how it had felt going into a lesbian bar for the first time.

"What sort of life was that?" Meg asked, wondering how she was meant to rebuild her own life.

"Well, for one, I never really liked men. So I explored being with a woman, and I discovered how much I like younger women. I bought an apartment in the middle of the arts district and go to all manner of art events. It felt like I was breathing for the first time," Anna replied, getting lost in the feeling of freedom before looking back down as Meg looked wide-eyed up at her.

"It sounds nice. I guess I can start over now. Maybe the bastard, I mean, asshole, argh shit, the mean man did me a favor," Meg said, trying to stop herself from swearing but struggling to think of an alternative. Anna felt herself swell on the inside as she watched Meg try and please her.

"Good girl. Little ladies like you don't need to use such foul language," Anna said, involuntarily kissing Meg's forehead.

"Sorry, I. You are just so sweet," Anna said, blushing as she thought she overstepped.

"It's cool. I like it. I like girls too," Meg said, making Anna laugh.

"It's been a long time since I've been called a girl," she replied, making Meg bite her bottom lip.

"I just meant," Meg began to say, stopping when Anna placed a finger over Meg's lips.

"I know what you meant, sweetheart," Anna said, closing her eyes and putting her head back.

"You can rest on me if you want, it's only fair after I pretty much just crashed on top of you without any warning," Meg said, seeing that Anna was tired. Anna smiled, keeping her eyes closed until she turned her head to look at Meg, opening her eyes slowly, happy that her gesture gave her the desired result, seeing Meg's eyes reflect her lustful gaze.

"It's ok, honey. I am very comfortable. Come here,"

Anna said, patting her lap, delighted at how Meg obediently lay back down, relaxing on Anna's lap as Anna stroked her back to sleep. Anna closed her eyes, feeling the girl's fluffy sweater under her fingertips as she too relaxed and fell asleep.

"Would you like some snacks?" Anna heard the air hostess ask as she made her way down the aisle. Anna looked at the screen in front of her, seeing that the plane was only a few hours off, landing back home.

"Yes, thank you," Anna said when the air hostess offered her the packet of chips, nuts, and a drink.

"Oh, wait a moment, I need some for, baby girl here," Anna said, referring to Meg laying on her lap. Unbeknownst to Anna, Meg had been awake for over an hour, and as Anna collected snacks for Meg, Meg smiled, feeling taken care of for the first time in a long time.

"Sorry, Ma'am, of course," the air hostess said apologetically, giving Anna extra as she recognized her from all the times she had been in first class.

"It's not like you to be sitting back here. Would you like me to move you to first-class?" The air hostess said, making Anna smile.

"No, it's fine, darling, but thank you. I am more than happy here," Anna said, patting Meg affectionately. The air hostess smiled and nodded her head and continued to walk down the aisle.

"You didn't have to turn down first class just to sit here with me!" Meg exclaimed, sitting up and looking at Anna like she had lost her mind.

"Oh, hello there, little miss eavesdropper," Anna teased, making Meg laugh.

"I go, first-class, all the time. It doesn't have anything on this," Anna added, making Meg shake her head.

"Thanks for getting me snacks," Meg said, picking up a packet of chips, realizing how hungry she had become while sleeping.

"My pleasure," Anna said, taking down the tray and placing the rest on top.

"So, where's home for you?" Anna asked, opening up a can of soda.

"Well, it was on the south side out of town. But who knows now. I guess I'll just crash at my friends' house until I figure out what the, what on earth I'm going to do," Meg said, smiling at herself for not swearing.

"I see. Well, here, take my number, and if you need anything, I want you to call me," Anna said, taking out her business card and handing it to Meg.

"Thanks, but I'll be ok," Meg said, taking the card and putting it in her skirt pocket.

"And I'm sure you will be, but just in case," Anna said, admiring the girl's slim legs. The seatbelt sign flashed on, and the captain called for the cabin crew to prepare for landing.

Anna smiled at Meg as she took her place back by the window, put on her headphones, and looked out onto the city below as the morning sun greeted them.

"Well, bye," Meg said, reaching out to grab Anna's wrist as the headed out of the tunnel and into the airport. Anna looked down to see Meg's hand and smiled.

"Goodbye," Anna said, her eyes dancing with desire as she tore herself away from Meg, winking at her as she turned her head and began to walk away.

"What was that about?" One of Meg's friends said, coming over to her. Meg continued to watch Anna leave, wanting to run after her, but not knowing what she should say when she reached her.

"I don't know, nothing, I guess," Meg said, shrugging her shoulders and turning to walk in the opposite direction.

Anna collected her bags, headed out to the car waiting for her, closed the door, and sighed as the car drove away. She closed her eyes, thought back to how divine it had felt to hold onto Meg, how her hair was warm and soft, and how sweet she looked sucking her thumb as she slept. Anna sighed once more, opening her eyes and shaking her head.

Well, that was lovely, she thought to herself, reaching for the bottle of chilled sparkling water and pouring herself a glass. She was headed home, but not before she ate breakfast at one of her favorite café s. The financial freedom is what she loved about the job, the seemingly unlimited funds to enjoy life at the level she so desired.

The car pulled into the street, stopped at the entrance at the café. The driver passed the keys to the valet, and both Anna and her driver walked inside. After flight café mornings had become somewhat of a tradition for the two, who never spoke to each other, but enjoyed their dynamic nonetheless.

"I'll take the scrambled eggs and sausages and a black coffee," the driver said to the waitress.

"And for me, I will have the Bircher muesli with fruits, and a green juice," Anna said, handing the waitress the menus back. They looked out the window and out onto the elegant street. Anna thought back to how she used to walk up this street years ago, wondering what it would be like to be one of the people in one of these café s, looking out and daydreaming about how perfect their lives were.

Is it everything I had hoped for? Anna thought to herself as she sipped her juice.

A few things are missing, she added, as she saw a couple holding hands and walking down the street. She thought back to how she had thrown caution to the wind in her younger days. The way she was always sweeping up those around her. In the hurricane, that was her life, somewhere between then and now, she had settled down and become grounded. Anna laughed to herself as she remembered the way she would dance and skip along with her friends as they walked down the street. Seeing that group of girls with Meg last night had reminded her of how she must have looked to strangers, and it made her smile as she fondly thought of all her youthful memories.

"Oh, to be 20 again," Anna said out loud, her driver smiling to himself and shaking his head. Anna liked that he never felt the need to engage her in conversation. When she was picking a drive that was one of the requirements, that they mustn't want to get to know her or talk to her for that matter, she appreciated that he kept his silence.

As they finished their breakfast, Anna paid on the business card, and they headed out the door to continue their drive. Anna took her place in the back seat, reaching into her phone, disappointed that Meg hadn't called.

She probably won't. You really shouldn't get your hopes up, Anna thought to herself as they veered out onto the road.

Chapter 4

Meg shared a taxi with her friends to the apartment where she and her ex used to live.

"Thanks, guys, this was an enjoyable trip. Sorry about the last bit," she said, paying her share and getting out of the taxi. She saw what was left of her stuff on the sidewalk and collected it in her arms. Her friends jumped out of the cab, offering for her to stay with one of them, but she declined. It was bad enough that she had to share the taxi with her backstabbing ex-best friend, she didn't want that bitch to know where she was going to stay.

"Do you want to come in? Here, have the key," Meg said to her as she looked into the taxi before throwing the key at her ex best-friend. Meg didn't wait to see what the response was as she took off up the street, only stopping when she was around the corner. Crying, Meg sat in the gutter and felt more lost than she had ever felt in her life.

Ok, I've got a couple of hundred dollars, my laptop, phone, everything that I took on my trip and this stuff here, Meg thought to herself, trying to calm herself down. She looked up at the gray sky and begged for it not to rain as she opened up her suitcase and put her stuff from the sidewalk in before closing it back up. Meg thought about the nice lady on the plane and tossed up the idea of ringing her.

She will think I'm so weird, Meg thought, taking the card out just to put it back into her pocket.

Fuck it, Meg thought, quickly taking it out again and ringing the number.

"Hello?" Anna said down the phone, Meg smiling as she heard the woman's familiar voice.

"Hi, um, it's Meg, the girl you were sitting next to on the plane?" Meg said, hoping that Anna would remember her.

"Meg, how are you? Lovely to hear from you," Anna said, making Meg smile.

"Um, so you know how you said if I needed anything, I should call you? Well, you wouldn't happen to be cool with me staying with you for a few days, would you?" Meg said, scrunching her face up as she heard how pathetic she sounded. Hearing Anna laugh down the phone was also not helping.

"Of course, I would be cool with you staying. I have a guest room set up, ready to go. Would you like to give me your address, and I can pick you up, or do you want to make your way here?" Anna asked, snapping her fingers at her driver just as he was about to get back into the car after dropping her off.

"I can make my way there. What's the address?" Meg said. Anna looked up at the driver, smiled, and waved him off before texting Meg the address.

"I will see you soon," Anna said, both surprised and

delighted at how her day was unfolding.

After receiving the address, Meg started punching in the details into her phone and began to follow the directions to get to Anna's house. She decided the most cost-effective way would be to take the two trains across town, knowing that getting stuck in midmorning traffic would make for a hefty fare.

She wheeled her heavy suitcase through the subway, ignoring the angry looks from people as she took up space they had decided she wasn't entitled too. After the 20 minute trip, she left one platform just to walk to another, feeling surprised that she felt light. It wasn't the fact that all her belongings now fit in one suitcase; it was the feeling of freedom.

Maybe this is what Anna was talking about, Meg thought as she boarded the second train. She put her headphones on and waited the next 30minutes, getting off in the art district and walking up to the street.

All those weight classes turned out to be good for something, Meg thought to herself as she dragged her heavy suitcase up the stairs, silently praying that it didn't break. When she reached the top, she moved to the side and checked her phone, letting it adjust before continuing to follow it down the street. Meg found herself in the middle of a place she never dared enter. Not because she felt like she didn't fit in or couldn't afford to live the lifestyle, but because she knew she couldn't. If it hadn't been for Anna's kindness on the plane, there is no way Meg would have continued to search for her apartment building number.

She's not like those snobby bitches, Meg reminded herself, remembering how gentle and tender Anna had been with her, somehow knowing what she needed. Meg stopped out the front of the number 29 Hamilton Avenue and looked up at the building in front of her.

Here goes, Meg thought, walking inside and pressing the elevator button. She rode the elevator up to level 8 and stepped out, walked down the marble corridor until she reached one of the two doors on the level, number 14, and knocked on the door. Meg waited impatiently, her stomach full of knots as she kicked her feet against each other, waiting for Anna to open the door.

"Darling, hello," Anna said, opening the door wide and walking out, embracing Meg and making her laugh.

"Hi, thanks for this," Meg said, feeling embarrassed. Anna shook her head, taking her suitcase and walking it inside.

"Not at all, I'm happy to help, and glad for the company actually," Anna said, allowing herself to give an honest answer.

"Did you find it, ok?" Anna asked, putting Meg's suitcase down by the door and watching as Meg looked around.

"Yeah, it was fine," Meg said, absentmindedly as she

looked at the high ceilings and luxury apartment furnishings.

"Your place is average," Meg laughed, teasing Anna and happy when Anna smirked.

"Yeah, it's a little run down, maybe you have some suggestions on how I can fix it," Anna replied, enjoying Meg's humor.

"The guest room is this way," Anna said, taking the suitcase and wheeling it down the hallway. Meg followed, wishing that she could sit down and relax but not wanting to offend Anna. Anna led the way past several rooms, all of which Meg was sure would have also been excellent, stopping when she reached one right at the end of the wide hallway.

"You can stay as long as you need to," Anna said, opening the door and letting Meg walk inside. The room overlooked the park with its floor to ceiling glass wall, the sheer drapes either side adding to the elegance of the room.

"Don't worry about closing them when it's dark, or when you get changed, I have a film on them that prevents people from being able to see in during the day and the night," Anna said, sitting on the bed.

"Also, that tablet there turns on the lights, movie screen, and the bathroom is just through those doors," Anna added, continuing to explain the room. Meg was somewhat overwhelmed and began to tear up, trying to hide it but failing to do so.

"Oh, darling, I'm sorry. Is this all too much for you?"

Anna said, standing up and walking over to where Meg stood, nodding her head and wiping her tears.

"Come on, come with me, I have something that will cheer you up," Anna said, enjoying being able to take care of the sweet girl. Anna led Meg back out into the living room and sat her down on the couch. She wrapped a heavy, fluffy blanket around her shoulders and poured her a glass of water, tipped some candied dinosaur shapes into a small bowl, and walked back over to Meg. Sitting down on the couch, a seat away, Anna placed everything down on the table and sat back, taking a bite of one of the treats.

"Thanks. You must think I am so weird or something," Meg said, her face blushing red. Here she was, sitting on the couch of a perfect stranger, being looked after because she couldn't get her life in order by herself.

"Not at all, honey," Anna said, reaching out and stroking Meg's cheek lightly.

"I like that," Meg softly said, wishing that her body wasn't betraying her.

Not everything has to be sexual! She thought to herself, wishing that her pussy wasn't getting wet from the attention the attractive older woman was giving her.

"I know you do. All little girls do," Anna said, taking a chance but feeling nervous the moment she let the words slip from her lips. Meg looked up at her, fear in her eyes but something else. It wasn't fear of Anna perse. It was fear that

Anna saw something in Meg that she tried to hide. Meg tried to speak, but the words didn't seem to want to come out, so she just smiled and rested her head on the back of the couch.

"What do you do for work?" Meg decided to say.

"I'm the CEO of Carson Lighting," Anna said, Meg, opening her eyes suddenly.

"Ok, wow," Meg said, making Anna laugh.

"What?" Anna asked, unsure of what Meg was meaning.

"Like, it's just perfect. Your place, your life, you. Everything is just so perfect," Meg said, wondering how long it would take her to get her life in order.

"Well, not everything is as it seems," Anna said, getting up and getting herself a glass of water.

"No? It looks pretty damn good," Meg said, getting a playful bop on the head.

"Don't say damn," Anna said, enjoying the redness in Meg's cheeks as she was corrected.

"I have all this yes, but I don't have anyone to share it with," Anna said, not wanting to scare Meg off by telling her that she wanted a baby girl to spoil and discipline.

"Is that why you let me crash here?" Meg laughed.

"Well, when you say it like that, it makes me sound desperate," Anna said, rolling her eyes at herself.

"No! I don't think you'd be desperate, look at you! I bet you could go out and pick up anyone you wanted in like, an hour," Meg exclaimed, making Anna think for a second before smirking at Meg.

Well, I managed to pick you up easily enough, Anna thought to herself, smirking before deciding she had nothing to lose by taking a chance to sleep with Meg.

"So, where would I go to find a fit, young girl that would want to have mad, passionate sex with me," Anna said, making Meg blush. Anna leaned forward, wrapped her arm around Meg's head, weaving her fingers through her hair. Meg battered her puppy dog eyes and slightly moaned, lifting off the seat as her clit began to throb.

"Yeah, that's what I thought," Anna whispered as she brought her mouth down on top of Meg's, kissing her deeply. Meg moaned into the kiss, finally feeling Anna's touch where she wanted to as the feeling raced to her pussy. Meg slipped her tongue into Anna's mouth, tasting her and pulling the blanket off herself, straddled Anna as she kissed her.

"Yeah?" Anna said as Meg pulled her top off, revealing her perky young breasts. Meg began to grind on top of Anna, making her panties wet.

"Yeah," Meg said, nodding her head, wanting nothing more than to have the woman whose lap she was sitting on, bring her to orgasm. It had been a long time since Meg had been with a woman, finding it hard to find the type of woman she found attractive. If she did find a MILF, they always came with so much baggage that Meg was turned off soon after meeting them. But Anna didn't seem to have any baggage as she shifted positions and lay Meg down on the couch, she knew that she was in for a treat.

"Do you know the traffic light system?" Anna said, reaching up Meg's skirt and feeling her wet slit through her panties. Meg nodded, causing Anna to moan in delight that she didn't have to give the girl a run down.

"Good girl," Anna cooed as Meg spread her thighs for Anna, wanting her touch as desperately as Anna wanted to give it. Anna pulled Meg's panties to the side, enjoying the view of her pink pussy.

"You still shave. I didn't think anyone still did that," Anna said, making Meg laugh.

"Yeah, I got it lasered like, way back when, so it doesn't grow anymore," Meg said, hoping that it wasn't a deal-breaker for Anna.

"Perfect," Anna said, her mind wandering, thinking of how sweet Meg would always look.

"Such a pretty little girl," Anna said, stopping herself from saying what she wanted to.

Don't call yourself Mommy whatever you do, Anna thought to herself as she tenderly spread Meg's pussy lips, slowing the pace. Meg moaned in frustration at the slowing pace, making Anna laugh.

"Oh, does somebody need to be touched here," Anna said, slapping Megs' pussy with the full palm of her hand and making her yelp.

"I like that sound," Anna said more seriously, spanking her a few more times before finally entering her.

"I just love the feeling of entering you for the first time. So tight, so wet," Anna said as she slowly pushed two fingers inside of Meg, stretching and filling her, making her gasp.

"Good girl, take it for me," Anna said, surprising Meg with how alluring her words were.

Oh fuck, Meg thought as she began to play with her tits as Anna slowly fingered her, pressing on her stomach and making Meg feel every stroke.

"Fuck," Meg gasped, feeling her pussy loosen and her juices beginning to flow more freely. Anna resisted the urge to slap her face, knowing that would be the punishment for swearing if she was Anna's baby girl. Instead, Anna pulled out of Meg, stripped herself down until she was wearing just her bra and thigh-high pantyhose and black heels.

"Do you know what happens to girls who swear?" Anna said, swinging her panties around one finger. Meg rested on her elbows, biting her bottom lip.

"No," Meg panted, wishing that Anna was still fucking her. Anna bent down over Meg, kissed her cheek, and lovingly stroked her hair before stuffing her panties in her mouth.

"They get gagged," Anna said, making Meg's cheek burn red as she tasted the woman's scent for the first time. Anna pushed Meg down with her foot, the heel digging into the younger woman's skin, making her cry out.

"Don't worry, baby girl," Anna said, spitting on her hand and going back to work on Meg's cunt.

"I'm not going to hurt you," Anna said, winking at Meg before rubbing her clit with her thumb as her two fingers re-entered Meg's pussy, making her close her eyes and roll her head back.

"Yes, cum for me," Anna said, watching as Meg writhed around on the lounge. The early afternoon sun came through the windows, warming Anna's back as she fucked the young blonde. She loved having Meg at her mercy. She imagined that Meg was already hers, making her feel more empowered and dominant than she had in a long time.

"Good girl," Anna said, feeling Meg push her hand away and reach up to pull Anna's panties out of her mouth.

There's no way I'd let this happen if you were mine, baby girl, Anna thought as she sat back and let Meg do what she wanted. Meg sat up, took the panties from her mouth, and placed them down on the couch.

"Woah," Meg said, the afterglow of such an intense orgasm flooding her being and making her numb.

"Did you like that?" Anna asked, already knowing the answer.

"Yeah," Meg panted, making Anna laugh.

"What? You think you're done?" Anna questioned, making Meg laugh. Anna grabbed Meg's hair and gently guided her down onto the floor.

"Stick out your tongue," Anna commanded, waiting for Meg to obey her. Anna slowly lowered herself down onto Meg's face, shivering as she felt the girl's wet tongue on her clit, repositioning herself so that it was her pussy that Meg would be tasting.

"Kiss me," Anna said, knowing full well that she wouldn't have to tell the girl how to eat her out, but enjoying doing so nonetheless. Meg obeyed, eating Anna out with a passion she had forgotten she had. Anna moaned and grinded her pussy onto Meg's face, relishing how the girl's tongue never stopped, feeling like a vibrator.

"Such a good girl," Anna moaned, reaching behind her and rubbing Meg's pussy, as Meg made her cum.

"Did I say stop?" Anna said, feeling Meg slow down, waiting for her to get up. Anna smiled as she felt Meg continue to lap up her juices, bringing on another slight orgasm. Anna knew that she wanted more; she wanted to own Meg. She wanted to bend her over, and strap-on fuck her until she was a limp plaything in Anna's arms.

Another time, Anna said to herself, not wanting to scare the girl away. Getting up, Anna laughed a she felt her legs almost give way, sitting on the lounge quickly as she felt the blood begin to flow back through her legs.

"That's what you get for being greedy," Meg laughed, teasing Anna. Anna smirked as she closed her eyes and waited for the pain to leave her body. Meg came up and sat next to

Anna, snuggling into her and kissing down her neckline, stopping when she reached her breasts.

"Do you want to see them?" Anna asked, Meg, beginning to blush. She wanted more than just to see them. She wanted to play with them, to suckle on Anna, and to lick her nipples for hours lazily. Meg always felt that she gave herself away whenever she played with a girl's breasts, she could be lost at them for hours and forget all about the sex the other girl thought she was going to get. Meg just blushed and shrugged her shoulders.

"Yeah," Meg said, her little voice escaping, making her blush even more.

"You don't have to, I'm not going to be offended if you don't want to," Anna said, sensing the change in Meg's expression.

"No, I want to," Meg quickly said, making Anna laugh and look at her curiously. Anna slowly took off her red lace bra, exposing her large, heavy breasts, making Meg's clit throb and something inside of her ache.

"They are nice," Meg softly said, reaching out hesitantly to touch them.

"Here," Anna said, taking Meg's hands and placing them on herself, showing Meg how she liked to be touch.

"They feel so soft," Meg whispered, she bit her bottom lip and Anna decided to take a shot in the dark.

"Do you want to suckle from them?" She asked Meg's

reaction all that she needed to know.

"Um, I don't, wouldn't that be weird?" Meg stammered, her face red with a mix of desire and shame.

"What's weird about, a Mommy nursing her baby girl?" Anna said, hoping that she had read Meg right. Meg eyed Anna, her mouth gaped open, and her stomach knotted.

"I thought so," Anna smiled, playing with her breasts. Meg looked down, only looking up when Anna lifted her chin.

"How did you know?" Meg quietly asked, Anna, laughing at the question.

"A good Mommy could see that a mile away. Plus, the thumb sucking, the cuddly way you wanted me to touch you. You were an easy read," Anna replied, making Meg sigh and look down at her breasts.

"It's been years since I have been with anyone like this," Meg nervously said, feeling out of her depth but wanting Anna with a frenzied desire.

"Then, it's about time you had Mommy take care of you," Anna said, pulling Meg onto her lap and rolling her onto her back before Meg knew what was happening. Anna held her breast over Meg's mouth, her nipple touching Meg's lips as she leaned forward and pushed her breast into Meg's mouth.

"Suckle on Mommy, baby girl," Anna said, making Meg's eyes glaze over, sending her into little space and making her instinctively begin to nurse. Both Meg and Anna moaned in pleasure as Meg started to suckle, Anna feeling her cunt ache. Yet, it was something deeper that seemed to ache with more intensity than Anna wasn't prepared for, and as she looked down into Meg's big eyes, her lips pursed around her nipple, she knew that she had denied herself Mommy space for far too long.

"Such a good girl," Anna cooed, watching as Meg placed both her hands on her breast and hold it in place. Anna reached down to Meg's pussy and began to rub her, smiling as she felt Meg wiggle against her hand.

"Do you like that baby girl?" Anna said, excited that Meg was enjoying herself.

"Yes, Mommy," Meg said, hesitating when she called Anna, Mommy, hoping that Anna didn't mind. The smile on Anna's face told Meg that it was fine.

"Mommy," Meg suddenly moaned, feeling Anna back inside of her.

"What? I told you that I wasn't finished with you," Anna said, quickly finger fucking Meg, loving how she sucked harder the closer she was to orgasm.

"You're not allowed to cum sweetie, don't do it," Anna said, making Meg's eyes go wide and hearing her groan in frustration as she was edged. Anna was curious to see how well Meg could control herself.

A little orgasm denial never hurt anyone. Well, mostly, Anna thought to herself, watching how the young girl in her lap gasped and groaned, trying to hold off.

"Wow, Mommy is impressed," Anna said, raising an eyebrow and watching as Meg continued to writhe under her touch. Anna knew that if Meg was forced to remain still, that she would have cum several times by now, but she found it endearing that Meg was so untrained and allowed her to continue to fight off her touch.

"Please, Mommy," Meg moaned in agony, desperate to cum. The sound also made Anna moan and nod her head before she realized she had, only noticing when her fingers were flooded by Meg's juices as she cried out.

"How beautiful," Anna said, knowing that she would have to do everything in her power to keep Meg under her roof and in her bed. Meg just panted as her pussy continued to drip, making Anna smile.

"You know, there's something I could put you in that would keep your pussy juices from messing up your pajama pants," Anna said, hoping that Meg would be down for some Mommy, little playtime. Meg just nodded her head, still in a daze.

"How did I get so lucky to meet you?" Meg softly said, making Anna smile.

"I feel the same way, sweet girl," Anna said, getting up and grabbing Meg's wrist. She didn't want to leave the girl alone and give her the chance to change her mind, and she led her into a room which made Meg stop and freeze on the stop.

"It's the nursey little one," Anna said, watching Meg's

face as she pulled her to the floor and onto the changing mat. Anna took out a pacifier, a pink diaper with stars on the front, and a onesie before returning to Meg's side.

"Oh, Mommy," Meg moaned as Anna pushed the pacifier into her mouth and held it in place.

"Don't take it out," Anna instructed, making Meg put her hands back down.

"Good girl," Anna said as she wiped the cum off Meg's pussy and thighs before she powdered her and fastened the diaper to her waist. She took the onesie, pulled it over Meg's head, and slid it down her body, smiling at Meg's thin frame.

"Mommy will have to get you something a little bit smaller, won't I?" Anna said. She had onesies in size small and medium, but Meg needed an extra small.

"I still like it, Mommy, it's snuggly," Meg said, making Anna smile. Meg looked around the nursery, seeing all the toys and then looked back at Anna.

"Do you want to play?" Anna smiled, watching as Meg nodded, and pointed to the stuffie high on the wall. There were three; free-standing shelves mounted to the wall, all of which had a collection of stuffies. Anna smiled and walked over to the top shelf, reached up and took down the cuddly crocodile, and gave it to Meg.

"You are just full of surprises, aren't you?" Anna said, making Meg giggle and nod her head.

"You are a little girl, aren't you, sweetie?" Anna said,

noticing that Meg was more and more non-verbal.

"Do you just want to be looked after when you're a little, sweetheart?" Anna said, sitting down on the floor and watching as Meg crawled over to her and sat in her lap.

"Yes, Mommy," Meg said, taking her paci out but putting it back in quickly.

"Well, Mommy can look after you for as long as you need and want. Does that sound like a plan?" Anna said. Meg's eyes grew wide, and she clapped her hands excitedly.

"This is such a typical lesbian thing to do. Move in together the moment you meet someone," Anna laughed as Meg played with her new stuffie.

Chapter 5

"So I work Monday to Friday, 7-6:30. They are long days. When I come home, I haven't had to worry about anyone but myself for a long time, so it might be a bit rough this week until we come up with a routine," Anna said to Meg the following morning over brunch. Anna had taken Meg out to a fancy brunch bar, and the two of them were waiting for their meals. Anna liked that Meg had ordered something healthy.

"Ok. They are long days," Meg said, wondering what she would do for all the time that she would be in the apartment alone.

"Tell me about your job?" Anna asked, her fruit platter being put down in front of her. Meg waited until her meal was also placed down before answering the question.

"Well. I am a freelance graphic designer. So I make book covers, a few logos, but mostly book covers," Meg replied, impressing Anna.

"You don't look old enough to have a degree," Anna said, smirking, clearly teasing Meg.

"I'm 26!" Meg said, taking the bait.

"Oh, that's endearing," Anna replied, loving how enthusiastically Meg had replied.

"How old are you?" Meg quietly asked, making Anna laugh.

"Older than 26," Anna replied, making Meg roll her eyes.

"I'm 45, my birthday is in a few months," Anna more seriously replied. Meg took no time at all to do the math.

"Ok, cool," Meg said, trying not to laugh, Anna never missing a beat.

"You laugh now, but let's see you at 45 missy," she said, playfully kicking Meg under the table, surprising her.

"I didn't say anything!" Meg insisted, Anna not believing her for a second.

"Ok, so. I usually get up at like 8, make a coffee and begin working until like 12, have lunch and finish for the day at 4, got for a run till five, and then chill out till 10 when I go to bed," Meg explained.

"Yeah, so I would have already been gone by the time you've woken up, and my day is over long after yours. I don't get home until 6:30, and I'm out of the house in the morning by 6:30," Anna said, feeling disappointed that her workdays were so long. Her schedule had been a deal-breaker for so many girls in the past. She hadn't realized until that very moment that she had given up looking for a permanent girlfriend.

"That's ok. I can maybe just run with your schedule for like a week and see how we go? I'd get so much work done!"

Meg giggled as she finished her brunch, sipping the champagne and looking around the space. The room was filled with the type of fancy people who always had looked down on her growing up. She had come from a hard-working, middle-class family who tried their best to put her through good schools. The problem was, that was all her parents could afford. They couldn't provide the money for the class trips, brand new uniforms, or money to do things with her friends on the weekends and over the summer. Very quickly, she was deemed a loser who none of the other girls wanted to be around. Sure she got a great education, but the cruel remarks and social isolation that she experienced still haunted her. Shaking off the thought, she looked back at Anna, who had been watching her.

"You're uncomfortable here," Anna said, rather than asked, tilting her head knowingly when Meg tried to dispute her remark.

"It's not that. It's just. I've never been good enough for these types of people," Meg said, feeling embarrassed that she let others take her power away so easily. She had always done that. She didn't seem to know how to stop it, that was what annoyed her.

"Hmm, let's go somewhere that you like then," Anna said, getting up and taking her glass of champagne with her.

"Can you leave with that?" Meg whispered as they made their way out the door.

"Darling, Mommy can do whatever the hell I want," Anna said, enjoying how the young girl looking up at her made her feel.

"Don't swear, Mommy," Meg teased, coping a playful spanking on her ass.

"So, where are you taking me?" Anna said, dropping her champagne glass in the sidewalk bin and reaching for Meg's hand.

"So, there's this place, it's a little run-down, but they sell great sweet treats. It's by the river," Meg explained. She loved how people got out of Anna's, and therefore, her way as they walked. Usually, Meg had to scramble through the masses, but with Anna, they seemed to part and made her way clear.

"I will have to remember that you can eat like a frat boy and still have that perfect body. Enjoy that, it goes, trust me," Anna said, making Meg laugh. They walked the three blocks, made a left turn, and head down to the water.

"You're right, this isn't my scene," Anna said, feeling vulnerable.

"Don't worry, I got you," Meg said, looking up at her. Anna reached out and touched Meg's face affectionately just as two guys entered the alley from behind them. Two other men then entered from the other side, and Anna felt her grip tighten on Meg's hand.

"It's ok Mommy, I'm not going to let anything bad

happen to you," Meg said reassuringly. Anna wanted to believe her, but as the men got closer, she wasn't so sure.

"Give me your wallet," one of the men said, taking out a gun and pointing it at Anna.

"She doesn't have the wallets, I do," Meg said, stepping forward. She looked around. Her parents owned a Krav Maga studio on the Westside, hardly the lucrative money machine, but it had taught her a thing or two. She knew that the guy with the gun was the only one she needed to worry about, the other three would run away the minute she had the gun in her hands. Meg slowly pushed Anna behind her and reached into her jacket pocket. She could tell the man with the gun was in a rush by the way he kept looking around, and as he looked over his shoulder, Meg quickly disarmed him and shot into the air above her head.

"Get out of here, or the next one is for you," she said, slowly bringing her arm down and pointing the gun at the leader's face and putting her finger back on the trigger.

"Run," Meg said, stepping forward and watching as the men scrambled back up the hill and out onto the street and disappearing. Meg turned back to Anna, who was in shock.

"Right, well, I will be tying you up if I ever have to punish you!" Anna said, making Meg laugh.

"I'm not like that all the time, just when I have to be," Meg said, shaking her head.

"Yeah, I see that," Anna said, taking the gun out of

Meg's hand and putting the safety on before putting it in her handbag.

"I thought you were going to throw it in the river," Meg laughed.

"No, I want to take it to the police. Who knows the horrible things those men have done. If there is a chance they can get caught, I want the police to be able to have that chance," Anna said, following Meg into a shop with a wooden door. Inside the shop, Anna smelt the sweet smell of candy from her childhood.

"Oh, you are such a clever little girl," Anna said as she saw the candy-filled jars behind the counter.

"Hi, how's it going?" The man behind the counter asked. He had that; old grandfather look about himself. The tall, jolly-looking man with a big beard and a white apron, the red and white stripe of his shirt made Meg smile.

"I haven't seen you in here for a while, Meggsy," the man said, making Anna raise an eyebrow.

"Meggsy?" Anna questioned, finding the name endearing but also somewhat disturbing.

"Anna, this is Phil. Phil, Anna," Meg said, introducing the two. Phil smiled warmly, came around the counter, and shook hands with Anna.

"It's a pleasure to meet you. Meggsy used to come here when she was a kid and stayed for hours. I gave her her first job because by the time she could work, she knew everything by heart," Phil said, the chuckle he had at the end of the sentence making his cheeks rosy.

"I love that. That's so sweet," Anna said, looking at Meg, who was smiling bashfully.

"We'll take two of everything from the top shelf," Meg said, turning to Phil, who was already making his way back behind the counter.

"Always the same," Phil teased.

"This used to be Meggsy's standard order back in the day," Phil said, filling two red and white striped paper bags.

"Thank you for taking me here," Anna said, enjoying the intimate act of letting her into Meg's world. Meg just gave her a sideward smile before trying to pay Phil, who declined.

"On the house," he said, waving his hands at her.

"Well, then, take the tip," Meg said, putting the money in the tip jar before hurrying out of the store laughing as Phil continued to try and protest.

"You are going to need to brush your teeth extra well tonight, young lady," Anna said, taking a bite of the pink sugar crystal-coated marshmallow and moaned in delight.

"I know right, pretty yummy," Meg said, tasting the smooth chocolate of her liquid caramel, chocolate shelled ball.

They walked back up to the street, straight to the police station and handed the gun in. Both Meg and Anna had to make a statement about how the weapon came to be in their possession and were walking back to Anna's apartment by 4 o'clock.

"What do you want to do now?" Meg said, holding onto Anna's hand like she hadn't only met her less than 48 hours earlier. Anna thought for a moment.

What I need to do is check my emails and go grocery shopping so I can meal prep for the week. Then I need to go to the gym and burn off all these calories. I wanted to go to the sauna as well, Anna thought to herself.

"I don't know, I had nothing planned," Anna decided to say instead, enjoying the feeling of spontaneity. They turned the corner and continued to walk, both yawning at the same time.

"I think I am about to be in a sugar coma," Meg laughed, causing Anna to reach down, take her paper bag and put it in her handbag.

"That's enough for you then," Anna said, an idea crossing her mind.

"Do you like the gym?" Anna asked, walking past the doorman and into the elevator.

"I guess. I don't have a membership to one or anything like that, though," Meg replied.

"The apartment has a gym, as well as a sauna. Want to go work out for a while?" Anna suggested. Meg couldn't remember the last time she worked out but shrugged her shoulders and nodded her head.

"Ok great," Anna said, opening the door to her home. Meg walked to her room, changed into something she was happy to exercise in, and made her way back to the living room to wait for Anna. She took out her phone while she waited, instantly regretting the choice.

Baby, I'm sorry. I made a huge mistake that I want to spend the rest of my life making up to you. You deserve so much better than me. I want to get professional help so that I can be the man you deserve, came the onslaught of messages from her ex. Meg turned her phone off before looking around the apartment and shaking her head.

This is what I deserve. Not some fuckboy who couldn't keep it in his pants, Meg thought to herself, jumping up when she heard Anna coming down the hall.

"Ready?" Anna asked, sitting on a chair and tying her shoes. Meg left her phone on the lounge.

"Yep," she replied, brushing off Anna's curious look.

"Wait. Tell me what's going on," Anna said, making Meg annoyed that she could tell something was up.

"Nothing," Meg said, trying to walk to the door, just to have Anna grab her wrist.

"Sweetie, don't lie to me," Anna loving said, bringing Meg into her arms and wrapping them around her.

"How can you do that?" Meg said in frustration, making Anna smile to herself knowingly.

"Because Mommy always knows," Anna said, taking

Meg to the couch and sitting her down.

"It's just Alex. He messaged me a whole bunch of texts saying how he is going to change and that he is sorry, and it just makes me so mad that I could have stayed with somebody so pathetic," Meg said, Anna, giving her her undivided attention.

"You don't need to be angry with yourself," Anna said, Meg, sighing and moving closer to cuddle into Anna.

"I'm happy that he kicked me out because if it hadn't been for him doing it, I would probably still be with the loser. When I could have been here with you for all this time," Meg said, hoping that Anna didn't think she was pathetic for sharing her feelings.

"It's just, I've never had somebody care for the way you seem to," Meg said, looking down, embarrassed that she felt so deeply so quickly.

"He will probably keep messaging you. Have you thought about blocking his number?" Anna suggested, Meg, shaking her head.

"May I then?" Anna said, holding out her hand to Meg and waiting for Meg to hand her the phone. Anna swiped a few times, finding his name and holding the phone up for Meg to see, watching her face as she blocked his number and then deleted it from her phone.

"There, Mommy made it all better," Anna said, rocking Meg in her arms.

Chapter 6

Anna's 5:30 alarm went off in the morning, unbeknownst to Meg, who had slept in the guest room Sunday night. Anna quietly walked around the apartment as she got ready, but the smell of her freshly made cappuccino woke Meg.

"Hi baby girl," Anna said, her appearance taking Meg by surprise.

"Oh my god, you're beautiful," Meg said, rubbing her eyes and trying to focus them. Anna wore her black heels, black pantyhose, a stylish black dress with a crisp white shirt underneath, a tan cape-scarf, and an elegant, bridle style black and brushed gold metal belt which clinched at her waist. Her makeup was flawless, her thick, wavy brown hair looked like it had been freshly blown out and as she stood with her cappuccino in one hand, and her other on her hip. She looked like a goddess.

"I'm happy you approve," Anna smirked, knowing that she looked amazing. Meg looked down at her pajamas, ran her fingers through somewhat messy blonde hair, and then looked back up at Anna.

"Oh, baby girl, you aren't meant to look like me," Anna said, checking her Rolex and sighing, knowing that her car and driver would be waiting downstairs for her.

"Mommy loves how little you look. But I have to go. There's food in the fridge, make yourself at home," Anna said, embracing Meg, kissing her passionately and grabbing her ass before she pulled herself away from the girl. She groaned in frustration at not having more time with her new favorite person before heading out the door and leaving Meg alone and standing in the spacious but empty apartment.

Well, now what? Meg thought, checking the time. She shrugged her shoulders, decided to make herself a coffee.

I can see how she found it hard to keep a girl around, Meg thought as she took her coffee outside and looked over the city. Sure, Anna's life was beautiful, she could buy anything she wanted, she could have anyone she wanted, but it came at a huge cost, and that cost was time.

I guess I just need to find my passions and get used to spending a lot of my time during the week without her. I'm sure I could get used to this, I got used to living with a lying dirtbag, this is an upgrade, Meg thought as she watched the city slowly come to life.

"Hi, baby girl, how are you?" Anna said down the phone. It was 3 in the afternoon, and Meg had been online all day.

"Hey, really good, I have so many things to tell you when you get home," Meg excitedly said.

"I can't wait to hear. I just wanted to check in to make sure you were ok," Anna said, silencing the person who came to her door.

"But I have to go now honey, I'll see you tonight," Anna said, hanging up the phone quickly.

"Lol, bye then," Meg said out loud before going back to her laptop.

"Honey, Mommy's home," Anna said at 7 pm. Although the drive to her office was just over half an hour in the mornings, it was less than 15 minutes during the evening.

"Sorry I'm late, I had to pick a few things up from the store. I could have gotten my assistant to do it for me, but I just love the feeling for doing a quick grocery shop," Anna said, smiling when she saw Meg in the living room.

"That's fine. What did you get?" Meg asked, her stomach growling.

"Oh, baby!" Anna said, coming to sit down next to her and rubbing her tummy.

"Mommy will get you a bottle, and that should keep you going until dinner," Anna said, kissing Meg on the head before standing back up and holding out her hand.

"Come on," she said, waiting for Meg to obey her, smiling when she did so.

"I bought some duck, some seasonal vegetables, and a herb rub I thought would be nice. It won't take me very long to make this all up," Anna said, sitting Meg down and beginning to make her a protein shake.

"Yummy," Meg said, making Anna smirk.

"I thought my little, sweet tooth would like it," Anna said, handing Meg the bottle.

"Tell Mommy about your day," Anna said, putting her hair up and rolling up her sleeves.

"So! I did some cool things," Meg said, her eyes sparkling.

"I made up a timetable of all the stuff I can do while you're at work so that I am not just waiting around losing my mind," Meg explained, making Anna laugh.

"Good. Keep going," Anna said, taking out pots and pans.

"So, I have a work schedule, I work 9 hours a day now, three hours on, half an hour off and I start this at 6:30 when you leave. I thought it might be nice to wake up together, you know, to have a little morning kiss," Meg said, Anna, coming behind her.

"Or a little morning fuck," Anna said, rubbing over Megs' breasts as she passed.

"Or that," Meg laughed.

"Then at 4:30, I head to the library because at five they have book readings. I don't care which book it is. I just thought it might be nice to hear that. Then after at 5:30, I go do something different each day until 6:30, and we get home at pretty much the same time," Meg said, feeling very proud of herself.

"My clever girl," Anna said, pouring herself a glass of rose wine as Meg handed her her bottle.

"I'm finished, Mommy," Meg said, Anna, taking the bottle and putting it in the dishwasher.

"I love that you have done this, it makes me feel like you want to be with me and I love that," Anna said, putting the duck and vegetables in the roasting pan before putting it in the oven.

"I do want to be with you," Meg said, lovingly smiling at Anna.

"Let's get you all cleaned up and out of those big girl clothes," Anna said, making Meg laugh.

"I don't feel very little night," Meg said, Anna, smirking.

"Oh, you will," Anna said, tickling Meg and making her squeal and run up the hallway toward the bathroom.

Anna ran Meg a bath, putting in bath toys, bubbles, and lighting some sweet-smelling candles.

"Armies up," Anna said, Meg, obeying her immediately.

She might have been right about me feeling little, Meg thought to herself, feeling her little self coming out with each passing second. Anna took off Meg's bra, frowning as she saw the bra lines.

"Mommy is going to take you shopping on the weekend

for new bras, I don't like that they cut into you like this," Anna said, running her fingers over Meg's skin, the touch painful, making Meg flinch.

"Ok, Mommy," Meg said as Anna helped her into the huge bathtub. Giggling, Meg ducked her head under the water, loving that the bath was more like a mini swimming pool.

"This is so nice!" Meg exclaimed, scooping up a handful of bubbles and blowing them in the air before laying back down in the warm water.

"Mommy's happy little girl," Anna softly said as she slowly undressed. She liked the way Meg's eyes were always glued on her when she was naked.

"Can Mommy join you, baby girl?" Anna asked, getting into the tub as Meg nodded.

"Oh, there she is," Anna said, enjoying how Meg became quiet, swimming over to her and cuddling in her lap.

"Cuddly baby," Anna said, holding onto Meg and sitting in the shallow end of the tub. Anna loved feeling Meg resting her head on her ample breasts, the water lapping just under her nipples.

"I love you, Mommy," Meg involuntarily sighed, darting upright and looking Anna fearfully in the eye.

"It's ok little one, Mommy isn't freaked out about that," Anna said, Meg, beginning to suck her thumb.

"You're not?" Meg asked, her eyes as wide as ever.

"No. I think, when it's right, it's right. And I feel so alive when I am with you. It is probably a lot to do with the fact that we just met and everything is new and exciting, but I also think that it is because of how open we have been with and to each other. I have never had a baby girl who has been as independent as you without being a little brat. I love that you let me look after you but, at the same time, spent the day making sure to look after yourself as well. You are the type of woman I have been looking for," Anna said, the smile on Meg's face said enough.

"Oh, Mommy," Meg said, burying her face in Anna's cleavage, just for Anna to reposition her in her arms and bring her nipple up to Meg's lips.

"Suckle on Mommy, little girl," Anna said, bringing Meg's head closer to her thick, hard nipple, smiling and happily sighing when Meg began to obey her.

"Good girl," Anna said, closing her eyes and resting her head on the towel she had positioned at the end of the tub. As Meg suckled, Anna thought back to their dinner in the oven and knew that they needed to get out of the tub shortly, but looking down to see Meg's wide eyes looking up at her, her lips pursed around Anna's breast and her hand grabbing onto Anna's body, Anna would have much rather stayed in that position until the water was freezing cold.

This is what I needed, Anna thought to herself. The emotional release she experienced having Meg on her breasts was something she knew she would never want to live without ever again. Patting Meg gently on her ass and placing her hands under Meg's arms, lifting her off, Anna stood up.

It could also be the fact that I am so needed, Anna continued to think, knowing that being needed was a big turn on for her.

"We need to get in some warm jammies, baby girl," Anna explained as Meg whined, pouted and reached for Anna. Looking down into the water, Meg nodded her head, making Anna smile, enjoying being craved as much as Meg craved her.

"Don't worry. You can have more Mommy cuddles before bed. But we will get sick if we stay in here for too much longer, sick and hungry," Anna lovingly explained, standing up and getting out of the tub, she guided Meg out and dried her off.

"I don't want you to crawl to the nursery, baby girl. The marble might be too painful on your little knees," Anna said as Meg got to the floor.

"But I'm tired, Mommy," Meg softly whined, rubbing her eyes, making Anna smile.

"I know, just a little bit longer, baby girl," Anna said, taking Meg's hand and leading her to the nursery.

"Lay down, honey," Anna said when they finally reached the nursery. Meg could smell the crispy duck and sweet vegetables in the oven, making her stomach growl and Anna laugh.

"Soon, little one. Let Mommy get you dressed and then

you can have yummy dinner and play or cuddle until bedtime," Anna said as she took out a diaper and a thick pad, sticking it onto the diaper before coming back down to the changing mat on the floor. Meg had found an aquarium mat and was busy kicking her legs in the air as she lay on her tummy and pushed the fish around.

"Rollover for me," Anna said, taking Meg's hips in her hands and turning her over, only for Meg to resist and try to roll back.

"Not, a good idea," Anna sternly said, reaching down and taking Meg's chin in her hand and making her look at her dead in the eye. Meg looked down in submission before Anna let her go and began to diaper her, making sure the diaper was on tight. Meg could feel the pad pressing into her pussy. Anna had made sure of that by opening Meg's pussy lips as she diapered her, knowing that it would rub on her clit.

"The more you wriggle, the more it'll rub," Anna said, pushing a paci into Meg's mouth as she rubbed her between her legs. Going back to the cupboard, Anna took out a matching set of duck pajamas and a pair of fluffy yellow socks. Meg giggled as she saw the outfit, clapping her hands and helping Anna as she got dressed.

"What a sweet little girl," Anna said, sitting back and looking at the adorable blonde playing in front of her.

"Mommy?" Meg questioned as she heard Anna leaving the room.

"Mommy is going to get out of this robe and into something more snuggly. Then we are going to have dinner. I'll come and get you after I'm dressed," Anna said, knowing what Meg's concern was before she even had to say it out loud. Meg smiled behind her paci before turning back around and continued to play. Anna left the room, hearing the timer go off on the oven, she walked to the kitchen and took their dinner out, leaving it to sit on the bench as she went back into her room to get dressed. She loved that Meg was so easily pleased that she was no trouble and was happy to be babied the way Anna liked. Anna hung her robe on the wall of her walk-in cupboard and walked around the room to where she kept her pajamas. Given, they were more her house clothes than pajamas as she preferred to sleep with only her panties on. She took out a pair of designer navy sweat pants and a white racerback singlet, her large, natural aesthetically looking yet fake breasts pressing the material out, making her smile. She took her hair out, put on some warm socks, and walked back out to find Meg sitting in the living room floor crying.

"Baby girl, what has happened?" Anna said, rushing over and bending down to see Meg clutching her foot.

"I hurt it, Mommy," Meg said, taking her hands away slightly, to show Anna. Anna gasped as she saw the small amount of blood coming through the sock.

"Baby, how?" Anna said, kissing Meg's cheeks before standing up and going to get her medical supplies, coming back almost instantly.

"I dropped my phone on it," Meg said, pointing to her phone, the shattered screen coming from it landing on the floor after it had cut Meg's foot.

"Oh, little one," Anna said, taking Meg's sock off slowly and cleaning her small wound.

"It's ok, little one, Mommy is here, I'll look after you," Anna cooed, wrapping Meg's toe in a bandage and going back to the nursery to take out another pair of socks.

"I'm sorry, Mommy," Meg said, beginning to cry again, worried that Anna would be angry with her for ruining her things.

"You don't need to be sorry, Mommy isn't mad at all, little girl!" Anna exclaimed, helping Meg over to the dining room table before placing her plate of food down in front of her.

"I'll cut it up for you, do you want me to feed you or do you want to do it yourself," Anna asked, sipping her wine.

"I can do it!" Meg proudly said, looking at Anna, making sure it was ok to start eating.

"Alright, sweet girl," Anna said, stroking Meg's cheek and beginning to eat.

After dinner, Anna took Meg back down to the floor, setting her up with the aqua mat, some blocks, and her crocodile stuffie she had name Sven.

"Mommy is going to tidy the kitchen. Then I want to have some chill-out time on the couch before bed, alright? Are you happy to keep playing there?" Anna asked from the kitchen, content with Meg's nod, and began packing the dishes into the dishwasher. Coming down to the lounge area, Anna poured herself another glass of wine, and began to scroll through her phone, checking her social media accounts and messaging with friends as Meg built Sven a castle.

Does it get any better than this!? Anna thought to herself, watching Meg play.

Chapter 7

At 9:45, Anna yawned and lay down on the couch. Meg turned around, looking at Anna, who was sleepily smiling and watching her.

"Mommy, is it bedtime?" Meg asked, resting her head on the couch close to Anna's face. Anna leaned forward, kissed Meg on the nose, and nodded her head.

"Yes, but I don't want the day to be over," Anna said, pulling Meg onto her and stroking her hair as Meg rested on Anna's breasts.

"But we can just do it all again tomorrow, can't we?" Meg questioned, feeling Anna's legs wrap around her.

"Yes," Anna replied, patting Meg's padded bottom and smiling.

"So, are you going to get up with Mommy tomorrow morning? Do you want me to undress you, or do you want to do that yourself? Mommy is going to go to the gym after work tomorrow. You can come down if you like?" Anna said, covering Meg's forehead with kisses.

"I can do it. I think that if I'm going to have such long days, I only want to be little in the night time. I can't be little and try to go out into the city, Mommy, I'll get lost!" Meg replied, making Anna laugh.

"And, yeah, I'll come to the gym with you," Meg added, Anna, smiling and indicating that she wanted Meg to sit up by the head tilt she gave her.

"Time for teethies and then bed," Anna said. She wondered if Meg would want to continue to sleep in her bed or if she would feel comfortable sleeping in Anna's.

You met her 48 hours ago. You've fucked her, regressed her, and let her move in with you, and you're nervous about asking her if she wants to sleep in your bed? Anna thought to herself, laughing out loud at how crazy her time with Meg had been.

"You're going to sleep in Mommy's bed from now on, alright, little one?" Anna said, smiling when Meg threw her arms around Anna's waist and held her tight.

"I am so happy you said that, Mommy," Meg said, letting her go as they reached the bathroom. They cleaned, flossed, and used mouthwash before they left, Meg watching as Anna put on night cream.

"This is how Mommy stays looking so good," Anna said, making Meg laugh. Anna then took Meg's hand and led her up into her bed, going back into the living room to get Sven before tucking Meg in next to her.

"Goodnight, little one," Anna said, kissing Meg on both her cheeks before letting her snuggle in close as they fell asleep.

The alarm woke Meg up with a start, making Anna laugh.

"Oh, baby girl, it might take some getting used to," she said, laughing. Meg looked around the room, one of the walls coming to life with a rainforest backdrop and birds flying across the screen.

"It's a virtual reality wall," Anna explained as Meg watched in awe.

"Of course it is," Meg laughed. She yawned, stretched, and looked down at her clothes and sighed.

"Don't worry. You'll be Mommy's little girl again soon enough," Anna said, kissing her forehead and beginning to unbutton her pajama shirt.

"Hey, I can do it!" Meg playfully exclaimed as she wriggled away from Anna, who just raised her eyebrow and smirked.

"Alright, then. Coffee and toast?" Anna asked as she walked into the cupboard, seeing Meg nod her head before she disappeared. Meg took off her pajamas and diaper, shaking her head almost as if to activate her adult self once more.

"So. What activity are you going to do today after the library?" Anna asked. Today was the first day Meg would put her schedule into place, hoping that she had given herself enough variety and breaks that it kept her well-paced and entertained. Today was Tuesday, and she had planned to go to an art gallery for an hour after the library.

"I'm going to the art gallery. I have no idea what's in there, but it's what I'm doing," Meg said, before running down the hallway, limping on her foot. She had forgotten all about her sore toe and moaned in frustration that it hurt. She put on a pair of jeans, her oversized cable knit sweater, and put her hair up in a messy bun, adding glasses to her look.

"Don't you look like an absolute picture," Anna said, coming out, enjoying the gaped mouth response Meg gave her.

"Nothing compared to that," Meg replied, looking Anna up and down.

"I wouldn't feel like you were my baby girl if you looked like Mommy," Anna said, making Meg her breakfast. Anna wore a tight pair of cropped blue jeans, a loose white silk blouse, and a long, light pink coat she wore open. She had a matching handbag and a Chanel brooch on her coat, her hair as immaculate as ever.

"Can you go into my room and get Mommy's cream, Fendi pumps, baby girl?" Anna said, buttering Meg's toast. Meg rushed down from her stool, and walked to the shoe cupboard, took out the heels Anna was referring to before coming back, and opening her mouth as Anna fed her a mouthful of toast.

"Thank you, baby," Anna seductively said, watching as Meg ate. Another alarm went off, Anna rolling her eyes and quickly put her heels on.

"Bye-bye honey," she said, kissing Meg's lips, enjoying

the salty, buttery taste of Meg's mouth and getting lost in the kiss before Meg pushed her away.

"You're going to be late," Meg laughed, watching as Anna came back for more.

"Fuck em," Anna said, putting her handbag down on the bench and wrapped Meg up in her arms as she passionately kissed her.

"I want that pussy tonight," Anna said, groping Meg's body, eliciting moans of pleasure from the girl.

"That's what I needed to get through this day," Anna laughed, stealing a few more quick kisses before walking to the door, turning back to face Meg and shaking her tits for her before she left the apartment.

"It's surprisingly easy and productive," Meg said down the phone as she made lunch.

"Good, I don't want this to be hard for you," Anna replied. She was on her lunch break and decided to call Meg after not hearing from her all day. She liked that Meg understood that Anna couldn't give her her undivided attention while she was at work. So many of her ex's had hated that when Anna was at work, she didn't want anything to distract her, which meant that they had to wait.

"I've only got a few more orders to do, and then I'm done for the day. I didn't think that I would be able to get through things so quickly but, here we are," Meg said. She had cooked a piece of salmon and a salad for herself, enjoying the array of ingredients in Anna's pantry and fridge.

"Have you thought about what you want to do when you have finished everything?" Anna said, eating the meal her assistant had picked up for her. A steak from one of the most famous steak houses in the city.

"Yes, Netflix!" Meg replied, making Anna laugh. She had half expected the girl to say, researching for new cover ideas, or upskilling but she smiled and appreciated that Meg was young.

"Oh, my sweet girl," Anna said, remembering just how sweet Meg was and licking her lips as she thought about the sex she was going to have that night.

"Well, my perfect girl, Mommy, has to get back to work. So I'll see you tonight. Don't forget. We are going to the gym together," Anna said, hanging up the phone. She was sure it was a power thing, to have the last word, but she loved that Meg didn't seem to mind that she always ended their conversations abruptly.

"See you then," Meg replied to herself, smiling as she continued her lunch.

Meg was already waiting for Anna in the gym. She walked on the treadmill as she watched a movie on her phone. Feeling the firm slap on her ass, she pulled her headphones down around her neck to see Anna standing behind her, smiling.

"Hey sugar," Anna said, the clear lustful look in her eye telling Meg that she wasn't only going to be Anna's baby tonight.

"Hey Mommy," Meg said, jumping down and hugging the taller woman.

"You look cute," Anna said, noting Meg's gray fitness tights, her pink t-shirt, and a gray sweater wrapped around her hips.

"Thanks," Meg beamed, as Anna got on the treadmill next to her.

"Wanna race?" Anna challenged, the look in Meg's eyes encouraging.

"I think I'd win," Meg teased, delighting Anna.

"Well, let's find out," Anna said, putting her machine up to level 12, only for Meg to do the same.

"Winner is the one who stays on the longest," Anna said, making Meg laugh.

"And every five minutes we go up a level," Meg added, surprising Anna.

"Alright, little one, let's see what you got," Anna said, beginning to run. Meg giggled as she ran, only becoming serious a few minutes in, deciding that she didn't want Anna to win. Anna, who thought this would be an easy win, felt her lungs heave as Meg's young, thin body seemed to float with each step.

"I ran track in school," Meg said, panting only slightly.

"Yes, but school for you was about two minutes ago. I ran track in school too, but that was a long time ago," Anna panted, refusing to give up as they upped the level.

"You're so stubborn," Meg said, wishing that Anna would let her win. Her toe had started to hurt, and she didn't know how much longer she could maintain the pace.

"I could say the same thing about you!" Anna exclaimed, reaching out to slap Meg on the ass. Meg laughed, coughing slightly and accepted defeat, stopping her machine.

"You. Win," Meg panted, Anna, stopping her machine and pacing around the room with her hands on her head.

"Yeah, but you didn't make it easy," Anna said, taking a sip of water from her bottle.

"Here," Anna said, noticing that Meg didn't have any water with her. Meg gratefully took the bottle and guzzled half before handing it back.

"So, I didn't tell you what the winner gets," Anna said, taking off her shoes and shirt, standing in front of Meg in just her tights and sports bra. Her flat but soft tummy glistened, her full breasts looked amazing in her sports crop.

"I think I can guess," Meg said, taking her shoes off.

"I told the front desk to reserve the gym for us," Anna said, taking Meg's hand and leading her to the weights room where she laid down an extra big towel and pushed Meg down.

"Stay," Anna said, taking her hair out and swaying her head a few times to loosen her wavy mane.

"I know that little body of yours will be tired, but you're going to have to keep going for Mommy, do you understand?" Anna said, feeling herself becoming particularly predatory toward Meg as she looked at her laying on the floor as Anna fastened her strap on harness in place.

"Mommy is going to make you cum until the pretty, slutty little body of yours can do nothing but lay there and take it, that pretty pussy leaking as you lay used and spent," Anna said stroking the cock as she bent her knees and knelt above Meg's face. Turning over, Meg felt the silicone push past her lips, making her gag.

"Such a pretty sight to see," Anna moaned, stroking Meg's hair and pushing herself further into Meg's throat.

"You'll learn," Anna said, placing her hand along Meg's throat and feeling how closed it was.

"You need to relax it," Anna said, guiding Meg gently as she pulled back just to slowly push forward once again, smiling as she felt Meg's throat open a little bit more.

"Just like that," Anna said, continuing to train her. Meg's eyes watered as she took Anna, gasping every time she pulled back, shaking her head, and not wanting anymore.

"Shh, you're ok," Anna said, holding Meg in her arms and rocking her gently.

"I'm going to stick it somewhere else now, are you going to be a good little whore for Mommy?" Anna questioned, laying Meg on her back and bringing her knees up to her chest.

"Yes, Mommy," Meg said, feeling her body accept Anna's thick cock, gasping in surprise.

"Did you think you'd be able to stop me, laying in this position?" Anna laughed as she filled Meg and held herself balls deep inside of her as she spoke.

"Nothing you do will be able to stop Mommy," Anna said, beginning to fuck Meg aggressively.

"I want to fucking own this cunt," Anna said, reaching down and pinching Meg's nipples, feeling the girl underneath her drip her cum onto Anna's thighs.

"Yes, Mommy's horny little girl," Anna said, pulling out of Meg, whose cunt leaked down her ass cheeks and onto the towel.

"Get your ass over here," Anna aggressively said as she sat on a bench, her cock sticking out and glistening in Meg's cum.

"Mommy, I'm tired," Meg whined, making Anna's clit throb.

"Oh, I know you are," Anna replied, taking Meg's wrists in her hands and turning the girl around, facing away from her.

"But that doesn't mean I am," Anna said, pulling Meg onto her lap and pushing her hips forward, spearing her cunt with her cock.

"Bounce on Mommy's cock," Anna said, watching as Meg strained to obey her but finding it hard as Anna continued to pull her arms back.

"Good girl," Anna said, beginning to bounce Meg on her lap herself.

"You like that, don't you, getting fucked like the whore you are. Mommy's little whore," Anna said, feeling herself cumming as the harness rubbed against her clit. She wrapped her arms around Meg, pushed her back to the floor and mounted her from behind, relishing the fact that she had to hold Meg up to stop her from collapsing on the floor.

"Just take it," Anna demanded as she pounded into Meg, making herself and Meg cum in unison before putting her down gently on the towel and pulling out of her. Anna smirked as she undid her harness, let it fall to the ground, enjoying Meg flinch as it landed close to her.

"Are you alright?" Anna said, lying down next to Meg, who was sucking her thumb. Anna and Meg had discussed tonight's sex scene, but it had felt different from how Meg had thought it would feel.

"Yep," Meg softly said, as she turned away from Anna.

"Hey. Don't run away from me. Talk to me," Anna said, Meg, turning back to look at her, her eyes filling with tears.

"I don't want to be a whore," Meg said, her tears rolling down her cheeks.

"Oh, sweetie," Anna said, sitting up and pulling Meg into her lap, wrapping her arms around her and holding her in a loving embrace.

"I'm so sorry, baby girl," Anna said, wishing that she had known that Meg had reached her limit and feeling awful.

"I'll never call you that again, sweetie," Anna said, reaching for Meg's hoodie and wrapping it around her body.

"I'm sorry I didn't notice it was affecting you. Why didn't you tell me?" Anna asked, holding Meg close to her breasts.

"Because I wanted to please you," Meg softly said, looking up at Anna.

"But it doesn't baby girl. You putting yourself in situations that you don't like doesn't please me at all. In fact, I feel the opposite," Anna explained, making Meg cry again and bury her face in Anna's breasts.

"Oh, my silly little girl," Anna said, rocking Meg in her arms until she settled.

"Let's go upstairs and get you all clean and settled," Anna said once Meg had stopped crying. Meg nodded and put her clothes back on, followed Anna in silence back up to the apartment and took a shower by herself. Coming out, she put on her pajamas and sat on the lounge where Anna was waiting for her.

"Do you know what you need? Can you tell me how I can make you feel better?" Anna asked. She had also showered and sitting in her normal house clothes. Meg smirked, knowing exactly what she needed and wanted, nodding her head.

"Well? Tell Mommy," Anna said, tilting her head down to meet Meg's gaze.

"I want to be mean to you," Meg softly said, Anna laughing, looking up at the ceiling and nodding her head as she looked back at Meg.

"Alright. Give me your best," Anna said, making Meg laugh.

"Come on. Tell me what you need to, that Mommy is a bitch, that I hurt your feelings," Anna said, sitting up tickling Meg.

"That you're the whore," Meg said, making Anna gasp and look at her wide-eyed in amusement.

"Ok, there you go," Anna said. She was so surprised by how she was reacting.

Wow, the old me would have never treated a girl like this, I would have been pissed she didn't tell me to stop and would have shut her down, but this is so much fun, Anna thought to herself.

"Wow, Mommy's a whore," Anna said, nodding her head and digesting the words making Meg giggle.

"You're not, Mommy," Meg said, smiling at Anna and melting her heart.

"No?" Anna said, opening her arms and having Meg cuddle into her.

"No. You're a predatory slut sure, but not a whore," Meg

giggled, Anna looking at her in shock.

"Do you really think so? That is the nicest compliment anyone has ever given me!" Anna joked.

"Yeah, but I like it. Coz, you make me feel all protected and safe," Meg said, snuggling into Anna.

"I'm glad I make you feel safe even though I pushed you too far tonight," Anna said, making the conversation return to a serious manner.

"I'll say something next time," Meg said, making Anna smile.

"I'd like that. And I will learn your limits the longer we keep doing this," Anna said, causing Meg to sit up.

"I don't want this to end," she said, looking fearful.

"No darling, either do I. I just meant that the more time I spend with you and your gorgeous body, the more I will learn how what your limits are. Oh god no, I don't ever want to give you up are you kidding me!" Anna replied, making Meg relax back into her arms.

Chapter 8

Meg had been dreading this day from the moment she had organized it. When one of her friends, Skyla, had messaged, asking if she and Meg could catch up for a coffee, Meg just knew that it would be some sort of ambush. She had learned that with these girls, and although she had wanted to be their friend, she had lost more than she had ever gained by being around them. As Meg got dressed, she tried to think back to the way things used to be, trying to decide for one last time if it was worth being in these women's lives or if it was best just to walk away.

They always treated you like an afterthought. They didn't care what they took from you, and they thought it was fun to have you around because you made them look cooler. You are clearly the most attractive out of all of them, that's probably why that bitch wanted your ex so that she could prove she was better than me or something, Meg thought to herself as she did her make-up.

But I mean, the worst part about the whole thing, is that I thought that was what I deserved! I actually thought I deserved to be treated like I was nothing, only to be used and then hurt like my feelings didn't matter. Why am I even fucking with the idea of seeing Skyla? She was one of the nice ones at the start, but that all changed, didn't it? Meg continued to think to herself as she walked out the door and checked her phone.

"Shit, I'm late," she said out loud as she pulled her coat around her tighter as a breeze picked up and swept the leaves up around her feet. Meg passed the stores and people, feeling the strange sensation of happiness for the first time without Anna.

I can't wait to tell her, Meg thought to her self, wondering what Anna was doing at that very moment. She reached into her pocket and took out her phone, just to put it back again, remembering that Anna didn't like to be interrupted when she was working.

In the past, that would have made me feel so sad that I couldn't contact the one person in the whole world that I wanted to. But look at me now, on my way to handle some shit, have my whole world in order, and everything seems to be going right for the first time. I feel like I am really getting this shit show sorted, Meg happily and proudly thought to herself as she pushed on the glass door to the café.

"Hey, sorry I'm late," Meg said, panting slightly. She took her coat and scarf off, pulled out the chair, and sat down.

"Babe, where the hell have you been?!" Skyla questioned, looking at Meg expectantly.

"So. You'll never guess, you remember that seriously hot woman from the airport last Sunday? The one who wanted the sugar and then who I ended up sitting next to?" Meg said, jogging Skyla's memory.

"Yeah, the one who was a bit older, with the eyes," Skyla said, remembering how piercing Anna's green eyes were.

"Yep. Well, after I got all my shit and walked away from you guys, I took out the business card she gave me and called her. And I've been staying at hers ever since," Meg said, looking over the menu as she waited for Skyla to process the information.

"Hold up. So you meet someone on a plane, and then they just put you up? Damn, the sex you must be giving her must be amazing," Skyla said, raising her eyebrows and shaking her head. Meg paused for a moment, mostly so that she wouldn't reach across the table and slap Skyla's smug face but secondly because she hadn't thought that Skyla would be so vicious so early into their conversation.

"It's not even like that. She is a. She gets me. I guess we are together actually," Meg said, realizing for the first time that she was potentially in a relationship.

"I like, don't mean to burst this happy bubble you've found yourself in, but like, what does she get out of having you there in her house?" Skyla seriously asked, putting her menu down and looking at Meg in the eye. This was not how Meg thought the lunch date would go at all. She had assumed that

Skyla would be subtle with her rudeness, but no, here she was, shooting Meg down without a care in the world about how it might make her feel.

"I can't get into it. But we give each other what the other person wants and needs. You wouldn't understand," Meg said before ordering a sandwich.

"No, what I understand is that you got with this woman, probably know next to nothing about her and haven't spoken to any of your friends in like, four days," Skyla said, folding her arms across her chest.

"I'm sorry you feel that way," Meg muttered to herself and shook her head.

"You know, I thought you'd be happy for me. Alex kicked me out, remember, I had nowhere to go and Anna," Meg said, getting cut off.

"Anna, what? Scooped you up off the street like you were some puppy in need of saving. Do you expect me to believe that?" Skyla said, raising her voice and frowning at Meg.

"You know what? I don't care what you fucking believe. She was there for me when no one else was, and I was prepared to put all the aside and try to start fresh," Meg said, raising her voice to match Skyla's.

"We told you that you could crash with any one of us," Skyla defensively said.

"Yeah. And I am so grateful I didn't take up the offer

you backstabbing, bunch of bitches who sided with that fucking slut. I saw the photos, Skyla. I know all about the party on Friday night. How all of you went around to Alex's place and hung out all together like it was no big fucking deal," Meg said, slamming her hand down on the table. She hadn't sworn in over a week, and she had to admit, it felt damn good.

"Whatever. This was a mistake coming here. I hope you and your old lady have a great time together," Skyla said, getting up just as Meg's sandwich was put down in front of her.

"Yeah, I'm going to need this to go," Meg said to the waitress, getting up to put her coat and scarf back on before heading to the counter to pay.

Meg walked to the park, trying to block out the words Skyla had used.

She's just jealous. They are all jealous. Anna is awesome who cares about how we met, Meg thought to herself as she found an empty park bench and took out her sandwich.

She doesn't understand. None of them would. It's impossible to find a Mommy. Let alone one who is super rich, super beautiful, and super amazing in bed and as a Mommy. And we have things in common. We both like movies, and we both think that bourbon is better than Scotch, Meg thought, watching as the people passed her. She continued to eat her sandwich, never checking the time until she got a phone call, her phone vibrating in her pocket.

"Hey baby girl, where are you?" Anna said down the phone. Meg smiled as she heard the concern in Anna's voice.

"Well, I'm sitting in a park, eating my sandwich that I got to go because all my friends are crap, and I hate them all," Meg said, feeling sorry for herself.

"Oh. Do you want some company? It's getting dark. Are you somewhere safe?" Anna asked. Meg turned around to see that the park was darker than she had registered it being, the park lights having come on long ago.

"Um, I'm just in the park, by the water on the side closest to our, your place," Meg said.

"Baby, it's your place too. Ok. Can Mommy come down and sit with you?" Anna said. She had planned a night of pillow fort making but figured that Meg would need a different kind of loving tonight.

"Yeah, I'd like that," Meg said as she sniffed back a tear.

See? Anna is perfect, Meg thought as she hung up and waited for Anna to join her.

"There you are," Anna said, jogging up to Meg.

"Were you out for a run?" Meg asked as Anna came to sit next to her.

"No. I just thought it would be quicker to run here than to walk," Anna said, wrapping an arm around Meg.

"So, talk to me," Anna said, taking out her Air Pods and putting them in her jogging jacket.

"So I met up with Skyla, and she pretty much just told me that it was weird that we only just met and moved in together like we were going too fast or something. She made it sound as though there was something suspicious about you or whatever," Meg said. She was annoyed that she had let Skyla get to her, as far as Meg was concerned she didn't have any friends anymore. They had all, for some reason, taken Alex's side. The various messages saying that she had been a shit girlfriend, that at least he was happy now and that she should try and just let it go so they could all hang out like old times was proof enough for her that those girls were never her friends.

"How do you feel about it all? I know it's a bit strange that we clicked right away, and it was fortunate for me, at least that you needed a place to stay. Do you think I crept on you too hard? Do you want me to help you get set up in your apartment?" Anna said. Hearing herself made her stomach churn.

Why am I suggesting any of this? I don't want to lose her, she thought to herself, sweeping the hair out of Meg's eyes.

"No. I don't want any of that. I just, I don't know. It just sucks that I lost all my friends," Meg said, bringing her knees up to her chest and holding onto them tightly.

"Can I offer a different perspective?" Anna asked, turning her body to face Meg and resting her arm on the back of the bench. Anna loved that her breasts pushed into Meg's arm, knowing that Meg would love it too and smiling when she put her legs down to snuggle into Anna.

"Sure," Meg softly said, holding onto Anna. Anna kissed the top of Meg's head, loving the sweet smell of her perfume.

"Maybe they weren't meant to be your friends forever. Maybe they were just friends until you found something more aligned with who you are and where you want to take your life?" Anna said, causing Meg to look up at her.

"But it hurts," Meg said, her whiny voice making Anna smile.

"Oh, I know it does, baby girl. I know it does," Anna said, rocking Meg gently in her arms as she remembered the countless people she had lost along the way. People who disguised themselves as friends only to let her down. Anna took a deep breath before kissing Meg on the cheek.

"Come on. Come home with me and let me look after you tonight," Anna said, holding out her hand to Meg.

"Why do you even like me so much?" Meg said as she got up and took Anna's hand, remembering the question Skyla had posed to her. Anna stopped walking and turned Meg by the shoulders to look at her. Meg knew that she was either in serious trouble for asking. Either that or that Anna was about to talk about something serious by the look in her eye. Either way, Meg knew that Anna was deciding on how serious she was about to be.

"You give my heart a reason to feel. Before I met you, sure I had my fun, but I never felt that my heart truly felt. You changed that. You give me an outlet to be soft, kind, loving, and gentle instead of overly dominating and viewing everything as a hunt. You bring out the best in me," Anna said, tears forming in her eyes. Meg gasped, surprised that Anna was being so forthcoming and stood frozen, processing the words.

"My walls just crumbled down when I met you," Anna said, wiping her tears away and smiling at Meg before retaking her hand and beginning to walk out of the park.

"You should see the way the other people at the office scurry out of my way, as though I will open my mouth and breathe fire on them. They call me the dragon lady. But knowing that I have the sweetest baby girl to come home to, I can feel myself transition in the car drive home, and by the time I am opening up that front door, I know who I want to be," Anna explained leading Meg out onto the street. Meg turned her head, surprised they were going the wrong way home.

"Um, Mommy?" Meg questioned, Anna, continuing to walk, her grip on Meg's hand tightening.

"I think we need to get you some new friends, and I know just the place," Anna said, smiling down at Meg. Anna loosened her grip, feeling Meg struggling to break free.

"So all that stuff you just said, that's how you feel about me?" Meg asked, making Anna laugh as she pushed the door open to a dark and rough looking pub.

"Yeah. I hope you can handle Mommy getting a little bit emotional now and then," Anna laughed as she felt Meg wrap her arms around her.

"I liked it," Meg replied, before turning her head toward the open door and looked inside the pub. It looked like a standard pub. Meg thought that Anna had taken her here for a drink, and although she wasn't one to make friends at a pub, she shrugged her shoulders and walked in.

"Get two of whatever you want, honey. I don't care what I drink," Anna said, handing Meg her card before disappearing. Meg smiled. She loved it when Anna gave her her credit card. She ordered two long island iced teas and waited for Anna at the bar. As she looked out over the crowd, she started to see it and smirked. This was no ordinary night at an ordinary bar, as Meg had first thought. It was some sort of kink enthusiast gathering. It was the subtle details that gave it away, a leather collar on a girl with a gorgeous pink cocktail dress who had the men watching her as she danced mesmerized. The way a man was standing next to a woman, as he waited patiently, looking at the ground while she spoke to a friend. Another woman was lazily petting the head of a man sitting on a bench as she stood next to him. As Meg's eyes slowly scanned the crowd, she saw Anna walking across the dance floor and join a group of women talking in a circle.

I guess they are the Mommies, Meg thought as she saw the cuddly figures of the women. Meg could also tell by the energy they gave off. It wasn't the stern or predatory gaze that the other groups of people had. It was soft, gentle, but with just enough control that you knew not to mess with them. Anna caught Meg's eye and winked at her before excusing herself and walking in Meg's direction.

"Baby girl, I want you to meet some of my friends," Anna said, taking her drink in one hand and Meg's wrist in the other.

"Ok," Meg replied, Anna, stopping immediately.

"Oh, I didn't think you would be shy about it. Do you get shy when you meet new people, baby girl?" Anna said, enjoying learning this about Meg, who nodded her head.

"Well. You don't need to be. There isn't any protocol here tonight, that's why there are so many people from so many kinks. It's just a night where everybody can make it as kinky or vanilla as they like. So just be yourself, and if your little self comes out, then Mommy will look after you, alright?" Anna said lovingly. Meg was wildly aware that the group of women were looking at her and bit her lip before nodding her head and walking behind Anna as they approached the group.

"This is Meg. This is Rachael, Belinda, and Carmen," Anna said, introducing the women. Meg politely smiled, sipped her drink as she listened to their conversation. Anna had known these women for a long time as Meg heard them sharing stories from years ago.

As the night grew on, Meg began to get increasingly drunk, enjoying the feeling of finally being able to relax.

"I've had the world's craziest week," Meg said to a guy she had just met.

"Really? Tell me about it?" He asked. Meg just laughed and shook her head.

"I don't even know your name!" She said, causing Anna to turn around, watching the two talk.

"It looks like you little one and mine are getting along," Anna said to Carmen, who turned to look as well.

"That's sweet. It's what you wanted, wasn't it? That Meg finds some people that she has something in common with," Carmen said as they turned back around to finish their conversation.

"I'm Garret. I'm with Carmen," Garret said, pointing to where she was sitting.

"Like with with, or like, with, you know," Meg said, beginning to blush.

"Like, yeah, she's my Mommy," Garret said. He rarely said that out loud, but hearing himself say it made him smile.

"So, now you know my name, what's yours," Garret asked, ordering another beer.

"Meg," Meg replied, sipping her drink.

"So my week went like this. I find out my boyfriend is cheating on me with my ex-best friend, I meet Anna in a café, and then we sit next to each other on the plane ride home and then she gives me her business card and says to call her if I need her," Meg said, pausing as Anna and Carmen came over.

"And then we lived happily ever after," Anna said, kissing Meg on the mouth.

"Dude, do you know how lucky you are?" Garret said, coping a whack on the back of his head.

"I know I'm lucky," Garret said, rubbing his head.

"No, my rude little boy is right," Carmen said, eyeing Garret.

"Anna has turned down many little offers, you must be something pretty special," Carmen said, smiling at Meg. Meg wrapped her arm around Anna's waist and hugged her tight. In her drunken state, she was worried that if she let Anna go, somebody else might come and take her heart.

"Ready to go?" Anna asked, paying the tab off and putting her card in her purse. Just as she saw a group of women in latex dresses, walk in catching Meg's eye.

"I'd say it was time for us to go too," Carmen said, laughing at the way Garret and Meg looked at the women.

"Where are they going?" Meg whispered to Anna as the women walked up the stairs of the outdoor area.

"Someplace where you are not. It's way past your bedtime," Anna said, making Meg giggle.

"Mommy," Meg cooed, trying her hardest to change Anna's mind.

"Don't Mommy me, young lady," Anna said in the tone that made Meg squash any desire to continue to test her. Anna held out her hand and smiled as Meg jumped down from her stool and walked out her with, onto to the street.

"We will have to have a play date sometime," Carmen said, holding Garret's hand. Garret was bigger than Carmen, and anybody looking at the pair would think their dynamic was the other way around, especially when Garret shoved a guy out of the way when he bumped into them.

"Watch it, bro," Garret said, looking at the guy with a challenging stare. Garret had big muscles from years as a personal trainer, and the other guy thought it better not to pick a fight with him.

"Oh, my sweet baby boy," Carmen said, kissing Garret's chest before turning back to Anna and Meg.

"Yeah, well. What about Tomorrow afternoon? That way, if the babies get too tired, you can stay over?" Anna offered, Carmen agreeing and the two women kissed each other on the cheek before they parted ways for the night.

"Mommy," Meg softly said as she walked alongside Anna, who was walking very fast to get out of the cold.

"Yes?" Anna said, looking straight ahead.

"What if I'm like, what if he is more of a real baby, and I'm like, a fake or something?" Meg nervously said. Anna wished it wasn't so cold so she could stop walking and give Meg the undivided attention the question begged.

"Baby girl. There is no right or wrong way to be little. I know littles who live the headspace 24/7, and I know littles who only have a stuffie. It's the same with Mommies too. Everybody is different, and even if Garret and Carmen do things differently to us, it doesn't make them right or wrong. It doesn't make us right or wrong, it just means that what we do is right for us, and they do what is right for them," Anna explained, grateful to be inside the elevator of the apartment.

"That makes sense," Meg softly said, thinking about the words Anna said.

"And anyway, you are such a baby, what are you even worried about," Anna teased opening the door to the apartment and looking over the mess of toys and bottles Meg had failed to tidy up before she had left the house.

"You know. Mommy did tell you not to leave the house looking like a mess, did I?" Anna said, the warning in her tone mixed with the alcohol running through Meg's veins, making her unsure if she was going to hate or love what came next.

"Yes, but I thought that I'd be home before you got home. I thought I had time to tidy it up," Meg said, impressed at the case she was putting forward.

"And yet, despite what you thought, Mommy still sees a mess," Anna whispered, stripping Meg of any confidence she had that she would get out of this situation without her ass being spanked.

Anna walked to the bathroom, stripped her clothes off, and put on her high heels, sighing in content as she ran her hands over her body. She walked to her bedroom, took out her flogger before walking back to the living room, where she saw Meg trying to tidy up.

"Oh, nice try," Anna laughed, enjoying the frenzied pace Meg was going.

"Get your ass over here," Anna said, her angry Mommy tone making Meg stop dead in her tracks. Anna sat down on the lounge, picked up Meg's paci, and patted her thighs, waiting for Meg to obey her.

"You know, little girls who break Mommy's rules make me mad," Anna said, pushing the pacifier into Meg's mouth and holding her arm around Meg's neck and her hand firmly placed on Meg's mouth.

"So this is what I'm going to do. Your little ass is going to be flogged until it is so red, that every time you think about breaking one of Mommy's rules, you remember how much this hurt and you do everything, and I mean everything in your power not to break my rules again," Anna said, bringing her flogger down on Meg's ass and getting turned on immediately by the squeal it elicited from Meg.

"That's what I want to hear little girl," Anna said, flogging Meg three more times before she stopped and rubbed her ass cheeks.

"Let Mommy see how red you are," Anna said, pulling down Meg's pants, smiling as she saw her pussy glisten.

"Does this turn the baby on?" Anna whispered as she slid her finger up and down Meg's wet slit making her moan against Anna's hand. Arching her back, Meg ached to be touched, making Anna laugh.

"Do you think, after you broke Mommy's rule, I am going to reward you by touching your pussy?" Anna said, pushing two fingers into Meg suddenly, making her moan.

"Is that what you want? To be fucked by Mommy," Anna said, pounding Meg hard and fast before pulling out of her just as she felt herself reach the edge of her orgasm. Groaning in frustration, Meg bucked her hips aggressively, stopping once she felt the flogger strike her ass.

"Don't get greedy," Anna said, waiting for the sting she knew Meg would have just felt subside slightly before flogging her again.

"So red, so wet, I bet you would do almost anything to stop this and have your pussy fucked instead," Anna said, kissing the top of Meg's head before flogging her again. Anna put her whip down, grabbed Meg by the hair, and pulled her into a room she hadn't been into.

"You are so lucky to be coming in here," Anna said, unlocking the door. Meg's eyes grew wide as she saw the space. Taking out her paci, Meg looked around the room.

"Mommy?" Meg questioned, seeing the BDSM

dungeon.

"I have a few kinks," Anna said, pushing Meg down on the bed. She cuffed Meg's wrists and ankles to the bedposts before standing back and looking at Meg.

"Such a beautiful little body," Anna cooed, taking a clit suction vibrator out of her cupboard. She replaced the paci with the dildo end of the toy, enjoying how Meg began sucking it straight away.

"Such a good girl," Anna cooed, watching her get it wet before taking it out and sliding it into Meg's pussy.

"You know how to take it, don't you little one," Anna teased, taking a pair of latex panties and gently dressing Meg, pulling them on over the toy, which was now also sucking on her clit. Anna loved hearing the moans coming from Meg, but worried that the neighbors might make a noise complaint, she took a gag and placed it in her mouth.

"Mommy is going to keep you like that while I finish tidying up the mess I shouldn't have had to see," Anna said, tenderly touching Meg's body and kissing her down her body before she shut the door leaving Meg in darkness as she was forced to orgasm over and over.

Anna knew that after ten minutes, Meg would be ready to fuck her way to freedom. She loved that about the girl, she sure knew how to use her body. Coming back into the room, Meg was blinded by the hallway light, closing her eyes as she felt another orgasm pulse through her body.

"What pretty little sounds," Anna cooed, coming to sit down next to Meg.

"Mommy doesn't think you've learned your lesson, I can see how hard your nipples are through your sweater," Anna teased, running her hands over Meg's breasts.

"No bra today? You were feeling little," Anna said, reaching under, delighted to find Meg's exposed breasts. Anna uncuffed Meg's ankles and wrists, happy that the girl stayed still once she was freed.

"Mommy has a special surprise for you. I must have known when I started taking the pills that I would have a little girl who needed me soon enough," Anna said, taking her top and bra off. She played with her breasts, loving how Meg moaned as she watched.

"Yeah, I know you love them," Anna said, wondering how she got so lucky to have this gorgeous creature so obsessed with her.

"Let me taking this off," Anna said, reaching for the gag, pulling Meg onto her lap and pushing her nipple into Meg's mouth, holding her head firmly in place. Anna smiled down at Meg as Meg's eyes grew wide, not expecting to taste milk.

"Now you won't have to drink from a bottle, you can drink from Mommy just the way you need little girl," Anna said, stroking Meg's face. Meg closed her eyes as another orgasm hit her, suckling hard as her body went rigid then fell limp in Anna's arms.

"I know baby girl," Anna said as Meg began to shake her head, signaling to Anna that her limit was wildly close to being reached. Anna loved that Meg held her breast with both hands as she rolled down the latex panties and pulled the toy from her cunt, leaving both of them in a pile on the bed.

"Mommy's pretty girl," Anna cooed, surprised at how connected she felt to Meg, who looked up at her with her big eyes as she suckled.

Chapter 9

"Is this ok?" Meg said, running down the hallway for the third time to show Anna her latest outfit choice.

"If I had known a simple get together would have turned into this, I wouldn't have suggested it," Anna said, the amusement showing on her face.

"Mommy, I don't have time for this, they are going to be here in like ten minutes," Meg half squealed as she twirled for Anna. This time she had opted for her combat boots, black denim mini skirt, and the fluffy pink sweater that Anna had first noticed her in.

"Well, if you want Mommy's clit to be hard for you the whole time, then yes, this is the outfit for you," Anna said, grabbing the hem of Meg's skirt and pulling her closer to her before touching her through her panties.

"Mommy," Meg whined, feeling Anna pull her panties to the slide and tease her pussy lips open just as a knock came from the door.

"Saved by the bell," Anna whispered in Meg's ear, getting up and walking toward the door.

"Guess that's what you are wearing," Anna said, turning around and winking at Meg before opening the door.

"Carmen," Anna greeted, opening her arms and warmly embracing the woman. Meg peaked her head around the corner.

"Oh, sweetie, Garret will be here shortly. He is just training a client at the moment," Carmen said, smiling warmly at Meg, who gave her a sad sideward smile before going out to the patio.

"So, drink?" Anna said, leading Carmen into the living room. Anna smiled at Meg, who sat on her phone in the afternoon winter sun.

"She's a sweet girl," Carmen said, eyeing Meg.

"Don't even think about it. She's all mine," Anna said, making Carmen laugh.

"Anyway, I'd of thought you'd have your hands full with Garret, quite literally," Anna said, drawing subtle attention to the monster she knew Garret was packing.

"Yeah. It's been a bit weird between us lately. I'm not sure what to think of it. Everything just seems so predictable," Carmen said, sipping the cocktail Anna had made them both moments before she had arrived.

"I get that. I worry about that with Meg, especially since it was going at 100 miles per hour, the minute we got together. I was worried for a moment that it would be a fast-burning candle and that it would be over as quickly as it started," Anna said, admiring how Meg's blonde hair was swept up in the wind.

"He has taken on more clients, working later than he ever has. He says it's because he wants to grow his reputation and client base, but it feels as though he is almost trying to get away from me," Carmen said, sighing.

"I don't know, maybe I'm being paranoid or something," Carmen quickly added.

"I don't think you are. These feelings often have some truth to them," Anna said, making Carmen laugh.

"That doesn't make me feel any better," she said, Anna just smirking.

"If you want to be soothed, let me get you a pacifier to suck on, you know me better than to bullshit with you," Anna teased making Carmen roll her eyes.

"You know. I know why Meg is so smitten with you, you are the only woman I know who can make another Mommy feel like a little with one sentence. That is some damn fine mind work you are wielding," Carmen said, getting up to get another drink.

"So, what do you think you should do?" Anna said, taking a strawberry from the bowl in front of her.

"I don't know any suggestions?" Carmen said, making Anna laugh.

"You know, you just don't want to do it," Anna said, looking up as she saw Meg walk through the glass doors. Patting her lap, Anna uncrossed her legs and smiled as Meg settled against her.

"You need to show him who is boss. Who he belongs to and what happens when he breaks a rule. It sounds to me like he has broken quite a few, not communicating his needs with you, withholding his truth, and the biggest one, wasting your goddamn time trying to figure out what his bratty, moody ass is up too," Anna said making Meg smirk.

"Mommy, you swore," Meg whispered, making Anna chuckle.

"Mommy can do what she wants, you on the other hand," Anna said, squeezing Meg tight.

"Withholding his truth?" Meg asked, turning her head to face Anna.

"We aren't at that stage yet, baby girl, it'll come but not yet," Anna said, reassuring Meg. She knew that Meg would be thinking about that for the next few hours, and Anna stroked her thigh lovingly, not wanting Meg to let her mind run off with thoughts that she wasn't doing something right.

"You're welcome to use the dungeon if you need to," Anna offered just as a knock came from the door.

"I might take you up on that offer," Carmen said, getting up to open the door.

"Hey, sorry I'm late," Garret said, walking into the room and passed Carmen. Anna wasn't impressed at the lack of attention he gave Carmen. She was even less impressed by how his eyes lit up when he saw Meg. As Garret walked over to greet Meg, Anna shifted her on her lap and held a foot out, stopping him.

"Go and kiss your Mama hello," Anna said, Garret's face falling before he turned and walked back to Carmen. Carmen and Anna had discussed how this afternoon would go, and as Anna looked at Meg's wide eyes, she knew that it was going to be fun.

"What is happening?" Meg whispered in Anna's ear as her head rested on her shoulder.

"This is what happens to naughty boys who don't listen to their Mommy's. It takes a village, after all, little girl," Anna replied, stroking Meg's back.

"But I've been good?" Meg asked, making Anna's heart swell.

"Yes, baby girl, you've been perfect," Anna replied, kissing her on the tip of her nose before turning her head to watch Garret and Carmen. Garret had leaned forward to kiss Carmen on the lips, wincing as she slapped his cheek.

"Try again," Carmen said, her frustration evident in her voice. Garret shifted from foot to foot, not wanting to get in wrong again and slowly bent his knees until he knelt before Carmen, who had her hand on her hips.

"Lower," Carmen instructed when Garret tried to kiss her pussy. He bit his bottom lip and placed his hands on the floor as he looked up from Carmen's feet, she raised eyebrow telling him that he finally got it right.

"Don't make wait any longer," Carmen said, watching as

Garret blushed and began to kiss her boot as her other foot rested on his back, keeping him in place.

"I didn't think littles would like that," Meg softly said, only realizing that she was sucking her thumb when she tried to speak. Making Anna hum happily.

"As I said, it depends on the people involved. Garret is a strong-willed little. He can be the best little boy in the world, but my god does he have a stubborn streak, and this has been the best way he has learned to correct that bratty behavior. There's always something you can learn about yourself, like how you learned you don't like being called a whore. He learned through experience that to get back to being good. He needs a strong hand," Anna explained as she watched Carmen switch boots.

"You know," Anna loudly said, winking at Meg and patting her bottom to get her to stand up before standing up herself and walking over to Carmen and Garret.

"I don't think he deserves these nice clothes you buy him," Anna said, reaching down and roughly stripping him. Meg was surprised at Anna's strength. She never used such a firm hand on her. Carmen crossed her arms and enjoyed watching Anna tear at Garret's clothes until he was naked.

"There. If you are going to act like a naughty little boy, that's exactly how you are going to be treated," Anna said, kicking his clothes away. Garret stood standing in front of the women naked, covering himself, which just made Carmen laugh.

"Oh, don't hide it away when you were so happy swinging it around to try and impress little Meg," Carmen said, making him blush.

"That's what I thought," Carmen said, looking over at Meg, who shifted uncomfortably.

"I didn't mean to make him think he had a chance," Meg said, Anna, smiling in amusement.

"Oh no, sweetie, that's just it. This naughty boy thinks he has a chance with everyone, don't you? Have you forgotten who looks after you? Who buys your clothes, who soothes you when you get nightmares and wipes your tears away when you feel scared?" Carmen said, turning back to face Garret.

"I. I'm sorry, Mommy," Garret said, feeling himself being pulled into little space. He sighed, finally feeling relief and dropped his head.

"There you are. Mommy's good little boy. Did all those weights and protein shakes and skinny girls in tight leggings make you forget that Mommy is the one who looks after you?" Carmen said, going softer on him than Anna would have.

"Yes, Mommy. I just," Garret said, blushing and looking up.

"I just thought I was the man and thought that I didn't need you to be my Mommy anymore. But I was wrong," Garret said, beginning to cry. Anna raised her eyebrow and headed back to Meg, who was standing as still as a statue.

"Come on, little one," Anna softly said, taking the bowl of strawberries in one hand and Meg's hand in the other and led her outside to the patio and curled up with her on the day bed.

"What just happened?" Meg asked before Anna put a strawberry in her mouth.

"Like, if he wanted to break up with her, why didn't he just say?" Meg said as she gulped the fruit so she could finish her question.

"He never wanted to leave her. It's kind of like. Sometimes when a little stays out of little space for a long time, they can start to be bratty because they miss being a little. They miss the relief of it. But work can get in the way, life can just happen so fast, and before you know it, you're a brat to try and push the other person into giving you attention because you don't know how to ask for what you want. It can happen when two people have been together for a long time. Then they start fighting and then sometimes if they don't fix it they break up. But this was easily fixed," Anna explained as Meg listened attentively.

"So, he never wanted to leave her? He just wanted to be little but couldn't get into little space?" Meg asked, clarifying what Anna just described.

"In this situation, yeah. But you need to understand, they have been together for ten years, they know each other well. They have the understanding that I can be a part of their dynamic to a certain degree. I know it seemed like it was all spontaneous, but it was all planned last night when you were asleep. I'm sorry I didn't tell you, do you think that I should have?" Anna asked, suddenly realizing that she really should have told Meg a few key points about the afternoon.

"Um, yes!" Meg exclaimed, laughing.

"Hello? I just saw a stranger naked," Meg continued making Anna laugh.

"Yeah, ok, my bad, can you forgive Mommy?" Anna said, making Meg laugh.

"I think you need to be punished, Mommy," Meg teased, getting tickled by Anna.

"Don't make it hurt too much, I have an important meeting on Monday," Anna laughed.

"Oh, no, I'm not going to hurt you there, we are going to go shopping," Meg giggled, Anna, raising an eyebrow.

"What, you told me that half the fun of punishment is the enjoyment it brings both people, and we both like to shop, so," Meg said as Anna began to nod in agreeance.

"Well, I guess we are going shopping," Anna said, watching as the sunset over the city.

Chapter 10

Carmen and Garret came out to the patio an hour later, just as Meg and Anna were about to come inside.

"Thanks, Miss Anna," Garret said, smiling at her bashfully.

"My pleasure, baby boy," Anna replied, reaching out and stroking Garret's face.

"Would you like to stay for dinner?" Anna asked Carmen, who smiled at her gratefully.

"Not tonight, I need to get my little prince home and tucked into bed. It's been a big day for him," Carmen said, hugging Anna affectionately before waving goodbye to Meg and leaving the apartment.

"I never want to be that naughty," Meg said once the door was shut.

"Oh, you'll be plenty naughty, you don't need to worry about that," Anna teased, grabbing at Meg's hem of her skirt.

"Now, where was I," Anna questioned playfully.

"Oh, yes," she continued, feeling Meg's wet slit.

"Mommy," Meg said, pushing Anna's hands away and shaking her head.

"Ok, dinner, bathies, and bedtime cuddles?" Anna said,

making Meg smile.

Anna tidied the kitchen, placing the empty bowl and glasses in the dishwasher before taking two pieces of salmon out of the freezer.

"Fish and chips work for you?" Anna called from the kitchen. Meg had run to the nursery and brought out the train set and was putting the tracks together.

"That sounds yummy, Mommy," Meg replied happily. She knew that it wouldn't be the standard fish and chips. Nothing about Anna was standard as she looked into the kitchen and saw the potatoes being cut and rosemary being sprinkled over the top, she knew that this dinner wouldn't be standard either.

Meg hadn't realized she had fallen asleep until Anna was gently rocking her awake.

"Hey there, little one," Anna said, smiling down on Meg. Meg scrunched her face up and rolled over, rolling onto one of her trains and was suddenly very awake.

"Ouch," she said, turning back to face Anna.

"What time is it?" Meg asked as she rubbed her hand.

"11:00. I wanted to let you sleep, but I need to get you ready for bed, and you weren't waking up," Anna replied, taking Meg's wrist in her hand and standing her up.

"Mommy," Meg said as Anna wrapped her arm around the girl and pulled her smaller body into hers.

"Gosh, you just fit perfectly in my arms," Anna said, stroking Meg's hair out of the way. Anna kissed Meg's forehead before walking with her down the hallway and into the bathroom.

"Just a quick shower tonight, little one," Anna said as she turned the water on before walking out the other side of the open shower and taking her clothes off.

"Mommy, can you help?" Meg said as she wearily pulled on her clothes, making Anna smirk.

"What's the magic word?" Anna questioned as she stood in front of Meg, who had somehow trapped herself in her sweater.

"Please, Mommy," Meg said, feeling Anna's hands on her body, giving her goosebumps as she helped her.

"There," Anna said, taking off Meg's skirt, panties, and bra. Meg had long since taken off her combat boots and socks, and she let Anna tie her hair up as not to get it wet.

"Here, clean your teeth in the shower as well. It'll get you into bed quicker," Anna said, passing Meg her toothbrush.

"Ok," Meg wearily said, wishing the Anna would brush her teeth for her, holding out the toothbrush to her and hoping that Anna would read her mind.

"Does the baby need Mommy to brush her teethies?" Anna said, rinsing Meg's body of any soap.

"Yes, please, Mommy," Meg said as she closed her eyes and melted into Anna's warm embrace as she brushed her teeth.

"Such a sweet little girl," Anna said, letting Meg spit the toothpaste out before turning off the shower.

"Mommy has put the towels on the heating racks baby girl, yours is the blue one," Anna said, pointing to the towel. Meg nodded and went over, taking it down and wrapping herself in it but drying her feet first, making Anna laugh.

"You sure do hate your feet or fingers not being dry, don't you," she said as Meg nodded.

"And other things," Meg said, causing Anna to tilt her head in curiosity.

"Like?" Anna asked as she wrapped her towel around her hips and walked to her bedroom, Meg, in tow.

"Like, I like my diaper dry too," Meg said, referring to a conversation she and Anna had had earlier in the week.

"I see. Still trying to tell Mommy that you're not going to wet your diaper?" Anna said, trying to hide her amusement.

"Yes," Meg said, nodding her head and looking very serious.

"Well, let's just put this on you, just in case," Anna said, taking a thick diaper and putting it on Meg, who huffed and looked away, crossing her arms over her chest.

"Oh, pouty little thing. Does Mommy have to correct that?" Anna said, grabbing hold of Meg's thighs and squeezing.

"No, Mommy," Meg gasped, remembering how long and tiresome Anna made her punishments.

"Good," Anna quickly said, getting up and going to the cupboard, taking out Meg's jammies.

"You are going to look so sweet in these. I picked them up on the way home this week but was waiting until we had some time so I could enjoy them," Anna said, showing Meg the crocodile print flannel pajamas. Meg smiled excitedly and reached for them.

"They have little Sven's on them, Mommy!" Meg exclaimed, melting Anna's heart.

"I know. I thought, who do I know who would like these? Do you know anyone?" Anna teased, pulling the pants over Meg's diaper and rolling them up until they were mid-calf.

"Me, Mommy," Meg squealed, making Anna laugh.

"You are so cute," Anna said, doing the buttons up on the front.

"If there was ever a little girl who could pull off crocodile jammies, it would be you," Anna said, looking at Meg's messy blonde hair, her sweet, ever so kissable lips and big innocent eyes.

"Come on, get under these covers and wait for Mommy to get ready," Anna said as she took both towels back into the bathroom. Meg waited with her thumb in her mouth, her eyelids growing heavy, and as Anna came back into the room, she sighed and smiled.

"Oh, baby girl," she softly said, turning the light off and

walking out into the living room.

It was nearing midnight, but Anna wasn't interested in sleeping. The tension she felt dominating Garret at even the small level she had that day had kept her blood hot, even now. Taking her phone out, she called Carmen, who she knew would still be awake as well.

"Hey. How did it go when you got home?" Anna said as she made herself a tea.

"So good. We had a long talk, turned out he needed me to give him more rules, he didn't think he was serving me enough, even as a little," Carmen replied, as Anna went to sit by the window.

"Aww, he just wanted to serve his Mommy," Anna laughed.

"That's quite sweet," she added.

"Yeah. It was. He was like, I don't feel like I have to do anything like you don't need me," Carmen said, piquing Anna's interest.

"Wow, no wonder he was acting out," Anna said, as she saw Meg walking out to her. Anna reached out to Meg, frowning when she didn't come to her, shaking her head instead.

"Babe, I've got to go. I'm glad it all worked out for you guys," Anna said, hanging up the phone. Anna looked at Meg for a moment, her initial anger that she was ignored fading when she saw the emotional look on Meg's face.

"Mommy," Meg said in her soft, little voice, looking down at her diaper. Meg held onto Sven's tail and sucked her thumb.

"Oh, baby girl," Anna said, lovingly smiling as she learned what Meg was trying to tell her.

"It's ok, sweetie. Mommy can just clean you up and change you," Anna said, standing up and walking over to Meg, who burst into tears.

"But I didn't want to," Meg said, Anna, bending down slightly and wiping her tears away.

"Sometimes, when we are relaxed, these things happen. Come on," Anna said, taking Meg's hand and leading her back into the nursery. Anna directed her to the mat, took off her pajama bottoms, and took off the wet diaper. She wiped Meg clean and sprinkled fresh powder over her, making her giggle as it tickled her body.

"There's my happy little one," Anna said as she fastened a fresh diaper to Meg's waist before pulling on her jammie pants again.

"There. That wasn't so bad, was it?" Anna said, Meg's pursed lips telling her that maybe it was.

"Do you want to cuddle Mommy while you fall back asleep, honey?" Anna asked, already knowing the answer. Meg rubbed her eyes and nodded her head. Anna walked back to the living room to put her mug in the dishwasher as Meg crawled into bed.

"Come to Mommy," Anna said, pulling Meg into her and taking her thumb out of her mouth, smirking when Meg whined.

"Don't whine baby girl, Mommy only takes things away when I'm about to give you something better," Anna said, pushing her nipple pasts Meg's lips and settling her as she closed her eyes and started to suckle.

"Mommy's pretty girl," Anna cooed as she patted Meg's bottom as she fell back asleep in the arms of her loving Mommy.

Mommy's Cuddles

Zara knew what she liked as an ABDL, and she knew she wanted an MDLG relationship. What she didn't know was that finding the perfect Mommy is hard

Tina Moore

Chapter 1

Zara just wanted to cry. It wasn't as though there was anything particularly troublesome or difficult in her life. The clients she had spoken to that day were okay. Her boss was okay and left her alone most of the time. Fiona had even told her that her outfit looked nice after a meeting, which was high praise coming from her. But something was very wrong, even if Zara couldn't put her finger on it.

Maybe I am just feeling a bit overwhelmed in general, like there's nothing specific, but something is wrong, Zara thought to herself. She had finished work for the week and walked down the main street, wishing she could blink and be home. She walked down the busy street, which was filled with bars and restaurants, and deeply inhaled as she smelt the delicious smells.

I know what I need, Zara thought, turning the corner and walking into a Chinese restaurant, hoping that the soul-warming food would bring her comfort. She ordered her usual spring rolls and cashew and chicken dish, before sitting down and waiting for her order to be made. While she waited, she watched the people passing by, all seeming to have somewhere very important to be or something to do that could not wait.

Zara had always loved to watch people. She wondered if she liked to watch them so she could learn how to behave in particular settings. As Zara sat there, she remembered how, when she was younger, she would go to the beach and watch how girls would flirt with boys as they played volleyball, wondering how it seemed to come so naturally to them. Nothing seemed to come naturally for Zara, and her mouth twitched as she looked down at her lap. Taking out her phone, she checked the time and knew that her favorite tv show would be starting soon and smiled as she heard her name being called.

"Perfect, thanks," Zara said as she took the paper bag and walked back out onto the street. She had noticed that when she was in one of these moods, where she felt like the simplest of stares would make her burst into tears, she would act tough. Really, tough. A lot tougher than she was, and she would glare people down until they got out of her way. She had learned that she had an aggressive type of resting bitch face and one which people often wanted to be away from, which suited her just fine.

Opening the door to her apartment, Zara flung her keys in the bowl on the hallway table and kicked off her heels, instantly sighing. Her heels acted like a trigger that when she put them on, her adult costume was complete and that when she took them off, she could finally be her little self. Zara walked to the kitchen, took a fork from the drawer, and sat on the sofa. She knew that she didn't have time to change before her show started, so bringing her knees up to her chest as she ate, she turned on her cartoons. It was during these times where she wondered what it would feel like to have a caregiver. She had watched all the vlogs, subscribed to all the online communities, and read all the stories about loving, tender, comforting Mommies but wondered why none of them seemed to want her as their own.

"I'm cute, right, Ducky?" Zara asked her stuffed duck, which sat next to her. She slightly smiled that she had, for a moment, genuinely thought her stuffie would reply. Shrugging her shoulders and biting into her spring roll, Zara watched her cartoons.

Argh, I've just got so many things on my mind, Zara thought to herself as she rubbed her temples. Although the weekend had been lovely, as she stayed in her blissful, little space, she still didn't feel rested as she sat in her office cubicle at work. The day was dragging on, and as Zara looked at the clock on her computer screen, she cringed.

Another six hours of this shit, she thought to herself, deciding to get up and make herself her third coffee for the morning. She walked passed the office gossips, wondering how they kept their jobs when they only did the bare minimum, reaching the refreshment station just as she saw Fiona come to stand beside her.

"You are going to give yourself a heart condition if you keep drinking coffee like this," Fiona, her colleague half-jokingly said. Zara just rolled her eyes and laughed.

"Well, anything to get me out of this place," Zara replied, stirring in the milk. She walked back to her desk, sat down, and sighed.

This is going to be a long day, she thought before continuing to work.

"Hey, we are all going out for some drinks after work. Apparently, there is a really cool band playing in a really shitty bar," Fiona said to Zara as the end of the day neared. Zara tilted her head, it was only Monday, and she thought it was humorous that they would go drinking so early in the week. She knew all the 'cool' people at work went to bars and clubs on a Friday after work, but she had never been invited. She didn't fit in with their 'look.' While she was naturally beautiful, Zara didn't feel the need to wear makeup or figure-hugging clothes. She preferred to be comfortable and relaxed.

"Okay?" Zara replied, unsure of what Fiona was trying to say, making Fiona roll her eyes.

"So, do you want to come with?" Fiona replied, spelling it out for Zara. Zara thought about the diaper and onesie which awaited her at home. She wasn't about to tell Fiona that, though. Fiona was the hot one at work. Every workplace has one, the ringleader of the 'cool' group. That seemingly untouchable woman who everyone either wants to be or wants to be with and Fiona was that woman. Zara thought it was odd that Fiona was trying to flirt with her, her battering eyelids, and the way her eyes smiled when she looked at Zara made her feel uncomfortable about the attention.

"Yeah, sure," Zara said, finding it hard to turn down a night out, smiling at the wide grin Fiona gave her.

"Great," Fiona said, practically bouncing away.

The bar was loud. Louder than Zara would have liked it to be. It was an unusual spot for young business and law employees to go. Still, they had transformed the smelt of stale beer into the smell of air conditioning, cologne, and money which hit Zara like a slap in the face as she walked into the bar, instantly regretted her choice.

Great, now I have to stay for at least a drink, she thought to herself, fake smiling as Fiona turned around and grinned at her. They found a tight corner and ordered some drinks, Zara grateful that her other colleagues had also decided to come because it meant that she didn't have to say too much. Zara was very good at faking laughing at their jokes, bopping around to music she hated, and generally looking like she was having a good time while wanting nothing more than to leave. Zara had become very good at blending into crowds. She often wondered if people even knew that she was an introvert because she masked it so well.

"Are you having fun?" Fiona asked. Zara could hardly make out the words, but nodded her head and gave a wide grin.

"Yeah, so much. Thanks for inviting me out," Zara replied, making Fiona roll her eyes.

"Come with me," Fiona said, taking Zara by the hand and walking out the back of the bar. The fresh night air hit them, making Zara feel light-headed almost instantly.

"Woah, I needed to get out of there," Fiona said, as Zara found a crate to sit on.

"I thought you were having fun," Zara said, pulling her coat around her.

"I was having about as much fun as you were," Fiona replied with a knowing look on her face. Zara smirked.

"I see," she said as Fiona sauntered toward her. Zara knew that having the hottest woman at work like you had its perks, but she also knew that Fiona wouldn't be able to give her what she wanted, she just didn't seem to be that type of woman that made Zara feel a connection.

"So, I saw the way you were looking at me," Fiona said, taking Zara's hands in hers. Zara sighed and bit her bottom lip.

It's probably a terrible idea to start something with her, Zara thought to herself as a gust of wind made Fiona stumble forward and into Zara's arms.

"Well, you're gorgeous," Zara said, beginning to blush despite the battle raging in her mind.

Maybe some harmless fun is a good thing. It's been ages since anyone has shown an interest in you, Zara thought, leaning forward to kiss Fiona on the lips. Fiona smiled into the kiss, wrapping Zara up in her arms and making Zara moan softly.

"Wanna get out of here," Fiona asked, breaking the kiss just long enough to speak. Zara nodded her head, feeling Fiona take her hand in hers and lead her out onto the street.

They walked quickly, Zara grateful for the pace, hoping that the alcohol would stay in her veins, she felt like she needed the liquid courage.

This is what normal people do, she told herself. Zara had always kept her little side a secret, ashamed of what someone might say if she told them. She certainly didn't want to tell Fiona. Zara imagined the most beautiful woman at work, laughing at her, and it made her cheeks blush red. As they neared Fiona's apartment, Zara inhaled deeply before stopping and kissing Fiona on the lips, wanting the hit of adrenaline to pump through her once more. As Fiona grabbed at her, Zara smiled, hearing her fumble with her keys as she struggled to open the door. Breaking the kiss long enough for Fiona to unlock the door, Zara giggled and followed her inside. She dropped her coat and bag, biting her bottom lip as she grabbed at Fiona's shirt, ripping it off.

"Wow, a little more passionate than I thought you'd be," Fiona said as she took off her bra and continued to walk into her room. Zara just smirked.

"There are a few things you don't know about me," she replied, taking her pants off and walking into Fiona's bedroom. Fiona lay down on the bed, now naked and backlit from the moonlight coming through the window.

"Why don't you show me then," she said, reaching out to Zara, who smirked. Zara lay on top of Fiona, feeling the warmth of her body before kissing her lips and snaking her way down her body, enjoying the wetness of Fiona's pussy as she stuck out her tongue and slowly licked her.

"Oh yeah," Fiona moaned, placing her hand on the back of Zara's head and pressing herself onto her mouth. Zara knew that Fiona would cum quickly as her moans filled the bedroom. Somewhat dissociated, Zara flicked and sucked Fiona's clit, fingering her at the same time as she came hard, almost surprising Zara. She hadn't realized that she was in her own world, somewhat forgetting that she was having sex, which made her laugh.

"Oh my god, it's usually so awkward the first time, but that was amazing," Fiona said, flipping Zara onto her back, just for Zara to push her off slowly. She didn't want to make Fiona feel rejected.

"I don't really feel like it," Zara said, worried that Fiona would think she was strange or something.

"Oh, did I hurt you or something? Are you ok?" Fiona asked, turning the lights on and almost blinding Zara.

"Yeah, I'm good. I don't know, I get weird sometimes like I just like pleasing girls or whatever," Zara said, trying to explain. Fiona looked at her curiously before trying to suppress the look in her eye. The look that would tell Zara more than she was ready to know. Fiona had had suspicions that Zara needed a different kind of experience, but she didn't want to push her into feeling more uncomfortable than she clearly already was feeling.

"Do you maybe want just to cuddle instead?" Fiona softly asked, taking Zara by surprise, the look in her eye telling Fiona that she was definitely onto something.

"Um, yeah, sure," Zara replied, happy when Fiona walked over to her, took her hand, and turned the lights back off.

Chapter 2

"Breakfast?" Fiona asked, waking Zara up. Zara blinked her eyes open, realizing that she had fallen asleep for the whole night and that it was, in fact, a work morning.

"Oh shit," Zara said, hurrying out of bed and putting her clothes back on.

"I can't. I have to go home and change. I can't go to work in the same clothes as yesterday," Zara explained, annoyed that she had let herself stay the night.

"You can just wear some of my clothes," Fiona said, walking to the closet and placing a bowl of yogurt and fruit down on the night table closest to Zara.

"Eat," Fiona said, taking Zara by surprise at the tone in her voice as she picked up the bowl.

"So, this could look cute. You can have a shower, and then we can go to work together," Fiona gleefully said, making Zara roll her eyes. Fiona had a way about her that made everyone fall in love with her almost instantly, and Zara, being as stubborn as she was, had decided to deliberately not fall for Fiona's charms. That, however, was proving to be quite a challenge.

"Thanks for this," Zara said, standing up after she

finished her breakfast and walked into the bathroom. She ran the hot water and stood under the tap. This was not the first time that Zara had felt torn up inside. She could feel her little self begging to come out, but as she rubbed shower gel over her breasts and stomach, she shook her head to try and refocus.

Getting out of the shower, she wrapped a towel around herself and walked back into the bedroom. Fiona was sitting on the edge of the bed, waiting for her.

"So," Fiona said, making Zara nervous.

Did I talk in my sleep? Oh god, what is she going to say? Just deny everything, I mean, heaps of people talk in their sleep. It's your word against hers, I mean, what she even have to gain from telling anyone about, you know, Zara thought in a slight panic.

"So?" Zara calmly replied, getting dressed and trying not to break out in a sweat of uncertainty. Fiona took her time to get up, slowly walked over to Zara, and kissed along her collar bone.

"So, do you want to be my girlfriend?" Fiona asked, making Zara freeze.

"What?" Zara questioned, unsure if she heard correctly, laughing as she looked Fiona in the eye.

"Do you want to be my girlfriend?" Fiona repeated, laughing that she had shocked Zara.

"Um," Zara said, turning back around and continuing to

get dressed.

"I have wanted to ask you for ages. How has everyone else in the office noticed me flirting with you, except for you?" Fiona said, Zara, sighing.

She is stunning. It's not the way I thought I'd find a girlfriend. It's a bit soon. You do like her, though, Zara thought to herself before picking her towel up from the floor.

"Yeah. Okay," Zara replied, kissing Fiona full on the lips, giggling at her squeal of delight. Fiona let her go and happily walked into the kitchen, leaving Zara alone in the bedroom.

"This was not how I thought my week would go," Zara quietly said out loud as she finished getting dressed in somewhat of a daze.

Fiona and Zara caught the train together, made subtle remarks to each other at work, but decided to go to their separate apartments that evening.

"I just really need to be in my own space for a while, babe," Zara said to Fiona in their lunch break.

"Yeah it's cool, I get it," Fiona said, somewhat disappointed that Zara wouldn't be coming over. Fiona always did this, as in got really attached to a girl super quickly. Zara, on the other hand, liked to take her time and really get to know someone before committing to them, which made her wonder why she had agreed to be Fiona's girlfriend in the first place.

"Thanks, I just like, my own bed and stuff," Zara said, kissing Fiona on the cheek before getting up to go back to her cubicle. She could hardly wait to get home, and she spent the next four hours fantasizing about what it would be like the moment she walked through the door.

These awful heels are coming off. I am taking a bath with bubbles and my duckies. I am going to put nuggies in the oven and my cartoons on. I'm going to wear the thickest diaper, and cutest onesie and my milk is going in a bottle. I am going to color and play and build my block towers, Zara thought as she typed away at her keyboard, realizing that for the first time in almost 24 hours, she was genuinely smiling.

Zara took the train home, walked quickly to her apartment, and sighed as she closed the door behind her.

"Thank fucking goodness," she said out loud, sighing as she kicked off her heels and shook her whole body, trying to almost shake the day out of her system. She stripped her clothes off as she walked to the bathroom and dumped them in the wash basket, before turning on the tap. She put the plug in the bath and squirted her pink, glittery bubble bath into the water and watched as the room became a steamy haze of sweet-smelling pink mist.

"Yes, this is what I was looking for!" Zara exclaimed as she lowered herself into the water, instantly feeling better. She slunk herself down and under the water, enjoying how being completely submerged made the world outside become quiet. She re-emerged and smiled to herself.

Maybe not everything is as bad as it feels, Zara thought to herself, playing with the bubbles. She dunked them into the water, tried to make shapes out of them, and splashed around until the water was cold and the mist had long faded. Getting out of the tub, she wrapped herself in her unicorn hooded towel and walked out into the kitchen. Taking out a tray, she set her nuggies out and put them in the oven before she walked into her bedroom and laid down on her bed.

"What should we wear, Ducky?" Zara said out loud, rolling over and taking her duck stuffie in her hands and wrapping her arms around it.

"That's what I thought!" Zara exclaimed, jumping up and walking to her cupboard and taking out a diaper, baby powder, and a light purple onesie. Zara quickly diapered herself, zipped up her onesie, and hung her towel in the bathroom before going back to the kitchen and checking on her nuggies, Ducky, in tow.

Chapter 3

Zara knew that things were going too fast as she approached her desk on Wednesday morning. The big give away was the dozen long-stemmed roses that were elaborately displayed in an elegant box. The other was the champagne and chocolates that proceeded to appear upon her arrival. Zara blushed as her colleagues looked on wistfully, not noticing that while this may have been their fantasy, it wasn't Zara's. As she opened the card which accompanied the gifts, she couldn't help but appreciate that this gesture was what most people would want. That Fiona was simply trying to seduce her, without knowing her well enough to know what would actually work.

I hope you have a beautiful day, sweetheart. I can't wait to see you tonight, read the card, making Zara frown.

What is happening tonight? She thought, racking her brain to try and remember if she had made a plan, remembering nothing.

"You got them then?" Fiona suddenly said, seemingly coming out of nowhere. Zara gasped, wondering how many more surprises she could handle.

"Yeah, I did. Thank you, everything is really lovely. But, maybe next time, a little more, low key?" Zara said, squinting as she said the words, not wanting to offend Fiona but trying to set up a boundary.

"You deserve more than low key. That's why we are going here," Fiona said, missing the subtle hint and making Zara bite her bottom lip, slightly annoyed.

"Where?" Zara asked, holding out her hand to accept the paper invitation that Fiona was waving. Zara looked over the flyer and tilted her head to the side.

"Fiona, really? I have nothing to wear to something like this," Zara said, rolling her eyes and handing it back to her before turning around in her chair.

"Okay, well, we don't have to go. What do you want to do instead?" Fiona asked, scrunching up the flyer and throwing in the trash. Zara thought for a moment, knowing fair well what she wanted to do and smirking to herself before deciding that telling Fiona that she wanted her to Mommy her all night would be way too much.

"Do you want to get take away Mexican and watch a movie at mine?" Zara offered, raising an eyebrow. Fiona, who clearly had to lower her expectations as to what she was expecting to do that evening, nodded her head before leaning forward to kiss Zara full on the lips, making Zara's eyes go wide.

"Text me your address. Oh, what? Nobody cares that we kiss," Fiona said, winking at Zara before getting up and walking away.

I fucking care! Zara thought to herself as she angrily turned around to face her computer screen.

Zara had spent the rest of the day wondering if she would bother to text Fiona her address, but at 4:30 in the afternoon that Fiona called back into Zara's cubicle and spun her office chair around.

"So, what time do you want me to come over?" Fiona asked, sitting on the edge of Zara's desk and folding her arms across her chest.

"Like, 7?" Zara said, writing down her address on a post-it note and handing it to Fiona.

"Okay. Sorry if I rushed you or something," Fiona said, taking the note and putting it into her pocket. Zara gave her a heartfelt smile, standing up and straddling Fiona's thighs as she embraced the other woman.

"I'm not like the other girls here," Zara softly said, kissing Fiona's cheek. Fiona looked at her with sad eyes and nodded her head.

"Yeah, I know, that's what I like about you," Fiona replied, wrapping her arms around Zara.

"Then, you'd know that I am quiet, I like, I don't know, quiet stuff," Zara laughed, enjoying how Fiona looked at her.

"I'll keep that in mind next time I decide to announce us to the entire office," Fiona replied, feeling guilty for making Zara feel uncomfortable.

"Thanks," Zara answered, sitting back down in her chair.

"See you tonight," she said, glad when Fiona took the hint and left her alone to finish her work.

What the hell was I thinking!? Zara thought as she whipped around her apartment, trying to hide any trace of her being a little.

Oh, great. Come over Fiona, just excuse all the cartoon themed pillows on my bed, Zara thought, collecting them all and throwing them into her cupboard before turning around and searching for anything that didn't seem fitting for a 29-year-old's room. Rolling her eyes to herself and shaking her head, she kicked Ducky under the bed as she saw his little tail sticking out.

"Sorry, Ducky," Zara whispered as she left her room and continued to de-little her apartment.

I need to stop buying so much stuff, Zara thought to herself as she put her princess printed blankets in the storage chest that she used as a coffee table.

"Okay. Good," Zara said out loud to nobody, trying to reassure herself but feeling like she was about to cry just as a knock came from the front door. Running to the door, she opened it and smiled as she saw Fiona.

"Low key enough?" Fiona said, opening her arms to show Zara her outfit. Fiona had her navy sweatpants on, her flip flops, and a gray hoodie over the top of a tight white t-shirt. Her red hair was in a messy ponytail, and she wore natural makeup. Zara smirked, she hadn't thought that Fiona owned anything apart from high-end luxury fashion brands and definitely didn't think she owned any natural-looking makeup. It was a stark contrast to her usual, almost runway model makeup she wore at work.

"Yeah, perfect," Zara replied, smiling excitedly and moving out of the way, so Fiona was able to walk inside, closing the door behind her. Fiona walked to the middle of the living room and stopped, turning around to face Zara.

"Come here," she said, taking Zara's wrist and pulling her to her as Fiona wrapped her arms around Zara and kissed her passionately, taking her by surprise.

"So, dinner?" Zara said, breaking the kiss and pulling away, making Fiona laugh.

"You sure do know how to keep me on my toes. Rejected twice in one day," Fiona said, only half-joking. Zara sat on the couch and took out her favorite take out menus.

"I'm not rejecting you. I am starving," Zara replied, glad when Fiona sat down next to her.

"So, which is your favorite?" Fiona asked, looking through the various Mexican menus. Zara felt herself give Fiona a little smile and promptly corrected herself before answering.

"I like these guys. They are a bit authentic, though, do

you mind? Or do you like more mainstream?" Zara questioned, her big eyes looking up at Fiona.

"Authentic is good," Fiona replied, taking out her phone.

"I'll ring," she said, dialing the number of the restaurant, unknowingly making Zara fight to not fall into little space as she watched Fiona take control. Fiona ordered, paid over the phone, and hung up, delighted that Zara had moved closer to her.

"Do you want to snuggle together when we watch the movie?" Fiona asked, almost causing Zara to clap her hands.

"Yeah, sure, whatever, if you like," came Zara's response trying to act cool, making Fiona laugh.

"We don't have to," Fiona said, trying to read Zara.

"Yes, I want to," Zara quickly said as she moved next to Fiona and wrapped her arms around her waist, making Fiona laugh.

"Okay, cool," she said as they began the movie and waited for their order to arrive.

Zara tried to steady her heartbeat as they watched the film, as Fiona started stroking her arm gently.

She doesn't even know what she is doing to me! Zara thought so loudly she was worried that Fiona might hear. As Zara slowly turned into Fiona, Fiona looked down into Zara's eyes and winked at her.

"Do you want a blanket?" Fiona asked, noticing that

Zara was cold, breaking their embrace and lifting the lid off the coffee table.

"No, I!" Zara exclaimed, jumping up and thinking she was about to pass out.

"What?" Fiona said, taking out one of the princess blankets from the wooden chest and draping it over her body, holding up the corner of the blanket and looking at Zara innocently. Fiona tried to hide her amusement as she watched Zara try to maintain her composure and sit back down, rigid and her breathing shallow. Fiona and Zara watched the film for a while, Fiona wondering how to approach the huge elephant in the room.

"Baby?" She softly said, making Zara's eyes go wide, and she turned her head slowly to face Fiona.

"Hmm?" Zara said, trying to act like she wasn't sitting under her princess blanket with the hottest woman who had ever been interested in her as they waited for their Mexican take out and watching a movie.

"Baby. It's alright. You don't have to pretend that you don't love this," Fiona said, indicating to the blanket.

"I don't know what you want me to say," Zara softly said, looking down and feeling deeply insecure.

"I like it," Fiona said, causing Zara to look up and wonder just how much of her private world she wanted to let Fiona into.

Maybe this is how you get a Mommy? Zara thought to

herself, as the doorbell rang, causing Zara to jump up and answer the door.

Well, that sucked, Fiona thought to herself, wishing that Zara would just open up to her. She had been looking for a baby girl for years, always seeming to scare them off. She wasn't sure what it was about her that was so off-putting to them. Sure, everyone seemed very interested in the beginning, but as they got deeper into a relationship with her, no one seemed to like her at all.

It's probably the hair, everyone says redheads have no soul, Fiona thought to herself as she saw Zara come back and place their food on the coffee table.

"Do you need any help," Fiona called from the living room as she saw Zara flutter into the kitchen to get glasses and plates.

"No, I'm good," Zara said, coming back to the living room and setting their food up.

"Can I pour you a drink?" Fiona asked, taking out the bottle of soda she had ordered as Zara nodded her head. Fiona picked up the glass, beginning to pour but then put it down suddenly, turning to look at Zara.

"Look. I know you're a little. I'm a Mommy. I can see it!" Fiona confessed, making Zara's eyes go wide as she slowly packed the paper wrapping into the bag and placed it on the floor.

"Oh, okay," Zara replied, unsure of what the correct

response was.

"Good, that's out in the open now," Fiona said, somewhat impressed with herself. They turned the movie back on and ate in silence, both wondering what it would take to make the awkward silence and energy of the room disappear.

She is beautiful, the type of woman like anyone would want to be with. She's a great kisser. She doesn't care that you're a little because she is a Mommy for Christ sake, what is your problem?! Zara thought to herself as she stared at the television, too nervous to look at Fiona.

"So, like, how long have you been into this?" Zara timidly asked as she paused the movie and turned to face Fiona. Fiona tried to suppress her smile, failing to do so as she looked at Zara.

"5 years. You?" Fiona asked, waiting for Zara to reply.

"I don't even remember," Zara softly answered. Fiona took her hair out of her ponytail, just to put it back up again before she spoke.

"You know, you don't need to be so shy with me. I'm not going to tell anyone, don't worry," Fiona gently said, reaching out and touching Zara's face. Zara looked up and smiled. It had been such a long time since somebody had shown her this type of affection, but something about Fiona still made her wary.

"We could try to do something, see if we both like it?" Zara suggested her desire to be babied, taking over and pushing all the red flag feelings she felt to the side. She knew that this might be a huge mistake, but she was so curious about what could happen that she couldn't help herself.

"What did you have in mind?" Fiona asked, finishing her food and looking at Zara with a mischievous twinkle in her eye. Zara just shrugged and looked around. She didn't want to have to be the person who decided, and Fiona picked up on that straight away.

"Well, for starters, this needs to come off. I know that you are far too little to be in such big girl clothes," Fiona said, taking Zara's hand, only for her to pull away.

"This is so awkward," Zara suddenly said, bursting out laughing, making Fiona laugh as well.

"I know," Fiona said, putting her head in her hands and shaking her head.

"What were we thinking?" Zara said, turning to face Fiona as she brought her knees up to her chest.

"We have zero chemistry!" Fiona exclaimed, clapping her hands as she emphasized her words.

"I know!" Zara replied, rolling her eyes.

"But like, you are so gorgeous. I should feel something, but I just don't feel it," Zara added, shrugging her shoulders.

"Oh, I feel the same way. It's just so hard finding a little, you know? You want to take every chance you can get," Fiona said, laughing when Zara shook her head.

"No, not really," Zara replied, smirking and making

Fiona give her a look.

"So, you want a beer or something?" Zara asked, suddenly feeling the stress of the evening fading and feeling more herself.

"Yeah, absolutely," Fiona said, getting up to follow Zara into the kitchen. She held the door open for Zara, who turned to look at her, with the same expression Fiona had written all over her face.

"I mean, you're already here, it would be a waste if," Zara slowly said as she put the drinks down and kissed Fiona, enjoying the sound of Fiona slamming the fridge door shut. Pushing her against the kitchen bench, Fiona pulled her hoodie off, her shirt coming off in the process.

"Can I pull your hair?" Fiona said between kisses, smiling as Zara nodded her head.

"Let me hear it, baby," Fiona said as she grabbed at Zara's clothes, ripping her shirt off and turning her around, pushing her down on the bench.

"Yes, pull my hair, but don't call me baby, call me sweetheart," Zara replied, not wanting to go into her little space too deeply.

"Good girl?" Fiona asked, biting her bottom lip as she kicked Zara's feet apart.

"Yeah," Zara gasped, feeling Fiona put her hands in her sports tights and feel her for the first time.

"Fuck yes," Fiona replied, pulling Zara's panties to the

side and stroking her slit, coating her fingers in her juices.

"Push that ass out for me," Fiona said, grinding against Zara's bottom as her fingers slowly entered her, making her moan and arch her back.

"So pretty," Fiona said, reaching forward and feeling Zara take her knuckle deep. Grabbing a fistful of Zara's hair with her free hand, Fiona felt her clit spasm as she looked at the beautiful woman under her control and moaned. Spreading her legs, Fiona grinded against one side of Zara's ass, feeling her clit being gently stimulated as she finger fucked Zara to orgasm.

"Oh fuck, sweetheart," Fiona gasped as she felt Zara coat her fingers, her cries of climax driving Fiona wild.

"Can I lick your pussy, sweetheart?" Fiona asked, wanting to taste Zara, who nodded her head and turned around, feeling Fiona rip her tights and panties off.

"So pretty," Fiona said, running her fingers through Zara's strip of pubic hair as she positioned herself under Zara's pussy, feeling her buckle forward as Fiona's tongue made contact with Zara's clit.

"Fuck," Zara gasped, grabbing Fiona's head and pushing her face into her cunt as she lapped up Zara's juices.

"Yes, just like that," Zara moaned as she arched her back and let her body take over, surprised that Fiona could drive her over the edge with her tongue. Not many people had been able to eat Zara out till orgasm. Pushing Fiona away, Zara grabbed the edge of the bench and held herself up, gasping as she kept Fiona away with her foot when she tried to come back for more.

"I'm done," Zara said, laughing as she shook her head and rubbed her pussy gently.

"That was fun," Fiona said as she got up, taking the beers, opening them, and placing one in Zara's hand before toasting and drinking it as she walked back into the living room. Zara couldn't help but admire the lithe body Fiona had as she drank her beer topless.

"You have really nice tits," Zara said, drinking her own beer after putting her panties back on, making Fiona laugh.

"You want to see them?" She offered. Zara seriously considered it for a moment.

"Nar, I'm good, I don't want this to get any weirder," Zara laughed, Fiona nodding her head, understanding where Zara was coming from and putting her shirt back on, before sitting on the couch next to Zara.

"So," Zara slowly said, wondering how to move forward.

"Yeah. Um, we can just pretend like this never happened if you want. Or we could I don't know, um, hang out sometimes," Fiona suggested making Zara laugh.

"It's okay. You don't need to babysit me, I'm good," Zara replied, smirking as she took her princess blanket and wrapped herself up in it.

"Alright. I didn't want you to think I was just using your

body or something. I liked fucking you, though," Fiona said, finishing her beer. Zara smiled.

"You did?" Zara asked, taking Fiona by surprise.

"Yeah. Why would you think I didn't?" Fiona replied, turning her body to face Zara.

"I don't know, I just sort of think that people don't notice me or find me attractive or whatever," Zara said, trying not to sound like she was fishing for compliments.

"I mean. You definitely hide yourself, but anyone would have to be stupid if they couldn't see your beauty," Fiona genuinely said, making Zara's heart flutter.

"Cool," Zara replied, her go-to response for when she felt happy but didn't know what to say.

"Cool," Fiona agreed, smiling at Zara.

Chapter 4

"Hey," Fiona hissed at Zara the next day in the office. Zara couldn't believe that it was only Thursday.

This week is next level crazy, she thought to herself as she looked around and saw Fiona standing by the elevators. Zara shrugged her shoulders at her, wondering what was going on that required such secrecy.

"You said this wouldn't be weird. Guess what, this. This is weird!" Zara softly exclaimed as she huddled over what Fiona was trying to show her.

"Weird, fun. It sort of all just blurs into one at some point," Fiona replied, causing Zara to scoff at her.

"Anyway. Here, there's an event, wanna go?" Fiona asked as Zara looked at her phone screen.

"What? Like, together?" Zara replied, confusion written across her face.

"No! Well, yeah, I mean. We could go together, but not like together together," Fiona replied, making Zara laugh.

"Yeah, okay. I hate going to things by myself anyway so, why not," Zara said, surprised at how quickly she could make a decision. Usually, she would have freaked out about doing something new and outside her box of "normal." Still, something about the way Fiona was able to maintain a completely neutral dynamic with her, made Zara respect her, trust her even.

"Sweet. Pick you up at 8?" Fiona asked, making Zara laugh.

"I'll make my own way there, but meet you out the front?" Zara quickly replied as the elevator doors opened before she scurried away.

"Looking good!" Fiona said, making Zara laugh. Zara wore a tight black dress, a flannel button-down tied around her waist, fishnet stockings, and black combat boots. Her hair was out and perfectly straighten, and her natural makeup completed the look.

"Thanks, I didn't really know what I should wear, so I figured this would work," Zara replied, smoothing down her dress over her torso.

"It definitely does! I would have thought you'd go for something, a little more girly. With all your princess stuff, I just thought," Fiona said, shrugging her shoulders.

"I just wasn't feeling all cute and girly tonight," Zara replied, before quickly giving Fiona a look.

"Anyway, why do you care? We aren't going to this, together together, remember," Zara said, sticking her tongue out and making Fiona laugh.

"Fair point," Fiona replied before walking toward the

entrance of the convention center.

"Have you seen this before?" Fiona asked, holding the door open for Zara.

"Only in movies," Zara replied, walking into the hall and seeing the woman skating around the track. The sounds overwhelmed her, and she found herself feeling small and wishing that she could reach out to hold Fiona's hand, forcing herself to resist the urge was more difficult than she had realized.

"Wow, so this is roller derby!" Zara said as she saw a woman being hip-checked.

"Pretty cool, huh?" Fiona said, sitting down and watching the bout.

"How did you know about this?" Zara said as she watched, smiling as the crowd cheered.

"I saw a flyer, the one I took a picture of to show you," Fiona replied, before cheering with the crowd. A player on the yellow and black team caught Zara's eye, and she felt her eyes glaze over. The woman was tall, her blonde hair had pink tips, and she moved through the pack with ease and speed. It almost looked like ballet instead of roller derby. Her athletic form was highlighted by the spotlight, which followed her around the track, and as she raised her arms in victory and the crowd cheered wildly, Zara cheering along with them.

How do I even talk to her?! Zara thought, as the woman passed her in the stands and winked at her, making Zara's stomach lurch and knot.

"That's Jill. Everyone actually calls her by her first name because she doesn't need an alter ego, she's made such a name for herself in the derby circuit, she doesn't need a scary name to threaten anyone, Jill is enough," Fiona explained, making Zara blush.

"Oh yeah, everyone thinks she's amazing, don't worry!" Fiona said, sensing that Zara was already under Jill's spell.

"Is she single?" Zara found herself suddenly saying, making Fiona laugh and taking her by surprise.

"I don't know, go and try to shoot your shot when the bout's over!" Fiona encouraged. Zara was surprised at how confident she had been feeling lately.

Maybe it is because Fiona knows I'm a little and I don't have to be worried about her finding out coz she's into this as well? Zara thought, deciding that it didn't matter why she was feeling so self-assured, she liked it, and that was all she was going to allow herself to think about the matter.
The bout ended with Jill's team losing by 3points, much to the crowd's disappointment.

"Boo!" Zara yelled when one of Jill's teammates was sent to the sin bin, allowing the opposition to gain the win.

"How could they call that!?" Zara yelled at Fiona, making Fiona laugh.

"I think I made you a fan," Fiona laughed as the crowd in the stands began to leave.

"Hey, you want to grab a drink?" Fiona asked, Zara, having to think for a moment before shaking her head.

"I think I might hang around for a while," Zara replied, a knowing smile forming across her face, causing Fiona to smirk.

"Alright, get it, girl!" Fiona said before waving goodbye and walking away. Zara turned around, taking a step just to bump into someone.

"Oh my gosh, sorry," Zara said, taking a step back to see who she had crashed into.

"It's fine," Jill said, causing Zara's eyes to go wide and her mouth to gape over.

"I, I, just watched you play," Zara said, shaking her head when she realized how stupid she just sounded, relieved when she saw Jill laugh.

"I know, I saw you, watching me play," Jill replied, enjoying Zara's cute choice of words. As an awkward silence came between them, Zara began to play with the sleeves tied up around her waist.

"You want to come and get a drink?" Jill asked, Zara, trying to subdue her excitement.

"Yeah, I heard that there was an after-party," Zara said, referring to the announcement she heard come over the speakers.

"Oh. Yeah, I didn't mean that. It'll be too loud, and I won't be able to hear you speak," Jill replied, making Zara smile. After a big night, she was happy with the idea of going somewhere quiet.

"Yeah, that sounds nice," Zara replied, smiling.

"Okay, give me 15minutes to get showered and presentable, and I'll take you out. I'm Jill," Jill said, extending her hand, Zara realizing for the first time that she hadn't introduced herself.

"Oh, I'm Zara," she said, shaking Jill's hand, noticing how small it made her feel as she closed her hand around Zara's.

As Jill went to get ready, Zara sat on the bleachers and flicked through her phone. There was nothing particularly interesting on her social media accounts, but it was better than having to dodge eye contact from strangers.

"There you are," Jill said as she approached Zara, starling her.

"Oh honey, I didn't mean to scare you," Jill affectionately said, hoping that Zara didn't mind the more nurturing side that she often chose to ignore.

"It's cool," Zara replied, shrugging her shoulder and trying not to get lost in Jill's eyes. They had a circle of navy around the outside, with hazel green in the middle and little flecks of gold reflecting from the lights, almost taking Zara's breath away.

"Ready to go?" Jill asked, placing her hand on her sports shoulder bag and running her fingers through her almost dried hair. She had washed it to get the rank smell of derby sweat out of her hair but hadn't bothered to dry it off completely. Zara nodded her head, and Jill fought herself not to grab the younger girl's hand and lead her away, instead, tilting her head and gesturing to Zara to follow her out of the arena.

On the street, people were still milling about, watching as Jill and Zara walked in silence passed them. Zara noticed that they all seemed to stare at her as she walked by, making her feel uncomfortable. Jill noticed, wondering how to best comfort Zara, not wanting her to be freaked out and reconsider getting to know her.

"So, tell me about yourself," Jill asked, as they turned a corner. Zara always hated this part of getting to know someone. She always wished that she had interesting hobbies or cool stories to tell. She thought for a moment before looking up at Jill, who could sense that there was something important Zara was about to say.

"So, I'm 29, I work as a success coach, and if you really want to end up with me, you should know I'm a little and if that isn't cool for you, then let's just stop right here," Zara said, almost feeling sick as she continued to walk. She never had, in all her nine years of identifying as a little, said it out loud, especially not to someone she had only just met.

"I don't know what that is," Jill said, lying. She had some idea of what it was but didn't want to assume and get

Zara's hopes up.

"For me, it's a lot of age play," Zara said, not wanting to get into it too deeply. She was still reeling for saying it out loud. Jill stopped walking, and Zara thought that she was going to turn and run.

"We are here," Jill said, indicating to Zara to go inside as she opened the door. Walking into the bar, Zara ordered a shot of vodka and a beer before walking away from Jill and finding a chair. She was sure Jill would follow her but needed a moment to get her head around what she had just done.

This is so typical of you. Everything is going fine, and you have to go and do something that makes you feel all fucked up again, Zara angrily thought to herself as Jill came to sit down in the opposing chair.

"So, if you were to explain it all to me in three sentences?" Jill asked, taking a sip of her beer. Zara crossed her legs on the chair before she looked at Jill, who was patiently waiting for her to respond.

"So, it's a sub-category of BDSM. It can be sexual or non-sexual, and comes in a whole lot of experiences and *flavors*," Zara said, surprised at how easy it was becoming to talk about her kink. Jill raised her eyebrows and nodded her head, making Zara glad she hadn't scared her off.

"Well, there you go," Jill said, processing it to the best of her ability.

"Did something happen to you as a kid or what?" Jill

asked, taking Zara by surprise.

"Um, no, not really. I just like how it feels to be looked after," Zara replied.

"So, like, you're not like, depressed or something?" Jill continued making Zara scoff.

"What? I just know a lot of girls who are subs are a bit fucked up," Jill said, as Zara tried not to be insulted.

"That's not very tactful," Zara said, finding it interesting that she was correcting Jill. She would have never spoken up about how something made her feel in the past.

"I don't really do tact. I'm not trying to insult you, I just don't sugar coat stuff," Jill said, seeing the way Zara pulled back from her.

"I can appreciate the honesty, but no. That's the misconception out there that bottoms, generally, are damaged, or something has gone wrong for them, but it's not the case. People, at large, have their shit, I think bottoms are just better at talking about it, in my experience," Zara said, looking around the bar and wondering why Jill had a smirk on her face.

"I agree. I guess I would identify as a top, and I constantly push my past and shit down, so no one sees," Jill said, taking Zara by surprise.

"So, what's your story then?" Zara asked, coming to sit down next to Jill and look her in the eye.

"Well, when you look at me like that, how can I refuse

to answer?" Jill said, placing her hand on Zara's thigh.

"I work in a casino, it's pretty basic, but it's fun. I have a cabin in the mountains that I go to in the wintertime. I never knew my Dad. He died in a motorcycle accident before I was born. My Mum remarried this prick who kicked me out when I was 16 because that's when I came out, and I've been on my own ever since," Jill said, finishing her beer and getting up to go to the bar.

"That's heavy," Zara replied as she approached the bar and bought her second drink. Jill just turned to look at Zara, surprised at how her defenses seemed to come down around her.

No girl has ever been able to do this to me before, Jill thought as she reached out and touched Zara's cheek affectionately.

"I feel so weird around you," Jill laughed before going back to sit down, taking Zara by the hand as she did so.

Chapter 5

"Well, this is me," Zara said as they approached her apartment. Jill would have usually taken a girl back to her house and be kicking her out by now, but she and Zara had talked all night. When they were kicked out of one bar because it was closing, they went to the casino and sat on the slot machines, not to play, but to chat. It hadn't felt right just to hit and quit on Zara, and as the sun rose behind her, Jill knew that Zara was somebody special.

"I'm going to read up on littles and ABDL," Jill said, wanting to keep Zara for as long as she could.

"What was the other one you said?" Jill asked as Zara beamed up at her.

"MDLG," Zara said, hugging Jill spontaneously and quickly walking up the stairs to her apartment. She was worried that if she stayed holding onto her any longer, she would melt into Jill's loving embrace.

"Okay, bye," Zara said as she opened her door and walked inside. She was exhausted. Not only because she had stayed awake all night, but because she had spoken about just about everything she had ever done. It wasn't that extreme feeling when she had met toxic partners in the past. Those ups and downs were like a roller coaster from hell. With Jill, it was calm, balanced, and even though they had not been able to say goodbye to each other until the early hours of the morning, it felt aligned.

Zara locked the door of her apartment and slowly undressed herself. She kicked off her boots, leaving them by the door and untied her shirt from around her waist. She walked to the bathroom and dropped it in the wash basket, pulled off her dress, and rolled down her fishnets, taking off the ankle socks she wore underneath. She turned on the water to the shower before she took off her bra and panties and closed her eyes as she stood under the water and sighed.

Well, that was unexpected, Zara thought to herself as she felt herself begin to relax under the pressure of the hot water.

Jill could hardly wait until she got home to begin looking up all the things she and Zara had shared. She liked the Zara didn't make her feel stupid for asking what felt like 10,000 questions.

She's certainly not like other girls. Jill thought to herself as she crashed onto her bed. Despite her desire to sleep, Jill stayed up searching MDLG, ABDL, littles, middles, bigs, looking at photos of events, following accounts, and joining pages online before finally falling asleep at 9:30 that morning.

My sleep schedule is going to be fucked up for days, was the last thing she thought before falling into a deep sleep.

Jill woke up to the sound of construction works outside her bedroom window and blinked her eyes slowly awake.

Fuck, what time is it? She thought to herself, grateful that she had the day off. She felt around the bed for her phone, remembering that she had been researching Zara's kink before she fell asleep. Finally, finding it under her pillow, she checked the time and smirked to herself. It was late afternoon. Groaning, Jill got up, had a shower, got dressed, and went to the kitchen. She opened her fridge and remembered that she needed to go to the grocery store, before rolling her eyes and slamming the door shut.

This is bullshit, she thought to herself as she grabbed her keys and headed out the door.

Jill walked down the street, trying to remember all the things she needed to get, but finding that her mind was elsewhere. After hours of searching, she had images of diapered women, playrooms, and all things adult-baby related running through her mind. She wondered what sort of play Zara enjoyed, how a relationship would look with her, and if she would ever feel like a Mommy.

She's so cute. I want to be with her, but I don't know if I can give her what she wants, Jill thought to herself as she entered the store. She absent-mindedly put things into her shopping cart. She imagined punishing Zara for breaking a rule, enjoying the image of her being strap on fucked and forbidden to orgasm.

Jill paid for her groceries and took out her phone on the way back to her apartment. She hoped that she wouldn't wake Zara up.

"Hey, it's Jill, from last night, and this morning actually," Jill said down the phone, surprised at how nervous she was when talking with Zara.

"Hi," Zara said, having only just woken up five minutes earlier, she hadn't bothered to call in sick, she just assumed they would figure it out when she didn't turn up.

"I hope I didn't wake you?" Jill said, concerned that she had disturbed Zara.

"No, it's cool, I was up. How are you?" Zara said, snapping Jill back into the confident person she was usually.

"Good. I was just thinking about you," Jill said, making Zara smile.

"That's nice," Zara replied, getting up out of bed and walking out to her balcony.

"Yeah, so, do you want to meet up sometime again? I read up on everything we talked about last night, and I think it could be really fun to explore that with you," Jill said, squinting and biting her bottom lip, hoping that she wasn't overstepping.

"Um, yeah, I mean. That could be fun to show you the

stuff I like. Do you want to come over tonight for a few hours, maybe come at six?" Zara said, feeling very proud of herself for the suggestion.

"Yeah, that sounds great," Jill replied, hanging up the phone and feeling herself getting hyped up.

Zara had spent the two hours before Jill arrived getting ready. She tided the house, took out some of her toys and laid them on her bed, and practiced what she would say to Jill. She got ready, deciding to put on her baby doll dress and her hair in a messy ponytail, and white ankle socks. Then she sat on the couch and waited, for what felt like an eternity. She was just about to lay down on the couch when she heard a knock coming from the door and excitedly jumped up and ran to it.

"Hey," Zara said, opening it up to see Jill standing in front of her.

"Hi. You look cute," Jill answered, smiling down at Zara, who blushed.

"You wanna come in?" Zara asked, stepping back and allowing Jill to enter her apartment. Jill walked in, standing awkwardly in the living room, making Zara laugh.

"You can sit down if you like," Zara said, causing Jill to look at her and sit bashfully.

"So, you didn't hate what you discovered?" Zara asked, sitting down next to Jill, immediately putting her at ease.

"No, in fact, I kind of liked it. From like, the Mommy

perspective," Jill said, blushing as she replied.

"Wow, that is really cool. Do you have any questions or?" Zara replied as she shifted in her seat.

"Yeah, heaps," Jill said, surprising herself. She had always been a more dominant type of woman, but this was different. It seemed to bring out in her a softness that wasn't familiar to her. Sure, she could imagine controlling and disciplining Zara, but the gentleness and care that coupled those feelings were strange and new but exciting to her.

"Like, how do you like to have adult relationships? What does a typical day look like for you? How do you balance what you need to do as an adult and still have enough time for age play? What do you look for in a Mommy, just to name a few?" Jill asked, looking at Zara seriously. Zara laughed. She hadn't expected this to go so well when she had told Jill, she was a little. It was a selfish act, something she was only doing for herself. She hadn't thought that Jill would be interested in it, or her after she had told her. She just wanted to say it out loud without any repercussions.

"Well. I guess I have adult relationships like everyone else. Sometimes things that people do trigger the little side of me and it comes out a little bit, but mostly I find it easy to keep both sort of separate, I just prefer to have them separate, it makes it easier for me to enjoy both. A typical day looks like me getting up and going to work. I like to have little time at night and on weekends, and that's how I balance, making sure that I have everything that I need. What I look for in a Mommy. I haven't ever given it much thought because I've never had one before. But I guess someone I'm compatible with! Everything else is just extra. Like, if we have that chemistry, and have a good foundation of friendship, I guess the relationship will progress naturally. Oh, I don't want to feel rushed, that's probably one of the big ones," Zara explained, enjoying that Jill was clearly listening. That was one of the things that Zara liked about Jill. Whenever Zara spoke, Jill gave her her undivided attention and didn't seem to listen just to reply, but really tried to understand where Zara was coming from. Jill took in the words Zara had said, nodding her head as she digested them.

"That sounds like, really standard actually. So, it's kind of like, for you, it's about having work and life balance, and then age play is what you do to unwind and relax and enjoy experiencing?" Jill asked, making Zara's heart swell. She loved how Jill seemed to see her.

"Yeah, exactly," Zara said, beaming. Jill nodded her head as she understood.

"So, do you want to show me some of the stuff you like?" Jill asked, somewhat timidly making Zara giggle.

"Yeah, come on," she said, taking Jill's hand and leading her into her bedroom. She sat on her bed and patted the spot next to her.

"Have a seat," Zara said, watching as Jill looked over

the things on her bed.

"What were you expecting?" Zara laughed as she saw Jill's face.

"I don't know," Jill laughed, looking at the blankies, stuffies, and adult pacifiers. Zara hadn't put out everything she liked, just a few things so that Jill wouldn't get freaked out.

"So, this is cute. You're just like a little girl in a sexy, grown body, huh?" Jill said, making Zara roll her eyes.

"Yeah, kinda," Zara replied, watching as Jill picked up a pacifier, playing with it.

"What other stuff do you like?" She asked, looking at Zara. Zara got up and opened her cupboard, letting Jill see the collection of diapers, onesie, and cute AB dresses and accessories. Jill got up and flicked through everything, looking at Zara when she was finished.

"I would have never guessed this," Jill said, making Zara nervous.

"Why not?" She asked, fearful that Jill wasn't as into it as she thought she would be.

"Because look at you!" Jill replied. Zara looked down at herself. It was true. She did look like a fashion model when she put in effort into her appearance, but that was what she loved about being a little. She didn't have to impress anyone, and no one expected anything from her. It was enough for her just to be herself. She had long learned to hide how gorgeous she was, disappointed that it seemed only to bring her misery when someone became interested in her. She had become comfortable with wearing little to no makeup, having her hair in messy buns or ponytails, and wearing baggy clothes. But when she was a little, she could be her naturally beautiful self because nothing bad could happen to her.

"Yeah, I know. That's what I like about being a little. I can look how I look, and no one expects anything from me. All I have to do is be a good girl," Zara said, feeling herself beginning to enter her little space being around all her things, she had to admit, it was very space triggering.

"So, you come home, have a shower or something, and then this is what you dress in around the house? Being in little space?" Jill asked, wanting to know how it all worked.

"Pretty much. I go to the gym after work on most days or go swimming. Then I come home, shower, put dinner on, and then I can start to get into my little space and only get out of it to do the dishes or put the washing on, for example. Sometimes on the weekend, I don't feel super little, but I still like to wear a diaper, I just like how they feel," Zara said as she closed her cupboard door.

"Do you use them?" Jill asked, sitting back down on the bed.

"No, I just like wearing them," Zara replied, coming to sit next to her. Jill nodded her head, and Zara was happy that she didn't seem too phased by anything she had just seen.

"So, I'm just going to come out and say it. I'd really like

to be your girlfriend," Jill said, making Zara laugh.

"What?" Jill said, tickling Zara involuntarily, making Zara giggle.

"Yeah, I kinda thought that we were both wanting that, that I was just showing you all this stuff so that you could make sure you wanted to be with me," Zara replied, crossing her legs.

"Oh. Well, good then," Jill laughed, realizing that she wasn't telling Zara anything new.

"I know it's kind of like, doming from the bottom, but you might need to help me like, make sure that I'm being a Mommy, the right way," Jill nervously said. Zara thought it was adorable that Jill was nervous, but didn't feel like teasing her for it.

"There's no right way to be a Mommy, but I get what you mean. I can show you, in time," Zara said as Jill nodded. She liked that Jill wasn't trying to rush into anything. It made Zara feel safe and calm.

"Do you want to watch a movie?" Jill suddenly asked, Zara's eyes going wide.

"Yes!" She exclaimed, her little side coming out and making Jill smile. She shifted on the bed, clearly wanting to ask something but not knowing how to form the sentence.

"Just ask," Zara whispered, tilting her head down to look up at Jill, who was now blushing.

"Do. Do you want to take a blankie or paci or

something?" Jill asked, biting her bottom lip. Zara nodded her head, grabbed her paci and princess blankie before taking Jill's hand, and putting her paci in her hand.

"You can put it in my mouth whenever you want," Zara said, looking at Jill with her biggest puppy dog eyes. Jill smiled, suddenly feeling her nerves shift and slowly pushed Zara's paci into her mouth, looking at her and feeling a new, strange sensation washing over her.

"You look really, sweet," Jill said, taking a moment to look at Zara before smiling in surprise.

"Come on," Jill said, standing up and holding out her hand to Zara, who eagerly took it. They walked out to the couch, and Jill sat down, letting Zara work the tv remotes.

"This feels really different. Like all soft and kind and cute and stuff," Jill said, surprised at how easy it was allowing herself to feel all the feelings of love, softness, and non-sexual affection.

"I'm glad you like it," Zara replied, letting Jill wrap the blankets around them both as Zara snuggled into her side. They started the movie, and Zara felt like she was in heaven. Jill's larger, soft yet athletic body made the perfect pillow, and as the movie progressed, Zara could feel herself falling asleep in Jill's arms. Much to Jill's surprise, she knew that she never wanted to let Zara go. She wanted her, craved her, and believed that no one could take care of her the way she could. It was a strange sensation to experience, so soon after meeting someone, yet one which she welcomed. As Jill looked down to see Zara clutching at her breast, sound asleep, Jill smiled and carefully reached for the tv remote, turning the tv off. She gently placed her arms under Zara and carried her like a princess into her bedroom. Pulling back the sheets, she placed Zara in bed, brushing the hair off her face as she stirred.

"It's alright, honey. You're safe. You're in bed," Jill whispered as she tucked in the stuffies that were on the bed around Zara. Jill looked down at Zara and smiled to herself. She loved that Zara had dared to open up to her so quickly, grateful to be allowed to look after another woman with such tender care.

This has always been me. I just never knew what it was called, Jill thought as she walked back out into the living room and sat down on the couch. She thought back on her past relationships and saw many similarities between what Zara was looking for and what she naturally gave. Her ex's had always loved her dotting and affectionate ways, but they always found that she wanted to do too much for them. One woman had even told her that she felt like her independence was being taken away. That comment still stung. It wasn't that Jill tried to be overpowering, it was just that, she wanted to make sure that her partner was taken care of to the highest degree. If a girlfriend said she needed new shoes for work or sport, Jill wanted to be the one to get them for her. If they said they didn't like their hairstyle anymore, Jill found the best hairdresser in their neighborhood for them. If they needed doctors' appointments, she organized it. She had dated sugar-babies before, thinking that would satisfy her need to look after someone, but they were really only interested in her money and not her.

But this, this just feels so right, Jill happily thought, taking out her phone and scrolling through content as she waited for Zara to wake up.

Chapter 6

Zara woke up with a start.

What happened? She thought, looking around her darkened room. She remembered that Jill had come over and they had watched a movie, gasping when she realized that she had fallen asleep as the movie had begun.

Oh my gosh, how embarrassing, she thought, getting up and seeing her stuffies all around her. Zara tilted her head, not giving it a second thought as her feet touched the ground, and she smelt the smell of fresh herbs and cooking coming from her kitchen. She walked out of her room to see Jill was still here. In fact, she was in the kitchen, cooking something which smelt delicious.

"Hey, sweetie, I thought you might be hungry after your nap," Jill said, spinning around to see Zara looking at her, a mix of shock and excitement on her face.

"I don't know what to say," Zara said, sitting down on the bench stool and watching Jill.

"I hope this is okay? I didn't just want to leave you," Jill said, stirring the pot on the stove.

"This is great. You're so lovely. You didn't have to do this though," Zara said, smirking as Jill passed her a bottle filled with water.

"You haven't had enough water today," Jill said, gesturing to the bottle. Zara liked that Jill seemed to be in her natural element, but what surprised her the most was that she felt as though she and Jill had been in a relationship for years. Everything seemed to flow so effortlessly.

"Here you go," Jill said, placing a bowl of warm beef stew on the counter in front of Zara. Zara was surprised. She had never had beef stew before but knew that it would become one of her favorites as the meat melted in her mouth.

"Oh fuck yes, this is amazing!" Zara said, making Jill laugh and frown at the same time.

"That's enough of that language, young lady," Jill teased, kissing Zara's cheek before getting up to get a drink for herself.

"You know, this feels really nice," Zara said, as she watched Jill. Jill smirked.

"Yeah. I can't believe I only met you a day ago. This feels right," Jill replied, causing Zara to smile in sheer happiness. She couldn't believe her luck. It all just seemed too good to be true.

"I feel the same way," Zara said as Jill sat next to her and began to eat dinner.

"I'm actually having a really hard time not jumping into this with you," Zara said, enjoying dinner. Jill laughed before looking at her.

"I know. Me too. But I don't want to ruin it by rushing in," Jill added, making Zara nod her head. She knew that she needed to take her time, let the relationship unfold naturally, but she just couldn't help but fantasize about how it would feel to be playing with Jill.

"Don't worry, I'm not going anywhere," Jill said, reassuringly.

Zara took leftover dinner to work on Monday, hardly being able to hide her smile as she walked through the office.

"Oh, somebody looks happy," Fiona said as Zara sat down in her chair.

"Do you just loiter around my desk, waiting for me to come in?" Zara laughed as she turned on her computer.

"No," Fiona scoffed, mildly offended. She moved to the edge of Zara's desk and crossed her legs, her thigh-split in her skirt, exposing her toned leg.

"Was she as good as me?" Fiona teased, making Zara roll her eyes.

"We didn't have sex," Zara said, taking Fiona by surprise.

"What do you mean?" Fiona asked, crossing her arms over her chest.

"We talked," Zara replied, turning around to face Fiona, who was trying to understand.

"Oh, wow. Well good, that's what you wanted,

somebody to take things slow with you. Good, I'm happy you found someone like her then," Fiona said, standing up.

"Fi," Zara softly said, sensing Fiona's disappointment. It was obvious now that Fiona was still interested in Zara, even though it had been awkward between them.

"She doesn't have your tits," Zara said, shrugging her shoulder and smiling as she saw Fiona perk back up, before winking at Zara and walking away. Zara just sighed and rolled her eyes. She liked that Fiona was who she was, but she wasn't the right person for Zara, and as heartbreakingly stunning as she was, she knew that truth deep in her soul.

Hey honey, I hope you have a good day. I saw this and wondered if you would like it? Came a message from Jill as Zara tried to get refocused on the mountain of work she had to get through. Looking at the picture she had sent, Zara gasped, as she saw the big, soft, multicolored Llama that Jill had sent.

Omg, YES!! Replied Zara, being barely able to control her excitement, smiling down at her phone, much to Fiona's disappointment. She had been watching Zara from her office, wondering what was so good about Jill that Zara wanted her as badly as she did.

Is it just because Zara said no? Am I just being possessive? It's not like we had any chemistry or anything. We both agreed that we aren't right for each other. Is it just coz I know she's a baby? Is it because I could get anyone I want, so I want the one person who doesn't want me? Fiona thought to herself as she angrily typed on her keyboard, wishing that she could shake the feeling of rejection from her bones.

Chapter 7

Zara went over to Jill's house the next weekend, excited to see her again after days of only messaging.

"Hi," Zara said as soon as Jill opened the door, jumping into her arms and snuggling in close as Jill wrapped her arms around her.

"Hi cutie," Jill replied, enjoying how it felt to have Zara's body pressed against hers.

"I'm glad you could come over," Jill said, taking a step back and breaking their embrace. Zara beamed up at her, melting her heart and finding it hard to keep her mind from wondering. Zara's body made her wet, but she knew she didn't want to scare her off and so cleared her throat and shut the door before leading Zara into her space.

"I guess this is how nervous you were when I first saw your place," Jill said as she looked back at Zara, who followed her.

"Yeah, a little bit," Zara said as they reached the back porch, and Jill gestured to Zara to sit down.

"This is really lovely," Zara said as she looked out over the backyard. The wooden porch had fairy lights strung up along one side, a hammock was set up next to a fire pit on the grass, and there was a garden bed with colorful flowers.

"Your place is really nice," Zara said, looking at the cake Jill had made as she cut her a slice.

"Thanks. It's not much, but it's cute, and the rent is cheap," Jill said, sitting down and pouring herself and Zara coffee.

"You don't seem like that, no-nonsense roller derby queen when you are off the track," Zara said, before taking a bite of the moist cake, savoring the flavor.

"I like derby because it gives me an outlet to be somebody I'm not usually. Like, I am pretty relaxed, but my ego still comes into play from time to time, and derby lets me be that center of attention, outspoken, loud, aggressive, and passionate, without it being a bad thing or upsetting anyone," Jill said making Zara smile.

"I like that. I like that you know yourself so well," Zara said, sipping her coffee. Jill sat back in her seat and tilted her head back, enjoying the afternoon sun on her face.

"You're really pretty," Zara said, biting her bottom lip as she finished her slice of cake. She ran her finger over her bottom lip, leaned back in her seat and pushed her pussy out toward Jill.

"I don't think you're ready for me," Jill said, excited that Zara had initiated sex.

"I'll be the judge of that," Zara said, standing up and walking over to Jill, just to straddle her lap, wrapping her arms around her neck and feeling her breasts against hers, making Jill's clit throb.

"Such a naughty little girl," Jill whispered, grabbing Zara by the back of her head and pulling her hair, making her moan.

"Fuck me, Mommy," Zara whispered in Jill's ear, causing Jill to spread her thighs, and take one of Zara's hands from around her neck and pushed it into her pants.

"First, you're going to give Mommy a reason to," Jill sensually said. Zara was surprised. Usually, she didn't have to do too much to be fucked, but she liked that Jill made her work for it, it made it feel more special. Jill put her hand over the top of Zara's and guided her fingers around her clit and into her pussy, holding Zara's hand there as she pushed herself forward, wanting Zara deeper inside of her.

"Nice and slow. Take your time," Jill said, bringing Zara's mouth down on top of hers. Jill reached under Zara's dress and smirked when she felt that Zara wasn't wearing any panties.

"Dirty little thing," Jill said, gently parting Zara's pussy lips and rubbing her knuckle over the girl's sensitive clit, enjoying how she shuddered as she was teased.

"Oh, does the baby like that?" Jill teased, flicking Zara's clit, making her gasp each time. Zara just closed her eyes and moaned as she felt Jill coat a finger in her pussy juices, before slowly sliding it inside of her. Jill was still working Zara's hand over her own cunt, smirking as she felt Zara struggle to focus as she was toyed with.

"Did Mommy say you could stop?" Jill whispered into Zara's ear as she filled her with a second finger, curling her fingers and anchoring Zara to her lap.

"No," Zara moaned, as Jill rubbed her clit with her thumb.

"No, Mommy," Jill corrected, feeling Zara's pussy clench as she heard the words.

"No, Mommy," Zara replied, beginning to grind on Jill's lap, desperate to cum. Jill smiled in satisfaction as she leaned further back and watched as Zara ached to cum, deciding that she was going to have to wait a little longer.

"I don't think you've done enough to deserve an orgasm, baby girl," Jill said, smirking as she pulled her hand from Zara, enjoying that look of disbelief on her face.

"Oh, don't worry, I'll show you exactly what you need to do to cum," Jill teased, shaking her breasts for Zara, who was speechless. She knew that the level of admiration she felt toward Jill was dangerous when she had to stop herself from saying that she would do anything Jill wanted.

"Tell me what I need to do, Mommy," Zara said, moving her body how Jill wanted her. Jill cradled Zara in her arms, moved one of her legs up on the table, the other one wrapped around Jill's leg, being held open and exposed. Jill wrapped an arm around Zara, supporting her head as her other hand lifted the hem of Zara's dress, uncovering her from the waist down. Her lips were open, her wet, pink pussy on full display. Jill pulled her top down, letting her breast fall out of her bra and pushed her nipple into Zara's mouth.

"Mmm, just like that," Jill said as she felt Zara begin to pull on her nipple with her soft lips, her tongue making it hard. Jill replaced her nipple with her fingers and watched how Zara made them wet before pushing her nipple back into the girl's mouth and sliding her fingers back into her pussy in one slow motion, making her moan.

"That's it," Jill said, as she saw Zara's eyes roll back. Zara wrapped her arm around Jill's body, her other one gripping Jill's thigh as she was fucked. Jill loved how Zara thrust up to meet her fingers as they reached her hilt, aching to be given release. Jill looked down. This is how she had fantasized about Zara. The beautiful woman, filled and at her mercy.

"Please let me cum," Zara gasped, her clit hard and throbbing, her cunt dripping wet.

"I shouldn't hear girls with Mommy's nipple in their mouths," Jill said, taking her fingers out of Zara and putting her heavy breast back in Zara's mouth before taking a toy from her pocket and sliding it up and down Zara's wet slit before beginning to tease her asshole with it.

"Just like we talked about. This is what you wanted, isn't it?" Jill said, referring to the multiple fantasies that they had shared over text message. Zara nodded her head, feeling the butt-plug press into her resisting asshole.

"Don't fight, Mommy," Jill said, holding it against her with her thumb and tapping on her clit with her fingers, making Zara tilt her head back and moan. She felt Jill add pressure, gasping as the butt-plug entered her, the pain mixed with the pleasure she was getting on her clit, making her head spin. Jill held her tight as she entered her pussy, making Zara buck her hips as she found her g-spot and refused to leave it alone.

"Should Mommy be mean and tell you that you can't cum, baby girl?" Jill whispered as Zara edged on the brink of orgasm. Zara's pleading eyes suddenly opened, and she looked desperately into Jill's eyes, hoping that she would be allowed to have what was sure to be a crushing orgasm.

"Mommy's not that mean," Jill said, bending down to kiss Zara, as her thumb began to work her clit.

"Cum for Mommy," Jill said, feeling Zara's body convulse immediately as she flooded Jill's hand and left out a high pitched cry before collapsing in Jill's strong arms, spent. Zara snuggled into Jill, burying her face in her ample cleavage before beginning to suck her thumb.

"Thank you, Mommy," Zara softly said, wriggling away from Jill's fingers, which were still in her pussy.

"Okay, little one," Jill said, taking the hint and taking her hand away.

"Do you need some downtime?" Jill asked, seeing Zara's little side for the first time. Zara nodded her head and stood up, her dress falling down as Jill smoothed it over. They had spoken about the kind of aftercare that Zara liked to have, and Jill had pre-emptively made sure she had everything that Zara had mentioned.

"Let's go inside. I can run you a nice bath," Jill said, taking Zara's hand and leading her into the bathroom. She gently undressed her, making sure to give her lots of cuddles as Zara became clingy and grabby. Jill took the butt-plug from Zara's ass and helped her into the bath. Jill turned the lights off, lit some candles, and sat by the bath, excited to be needed at the level she desperately required. She hadn't even considered that she needed to be a Mommy Domme before meeting Zara, but as Zara reached up for her, she knew this was exactly the type of relationship she had been searching for for so long.

"Mommy," Zara softly said, getting taken out of the bath and wrapped in a towel. She rested her head on Jill's breasts, her thumb in her mouth, and Jill tenderly dried her body. Zara was pleasantly surprised that she was able to go so deep into her little space, with Jill. Although she always seemed to keep a foot in both her little space and her adult space, being able to get into little space as quickly as she had made her happy.

"I've got you," Jill lovingly said, as she wrapped her arm

around Zara and walked with her to her bedroom. She lay Zara down on the bed and went to her chest of drawers, taking out a diaper and onesie. Jill had never diapered another adult before but knew that it was something she wanted to do, especially because she knew that it would make Zara happy. She had seen videos on social media of Mommies diapering their adult babies and felt quietly confident.

"Really?" Zara asked as she saw Jill come back with the diaper in her hand.

"Yes, baby. What else would I put you in? You're too little for big girl panties," Jill said, finding that the words came from her mouth easily. She smiled. It felt nice to have so much control and authority in a relationship. Jill placed everything she needed down on the bed and began to lay the diaper out on the bed. She moved Zara on top of it, sprinkled powder over her, and made sure it covered her so that she wouldn't rub anywhere. Fastening the tabs, she enjoyed the feelings washing over her. It had been months since Jill had been in Mommy space, and she smiled to herself as she took the onesie, gently dressing Zara before sitting back and looking at her.

"You're really cute," Jill said, slightly unsure what to do next. Zara noticed and crawled over to Jill, hugging her tightly and nestling her face into Jill's neck.

"Can we snuggle together in bed, Mommy?" Zara asked, laying down and half pulling Jill down with her.

"Of course," Jill said as she pulled back the sheets and turned off the lights.

Chapter 8

Jill was working double shifts for the next few weeks, as the floor was understaffed, which meant that she and Zara could only text and call. Zara didn't mind. She was happy the relationship was able to go at a slower pace and learn about Jill, without the ability to jump her bones.

"How was work?" Zara asked Jill on a Friday night. Jill had told her that she would call when she had time, but if Zara missed it because she was in bed or asleep or at work, that was fine. They had played phone tag for the last two days, and Zara had almost missed the call as well, having to jump out of the shower and run to her phone.

"It was fine. I am tired, though. I'm glad there is only one more week of this shit," Jill replied, pouring herself a drink and sitting down on the floor next to the ceiling window, which overlooked the city.

"I bet. I'm sorry I can't come over and help you feel better," Zara replied, making Jill laugh.

"Shouldn't it be me looking after you?" Jill questioned, sipping her drink. Zara shook her head, even though Jill couldn't see her.

"No, Mommy, sometimes I can look after you too!" Zara

exclaimed.

"Oh yeah, what would you do?" Jill said, finishing her drink and laying down on the carpet. Zara thought for a moment before smirking.

"First, I would take off your work clothes. Starting with your shoes and socks. Then I'd unbuckle your belt and pull your pants down slowly. I'd loosen your tie, unbutton your shirt and push you back on the bed in just your bra and panties," Zara said, making Jill undress herself the way Zara was describing.

"And then," Jill said in a husky voice, caught in the daydream of Zara's fantasy. Zara giggled and bit her bottom lip before continuing.

"Then I would slowly get on top of you. I'd run my fingernails up your tummy and around your body, unclipping your bra and kissing down your collar bone until I reached your breasts. I'd gently grab them, playing with them and sucking on your nipples as my hand slid into your panties," Zara teased. Jill had run her hands down her body, following the path Zara was paving.

"Do you like it, Mommy?" Zara said, making Jill smirk.

"Yes. Keep going baby girl," Jill softly moaned, closing her eyes.

"I'd slowly part your lips, circling your clit and sliding my little finger into your pussy, knowing that you'd be wet enough. Then I'd play, doing nothing, in particular, just teasing you, feeling you. I'd kiss your inner thighs, licking your clit and sticking my tongue into your pussy, but nothing so constant that you could get off. I'd want to see how long I could tease you. How long I could play with you before you grabbed a fistful of my hair and held my mouth against you. Forcing me into you and grabbing at my throat until I gave you what you wanted," Zara said, stopping as she heard Jill's labored moans and gasps down the phone.

"I know you like that. I know you need me to look after you sometimes, Mommy," Zara said, hearing Jill's orgasm as she called her Mommy and smiled to herself, satisfied that she had given Jill pleasure.

"You are such a good girl," Jill said, opening her eyes, surprised that their phone call had turned out this way.

"Are you free tomorrow? I want to take you out for the day," Jill said suddenly. Zara frowned.

"I thought you said you'd be too tired. That you just wanted to sleep on your day off," Zara replied, as the rain began to pour outside.

"I thought I was going to be too tired too. But I suddenly have all the energy in the world," Jill laughed, hearing the rain.

"But maybe, we do something indoors. I can pick you up at ten if you'd like?" Jill asked, thinking of what she and Zara could do.

"Ten would be perfect," Zara said, smiling down the

phone and hanging up.

Zara wasn't sure what she wanted to wear. She had taken a long shower, put on her fanciest lingerie and did her makeup, excited to try the new eyeliner she had bought earlier that week. She walked around her apartment, her hair flowing in the cool breeze as she sipped her coffee by the window seat.

This feels really lovely, she thought to herself, checking the time and running her fingertips over her soft skin. She looked out the window, watching as the people on the street hurried about their day. They always looked like they had so many important things to do, making Zara smile.

It's a Saturday, and I don't have to work, she thought, remembering how she used to spend her weekends before she had graduated from college. Back in those days, she worked at a fancy shoe store, selling only the highest quality of products. She hated it there. The people were so entitled, the job was incredibly repetitive, and she could predict what her day would be like, months in advance. She knew she had to get out of there, but she had college, which meant that she had to stay working there for several years before she could leave. She still remembered her last shift. She had stolen a pair of shoes that she had always admired. She wasn't sure if it was because these were the most expensive shoes in the store or if she did, in fact, like them. All she knew was that she felt like she deserved them, and so she took them. She hadn't done too many other naughty things in her life. This was the biggest one. Zara smirked at how brazen she had been. It was a similar attitude she had when telling Jill that she was a little.

Sometimes, the juice is worth the squeeze. She thought to herself as she got up, finished her coffee, and headed into her bedroom. She took out her black stockings and pink dress, her black jacket, and those black heels she had stolen. Dressing herself, she looked in the mirror and knew that she looked good, just as she heard her doorbell chime.

"I'll be down in a minute," Zara said, pressing the intercom and quickly grabbing her keys, handbag, and heading out the door. Zara walked downstairs, opened the door, and stopped in her tracks when she saw Fiona standing in front of her.

"You're not Jill," Zara said, confused and tilting her head.

"Good observation," Fiona smugly replied, staring blankly at Zara.

"Well, um, what do you want?" Zara asked, knowing that Jill would be there any moment.

"I wanted to talk about us," Fiona said. She had her usual, don't mess with me, look about her, and Zara thanked herself for not getting too involved with Fiona.

Clearly, things hadn't worked out between the intern, Zara thought, remembering how Fiona had been flirting with a particularly sweet new intern, before shaking her head and looking mildly angry at Fiona.

"There is no, us, Fi," Zara replied, annoyed that she thought there was a chance that they would be together.

"Yeah, I know that. But I think we just got off to a bad start. Everything is awkward at the start. I'd like to try again with you," Fiona said, just as Jill drove to a car space on the street.

"I don't, though. Sorry Fi, but I'm not interested in being with you. You're beautiful, funny, kind in a bitchy sort of way, which is really fun to be around, but I don't want to be with you," Zara said, looking at Fiona apologetically.

"I have to go," Zara said, smiling at Fiona pitifully before walking away and getting into Jill's car.

"Just drive, and quickly," Zara said as she sat down in the passenger seat, Jill following her request.

"What's going on?" Jill asked when they were around the corner. Zara had seen the excited look on Jill's face as she got into the car, feeling guilty that she hadn't been able to greet her the way she had planned.

"So, that woman I was with. Her name is Fiona. We work together. Before I met you, we tried to be together, but it was just so weird and like, there was no flow, and it just sucked. But she wanted to try again with me. So I was just telling her that that wasn't going to happen," Zara explained, Jill putting her hand on Zara's thigh.

"Sucks to be her," Jill replied, making Zara laugh. She

loved that Jill was so self-assured and didn't feel threatened or annoyed, and Zara reached for her hand, holding onto it tightly as Jill drove them to their first destination.

"Where are we going, actually?" Zara suddenly asked, realizing that Jill hadn't told her what they were going to be doing.

"Well! Now that you are here, I can tell you," Jill enthusiastically replied.

"We are going to do a few things today. And seeing as it's probably going to rain, I figured we should do the outside stuff first," Jill said, turning into the zoo parking lot.

"Love it, nice, good call. Can I get a stuffie?" Zara said, feeling herself drift into little space. Jill noticed, too, and smiled. She liked that Zara didn't try to hide herself from her.

"Only if you are a good girl and hold Mommy's hand," Jill replied, parking the car and getting out. Zara playfully skipped over to Jill after she got out of the car, delighting that there were only a few other people around.

"I guess not many people want to go out when it's overcast and rainy," Zara said, reaching for Jill's hand.

"No, which is perfect because it means there will be fewer people, more opportunity to be Mommy's baby girl," Jill whispered into Zara's ear. Zara giggled as they walked toward the ticket booth, Jill paying, and both of them walking in.

"I do think it's cruel that they cage up the animals, though," Zara said, looking at a jackal, noticing a bandage around its leg. Jill smiled.

"So do I. That's why I took you to this one. It's not like a normal zoo. It's a rehabilitation center. So, not all animals are here all the time. Like, I think I read online that there are no coyotes here at the moment because none have been brought in that need to heal. Only sick animals come here, and they stay only as long as they need to before being put back into the wild," Jill explained, delighting Zara.

"That is amazing!" Zara replied, happier to be here supporting the center.
They walked around the enclosures, looking at the animals and watching exhibits on snakes, flying foxes, and raccoons.

"I like that the lady said that even though raccoons are seen as a pest, that if an animal needs help, they provide it," Zara said as they looked at a bear who had been hit by a car. It had a bandaged side and was walking slowly towards a tree that had food strung up to it.

"Yeah, just like you. I still look after you, even when you are a pest," Jill teased, making Zara laugh.
They went to a food stand and bought hotdogs and soda before finding a spot underneath a tree that was dry.

"So, have you thought about what you want from the gift shop?" Jill asked, opening Zara's soda for her. She loved that she knew she could be her normal, caregiving self toward Zara without Zara feeling as though her autonomy was being taken away.

"Hmm, I think I just want a stuffie," Zara replied, snuggling into Jill as she ate her hotdog and watched a mountain lion being taken for a walk. It had a sore paw, and Zara watched as the handler walked slowly beside it.

"I think it would be really cool to work here," Zara said, imagining herself doing this job.

"Yeah, but just as you get attached to the animals, they would leave. I think I'm too much of a softie to do this job. I'd cry all the time," Jill laughed. Zara nodded her head, deciding that she would probably be just as emotional.

"But it would be so good because you would know that they are going back to the wild, where they belong. Animals don't belong in cages. Only for when they are sick and getting treated," Zara said, catching the way Jill was looking at her.

"What?" Zara whined, giggling as Jill continued to stare.

"Oh, nothing. You are just so cute. Come here, my little animal," Jill said, pulling Zara into her lap and holding her tight.

"Hey!" Zara giggled, Jill, letting her go and finishing her hotdog. There was something special about the way that Jill held her that made Zara feel as though nothing bad could ever happen to her, and she snuggled into the embrace, wishing that Jill never had to let her go.

Jill and Zara spent far longer in the gift shop than either of them had expected.

"Mommy, I can't decide," Zara whispered in Jill's ear. Zara had gone around the store several times, narrowing her choice down to two stuffies. One was a mountain lion, and the other was a bear.

"I think it's sad that they get hit by cars so much that they have these available all the time," Jill said, more to herself than anyone else, as she watched Zara loop the store once more.

"Baby," Jill said, catching Zara as she walked passed her.

"Yes?" Zara said, wide-eyed, making Jill laugh.

"Let's just get both. We have to get out of here. There are still things I have planned," Jill said, delighting Zara.

"Really?" Zara said, cuddling into her soon to be new stuffies.

"Yes, come on," Jill said, putting them on the counter before paying the lady.

Zara walked out of the zoo, cuddling both her stuffies. Jill gently put her seat belt on as Zara continued to play with them.

"I'm so happy you are having a good day!" Jill exclaimed, driving back onto the road.

"So, where are we going now?" Zara said as the rain began to fall on the windscreen.

"Wow, that was great timing," Jill said, turning on the

heating.

"I'm surprised how cold it gets when it rains, it's icy," Zara replied. Jill reached into the backseat and grabbed the blanket that she had packed.

"I thought we might need this later, but I guess you need it now, baby girl," Jill said, giving it to Zara. Zara snuggled into the thick blanket, warming up in seconds.

"So, where are we going now, Mommy?" Zara asked, yawning and turning her body to face Jill.

"The movies," Jill replied, making Zara's eye go wide.

"This really is the best day ever!" Zara exclaimed, clapping her hands in excitement.

Chapter 9

Zara was surprised how quickly the months seemed to pass by. Before she knew it, she and Jill were living together, had set up a dynamic that suited both of them, and were enjoying life at a level they hadn't thought possible. Zara's work with her clients had improved, and she felt as though she was able to understand them on a deeper level, especially where their relationship problems were concerned. Fiona had even settled down, having found herself another intern to occupy her time with, life was as close to perfect as it had ever been.

"Hey, hey," Fiona said, walking up to Zara at the refreshment station. Zara had taken to allowing Jill to decide what she wanted to wear, and it showed. Jill had taken her shopping for new work clothes, and Zara's slim-fitting skirt and plunging neckline knitted pullover had caught Fiona's attention the moment she laid eyes on her.

"Hi, Fi," Zara said, amused that under different circumstances, she could have called Fiona, Mommy.

"You look nice. I see Jill has taught you a thing or two," Fiona playfully teased, noticing how Zara's makeup was significantly more flattering than usual. Zara just rolled her eyes at Fiona, making her laugh.

"What makes you think that I didn't do this myself?" Zara replied, stopping what she was doing and turning around to look at Fiona, taking small sips of the hot chocolate she had just made herself.

"I don't know. I just thought maybe you'd have given that up?" Fiona said, beginning to make herself a coffee.

"Given what up?" Zara asked, happy that she had someone to talk to who understood, to a certain extent, the dynamic of her relationship. She had always hated having to give generic answers when people asked her how Jill was when she knew they wouldn't be able to handle the truth.

"Given up power over your appearance," Fiona said, a wicked smirk on her face.

"No. This is for me. Jill does enough," Zara said, walking away just to have Fiona grab hold of her upper arm, causing her to look up in surprise.

"Just be careful with how much you give up, alright? I have heard she has a propensity for demanding more and more," Fiona said before letting Zara go and kindly smiling at her that she wasn't used to seeing. Fiona always had an aura of superiority around her that it was almost unnerving to see her softer side coming through. Zara looked at her with a slight frown before going back to her desk, but Fiona's words were ringing in her ears. Zara thought back to the conversations she and Jill had, the way Jill had gotten Zara to write down the things she was happy to let her take over. It didn't feel like a power strip. It felt nice not to have to think about all the bills as they had a joint bank account in which both their pays went into. They both kept $800 a month for themselves, which they could spend any way they wanted. Zara had told Jill that she could be in charge of the food they ate, and she had never eaten better in her life. Jill had even helped her to buy a new car, letting Zara put her name on the insurance and ownership so that the premiums would be lower. Sure, Zara could see how, in a toxic relationship that there could be an abuse of power, but that wasn't Jill. She was a good person. She wasn't like that.

Zara brushed off the thoughts Fiona had put in her head, deciding that Fiona was probably just jealous as she got back on with her job.

Zara arrived home before Jill and collected the mail from the mailbox. It wasn't much, but it was something Zara loved doing because it made her feel grounded, that this was her home, and she belonged here. Jill had bought the house when they wanted to move in together. Zara had felt bad that she wasn't able to contribute much to the deposit, feeling spoilt and slightly embarrassed when Jill still put her name on the ownership paperwork. They had planted a strip of lavender up the garden path to the front door, and as Zara walked toward the door, she put out her hand and let it sweep past the lavender. They had planted it because of the bees it attracted, and on more than one occasion, Zara had been stung. For her, it was worth the risk. The warm afternoon sun shone down, warming Zara's hair by the time she arrived at the door, taking out her key but noticing the door was already unlocked. She frowned, everything in her body telling her not to go inside, she took out her phone and called Jill, happy when she heard her phone ringing inside. Still hesitant, she waited for Jill to pick up the phone.

"Hey baby," Jill happily said, making Zara walk into the house.

"Hey," Zara replied, seeing Jill in the living room, a cardboard box on the couch.

"The door was unlocked, I didn't think you would be home this early," Zara replied, putting her bag down and walking over to Jill, collapsing on the couch and kicking her heels off.

"I know that you have been struggling to maintain your fitness routine, so I thought this might help," Jill said, tilting her head toward the box. Zara looked at her suspiciously, peeking into the box, and squealing with excitement.

"A puppy!" Zara exclaimed, taking the German Shepherd puppy out of the box.

"A guy at work had a litter and asked if I wanted one. She's been vet check, and she's in great condition. You can call her anything you want," Jill said, watching as the puppy excitedly licked Zara all over.

"Mommy, I love her!" Zara said, disregarding the last trace of fear from her mind that Jill was an overbearing partner.

"Anything I want?" Zara asked, causing Jill to smirk.

"As long as it's not a silly name," Jill replied, stroking the dog's soft coat. Zara thought for a moment, snuggling into Jill and letting the puppy climb over the top of them. "Okay, what about Freya?" Zara asked, playing with the puppy's paws. She felt Jill kiss the top of her head.

"Freya it is," Jill said, surprised at how much the name suited the dog.

"So, I bought a few things that she'll need. You can take her for a walk now if you want, or a run?" Jill said, making Zara frown. Sure, she hadn't exercised in a while, but it seemed that Jill was trying to say something.

"And if I don't?" Zara said, as Jill got up and took the dog leash out of the bag.

"Well, we agreed that you would work out every day. So if you don't, you'll get this on your ass," Jill said, putting up her hands.

"Your choice," she said, as Zara reached out and took the leash, clipping it onto Freya's collar and putting her on the ground.

"Fine," Zara said, Jill just raising an eyebrow and heading into the bathroom to have a shower.

After that day, Zara couldn't shake the feeling that Jill was trying to take too much of her autonomy. She tried to ignore it, being annoyed when Jill controlled her little outfits at night even though she had been the one to suggest it in the first place.

Maybe I'm just moody tonight or something? Zara thought to herself, fussing, and testing Jill's patience.

"I don't wanna!" Zara yelled as Jill pulled her arm through the onesie.

"You're on your way to getting your ass spanked, little one," Jill sternly said as she rolled Zara onto her tummy and gave her a taste of what she could expect.

"But Mommy," Zara whined, trying to shield her ass from Jill's firm hand, with no avail.

"No. You've been a brat for days, and I am not putting up with it anymore," Jill replied, grabbing Zara by the upper arm and dragging her into the living room.

"Stand there," Jill said, turning Zara around and making her face the wall. Taking her wrists and putting them behind her back, Jill began to walk away.

"Don't you fucking dare of think of moving. You stay there until you decide to be a good girl for Mommy," Jill said, turning the light off and going back into the bedroom.

Well, at least I'm not getting spanked, Zara thought as she sighed deeply.
Jill sat at the edge of their bed and put her head in her hands.

What the fuck is going on? She thought to herself, disappointed at how the last few days had been. She thought back to all the times Zara had complained about following the tasks and boundaries that they had both agreed to and sighed.

Maybe work is really hard for her right now or something? Jill continued to guess, trying to figure out how their perfect world had turned so sour almost overnight. She was worried that her relationship with Zara was fast becoming like the relationship she had experienced time after time where everything was fine until it wasn't. As she lay on top of the bed, she knew that she needed to talk to Zara, but she wasn't sure how. When she had spoken to her about her concerns on other topics, Jill felt as though Zara would hide her true feelings and just agree to whatever Jill said. Jill rolled over and checked her phone. Zara had been out there for ten minutes, so Jill got up and walked out into the living room.

"Baby girl?" Jill asked as she turned on the light and looked at Zara.

"I'm sorry, Mommy," Zara said, feeling Jill come and cuddle her from behind.

"I know you are, baby girl," Jill said, sitting down and pulling Zara into her lap. Jill wrapped her arms around Zara and rocked her gently, wondering how to bring the issue up.

"Are you happy with how things have been this last week?" Jill asked, Zara, turning around in her arms.

"Yes, why?" Zara said, making Jill hold her breath.

"Because I think you're lying," Jill said, biting her bottom lip. Zara looked like she had just been busted sneaking a cookie she wasn't meant to be eating.

"Um, no. Why would I lie?" She replied. In her heart, she knew that she wanted to talk about her feelings. She just didn't know what words she should be saying. Jill sighed and pulled her knees up to her chest.

"It's just that. You can't tell me this week hasn't felt a bit. I don't know. A bit weird. Like you are pulling away from me. Am I doing something wrong?" Jill asked. Zara both loved and hated that Jill was so good at seeing her for all that she was, and she rolled her eyes and sighed.

"I just think that maybe I gave away too much power, and I want some of it back," Zara said, feeling the knot in her stomach tighten. She had always hated confrontation and had actively tried to avoid it. But she had slowly realized that there was a difference between avoiding confrontation and denying her own reality.

"Oh, really. Okay, then let's talk about what things you want control over then," Jill said, making Zara burst into tears. She hadn't thought that Jill would be so supportive, and she crawled into Jill's lap and cried into her chest.

"It's alright, sweetheart. Did you think I was going to get mad at you?" Jill lovingly asked as she rocked Zara. Zara just nodded her head as Jill soothed her.

"I don't want you to get mad at me," Zara said, feeling

her eyes sting. Jill continued to rock Zara, stroking her hair and wiping her tears away.

"Do you still like Mommy's cuddles?" Jill asked when she tried to put Zara down and was met with a resisting Zara.

"Yes," Zara softly replied, wanting to be held. Jill smirked to herself and wondered how Zara managed to live without her for all these years before they met.

She sure is a baby. She can tell me she wants all the independence in the world, she still needs Mommy, Jill thought to herself as she held onto Zara. She bent her head and kissed the top of Zara's head, enjoying the soft happy sounds that Zara made as she began to fall asleep.

Chapter 10

Zara wished that she didn't feel this way. It had been two weeks since she and Jill had decided on what Zara was going to reclaim control over, but she still felt as though something was not right. She looked over at Jill, who was sleeping next to her, wondering how much longer they would be together.

It's not even that she's bad or anything. I'm so lucky to have a Mommy, and I still feel this way, Zara thought to herself. She knew that she should be happy with Jill, but something just didn't feel right. It wasn't that she was doing something wrong, but something was missing. Jill stirred, causing Zara to beg that she wouldn't wake up.

I think I need to break up with her, she thought to herself before closing her eyes and squeezing them tight, trying not to burst out crying. Zara put her jacket on before closing the door to the apartment and walked down the street.

Maybe I just need some perspective, she thought to herself, not wanting to believe that she needed to break up with Jill. Zara passed people on the street as quickly as she could, wanting to be down by the park.

I wish I could just be happy. Why do I always have to feel as though I am searching for something? Zara thought as she walked through the park gates and toward her favorite spot by the water fountain. The day was one of those days that she knew she would never forget, not because it was anything particularly special, but because of the contrast between the weather and her feelings. Everything seemed to be the opposite. She was feeling torn up and confused on the inside, almost as though she was looking at her life through a window rather than being able to feel it. Yet the day outside of her was sunny, calm, and breezy enough to keep her at an even temperature. This was the type of day that was meant to be filled with laughter from friends at a barbecue or enjoyed with the person she loved, but her reality could not be further from the truth.

I hate this. I hate all of it, Zara thought as she wasted the day away.

"Baby girl, Mommy's home," Jill called as she walked into the house. She dropped her bag by the door and smiled as she heard music coming from their bedroom. Walking down the hall, Jill slowly took her scarf and coat off as she walked, stopping when she saw Zara in the middle of a huge pile of clothes.

"Mommy," Zara said, looking up at Jill, surprised to see her home so early. Zara commanded the music to stop and scrunched up her face.

"I didn't think you'd be home so early," Zara

apologetically said as she turned and looked at the huge mess on the floor.

"I can see that. What have you been up?" Jill said, putting her things away before sitting on the bed. Zara got up to join her, placing her hand on Jill's thigh as she snuggled into her.

"I wanted to find some new outfits, but I can't seem to make anything look good," Zara said with annoyance in her voice. Jill tried to suppress a smirk as she saw Zara's pouty face.

"Well. What sort of look were you going for?" Jill gently asked, sensing that this was a delicate topic.

"I don't know!" Zara dramatically exclaimed before she threw herself down onto the bed. Jill rubbed her back as she listened to Zara yell into the pillow.

"Okay, come on, show Mommy what sort of outfits you like," Jill said, deciding that Zara had been given enough time to feel sorry for herself. Zara let out a loud sigh and sat up, passing Jill her phone. Jill looked at the outfit styles as she flicked through the screenshots and nodded her head as she became more and more aware of the look Zara was trying to achieve.

"Okay. So, let's get all these clothes off the floor and see what we have to work with," Jill said, putting the phone down.

"But I've already tried that," Zara whined, getting a look from Jill.

"Move it," Jill said, pointing to the clothes. Zara got off the bed reluctantly and began to put the clothes on the bed. When she was finished, Jill helped her sort the clothes into the different looks, making a list of the things that Zara needed to complete the look.

"Thanks, Mommy," Zara quietly said as she snuggled into Jill, looking at the bed with all of the outfit choices.

"It's okay," Jill said, kissing the top of Zara's head and passing her a handful of coat hangers.

"Now put everything back on these and come out to the living room. I'm going to make a start with dinner," Jill said, patting Zara on the ass.

"Little one," Jill said, coming into the kitchen an hour later. Zara sat at the bench, her stomach in knots.

"I think we need to break up," Zara blurted out, taking Jill by surprise. Jill stopped walking and froze. This was not what she was expecting.

"Um, why?" Jill asked, coming to sit by Zara. Jill's hair falling to one side.

"Because I don't think this is working for me anymore, it just feels flat," Zara said, bursting into tears. Jill sighed and looked around the room, trying to process what Zara was telling her.

"It can get like this sometimes," Jill said, standing up and making herself a coffee. She looked out the window and rubbed her breasts as she waited for the water to boil in the kettle.

"I don't want to lose you," Jill said once the light went off, signaling that the water was ready for the coffee sachet.

"I know, I don't want to lose you either, but I also don't want to keep feeling this way. I don't know what I'm looking for, but I just feel like I can't get into little space with you at the level I want and need," Zara said, wishing that she didn't have to have this conversation.

"So, do you want to try and work through this, or do you want to go our separate ways?" Jill said, coming to sit down next to Zara.

"I kinda want to go our separate ways, but I really don't want it to be like a mean break up. I don't want to get into a fight with you," Zara fearfully said, making Jill tilt her head to the side.

"Zara. I am not going to get mean with you, sweetie! Of course, I am sad that we are ending this, but I'm not going to make it any harder than it is already going to be," Jill said, feeling her heartbreak.

"I can move out if you need me too. I can pay my half of the rent for the rest of the contract if you want," Zara said, feeling somewhat relieved that Jill was so civil.

"You can stay as long as you want Zara, I'm not about to kick you out onto the street," Jill laughed buttoning up her pajama skirt. Zara noticed the subtle way she was pulling away emotionally.

What were you expecting? She needs to protect herself as well, Zara thought to herself.

"I might move into the spare room tonight if that's cool?" Zara said, Jill just nodding her head and quickly standing up, going over to the sink and putting her coffee cup down.

"Do you want help? If not, I might go out tonight," Jill said, sadly looking at Zara.

"No, it's cool. I can do it myself," Zara said, Jill, forcing a smile and walking into their bedroom.

Fuck. I hope this was the right decision, Zara said to herself as she sat in the kitchen by herself.

Chapter 11

"Thanks for coming," Zara said as she opened the door to Fiona. Fiona stood in the doorway with her usual flamboyant outfit and resting bitch face.

"Anytime, I told you that," Fiona replied, suddenly changing into the sweet and kind person Zara had learned that she could be when the situation arose. Zara smiled, moved out of the way, and waited for Fiona to come inside, closing the door behind her.

"So, what's going on?" Fiona said, sitting in the living room and seeing the afternoon tea that Zara had set on the coffee table. Jill hadn't come home last night. She had text Zara saying that she would be staying with a friend for a few days. So Zara had invited Fiona over. Zara wasn't really sure what she expected from the afternoon, but she just knew that she needed a friend who understood what she was going through. Zara sat down on the couch, offering Fiona tea and cake and serving her before she got into the details as to why Fiona had been invited over.

"So. Things haven't been the best between Jill and I lately," Zara said, running her hand through her hair. Fiona raised an eyebrow.

"But you always seem so happy at work?" She questioned, enjoying the red velvet cake Zara had made. Zara sighed, nodding her head and wondering how she was going to explain the situation.

"I know. And for the most part, it is great. But, and I'm not blaming you, but ever since you asked if I was giving too much of myself up, I have felt all, I don't know, weird," Zara said, shaking her head and being disappointed that she wasn't able to articulate her feelings any better. Fiona looked shocked and disappointed.

"I'm so sorry. I didn't mean for you to take it like there was something wrong with how you guys were doing stuff," Fiona said, putting her plate down and looking concerned.

"You know I say stuff off the cuff," Fiona added, taking a sip of her tea.

"Yeah, I know. But I think you were right. And now, I just don't want the dynamic to continue to go the way it was going. I, I kinda don't want to be her baby anymore, and so I broke up with her, but I don't even know if that was right decision either," Zara said, putting her hand over her mouth after she heard herself. Fiona just shrugged her shoulders. Clearly, she didn't find this to be as shocking as Zara had.

"Then tell her that. Who cares if you don't want to be her baby anymore? That's ok, just break up with her. It's better to make a clean cut than to drag it out and cause both of you unnecessary heartbreak. But if you want to be with her, you better find a good apology gift," Fiona said, looking at Zara expectantly. Zara crossed her legs on the couch and thought for a moment.

"And that's the thing, I still like a lot of what we do, I just, I don't know, I want more control," Zara half yelled, getting frustrated, which made Fiona smirk.

"Have you thought about how much of a moody teen you sound like?" Fiona asked, the look on her face making Zara annoyed.

"Why do you find this so funny?!" Zara yelled, storming off into the kitchen to get a glass of water before coming back and sitting back down.

"Look. Has it occurred to you that maybe, just maybe, you are more of a middle than a little? And that maybe you felt more little when you had to care for yourself, but now that you have a Mommy and don't need to do everything yourself, you feel a little bit bigger?" Fiona asked, coming over to sit next to Zara, wrapping her arm around her.

"No," Zara said, the pout on her face making Fiona laugh.

"Maybe try it out, see if you like it. You can still wear diapers. You can still snuggle with a paci and a bottle, you can still have your train set, for example. But you can also do other things like deciding what you want to wear, what you want to eat, how much you work out, maybe have some different hobbies. I don't know, all I'm saying is that maybe you shouldn't limit yourself and therefore your relationship to just one thing. I like to think of it all as more of a spectrum and depending on the day, depends on how far along the spectrum you want to swing. If that makes sense?" Fiona said, smiling as she felt Zara reach out and hug her tightly.

"Thank you," Zara said, wishing she knew how she was going to word this so that Jill understood what she wanted.

After Fiona left, Zara finished moving her belongings into the spare bedroom.

I didn't realize how much stuff I had, Zara, though, as she collected the last of her things from their old bedroom just as she heard Jill coming home. Quickly running into her new room, Zara dumped the armful of little things on the bed before walking out to the living room.

"Hey," she said, seeing Jill coming through the door with two big shopping bags.

"Hi," Jill replied, putting the bags down on the kitchen bench, without looking at Zara.

"I moved my stuff out," Zara said as they looked at each other awkwardly.

"Okay, great," Jill said, feeling her stomach knot as she began to put the groceries away.

"Can I help?" Zara said, Jill, sighing and putting a bag of pasta down on the bench before turning to look at Zara.

"Yeah, sure," Jill sighed, before turning back toward the

pantry.

"Look. This is going to get really hard before it gets better," Jill suddenly said. She had spent the day at a café, reading every newspaper she could get her hands on and thinking about Zara, where their relationship had gone wrong and generally licking her wounds. It had been what she needed to spend the time to try and process the feelings she was feeling, but nothing had prepared her to feel the disappointment she now felt.

"I think maybe it would be good if you moved out. As I said, I'm not going to kick you out. I'll help you find a place if you like. I'm not just going to dump you on your ass, but I think it would be better for me if you were happy to move out," Jill said, wishing that she didn't feel the emotional pull toward Zara. Zara just nodded her head. She understood where Jill was coming from and didn't want to make it any harder for her than it would be already.

"That makes sense. I can look for a place tomorrow," Zara said, fake smiling. Jill returned the gesture, and they both stood in the kitchen in silence, looking at each other.

"This sucks," Jill laughed, shaking her head, enjoying a moment of relief from her broken heart.

"Yeah, I know. I'm sorry I was the one to do it," Zara said, feeling guilty. Jill just shrugged her shoulders.

"It happens. Maybe if I had given you more attention or done something differently, it wouldn't be the case, but it is so," Jill said, Zara, tearing up and shaking her head.

"I don't think so. I don't think it had anything to do with you or me doing or not doing something. I just think we want different things," Zara said, causing Jill to tilt her head in curiosity.

"What do you mean?" Jill said, feeling herself have a faint glimmer of hope in her heart that she could get Zara back.

"Like. I like diapers and baby stuff, but I kinda don't at the same time," Zara said, causing Jill to roll her eyes.

"Oh my fucking god, are you kidding me?" Jill said, raising her voice and somewhat starling Zara.

"What?" Zara defensively replied, feeling attacked.

"Maybe, you are more of a middle than a little? That could explain why you don't want super baby things anymore. Maybe I did such a great fucking job of looking after you that you moved up in your little age. It happens sometimes. I read about it," Jill said, rolling her eyes. Zara smirked for a moment, enjoying that the Mommies in her life understood things that had clearly escaped her.

"Would you be interested in trying it out with me?" Zara asked, making Jill laugh.

"Fuck me, darling. You sure know how to turn my life absolutely inside fucking out," Jill said, making Zara laugh.

"Imagine what goes on inside my head then," Zara laughed, feeling light for the first time in a while.

"Sure, why the hell not. Let's try it for a while and see if it's something we both like," Jill said, feeling her heart pounding in her chest as the emotional turmoil that she had experienced all day caught up with her.

"Can you stay in the spare room tonight, though? I need a minute to process everything," Jill said, taking out a bottle of wine and pouring two glasses.

"Here," Jill said, shaking her head as Zara laughed.

"Sorry," Zara genuinely said, feeling embarrassed, apologetic, and relieved at Jill's response. Jill laughed and shook her head.

"I feel so sick," Jill said, going to the couch and laying down. She put her arm over her eyes and sighed, letting the feeling wash over her.

"Can I be honest?" Zara asked, making Jill laugh.

"I think I can only take so much of your honesty for one day," Jill replied, feeling Zara sit down on the floor and put her face close to Jill's thigh.

"I didn't think you liked me that much," Zara whispered, causing Jill to sit up and look at her with a shocked expression on her face.

"What do you mean?" Jill questioned, surprised that Zara would feel that way.

"Well, like I just didn't feel like you did. I thought you weren't like super into me or whatever," Zara said, Jill, feeling like she was losing her mind.

"Mommy needs another drink," Jill said, getting up, Zara watching her from the floor.

"Zara. I fucking adore you," Jill said, taking a sip and coming back to the couch with her glass in one hand and the bottle in the other.

"Damn, we really have a few things we need to work on," Jill said as she drank. Zara just laughed.

"Have you heard of love languages?" Zara asked, watching as Jill placed her glass down.

"Not really," Jill replied. Zara stood up and moved to the couch, sitting down next to Jill and taking out her phone.

"Okay, so it's like everyone has their own love language. You can do a test to figure out which one is yours. Mine is gifts. So I feel most loved when I get gifts," Zara explained. Jill wrapped her arm around Zara, smiling when Zara snuggled into her.

"I think yours will be affection but do you want to do the test and find out? That way, we can start to do stuff that speaks the other person's love language?" Zara suggested, smiling as Jill nodded her head and took the phone in her hands.

Chapter 12

"How are you going?" Jill's friend Mike asked her a week later. Jill learned that her love language was primarily quality time, so she and Zara had tried to incorporate both of their love languages into their dynamic. Their dynamic had also taken on a different tone, with Zara doing a lot of different things such as listening to music more frequently, learning dances, and watching shows that were more stimulating than her previous cartoons.

"It's been good. I must say, it took a minute to feel better after she 'broke up' with me. I kind of felt like I didn't want to give her another chance because I was hurting, but when I realized that it was just her cute, dumb ass freaking out about not knowing how to communicate, I got over it," Jill explained making Mike laugh.

"I really don't know how you do it. I mean, I would lose my mind if somebody like Zara had me on an emotional roller coast like that," Mike said, taking a sip of his coffee. Jill just laughed.

"Yeah, but it's not like she does it on purpose. I really don't think she can help being a little bit, I don't want to use the word unstable, but I mean, she's learning how to control her emotions and learning about herself, and that sort of thing takes a while to figure out," Jill replied shrugging her shoulders. She smiled to herself, understanding that it was okay that Mike had no idea how she could manage it. The thing was, Jill didn't feel like she was simply managing. She felt as though as she was helping build and maintain her relationship with Zara.

"I mean, relationships take time to build, they change, and they develop. How boring if everyone just stayed the same. I'm happy that we are in a situation where we can build on our foundation. I'm in this for the long haul with her," Jill said, making Mike wonder if it was herself that she was telling this too and not him.

"I get that. But is that how Zara feels? If she was so quick to break up with you, maybe she isn't in it for the long haul like you are?" Mike asked. Jill thought about the comment for a moment before shaking her head.

"No, she is, she just never had somebody who was prepared to stay with her as she went through growth periods. She thought that the best way to evolve was to leave," Jill explained. Mike just shrugged his shoulder and made a face that told Jill that he accepted her answer, even if he didn't really understand it. Jill smiled as well and looked out the window, excited to get home to Zara. They had decided to spend the weekend in

Jill's cabin in the woods and Jill knew that she wanted to get home before sundown.

The wind was blowing stronger than Jill had thought it would as she looked out over the rolling hills. As the sun came down and the sky shone in muted hues of pinks and purples, she knew that she needed to get inside and start the fire.

"Zara?" Jill called as she passed the horses of her neighbor and walked inside. She had stayed with Mike longer than she had thought she would, and was worried that Zara would be a hangry little mess by the time she saw her. Shutting the wooden door to the cabin, Jill shivered as she looked around.

"Baby?" Jill called again, as she saw Zara walking out of their bedroom with her earphones in, startling when she saw Jill.

"Mommy!" Zara exclaimed, holding onto her chest.

"Oh my gosh, feel my heartbeat," Zara said as she ran over to the older woman. Jill smirked as Zara pulled up her t-shirt and placed Jill's hand on her chest.

"I have a sneaky feeling you want me to feel more than just your heartbeat," Jill said as she groped Zara's breasts, making her giggle.

"Maybe," Zara said, pulling back slightly when she saw the look in Jill's eye.

"So, have you done your chores?" Jill asked, looking around the living space. Zara beamed up at her, before running over to the fridge and taking her sticker chart in her hands and coming back over to Jill who was busy lighting the fire.

"Yep. See," Zara said, holding it up proudly. Jill looked over the sheet and smiled, patting Zara on the ass lovingly.

"I think that you need some new stickers," Jill said, taking it from Zara's hands and putting it back on the fridge. Zara was standing next to the fire, Freya coming to lay on the rug in front of it and warmed herself as Zara listened to Jill.

"Can we go into town to get them tomorrow, please, Mommy?" Zara said, turning her hands over as Jill came to stand behind her. Wrapping her arms around Zara's body, Jill rested her head on Zara's shoulder and kissed her cheek affectionately.

"We have to see. Mommy has a few things to do tomorrow," Jill replied, Zara, trying not to feel disappointed that it wasn't a straight yes. Nodding her head, Zara turned around in Jill's arms and snuggled into her breasts.

"What is it, baby girl? You've been a bit off all day, haven't you?" Jill questioned. Zara had spent the day trying to fight herself to remain happy and feeling balanced, but the day hadn't gone to plan at all, which meant her routine had been thrown into disarray. Usually, when this happened, she could just go for a run and almost reset herself, but as the winter winds had picked up early this year, the bite of the cold was too much to bear.

"I don't know. I just feel so, yuck," Zara said, sighing deeply.

"I don't want to feel like this, but I just don't feel right," she added, sitting down on the couch.

"Well. How about Mommy takes you out for takeout, and then we can come back and watch a movie?" Jill asked, hoping that would be enough to make her little one smile again.

"I'd like that. I just hate feeling this way," Zara said. Getting up, Zara walked into the mudroom and put her boots on. Jill had decided to keep the fire burning, and while they were out, Freya laying comfortably on her rug as the house warmed.

"My little snow bunny," Jill said, seeing the pink bandana Zara was putting on over her ears, it matched her blonde her perfectly.

"Burgers and shakes?" Jill asked, knowing that she would need to go for an extra-long hike the next morning to work it off.

"Perfect," Zara said, standing by the door. Although she was only eight years younger than Jill, Zara's youthful appearance kept Jill in Mommy space almost permanently. Looking at her beautiful girl waiting by the door, Jill knew why. Zara's long, wavy blonde hair, her tight figure, and firm but generous curves looked divine in her adult clothes and her little clothes. Jill smirked, wondering if Zara was in the mood for some playtime and grabbed the back of her jeans, pulling her back into her.

"Why have you got big girl panties on, baby girl?" Jill whispered in Zara's ear, roughly rubbing her through the front of her jeans. Jill loved how Zara instinctively began to bite her bottom lip and accept Jill's touch.

"Because I had to go into town today, Mommy," Zara replied, bending over and placing her hands on the wall as Jill unbuttoned the front of her jeans and cupped her pussy. Jill's hands were cold, and she smiled as she heard Zara gasp and try to get away from her touch.

"Where do you think you're going?" Jill said, pushing Zara's panties into her pussy and rubbing her gently. Zara just moaned as she was toyed with, feeling Jill's hand on the back of her head, keeping her face against the wall.

"Take these off, Mommy is going to put you in something more appropriate," Jill ordered, standing back and folding her arms across her chest. Zara turned around slowly, looking up at Jill with her innocent eyes as she obeyed her commands. Her jeans fell to the floor, Zara bending down to pick them up and hand them to Jill, who had her hand out waiting. Next, Zara slowly slid her panties off, her legs getting goosebumps as they were exposed.

"Go lay on Mommy's bed," Jill said, as Zara handed her her panties, before following the instruction. Zara walked into their room, crawled up onto the high bed, and waited for Jill.

She knew what was coming, and she felt butterflies of anticipation in her stomach as she waited. Jill loved diapering her when they were going out for small trips, enjoying how it made Zara feel small and cling to her. Usually, Jill would put her in a pull-up so that Zara could still wear her skinny jeans over the top, but tonight Jill had something else planned.

"We aren't getting out of the car tonight. So," Jill said, taking out a thick diaper and almost giving Zara a heart attack.

"Mommy, I can't wear that! What if someone sees?" Zara questioned, her eyes going wide as she tried to protest.

"Now, listen to me. If someone sees you, they are just going to think what a sweet little girl you are," Jill replied, enjoying the resistance in Zara's squirming body.

"Stay still for Mommy, or you'll get a spanking, and it'll still go on, is that what you want?" Jill said, placing the thick, crinkly diaper under Zara who just pouted.

"It's not fair," Zara whined, making Jill smirk. Zara crossed her arms over her chest and pouted as Jill sprinkled fresh baby powder over her and stuck the tabs of the diaper down.

"There, doesn't that feel nice, baby girl?" Jill questioned, going into the cupboard and taking out Zara's pink sweatpants and pulling them up and over her diaper. Rubbing her hands over the pants, Jill enjoyed watching as Zara resisted the pull into little space, deciding that she was going to be a brat instead.

"You know, I'm not happy with how snarky you've been tonight," Jill whispered in Zara's ear as she took her wrist and pulled her into the corner.

"So you can stand here until you fix that attitude, young lady," Jill said, putting socks onto Zara's feet before turning her body to face the wall. Zara just sighed dramatically before crossing her arms over her chest and resting her weight on one foot.

"Oh, is that what you thought you'd be doing with your hands?" Jill said, taking Zara's wrists and tying them behind her back, pulling them tightly.

"Mommy!" Zara whined, her little voice escaping and making her pout in defeat.

"That's better," Jill said, patting Zara on the top of her head before walking out of the room and leaving Zara to stand in the corner. Jill walked out to the living room and sat down, enjoying how warm the space was, and she lay down on the couch and took out her phone. Flicking through social media, she came across an account that had some half-decent content. Jill smiled as she scrolled through the photos and stopped when she saw a few scenes that she knew she wanted to explore with Zara. Putting her phone down, Jill got off the couch and walked back to the bedroom and looked Zara in the eye.

"Still feeling like you want to be bratty for Mommy?" Jill asked, already knowing the answer.

"No, Mommy," Zara said, shaking her head and looking up at Jill and trying to grab at her wanting to be held.

"Good girl," Jill said as she opened her arms and held onto Zara, who snuggled into her like her life depended on it.

"You know, Mommy had a few ideas while you were fixing your attitude," Jill said with a wicked grin that told Zara everything she needed to know.

"Mommy," Zara whined as she watched as Jill took off her shirt, knowing that she was in for a wild ride.

"Oh yes, that's exactly what I want to hear, little girl," Jill replied, cupping Zara's chin in her hand and forcing her eyes to look up at her. Zara felt Jill begin to grab at her sweat pants, pulling them down roughly, Zara kicking them off.

"I don't know why I didn't just do this in the first place," Jill said, sitting down and bending Zara over her knee.

"Girls who are rude need to be taught a lesson," Jill said as she spanked Zara firmly, leaving red handprints all over her thighs and making her ass sting, even though the diaper. Zara knew that she needed to stay quiet, or she'd get extra spanks, but as Jill landed the final blow, she yelped.

"Oh, you know what that means," Jill said, taking a gag from the bookshelf and pushing it into Zara's mouth, securing it around her neck and continuing to spank her. Zara wriggled on Jill's lap, causing Jill to hold her down with her forearm as she spanked Zara's thighs.

"If you had been a good girl, instead of a bratty little

slut, I wouldn't have to do this," Jill said, enjoying being able to be more firm and aggressive with Zara's punishments. Zara stopped thrashing around on Jill's lap, making Jill begin to rub Zara's diapered ass and thighs between spanks, eventually slowing them down until she was only stroking Zara. Taking the gag from her mouth, Jill pushed Zara to the ground and pulled her panties off before bringing Zara's mouth to her pussy.

"Don't make me wait," Jill said, holding Zara firmly in place as she began to lap at Jill's cunt with enthusiasm.

"There's my good girl. Did your moody little ass need to be reminded who was in charge?" Jill moaned as Zara expertly fucked her.

"Put your hands behind your back," Jill instructed, pulling Zara's head back to slap her cheek.

"Look up at me," Jill commanded, looking down into Zara's eyes and was edged closer and closer. Zara could feel herself slowly coming out of this space and wanting this to stop, grateful when Jill came quickly, pulling her head backward.

"Mommy," Zara softly said, Jill, looking down to see Zara needed to stop.

"It's ok, sweetie. Mommy is here," Jill said, picking Zara up from the floor and bringing her into her arms. Jill hadn't been so rough with Zara before and knew that their dinner plans would need to wait.

"Shh, Mommy's here," Jill cooed, feeling Zara snuggle into her. She was secretly happy to have Zara become so needy for her once again, not having realized just how much she had missed having her grabby hands reaching for her.

"Bath and quiet time?" Jill said. Zara just nodded her head and thought for a moment.

"Maybe a shower, though," Zara replied, Jill, smiling to herself. She was still adjusting to Zara feeling more grown-up than the little she had first been when they started their relationship.

"Okay. Do you want me stay or go?" Jill asked as they walked to the shower.

"You can stay," Zara said, turning on the water before undressing herself. Jill sat on the wooden stool in the bathroom, and watched as Zara put her clothes in the wash basket, set her diaper aside and stepped into the shower. The water ran down her body, and Jill smiled to herself as she looked at her beautiful girlfriend.

"I think I want my new pajamas. Tonight, Mommy, but like, a diaper still, for when we go out," Zara said from the shower.

"Could you get them for me, please?" She added, smiling as she saw Jill stand up.

"Sure, sweetie," Jill said before walking into the bedroom. She took down a diaper and rummaged through Zara's section of the cupboard before finding the pajamas she wanted just as Zara walked into the room.

"Can Mommy do it for you?" Jill asked, holding up the diaper, happy when Zara nodded.

"Okay, lay up here for me then, princess," Jill said, patting the stop on the bed that she wanted Zara to lay down. Obediently, Zara moved to where Jill wanted her and moved her body at Jill's command while she was diapered.

"I can do this myself, though," Zara said, putting her pajamas on and putting her hair in a messy ponytail. Jill smiled and watched as Zara took over, happy that she hadn't lost her baby girl.

I guess that's the thing with growing with someone. They will want new things, you'll want new things, and finding the happy medium in the middle with where the hard work comes in, Jill thought as she watched.

"You're a cutie, baby girl," Jill said, as Zara snuggled into her, coming to sit in her lap. Zara took out her phone and gave Jill an AirPod before turning on a movie.

"Yeah, I might be a big girl, but I will always need Mommy's cuddles," Zara said, as Jill ordered their dinner online and turned off the light as the movie began.

Mommy's Got You, Honey

Scarlett wasn't looking for a Mommy, but when she found someone who opened her up to a loving and supportive MDLG dynamic, she couldn't hide her ABDL side any longer

Tina Moore

Chapter 1

"Dude, just take it. No one is even looking," Scarlett's friend Scott whispered to her as they walked through the aisles of the supermarket. Scarlett had been between jobs for the last two months, and it was starting to take its toll. She had enough money to pay for rent and a few utilities, but she had been losing weight as a result of not having any money left over for food.

This was typical of her life, three steps forward, and two steps back. Maybe it had something to do with the fact that Scarlett lived her life walking the line between right and wrong for as long as she could remember. It wasn't that she tried to be bad. It was just that every time she tried to be good, something bad would happen. She tried to make friends, and they would turn out to be into drugs. She tried to get a job. Her boss would bully her. She tried to do well in school. The popular kids would beat her up and spread nasty rumors about her. So in the 24 years that Scarlett had been on earth, she had learned to only depend on herself. The problem was, depending on yourself when you are between jobs can be somewhat of a tricky situation.

"I can't. The cops said that next time they catch me, it'd

be jail time. You don't get it," Scarlett replied, pushing her hands in her pockets. She watched as Scott boldly turned and swiped a large can of tuna from the shelves, putting it in the front pocket of his hoodie and shrugging his shoulders.

"It's not like we are stealing alcohol or candy or cigarettes. We are literally just trying to survive," Scott sassed, making Scarlett roll her eyes and continue to walk through the store toward the cold food section.

It was true. In all the time that Scarlett had known Scott, he had never robbed a family or an old lady. He only ever took things from huge franchises that he knew would be okay if a 90cent can of tuna or corn or something like this, was taken. Scarlett shrugged her shoulders as she felt the rumble in her stomach and picked up a packet of cheese.

"I hope you're ready to run," Scott said as he saw the store security approach them as they headed toward the door.

"Let's go," Scarlett reluctantly nodded before breaking into a sprint and sidestepping the security. They raced down the streets, dodging other pedestrians and feeling the wind in their hair, laughing as they reached the park and turned around to see that the security guard had stopped chasing them and was walking back into the store.

"Nailed it," Scott panted, slapping Scarlett on the back. She was doubled over and felt as though she was going to be sick.

"I wasn't sure I'd make it. I am so hungry I was worried

my legs would give way," Scarlett said as she stood up and began to walk through the park, towards her apartment.

"Want to come in? I've got some bread. We could have tuna and cheese sandwiches?" Scarlett offered, a delighted Scott beaming at her.

"Sounds perfect!" He exclaimed as they walked out of the park and onto the street.

"You there, stop," Scarlett heard an angry male voice as she was grabbed and pushed against the side of a brick building.

"You're under arrest. You have the right to remain silent," the male voice boomed as Scarlett saw Scott take off down the street, looking back in distress as he saw Scarlett being frisked before being pushed into the back of the police car.

That was two years and fifty-one weeks ago. Scarlett had successfully stayed out of trouble in jail of all places by keeping a low profile and following the rules the top dog demanded. She had even found herself a girlfriend who had some status, so for the most part, everyone had left Scarlett alone.

"Hey baby," Ross, Scarlett's girlfriend, said as she walked into the yard. Scarlett knew the drill. She walked over to Ross, kissed her passionately while letting Ross grope her before sitting on her lap and being put on display. Scarlett didn't really care. She had seen what happened to girls who didn't have the protection. They either ended up being used as mules for the top dog and all her friends or by the guards as fuck dolls. Both choices, Scarlett found to be less pleasant than being Ross's plaything.

"Hey, Daddy," Scarlett replied. Ross had told her that's what she liked to be called. Apparently, it turned Ross on and made her feel tough, but it did nothing for Scarlett.

"You're getting out in a week, aren't you?" One of the women standing around them asked.

"Yeah, we will have to see about that," Ross replied before Scarlett had a chance to speak. Ross cupped Scarlett's pussy predatorily while she sucked her bottom lip before slapping Scarlett's thighs and standing up behind her.

"See you later. I have some things I need to do," Ross said to Scarlett before she walked away, her friends following and leaving Scarlett standing alone in the yard. It didn't bother her, but as she looked around and up to the warden's office, she couldn't help but notice the warden looking down on her.

Fucking creep, Scarlett thought to herself before going back inside and heading to her cell.

"D block, showers," a guard aggressively yells as he walks down into the seating area. As the women start to file down the stairs, Scarlett looked for Ross. Usually, Ross made sure she got to shower with Scarlett and would find her along the way to the shower block, but as Scarlett approached the block, Ross was still nowhere to be seen.

Scarlett walked into the shower block. She noticed Ross leaning against the wall.

"Hey, baby girl," Ross almost snarled. Scarlett tilted her head, surprised at the venom in Ross's eyes as she felt a blow come down on the back of her head. Falling to the ground, Scarlett felt the kicks on at least four of Ross's friends as they stomped on her body and kicked her until she was a wailing mess on the floor. Ross snapped her fingers, and they stopped, leaving Scarlett writhing on the floor, clutching her stomach.

"What the fuck, Ross?" A guard grunted, picking Scarlett up and glaring at Ross. Not because he was annoyed that Scarlett was hurt, but because now he had to explain it to the warden.

"What, she slipped," Ross said, shrugging her shoulders and walking into the shower cubicle. Scarlett was picked up under her arms and marched to the medical block, where the guards pushed her onto a bed.

"She fell," one of the guards said to the nurse who was looking unimpressed by the situation.

"Yeah, I see that," the nurse sassed, as she closed the door behind the guards.

"What really happened, sweetie?" The nurse gently said as she began to disinfect the cuts over Scarlett's face and arms.

"I slipped," Scarlett whispered, making the nurse nod her head, understanding how the situation went.

"Alright, let's get you all fixed up then," the nurse practically cooed as she began to treat Scarlett.

Scarlett stayed in the medical block for a few hours before she saw the guards coming back.

"She's not ready to be taken back," the nurse said as the guards began to pull Scarlett from the bed.

"She's not going back. Warden said to put her into solitary to keep her out of trouble," the guard replied, tightening his grip on Scarlett's upper arm as she tried to pull away.

"I don't want to go in there," Scarlett yelled, the fear in her voice upsetting the nurse.

"Don't worry. You'll be out in a week. Think of it as a silent retreat before going back into the real world. Now move!" The guard bellowed, pushing her forward and out into the corridor. It felt like a blur to Scarlett as she was bustled down the corridor after corridor. The nurse had given her some pain killers that had made her sleepy, and as she was pushed into a small, dark room, she collapsed on the bed as heard the door slam shut.

Now what? Scarlett thought to herself as she closed her eyes and went to sleep.

"Scarlett," a woman's voice affectionately called, causing Scarlett to wake up. She had no idea what time it was, as there were no windows and, therefore, no natural light. The singular ceiling light was broken, and as she slowly sat up in darkness, she could feel that someone was sitting next to her.

"It's okay, Scarlett. I'm not going to hurt you. It's me, Warden Healy. But you can call me Esther," Esther explained.

"Why are you here?" Scarlett softly asked, not wanting any more trouble. It was bad enough that she would have to spend the next seven days locked up here. She didn't need to make matters worse by the warden taking an interest in her.

"I wanted to make sure you were alright. We both know you didn't fall," Esther simply stated. Scarlett shook her head, seeing the door begin to open and shielding her eyes from the light.

"Oh, good. I was hoping that it wouldn't take you long to fix this light," Esther declared as she watched the repairman begin to set his ladder up and tinker with the light fixture.

"Why are you doing this?" Scarlett whispered, slowly taking her hand away from her eyes and looking at Esther. What she saw surprised her. Usually, Esther's hair was in a tight, slicked-back bun, her uniform impeccable and a look for sheer domination on her face. What greeted Scarlett was anything but dominating. Esther had her long brown hair out, the waves softening her face, which had a natural covering of subtle makeup. She wasn't in uniform. Rather she was wearing casual clothes, the type that you would comfortably wear around the house. Her eyes didn't try to pierce through

Scarlett's soul either. They were kind, gentle, almost loving. Scarlett shook her head, feeling herself being drawn to the woman. Esther noticed how Scarlett's pupils dilated as she took her in, and she tried to hide a satisfied smirk. This was the reaction that Esther was hoping to elicit from Scarlett.

Over the last, almost three years, Esther had watched Scarlett. How she interacted with the other inmates, the types of activities she enjoyed participating in, and the way she would snuggle into her blankets when she thought no one was watching. But Esther was always watching, and if there was one thing Esther knew how to spot, it was a little. However, the risk of trying to start something with Scarlett was far too high, for multiple reasons. Firstly, it was completely unprofessional and an abuse of power. Secondly, it could put Scarlett at risk, and thirdly, she could lose her job over it. Not to mention, if Scarlett didn't reciprocate the feelings, it would be disappointing. Yet now, with Scarlett in solitary confinement, and about to be released, Esther thought that the risk was justified.

"Thank you for fixing that," Esther said to the repairman as he tested the switch, turning the light on before nodding and leaving.

"You can go to, you know," Scarlett snarled. She knew that having the warden's attention could only ever end in disaster and wanted to be as far away from her as she could.

"I'll go, but before I do, I thought you might want this,"

Esther calmly explained, taking Scarlett's blanket from behind her back and handing it to her. Scarlett couldn't contain her excitement and reached out to take it and brought it close to her face, burying her face in it before looking at Esther fearfully.

"It's alright, I'm not asking for anything," Esther reassured Scarlett before standing up and walking out of the cell, closing the door gently behind her.

Chapter 2

Scarlett fell asleep curled up in her blankie, only waking to the muffled sound of inmates yelling and bouncing a ball outside her cell.

Must be yard time, Scarlett thought as she rubbed her eyes. The room was still dark and cold from the night, and Scarlett was glad she had her blankie to wrap around her tightly. She uncurled herself from her sleeping position and stretched. It felt strange to be by herself. Strange in the sense that she felt safe for the first time, as though she didn't have to be on guard. Walking toward the wall, she found the light switch and turned it on, happy that she had control over that.

I guess it's the little things, Scarlett thought to herself, wildly aware that not all cells had a switch that the inmate could control. She blinked her eyes until they adjusted to the brightness of the room and felt her way back to the bed. Sitting down, Scarlett sighed again, shaking her head and beginning to cry into her hands. This was the first time that she had cried in three years, and the tears stung her eyes as they fell into her hands.

"Shh, there there, it's okay, sweetie," came a voice that made Scarlett freeze. Looking up, Scarlett saw the face of

Esther looking back at her, and she fearfully looked behind her to see that the door to the cell was closed.

"How?" Scarlett began to say as she tried to pull away from Esther and wipe her tears away.

"You didn't hear me come in?" Esther asked, reaching out and wiping Scarlett's tears from her cheek. Scarlett hated herself for pausing for a moment to let her before flinching and moving back, sitting with her knees to her chest against the wall.

"No," Scarlett replied, glaring at Esther. Esther looked at Scarlett, with a look of amusement and desire in her eyes.

"What?" Scarlett aggressively yelled, annoyed that her body was craving the gentle touch of the woman sitting opposite her. Everyone knew that a guard's affectation was dangerous. It didn't take a genius to know that interest from the warden was even riskier.

"Nothing, I just can't believe that you'll be out of here soon," Esther replied, shifting closer to Scarlett.

"Yeah, thank fuck. I'm sick of this shit hole," Scarlett replied, making Esther laugh.

"Yes, I would be too if I had to live in here," Esther said, taking Scarlett by surprise.

Don't fucking do it. Don't do it! Scarlett internally screamed to herself, feeling the emotional pull toward Esther and hating herself for it.

"Well, I'm glad that you are up. Enjoy your day," Esther

said, slapping her hands down onto her thighs before getting up, walking to the door but then turning and facing Scarlett.

"Can I get you anything?" Esther asked, making Scarlett frown.

"No," Scarlett replied, annoyed that Esther was so seamlessly creeping into her mind. Esther winked at Scarlett before she opened the door, only to close it again, locking it and walking back down the corridor.

"I'm so fucked," Scarlett said out loud as she lay back down on the plastic mattress and closed her eyes shut, hoping just to sleep the day away.

Scarlett spent the rest of the day trying to build a routine. She did push-ups, sit-ups, planks, and squats. She took naps and tried to make her meals last for as long as they could. Yet, no matter how hard she tried, she couldn't get the image of Esther out of her mind. Never before had she spent any time thinking about her, and yet, within two days, Esther had become all she could think about.

Relieved when the run went down, Scarlett finished her dinner, curled up in bed, and wrapped her blanket around her.

"Another cold night," she said out loud, wishing that she was already free and on the outside.

"Fuck off," Scarlett yelled as she heard the door to her cell open, assuming it was one of the guards. They had a habit of making getting a good sleep impossible.

"That's no way a young lady should be speaking," Scarlett heard, smiling despite herself as she realized that it was Esther standing in the doorway.

"Oh, sorry, I didn't think it was you," Scarlett replied, having to shake her head once she realized what she had said.

"That's better," Esther remarked, delighted at the change in Scarlett's voice and tone once she knew it was her.

"What is it?" Scarlett replied. She had decided that as long as she stayed in solitary than having a fling with the warden couldn't do her any harm, and had been planning on how she was going to seduce Esther if she insisted on continuing her visits.

"I thought you might need a friend. It's a cold night," Esther explained, closing the door behind her but keeping the lights off.

"Couldn't you get in trouble for this?" Scarlett asked, feeling Esther sit down next to her. As Scarlett tried to get up, she felt Esther reach out and push her back down on the bed, making her gasp but comply.

"Good girl," Esther cooed, placing a soft stuffed toy next to Scarlett.

"I know you only have a little bit of time left with us, and I wanted to make that time special for you. I know that you are a baby, I can see it in your eyes," Esther said, making Scarlett blush. She was happy that the room was dark. The last thing she wanted was to give Esther the satisfaction of knowing she was correct.

"Whatever," Scarlett replied, rolling over just to feel Esther's hands on her body, rolling her back, so she was facing her. Scarlett whined and wriggled, making Esther smile, her noises moistening her cunt and giving her the predatory edge she loved to experience.

"Shh, don't fight Mommy, little one," Esther said, stopping Scarlett in her tracks. Her heart skipped a beat, hearing those words from Esther, and she froze, unsure of what to do next.

"That's what I thought. Now come on, come and cuddle with Mommy and let's get that little body all warmed up," Esther said, placing another big blanket over Scarlett and coming to lay down next to her. Scarlett hated herself for turning into face Esther, her perfume soft, and her touch melting. Esther held Scarlett close to her chest, smiling when Scarlett reached her hand up to touch Esther's breasts.

"Yes, good girl," Esther said, kissing the top of Scarlett's head and gently beginning to rock her. Esther snaked her hand down Scarlett's back, over her ass and around to her pussy, making Scarlett gasp as she was touched. She wasn't used to being taken so gently. Ross had always been so rough and aggressive, Scarlett found the emotions that came with Esther's tender touch startling.

"Mommy isn't going to hurt you. Not like that awful woman you've been letting fuck you for protection," Esther said, still gently cupping Scarlett's pussy over her pants. Scarlett bit her bottom lip and tried to move away from Esther, Esther only laughing and pulling her back.

"I said I was gentle, not that you weren't going to give me what I came for," Esther explained, the feeling of being used, painfully familiar to Scarlett.

"Just get it over with then," Scarlett sighed, the hurt in her heart feeling more intense than she thought it would be. Esther began to rub her, putting her hand down Scarlett's pants and kissing her neck.

"It's no fun if you don't want it, I'll be back when you're more in the mood," Esther said, standing up and walking to the door. Scarlett lay silent on her bed. She wasn't sure what she was meant to say.

I don't know if I like it more, her being here or her leaving me alone, Scarlett thought as she saw the cell door open, closing swiftly and leaving the room silent and in darkness.

Chapter 3

What the fuck is all this? How am I supposed to deal with it? Surely she could find someone to be with on the outside? Why does she have to make me so fucking horny? Scarlett thought to herself over breakfast. Her bruising was healing as it should, and she knew that she only had a few more nights before she'd be able to be released.

I don't want her to come back. She'll probably be really mad if I refuse her again, Scarlett thought, wondering how to put off fucking Esther.

It's not that she's ugly or something, but I just wish she wanted me for me, she only sees me as a fucktoy, just like Ross does, Scarlett continued to think, feeling stupid that for a moment she thought that someone would actually want her for her, not for the innocence that they saw in her. She had always thought it was strange that women seemed to get high off taking her. As though by ruining the innocent and vulnerable sides of Scarlett would somehow feed their rotten souls or something.

"I just want to go home," Scarlett said softly to herself, wishing that it would come faster. The thing about jail is that Scarlett had never felt safe. She knew that someone was always sizing her up that she couldn't trust anyone and that, evidently, even the people who were meant to protect her, and were only interested in their own motives. She imagined what getting out would mean. Feeling the soft grass under her toes, the wind in her hair, and being able to close her eyes and know that nothing bad could happen to her filled her with hope and excitement.

"You look pleased with yourself," Esther said, opening her cell door and making Scarlett open her eyes.

"I was just thinking of what I'm going to do when I get out of here," Scarlett replied, moving over to that Esther could sit next to her.

"And what is that?" Esther asked, placing a hand on Scarlett's thigh, high enough to make Scarlett look at Esther with questioning eyes.

"How about you lay back and let Mommy look at you?" Esther knowingly said, pushing Scarlett down. Scarlett bit her bottom lip, deciding that letting Esther have her fun was a better idea than annoying her.

Sure, she's not your first pick, but she's okay, and she's been gentle with you so far. You might as well let her, Scarlett thought to herself as Esther pulled on her pants.

"These can come off. Oh, baby, they really did a number on you, didn't they?" Esther said, kissing the bruises along Scarlett's thighs, making her shiver.

"I fell," Scarlett said, a tear escaping her eyes.

"Yes, I know you did, princess," Esther replied, pulling Scarlett's panties down and quickly licking her slit and making her gasp.

"Sweet little thing," Esther said, parting Scarlett's pussy lips with her tongue and tasting her deeper.

"Shh, it's okay, baby girl," Esther cooed as Scarlett gasped and tried to pull away from her.

"I'll be gentle, don't worry," Esther said, pushing Scarlett back down and gently licking and teasing her. Scarlett had to admit, it felt more loving than anything she had experienced in here, and as she let Esther have her way, she closed her eyes and gave in to the sensations.

Sure, it's a bit of an abuse of power, but it still feels so good, Scarlett thought, arching her back and pushing Esther's head away as she came, quickly huddling in the corner and looking at Esther with a frown on her face.

"You don't need to be scared, little one. Mommy isn't going to hurt you," Esther gently said, opening her arms to Scarlett, who slowly moved into them. Esther held onto Scarlett until her body relaxed, and she began to snuggle into the neck of Esther.

"I want my pants back on," Scarlett whispered, making Esther smile.

"Here, baby girl," Esther replied, reaching down and putting Scarlett's clothes back on her body. Scarlett reached for Esther once she was dressed, and Esther smiled as she finally had a compliant Scarlett wanting and needing her embrace.

"Mommy has to go now, baby girl," Esther said, enjoying the soft whine that came from Scarlett as she affectionately pried her hands off her.

"Will you come back?" Scarlett asked, the desperation in her eyes and voice filling Esther with the feeling of power and domination she longed to feel.

"If you're a good girl and play with yourself for me, I'll be watching," Esther said, tilting her head to the corner of the room where a camera was recording.

"Okay," Scarlett replied, biting her bottom lip and watching as Esther left her cell.

Scarlett waited a few minutes before timidly reaching into her pants and touching herself. It was one thing to pleasure herself when she knew no one was watching. It was a different thing entirely when she knew that Esther would be looking. The last night of her incarceration would be that night, and she thought about all the things she would do with her freedom. Feeling a shiver flow over her body, Scarlett teased herself, hoping that it was only Esther who was watching.

I guess I'll get out of here and use the $15 I have for a bus fare to the city. Then stay at Scott's place for a few nights while I try and get a job, save up a bit and then get my own place and take it from there, Scarlett thought to herself, arching her back, annoyed her wrist wouldn't flex enough to allow her to hit her g-spot. The only thing that she wasn't looking forward to doing on the outside was the mandatory therapy sessions that she had 50 hours during her probation period. Thinking about that made her angry, which in turn made her stop playing with herself, getting herself out of the mood almost instantly. She rolled over to face the wall and closed her eyes.

She had been told to go to therapy countless times in the past, always deciding that it was better to keep her fucked up ways to herself. It wasn't that she thought what she kept secret was particularly bad, but it was something that she would rather no one know, ever.

Maybe Esther wants to continue this on the outside. Maybe I will finally have something that I want, Scarlett thought to herself as she opened her eyes on the day of her release. Esther had come back that night to say goodnight and for a cuddle, telling Scarlett that she would be released in the morning and that she was a good girl for following Esther's request to pleasure herself. Scarlett loved how it felt to allow herself to slip into little space, even at the shallow level that Esther seemed to bring out of her so easily. Scarlett's thoughts were interrupted by the sound of the guards opening her cell door and telling her that her time was up.

"Pretty nice show you put on last night. Never had a girl submit so easily," one of the guards sneered, causing Scarlett to feel a knot in her stomach instantly.

Don't say anything, just get out of here, she said to herself, feeling her eyes well up.

How could she, the fucking bitch, Scarlett internally screamed as she was given her belongings, processed and suddenly outside the prison gates and looking out onto the street.

"Okay, so, fuck," Scarlett said out loud, feeling overwhelmed and wishing she had somebody to turn to. She turned around, looking at the big building, surprised that for a moment, she wished she was back inside.

At least I knew what the rules were, she thought, deciding that she needed to wipe Esther from her mind and focus on what she was trying to do.

Get your life back, that's the only plan, she thought as she walked out into the sun and tried to find the bus station.

Chapter 4

Scarlett decided that it was better just to let go of the idea that she and Esther would have anything to do with each other on the outside.

She could do what she wanted in there, that's not the sort of person you want to be with, Scarlett told herself as she walked up to Scott's front door. He had obviously done alright for himself, as she stood on his doorstep and waited impatiently.

"Hello?" A voice said, causing Scarlett to turn around, her eyes going wide as she looked at the beautiful woman standing in front of her.

"Oh, hi. I'm looking for Scott," Scarlett said, trying with all her might not to look at the woman's breasts in the tight, fluffy light pink sweater.

"You must be Scarlett," the woman said, opening her arms and pulling Scarlett into her. Scarlett held her breath and bit her lip, looking up at the sky and trying not to blush as she felt the woman's firm embrace.

"Yeah," Scarlett replied, slowly pulling away.

"I'm Emily. Scott's girlfriend, he mentioned that you would be staying with us for a while. He said that you two used to get up to all sorts of mischief and that you took the fall for him a few years ago," Emily said, taking Scarlett's hand and walking her inside, shutting the door behind her and giving her a moment to take in her new surroundings.

"Nice, huh?" Emily laughed, putting Scarlett at ease. Scarlett liked that Emily hadn't brought up the whole jail thing, she seemed to know how to talk without triggering her in any way, and that made Scarlett instantly like her.

"Scott is just out getting a few things, he should be back in about 30minutes or so," Emily explained, leading Scarlett through the house and to a guest bedroom. Scarlett didn't want to say that this was the nicest place she had ever been. She thought her silence and facial expressions made it clear enough.

"Do you want a shower? Sometime to unpack and relax? Tell me what you need, honey," Emily said, affectionately stroking Scarlett's arm and looking at her with the warm and lovely eyes that made her stomach knot and churn.

Scott is one lucky son of a bitch, Scarlett thought as she cleared her throat.

"Maybe a shower, yeah. I'd love to get out of these clothes. I kinda just want to burn everything and start from scratch," Scarlett replied, surprised that she was so open with Emily.

"Well, I can't let you burn them, but we can absolutely

throw them out and get you some new things. Do you want to go to the shops with me tomorrow and we can get you everything that you'll need?" Emily said, stopping when we saw Scarlett sit on the bed, smiling up at her.

"Yeah, that'd be great," Scarlett replied. She figured she'd just buy a few pairs of panties, that way she could continue to wash her clothes until she had enough money to buy new ones. Scott had told Emily that Scarlett was attractive, but he had obviously not seen her for a few years, because she was stunning.

I bet jail was hard for you, cutie, Emily thought as she looked into Scarlett's big eyes.

"Okay, enjoy your shower," Emily said, reaching into the cupboard and passing Scarlett a navy towel before turning and walking out of sight.

Scarlet walked into the shower, turned the tap on, and looked around the room.

Shit, this is so nice, she thought to herself, looking at the shower gels, shampoos, and conditioners.

He made it. I wonder how they even met, Scarlett thought as she tried to wash away three years of bad memories.

She heard Scott come home, smiling as she wondered how he would look and what sort of person he was now. He had never visited, but they had talked on the phone while she had been away. Getting changed into her old clothes, she nervously walked out to see him standing in the living room.

"Hi," Scarlett timidly said, waving at him and relaxing once she saw his face light up.

"Scarlett!" Scott exclaimed, rushing over to her and bear-hugging her, making her laugh. He had changed. He had a beard, he seemed taller, and he wasn't that hungry kid she remembered. He was muscular, thick-set, and strong.

"Wow, you've changed," Scarlett said, taking a set back and looking at him.

"Yes, I know how to look after my man," Emily said, walking into the living room with a plate of meats and cheese, crackers and fruit. Placing it down on the table, she offered Scarlett a glass of wine.

"Oh, I um, can't," Scarlett said, blushing but making Emily beam.

"Such a good girl," she said, passing Scott a glass before the three of them sat down.

"So, you've come pretty far from what I remember you being like," Scarlett said, breaking the silence that had fallen between them.

"Yeah. I met Emily at a bar two years ago. I was down to my last \$5, and I just thought, fuck it, I'll just drink it and deal with the consequences later. And she saw me and hasn't let me out of her sights since," Scott said, gently placing his hand on her thigh. Scarlett nodded her head.

"So, what's your plan?" Scott asked, catching Scarlett off guard and making her roll her eyes.

"I just want to get a job, get some money, and get my own place. I haven't thought of anything past that because it's a hard enough plan to make work. Not many people want to employ a felon," Scarlett explained, making Scott laugh.

"I'm kinda tired, guys. Thanks for all of this," Scarlett said, grabbing a piece of fruit and standing up.

"Have a nice rest, baby," Emily said as Scarlett walked down the corridor and into the guest room. Closing the door, Scarlett lay on the bed and felt her eyes well with tears.

Oh fuck off, Scarlett thought to herself, trying to push the gentle touch of Esther out of her mind.

"So, what sort of style are you going for?" Emily said, making Scarlett laugh. She had never thought about her style before, and certainly not for the last three years.

"I can only get a few things, Emily," Scarlett replied, embarrassed that she still felt like a prisoner. Sure she was on the outside but, it's not like she could just go and do whatever it was that wanted or buy whatever it was that she wanted either. Emily looked at Scarlett and tilted her head.

"Baby, I might not have made myself clear. Scott and I are going to get you everything you need to set you up because of what you did for him," Emily whispered into Scarlett's ear, making her shiver. Scarlett wasn't used to people being this kind to her, especially without wanting something in return, and as far as Scarlett could tell, Emily wanted nothing.

"Oh, that's okay, I don't need so much stuff anyway," Scarlett replied, feeling embarrassed by the look Emily was giving her. It was a mix of disbelief and something else that Scarlett couldn't seem to work out.

"No, I insist. Give me these, and go and get all the things you actually need and want. If you don't, I will, and I might not choose the things you like, so off you go," Emily said, gesturing to go back onto the shop floor and pick out more clothes. Scarlett hated to admit that Emily caring for her, made her wet.

You can't fuck your mate's girlfriend. She is probably just being nice, and you just think it's something more because that's how you think. But it isn't, and she's just nice, Scarlett said to herself, not wanting to stuff up her situation. The last thing she wanted to do was ruin something good, just because she seemed to only attract people who wanted to use her.

Scarlett ended up getting two outfits to wear for when she was applying for jobs, a selection of jeans, shorts, t-shirts, and sweaters, and a jacket. She got underwear, socks, and a few pairs of sneakers, a pair of ballet flats and sandals, as well as a pair of boots.

"This is really lovely of you guys, thank you," Scarlett said, as Scott helped unpack the car.

"No, dude, thank you. You could have ratted me out, but you didn't. I mean, I'm pretty sure that I would have been locked up as well after all my priors. This is the least I can do," Scott explained, making Scarlett's heart swell.

"Yeah, well, I was always looking out for your ass, wasn't I?" Scarlett joked as she walked inside the house, happy that her life seemed to be going in a positive direction for the first time in a very long time.

"How's the job hunting going?" Emily asked Scarlett as she came home late for the fifth night in a row. Scarlett exhaled loudly, made a dramatic collapse onto the couch and groaned.

"I swear, there is nobody hiring in this fucking city," she replied, smiling as she felt Emily put a blanket over her.

"Then have a little rest before dinner. Try not to stress about it, you'll find something," Emily said, stroking Scarlett's forehead. Scarlett hated when Emily was affectionate like this to her. It reminded her of everything that she wished she could have for herself.

Trust Scott to end up having the most beautiful, affectionate partner on the planet, Scarlett thought to herself pouting, before remembering that Emily was talking to her and was expecting a reply.

"Yeah, I'll try," Scarlett said, thinking about how the only thing worse than not having found a job yet was that fact that she had her first mandatory therapy session in the morning.

Scarlett sat in the waiting room of the therapist's office, wishing that the floor would open up and that she would be able to fall through and out of this situation. She hated shrinks. They always tried to make her issues seem like something they weren't.

"Scarlett," a woman in her late 30's called from the corridor.

Here we fucking go, Scarlett thought to herself.

At least my clothes are comfy, she added, walking passed the woman, not being able to miss the sweet and sensual scent of her perfume.

"Hi, I'm Rachel," the woman said, gesturing to Scarlett to sit on the couch. Scarlett looked around the room.

These rooms always look the same. Some abstract art on the walls, office furniture, the feeling of being observed, she thought, picking at her cuticles.

"So, you're here for your mandatory 50 hours. Is there something that you'd like to talk about specifically?" Rachel asked, enjoying having a new client. Rachel had been a psychologist for the last 15 years, deciding that her passion for working with ex-cons was her calling.

"No," Scarlett replied, looking around the room. She hated to admit. Her shrink was gorgeous.

"I thought that might be the case. Well, you're here for an hour, you can sit in silence if you like or we can get to know each other a little bit," Rachel offered, tilting her head at the bottle of water on her desk and offering Scarlett a glass.

"No thanks," Scarlett replied, her guard up higher than she knew it could be. There was a difference between being tough in prison than being on guard in the real world, and Scarlett was feeling the difference.

"You go first then," Scarlett said, a glint of mischief in her eyes, she had already figure out what she was going to say to whatever superficial crap Rachel replied with and was excited about starting the game.

"Well, I'm 38, I have a dog called Henry, and I'm not married because I like having sex with all sorts of different people," Rachel replied, taking Scarlett by surprise and ruining her smartass comeback that she had planned.

"Cool," Scarlett replied, being taken aback and somewhat impressed.

"Maybe this could be fun after all," Scarlett added, enjoying the smug expression on Rachel's face.

"Don't be too quick to judge me, baby girl," Rachel said, noticing how Scarlett's eyes glazed over at the words.

"Don't call me that," Scarlett whispered, looking into her lap.

"Pardon," Rachel said, leaning forward to hear better.

"I said, don't fucking call me that," Scarlett yelled,

getting up and pacing the room. Rachel liked that she had hit a nerve, and was curious to find out why it pained Scarlett so much to be called that. Scarlett moved to the corner of the office, looking out at Rachel with hurt in her eyes.

"Want to tell me what happened?" Rachel softly asked, slowly walking over to Scarlett and reaching out her hand. Scarlett moved away, pushing Rachel's hand away, just for Rachel to continue.

"It's alright, honey," Rachel said, as she made contact with Scarlett. Scarlett flung her arms around Rachel, burying her face into the woman's soft neck and feeling her heart finally be able to have a break. It had been years since Scarlett had felt as though she was safe, and in the soft arms of the older woman, Scarlett didn't even care that this wasn't the right thing to do in a session. She was surprised to find herself holding the woman, feeling as though her heart was a hot coal, put into a bucket of water.

"I've got you, honey," Rachel gently said, walking Scarlett back to the couch and holding her, cradling her in her arms.

"I'm sorry," Scarlett said, smiling as Rachel placed her hand over her mouth.

"You don't need to say sorry, honey. That's what this is all for, for healing. You can cry," Rachel affectionately said. Scarlett hated herself for letting this woman see a side to her that almost no one ever saw. But what she couldn't shake was the feeling of surrender. Almost as if, if she just allowed herself to be nurtured by this woman, that everything would be alright in the end, if the hurt she carried with her ever ended.

Chapter 5

Scarlett left the session feeling more lost than she did before it, making her mad as she replayed what had happened.

She's going to think I'm so fucking weird. I can't tell her that. I just can't, Scarlett thought to herself. She decided it was better to find something she wanted to work on, so the topic of her sexual appetite didn't come up. Scarlett got the vibe off Rachel that Rachel would stop at nothing to uncover Scarlett's most private secrets, and that wasn't something Scarlett wanted to give up.

Everyone just uses it against you. It's like, they see the soft side and then want to ruin it or something, Scarlett thought, trying to regain her composure as she walked through the door and into Scott and Emily's house.

This is going to be a good day. I can just feel it, Scarlett continued to think, deciding that she was going to go out and try to find a job, this time not taking no for an answer.

"Hey, good news," Scarlett said as she walked into the next session. She hated that Rachel wore her hair down, making her instantly have to hold her breath. Scarlett knew what it was about Rachel that had her unnerved. It was her aura. The whole, Mommy vibe that she gave off. Her generous breasts, her long brown hair, her happy and gentle eyes and smile, and the way her clothes seemed snuggly and welcoming.

Just fucking stop it, Scarlett whined to herself, as she found herself looking over Rachel's body. Rachel noticed Scarlett's untrained gaze, enjoying that the outfit she had deliberately worn, had paid off.

"What is it?" Rachel said, sitting down and getting out her note pad.

"I got a job," Scarlett replied, crossing her legs on the couch. Rachel smiled and wrote something down.

"That's great. Is it something that you wanted?" Rachel asked, making Scarlett scoff.

"No. It's washing dishes. But the people who will willingly employ an ex-con are few and far between. I think I'm going to get some money together and then get a new job. Hopefully, I can keep my past from following me," Scarlett said, folding her arms across her chest.

"That all sounds really positive," Rachel said, putting her note pad away. They sat in silence, Scarlett looking anywhere but Rachel, amusing her.

"What is it?" Rachel asked, looking inquisitively at Scarlett, knowing exactly what had unnerved Scarlett.

"Nothing," Scarlett said with an attitude. Rachel thought for a moment before getting up and coming to sit next to Scarlett, instantly making her hold her breath.

"Well, this, this isn't nothing," Rachel said, referring to the way Scarlett tried to distance herself.

"What are you afraid of?" Rachel gently asked. Scarlett glared at her, angry that she could see past the cool and somewhat aggressive exterior that she thought she put up so well.

"Fucking nothing," Scarlett whined, annoyed that Rachel wasn't being deterred by her hostility.

"Tell me about your childhood," Rachel asked, remaining in her spot next to a cowering Scarlett.

"What fucking childhood. I was on my own for most of it," Scarlett said, frowning and not wanting to cry.

"Are you going to write that down in your fucking book?" Scarlett mocked, wiping a rouge tear that fell onto her cheek.

"No," Rachel slowly replied, looking at Scarlett.

"Scott was all that I had," Scarlett said, getting used to feeling Rachel so close to her.

"Do you want to talk about him?" Rachel asked, hanging Scarlett a tissue.

"There's not much to say. I took the fall for him, he got himself a lovely little set up in the best part of town with his gorgeous girlfriend, and I have to come here and talk about my fucking feelings," Scarlett angrily replied, bringing her knees up to her chest and feeling more alone than she knew she could feel.

"That's probably why I am so fucked up," Scarlett said, looking up at Rachel, with nothing but fear in her eyes.

The angry ones are always the sweetest, in the end, Rachel thought watching how Scarlett's fierce guard came down and her big baby girl eyes looked up at her.

"You wanna talk to me about it?" Rachel asked, smiling kindly down at Scarlett and making her roll her eyes.

"I can't," Scarlett whispered, wishing that she could say the words she so desperately wanted to say.

"Yes, you can," Rachel said, suspecting that Scarlett's big reveal was that she liked the MDLG kink on some level. Rachel had been a Mommy Dom for long enough that she could spot a baby, or even a potential baby from a mile away. They all had a few things in common, that subtle look of longing in their eyes, no matter how much ego, aggression, or bravado they tried to mask it with. Scarlett was no different. Her whole, I fucking hate the world, but please love me, vibe gave her away the moment Rachel saw her.

"Is it that you want to feel safe?" Rachel softly asked, her eyes smiling as she saw Scarlett gently nod her head.

"Is it that you want, you want Mommy?" Rachel asked, Scarlett's eyes darting up to look at her, like Bambi in the headlights.

"It's more common than you'd think," Rachel said, soothing Scarlett's fears.

"I have to go," Scarlett said, wanting to get out of there,

now that her secret was out in the open.

"You don't actually. There's still 25minutes left," Rachel answered, watching as Scarlett once again paced around the room.

"Fine," Scarlett said, sitting down again and refusing to look at or talk to Rachel until their time was up.

Rachel went home after a long day of thinking about Scarlett.

You know what you are doing, and you need to stop, she said to herself as she showered. The room was steaming up as the hot water poured over her body. She knew that she shouldn't, but Scarlett just made her feel so deeply.

She is in a vulnerable position. She's trying to get her life back. You can't do this to her. Just wait until she's finished her sessions and then, maybe, see if something could work, Rachel said, finding that her hand had slipped between her thighs, pressing her fingers into her as she thought about how it felt to hold Scarlett. Rachel hated herself for her predatory ways at times. She felt like a dirty, dangerous predator as she remembered how hot it had made her, making Scarlett to submit to her.

Just go out and find someone who is already down for this, she thought, knowing that she could have a playmate in seconds if she went online.

"But I want her," Rachel hungrily said out loud, her eyes opening and their dominance reflecting in the mirror.

Rachel knew how to seduce Scarlett, but she also knew that she needed to do the right thing by her.

"Why are you like this?" Rachel asked herself in the mirror, half expecting a reply. She rolled her eyes and walked out of the bathroom into her bedroom and put on some loungewear. She went online, saw the different girls who were looking for an online play partner, but she soon put her phone down, and closed her eyes. Reaching into her leggings, Rachel smirked to herself as she replayed Scarlett's face and her moody attitude that subtle, untrained bratty behavior making Rachel wet as she thought about how she was going to turn her into her good girl. Rachel imagined tying Scarlett up, her arms behind her back as she groped her breasts, kissed her lips, and touched her pussy, making sure that Scarlett knew that she was owned.

"Mommy's good girl," Rachel imagined herself saying, moaning in sexual relief as she began to circle her clit and play with her own breasts. She imagined Scarlett, sticking her tongue out and tasting her for the first time, her sweet little lips pressed against Rachel's wet mound.

"Fuck," Rachel said out loud, opening her eyes and rubbing herself with a desperation that didn't seem to end.

"This isn't going to end well," Rachel moaned as she came, fully aware that what she wanted with Scarlett was forbidden.

"Woah," Rachel said as Scarlett stormed in for their next session.

"You know what is fucking bullshit?" Scarlett angrily said, looking at Rachel and waiting for her to reply.

"Tell me," Rachel said, pulling her cardigan across her breasts, distracting Scarlett for a moment before her rage found her once again.

"That everything is so hard," Scarlett said. She had been furious until she had seen Rachel, but something about her soft, loving way made Scarlett forget that she was angry. Rachel smiled as she noticed this as well, feeling herself slowly fill with desire.

"What's hard?" Rachel asked, tilting her head and licking her lips.

"Oh, just this online course I'm doing right now. I want to become a security guard," Scarlett calmly said, completely disarmed.

"I think that's a great idea. You'd love that a lot more than doing dishes," Rachel said, making Scarlett smile.

"Yeah, I know," Scarlett replied, sitting on her hands and looked around the room. Rachel waited for the silence between them to settle before speaking.

"So, I was wondering if you'd like to try a different type of therapy with me?" Rachel asked, Scarlett's eyes curious and questioning.

"It's called cuddle therapy, have you heard of it?"

Rachel questioned, Scarlett, shaking her head and wondering if this is just all she had needed all along.

"It's especially good if you don't have a history of physical touch, which is important to soothe the nervous system and maintain a healthy mental balance. There's a thing call touch starvation, and it can have negative side effects," Rachel explained. Scarlett clenched her calves and didn't really know what to say.

"I haven't heard of it," she decided on and waited for Rachel to make the next move.

"Would you be interested in trying it? Obviously, we can stop at any time?" Rachel reassuringly said, watching as Scarlett timidly nodded her head.

"Okay. I'm going to come over there and lay on the couch, alright?" Rachel said, standing up and slowing, walking over to the couch. Scarlett stood up and got out of the way, watching as Rachel lay down. Rachel pulled her hair out from her bun, letting it tumble down, and her cardigan opened, showing off her grey sweater, making Scarlett bite the side of her bottom lip.

"Do you want to come and lay next to me?" Rachel asked. Scarlett moved slowly into her arms and felt like she would burst into tears the moment she felt Rachel's arms wrap around her. Scarlett lay rigid, trying to keep her breathing regular but finding that her breaths were short and shallow, her heart racing.

"It's alright, Scarlett," Rachel cooed, beginning to stroke Scarlett's hair, smiling as she felt the younger woman cautiously being to relax. Scarlett hated that this felt so nice, she was uncomfortable with Rachel's caring touch and gentle ways. Rachel repositioned herself so that she was slightly over Scarlett and able to look down at her, seeing her eyes begin to well up.

"You're safe here," Rachel whispered, stroking Scarlett's frowning forehead, the fear in her eyes still present. Tears began to stream from Scarlett's eyes, her silent crying breaking Rachel's heart.

"Oh sweetie, it's alright, Mommy's got you," Rachel involuntarily said, smiling as Scarlett snuggled into her. Rachel hadn't realized that she was so deep in Mommy space, delighted that Scarlett hadn't tried to push her away, and in fact, snuggled in closer to her chest.

"Do you want to suck your thumb? Rachel affectionately asked, Scarlett's aqua eyes looking up at her and timidly nodding her head.

"There's a good girl," Rachel cooed, taking Scarlett's hand in hers and bringing her thumb up to her mouth, watching as Scarlett looked at peace for the first time since their sessions had started.

Chapter 6

That was so amazing, Scarlett thought as she walked out of Rachel's office and out onto the street. She felt light in her heart, her fears of being touched seemed to disappear, and she felt as though everything was going to be alright for the first time in her life. Rachel had held Scarlett's timid body, gently rocking her like a Mommy and patting her affectionately as she snuggled into her breasts, getting lost in the feeling of safety and love for an hour, smiling at her as she became more confident and soften in her expression and attitude.

Rachel had closed the door behind Scarlett as she left, feeling her wet pussy rub against her panties as she sat back down on her office chair and recalled how Scarlett had voluntarily closed her eyes and relaxed into her arms.

Oh, my sweet girl, Rachel thought as she replayed the image, rubbing her breasts and gently pinching her nipples as she remembered Scarlett's soft breath hardening them under her bra.

"Dude, what's up with you?" Scott asked as Scarlett floated into the house and crashed on the couch.

"My therapist is fucking amazing," she replied absentmindedly, her mind was still in Rachel's office, enjoying the feeling of somebody touching her without making her feel as though she owed them for their kindness.

"That's good," Scott replied, unsure of what the appropriate response.

"I'll be out of your hair in about three weeks," Scarlett called as she saw Emily come home with the groceries. Emily had taken to calling Scarlett, baby, and it had made her wet countless times.

"That's alright, baby, whenever you're ready. Come and help me with this," Emily said, putting the groceries on the bench and waiting for Scarlett to get up and follow her instruction.

"You know that Scarlett's a baby, just like you are right?" Emily questioned Scott as they got into bed that night. Emily had diapered Scott and put him in a dino onesie, before letting him in their bed and stroking his hair as he snuggled into her.

"Really?" He asked, putting his thumb in his mouth and grabbing at Emily's pajama top. Emily just smiled as she looked down on the sweet boy she had all to herself.

"Yeah. How would you feel about Mommy seeing if she wanted to stay a little longer?" Emily asked. She had fantasized about having Scarlett and Scott in each arm, both nursing on her as she cuddled in bed.

"No, Mommy, I want her gone in the three weeks she said she'd go so I can be little again. But you can be cute with her if you want," Scott pouted, making Emily smirk.

"Mommy's greedy little boy. Alright then, I'll be cute with her," Emily replied, enjoying Scott's wording and continuing to think about how adorable she'd make Scarlett as she patted her baby boy to sleep.

Emily woke to the soft sounds of distress coming from the guest room, where Scarlett had been staying for the last two weeks. She slowly got out of bed as to not wake Scott, and quietly walked down the hallway, opening the door to see Scarlett having a nightmare.

Sweet baby, Emily thought as she saw Scarlett toss and turn. Walking into the room, Emily gently sat on the bed and placed her hand on Scarlett's chest.

"It's alright, sweetie, it's just a bad dream," Emily whispered, waking Scarlett up and looking around in a panic.

"Hey, there, honey. You're alright," Emily said, calming Scarlett, who was now able to focus her attention.

"Sorry, was I too loud? Did I wake you up?" Scarlett apologetically said, blushing and bringing her knees to her chest.

"No, not at all," Emily replied, smiling at Scarlett and pulling her bedsheets back.

"Come on, let me tuck you back in and pat you back to sleep," Emily said, taking Scarlett by surprise.

"Oh, it's okay, you don't have to," Scarlett said, moving her body under the sheets anyway.

"Good girl," Emily said, pulling the sheets up around Scarlett and tucking her in.

"Roll over sweetie, onto your tummy for me," Emily said, happy when Scarlett obediently followed her instruction as Emily began to pat her back, putting her to sleep in no time at all. Emily had a firm touch, far firmer than Rachel had, and Scarlett replayed the gentle ways that Rachel had positioned her in their last session together.

I wish this was Rachel, was the last thing Scarlett thought as she put her thumb in her mouth just as she fell asleep.

Scarlett woke up the next morning, knowing that she had to go to therapy and trying to find any excuse to get out of it.

"Do you want me to wash your cars, or do we need something from the store, I can get it," Scarlett said over breakfast. Scott just looked at her curiously.

"No, we have everything we need. Don't you have therapy and work today?" He asked as Emily filled up their water glasses.

"Yeah," Scarlett replied, looking down and digging her fork into her pancakes.

"What's the problem?" Emily asked, taking Scarlett's fork and feeding her a mouthful, making Scott jealous.

"Don't look at me like that, baby," Emily said, the warning in her voice making Scarlett curious and Scott annoyed.

"I don't want to keep going to therapy, she is getting to know me way too much," Scarlett replied, jumping when Scott loudly threw his plate into the sink.

"Everyone has things they have to do even if they don't want to. Get over it," he loudly said, walking away into the bedroom, and leaving Scarlett looking confused.

"Don't worry about him. He's grumpy when I get the final word about something. That has nothing to do with you," Emily reassuringly said, coming over to Scarlett and placing her hands either side of her face and kissing her forehead.

"Go, it'll be good for you," Emily lovingly said, before following Scott into the bedroom and closing the door behind her.

I think I'll still give it a miss, Scarlett thought as she finished her breakfast and went to get changed.

Scarlett ignored the session reminder, the phone call, and text from Rachel, putting her phone in her back pocket and headed to the shops.

They might not need anything, but I need a drink, she thought, only to remember that she wasn't allowed to drink until her probation was over.

This is fucked, she whined to herself, passing the liquor store and going to a corner shop, deciding to buy a packet of chips instead.

"Well, at least I know you haven't been run over," a voice said behind Scarlett. Scarlett froze, feeling like a naughty girl who had just been caught doing something she knew she shouldn't.

"Um," Scarlett replied, turning around slowly. Rachel looked different outside her office. She seemed to be taller, but somehow, even in her casual clothes, she looked domineering and strong. It was a different type of energy, one which Scarlett hadn't experienced before because as fierce and intense as Rachel was, the kindness and affection that seemed to flow from her made Scarlett's head spin.

"That's what I thought," Rachel said, taking the packet of chips from Scarlett's hands and walking to the cash register.

"Hey, I can buy these myself," Scarlett whines, hating herself for getting turned on by Rachel's wide hips and thick-set thighs.

Mommy, Scarlett, whined out of frustration and lust to herself, feeling her desire to be Rachel's center of attention, beginning to take her to a space she wished she could fight.

"I'm sure you can, but I think I need to remind you who is in charge. You do know that these sessions are mandatory. Meaning that if you don't come, you'll be in a lot of trouble. I haven't told anyone you decided to bail, but I'd like to know why," Rachel said, paying the cashier, opening the bag and passing Scarlett the packet.

"You make me feel weird," Scarlett mumbled. Rachel reached out and lifted Scarlett's chin until their eyes met.

"Pardon?" Rachel asked, raising an eyebrow and looking down at Scarlett.

"You make me feel weird," Scarlett replied, her eyes looking fearful, the way that turned Rachel on.

"Well, let's go talk about this then," Rachel commanded more than said, wrapping an arm around Scarlett and leading her to her office. Scarlett smirked to herself as they walked.

This is the start of so many porn videos, she thought, enjoying her chips and Rachel's firm but gentle embrace.

Rachel sat in her office chair and looked at Scarlett, sitting across from her.

"Talk to me," Rachel said, Scarlett beginning to pull at her cuticles.

"It felt weird when we hugged and stuff," Scarlett softly said, beginning to blush. Rachel had tied her hair into her signature bun, showing off her collar bones and model-like neck. Scarlett could almost detect the faintest of smirks coming over Rachel's face.

"Weird good or weird bad," Rachel asked, fighting her urge to sit next to Scarlett.

You just need Mommy, don't you baby, Rachel thought, eyeing Scarlett.

"Weird good," Scarlett softly said, annoyed at herself for feeling like she was falling into little space as she fidgeted with her fingers.

"Then come here," Rachel replied, taking Scarlett by surprise as she patted her lap. Scarlett slowly got up and made her way across the room.

"This isn't like, normal therapy is it?" Scarlett said as she felt Rachel's hand on her wrist, pulling her down and smiling as Scarlett wrapped an arm around her shoulders.

"Why would I give you 'normal' therapy? You told me that you didn't need therapy, remember?" Rachel sarcastically remarked, making Scarlett laugh and relax into her.

"Have you heard of MDLG before? Because I think that you'd love it," Rachel said as she began to rock Scarlett on her lap and wrap her arms around Scarlett's waist.

"Maybe," Scarlett said, giggling and burying her face into Rachel's neck. Rachel held Scarlett's head in place as she rocked her, enjoying feeling her relax and melt onto her lap.

"I thought so," Rachel replied, smiling to herself. Scarlett began looking at Rachel's neck, the long lines, and bits of hair that had fallen, causing Rachel to reach up and pull it out, letting it flow down her back and tickle Scarlett, making her laugh.

"Such a sweetheart. You're not so big and tough, are

you, little one?" Rachel said, smirking as she saw the mischievous look in Scarlett's eyes and the cheeky smile on her face.

"No, I just always had to be," Scarlett replied, shaking her head and shrugging her shoulders.

"But not anymore," Rachel quickly added, taking out a paci from her top drawer and pushing it into Scarlett's mouth, taking her by surprise.

"You leave that in little miss," Rachel said, pushing it back in as Scarlett took it out.

"You're going to be a good girl for me," Rachel warned, causing Scarlett to place her hand on Rachel's breast, taking her by surprise.

"Cheeky girl," Rachel said, smiling and letting Scarlett gently grab at her. Rachel leaned back against her chair and let Scarlett begin to explore her body. She loved seeing Scarlett get lost in her and imagined taking her home and babying her for the night, just as Scarlett sighed and resting her head against Rachel's chest.

"You're so lovely," Rachel sighed, stroking Scarlett's back and almost putting her to sleep.

"I should probs see another shrink now, right?" Scarlett said as the alarm went off on their session. Rachel had rocked Scarlett on her lap their whole time together, enjoying Scarlett's little outburst of tears, as she was loved and nurtured.

"Well, that's something that I wanted to talk to you about. How would you feel having a play session here, so still coming here, and I can just sign you off as coming, but we play instead? If you want to actually commit to therapy, then yes, you should see another therapist," Rachel said. Scarlett just gave her a one-sided smile.

"I kinda don't want to. I don't think I need therapy. I think I might need this," Scarlett softly replied, looking at Rachel timidly, not wanting to be rejected. Rachel stood up and walked to where Scarlett was standing. She reached out and ran her fingers through Scarlett's hair, holding her head back and making her look up at her. The look of lust and passion in Rachel's eyes was reflected in Scarlett's, and the two of them stood as time seemed to stop around them.

"Yeah, I'd love that," Scarlett replied, breaking their eye contact and picking up her wallet and walking out the door.

Chapter 7

"Tell me some of the things that you'd like to try," Rachel said down the phone Saturday night. Emily and Scott had gone out to a restaurant, meaning that Scarlett had the whole house to herself for a few hours.

"I don't know, I like cuddling with you," Scarlett said, letting her fingers play with her panty covered pussy.

"Tell me what you are wearing," Rachel sensually instructed, making Scarlett giggle.

"Do you like it when I tell you what to do?" Rachel asked, making a mental note.

"Yeah," Scarlett replied, feeling her wetness between her pussy lips.

"Yes, Mommy," Rachel corrected, smirking as she heard Scarlett's breathing come in short sharp pants.

"Yes, Mommy," Scarlett repeated, rubbing her clit. She closed her eyes and arched her back, aching for release.

"Mommy wants you to stop playing with yourself now," Rachel sternly said, causing Scarlett's eyes to open as she reluctantly took her hand away.

"Good girl," Rachel said, hearing her soft whine in frustration.

"Tell me what other things you like. I already know you like a paci, do you like coloring and making things?" Rachel asked. Scarlett bit her bottom lip as she thought about the different things that she had only ever thought of doing and smiled.

"I guess. I haven't ever really explored it too much before, I kinda just like calling you Mommy. I don't know what else I like," Scarlett honestly replied, making Rachel's heart swell.

"Okay, well would you be happy to let Mommy take the lead tomorrow, and you can say you want it to stop whenever you want," Rachel said, Scarlett, giving her puppy dog eyes and nodding, even though they were on the phone.

"Alright, see you tomorrow," Scarlett replied, hanging up the phone and going back to touching herself. She couldn't believe how her life was turning out. Sure, the start was a bit hit and miss, but now she had the type of Mommy she had dreamed of, was almost ready to move into her own place, and had a killer wardrobe.

Not so bad, for a bad kid, she thought as she pleasured herself, not hearing the front door open. Scarlett teased her clit, running her fingers down the sides and into her pussy, closing her eyes and rolling her head back as she arched her back, wanting a deeper penetration.

"That's not what good little girls should be doing," Emily said, leaning against the wall and making Scarlett gasp and freeze.

"I, um," Scarlett stammered as Scott peered around the door, seeing his friend in just her t-shirt and panties.

"Emily, I'm really sorry," Scarlett apologetically said. It had been clear from the first day that she was there that Emily ruled this household, and even though she did it nicely, there was no question in Scarlett's mind, Emily was the boss.

"Scarlett, do you want to play with us?" Emily said, walking into the room and sitting on the end of the bed, gently taking Scarlett's hand from her pussy. Scarlett couldn't deny that Emily was gorgeous, but she didn't really know how it would make her friendship turn out with Scott.

"Oh, don't worry about him, I know you don't want his cock," Emily said, making both Scott and Scarlett laugh.

"Yeah, okay," Scarlett excitedly but nervously said, smiling and wondering what would happen next.

"Good," Emily replied, kicking off her shoes and smirking at Scarlett.

"Scott, sit on the floor. You're going to find this torturous, and I am going to love every moment of your pain," Emily said, her voice changing and making Scarlett frown.

"Take off the rest of these clothes," Emily said, turning to face Scarlett. Scarlett felt the dynamic shift as Emily went from the authoritarian but soft and gentle woman she had come to know, into somebody harsher, with a cruel look in their eye. She tried to brush it off, telling herself that she could leave at any time she wanted.

"Kneel on the bed for me," Emily said, interrupting Scarlett's thoughts, her body moving to Emily's request.

"Like this," Emily sternly said, grabbing Scarlett's arms and putting them behind her head and pushing her thighs apart.

"I'd be lying if I said that I hadn't thought about you in that position for days," Emily said almost to herself, reaching out and cupping Scarlett's pussy, causing her to gasp and pull away from her.

"Where do you think you are going?" Emily said, gently slapping Scarlett's ass and putting her back into the position. Scarlett bit her lip, feeling herself become aroused by Emily's aggressive manner, moaning as Emily felt how wet Scarlett was, smiling as she did so.

"I knew that you'd like this," Emily whispered into Scarlett's ear, only leaving her pussy to begin to rub her breasts. Scarlett thought about Rachel. Her soft embrace, the way she held onto Scarlett as she had cried. Her sweet but subtle smelling perfume that seemed to calm Scarlett's tortured heart, just as she felt Emily's leather flogger on her ass.

"Ouch," Scarlett involuntarily said, snapping out of her daydream and looking at Emily's face.

"I said, turn around," Emily commanded, making Scarlett laugh.

"Yeah, um, I'm out. I don't want to do this anymore," Scarlett said, getting up and beginning to put her clothes on, clearly surprising Emily.

"Oh, okay then," Emily said, snapping her fingers at Scott, who followed her out of the room. Scarlett pulled on her house clothes and lay on the bed, taking her phone out and wishing that Rachel had messaged her.

She's just doing her job. It's not personal. She doesn't want you, Scarlett told herself, trying to stop any transference she was feeling from taking over her mind.

But I mean, we do play a little. Like, calling her Mommy is amazing, Scarlett continued thinking, wondering if she was reading more into it than Rachel was intending, or if she was reading it correctly.

"Knock, knock," Scarlett timidly said as she saw the door to Rachel's office slightly opened the following day.

"Hi, sweetie, come in," Rachel said, jumping up from her black office chair and standing up, just as Scarlett walked into the room.

"Um, what's all this?" Scarlett said as she looked around at the play gym on the floor. Rachel smiled and sat back down, placing her hands in her pockets.

"Well, I thought that maybe you would want to try going a little further. I know that you liked cuddling, I wondered if you'd like this as well," Rachel explained, making

Scarlett laugh.

"I don't really feel in that sort of headspace today. The people that I'm staying with, well, we tried to have sex last night, and it was just, really bad," Scarlett replied, Rachel, raising an eyebrow, her curiosity piqued. Although she knew that Scarlett wasn't hers, Rachel was taken aback and had to check herself before she continued to speak.

"Why was it bad?" She asked. Scarlett sighed and sat back on the couch, looking at the play gym mat with its cartoon animals and colorful shapes.

"She just got really rough, and like, I wasn't down for it," Scarlett said, folding her arms across her chest.

"Did it remind you of something?" Rachel said, coping a glare from Scarlett.

"I just mean, I can't imagine prison was easy for you. Could it have been that the rough sex that she was wanting made you remember your time in prison?" Rachel backtracked, happy when Scarlett's expression softened.

"Maybe," she answered, making Rachel smile as she watched Scarlett look at the gym.

"Do you want to cuddle again?" Rachel asked, seeing Scarlett pulled her arms closer around herself. Scarlett subtly nodded, surprised that Rachel could bring her into her little space with almost no effort at all.

"Come here then," Rachel said, turning her chair and holding out her hand to Scarlett. Scarlett sat on Rachel's lap, enjoying how it felt to have her gentle touch as Rachel rubbed her back. Scarlett dropped her head, closed her eyes, and relaxed into Rachel's embrace.

"I wish you were my Mommy," Scarlett involuntarily said, gasping and looking up when she realized what she had said.

"Sorry, I," Scarlett said, trying to get up, surprised when Rachel held her in place.

"You don't have to run away from me," Rachel replied, smiling, happy that Scarlett had just confessed her deepest desires.

"I wish you were my baby girl, too," Rachel confessed, taking Scarlett by surprise. They stayed like that, Rachel holding onto Scarlett for the longest of times before Scarlett began to wiggle on Rachel's lap.

"Do you want to hop down, little one?" Rachel asked, Scarlett, giving her her big puppy dog eyes and smirking.

"I wanna play with that," Scarlett replied, pointing at the play gym. Rachel took her arms away from around Scarlett's waist and let her hop onto the floor, kicking her shoes off as she did so.

"Can I come down and play with you?" Rachel asked, Scarlett, nodding her head as she hit the toys which hung overhead.

"I didn't know they came in such big sizes," Scarlett happily said, touching all the hanging toys. Rachel couldn't help but fall for Scarlett's happy face and playful personality, deciding that it was best that Scarlett see another therapist.

"Baby," Rachel said, getting Scarlett's attention.

"Would you be interested in getting to know me a little bit more, maybe, have dinner with me?" Rachel asked. In her time as a therapist, she had never fallen for a client as hard as she had Scarlett, and the thought of not having Scarlett as her own filled her with disappointment. Scarlett thought for a moment, surprised that Rachel was trying to move their dynamic forward. She looked at Rachel, wondering how to respond correctly.

"You can say no if you want, that's absolutely no problem, and we can keep doing what we are doing here. If that makes you more comfortable?" Rachel began to say, not wanting to push Scarlett too far out of her comfort zone.

"No, I would really like that," Scarlett suddenly replied, not wanting Rachel to take the offer away and giving Rachel one more cheeky smile before going back to play with the play gym.

Chapter 8

Rachel looked at the clock on her wall and smiled, knowing she still had 30minutes with Scarlett before their session ended.

"What are you playing with, baby?" Rachel asked, looking at Scarlett and brushing the hair out of her eyes.

"The lion," Scarlett replied, surprising Rachel when she put it down and looked at her seductively.

"But I want to play with something else," Scarlett smirked, looking at Rachel and casually putting her hand on her thigh. Rachel raised an eyebrow. It wasn't the first time that a client had wanted to have sex with her or vice versa, but it was the first time that a client had instigated sex.

"Are you being a cheeky girl?" Rachel said, laughing at Scarlett's innocent face.

"Maybe," Scarlett softly said, giggling as Rachel, flipping her onto her back and knelt over her face.

"Do you do this with your other clients?" Scarlett asked. Rachel just shook her head before slowly bringing her lips down to touch Scarlett's, enjoying the gasp of surprise that she elicited.

"Is this what you wanted?" Rachel asked, allowing her

body to fall onto Scarlett's gently. Scarlett moaned as she kissed Rachel back, feeling the older woman's hands gently touching her body and fanning the fire that had been building for weeks.

"Yes," Scarlett desperately moaned as she arched her back and rolled her head back, feeling Rachel kiss her again, more passionately this time. Scarlett loved that she could feel Rachel getting lost in their kiss, feeling her hands softly grabbing at her breasts and thighs and taking her to a place of safety and arousal.

"Does that feel good, baby?" Rachel seductively whispered into Scarlett's ear as she slowly felt over Scarlett's clothes.

"You are making Mommy horny sweet girl," Rachel said as she stopped herself, wanting to pull off Scarlett's shirt.

"You can," Scarlett replied, helping Rachel do so.

"Honey, take those hands and put them behind your head for Mommy," Rachel said, climbing on top of Scarlett.

"You'll be a good girl for me, won't you?" Rachel moaned as she began to slowly take off Scarlett's shirt and bra, kissing along her collar bone.

"I don't want to go any further," Scarlett said, gently pushing Rachel away, worried that she would be angry just like Emily.

"That's alright, honey," Rachel replied, pulling Scarlett into her arms and holding her tightly. Scarlett was surprised at how okay Rachel was with ending their play. It wasn't conditional like with Esther or Ross, and she wasn't super angry about it like Emily had been.

"I guess this isn't what you're meant to do with your clients, huh?" Scarlett said, turning in Rachel's arms and looking up at her.

"No, and if I'm being honest, I could be in a lot of trouble for this. But you're worth it," Rachel laughed, before becoming serious.

"But I still think it's a good idea for you to go to another therapist because there are some things that you need to sort through, but I just want a different role with you, and from the looks of things, you want that too," she added beaming down at Scarlett.

"Yeah, I think that might be a good idea. I also think that I'd like to take you out somewhere nice and get to know you better. I guess this whole thing isn't really starting the way it should. Can I change the tempo a little bit?" Scarlett asked, Rachel, tilting her head to the side and curiously looking at Scarlett. Scarlett was surprised that she felt like she had so much control in the dynamic that she was creating with Rachel.

Usually, I would just let her do whatever she wants. I just let anyone do whatever they wanted. It feels good to have some control and for that to be respected, Scarlett said to herself

"Yeah sure, tell me about what you want," Rachel said, smiling as she saw Scarlett feeling empowered.

"Okay. I want to take you somewhere nice and just talk like adults. I don't want any teasing or suggestive stuff. Then I want to see if we click outside this dynamic of doctor and patient and then maybe start something with you. I want to backtrack a little bit. I hope that's alright?" Scarlett said, holding her breath and hoping that by setting her boundaries, she wasn't going to lose Rachel.

"That sounds like a very wise decision," Rachel replied, nodding her head and putting all of Scarlett's fears aside.

"Can I just say one more thing before I go?" Scarlett added, getting up and walking to the door. Rachel could see the cheeky look in Scarlett's eye and knew that whatever was coming next would be good.

"Sure," Rachel said, trying to hide her excitement.

"Your tits are amazing," Scarlett said, reaching out and playing with them, making Rachel laugh. She allowed Scarlett to have her fun before taking her hands in hers and holding them behind her back.

"That's enough now, you've had your fun, now let's try to keep to those rules you just set," Rachel said, opening the door and walking Scarlett out of the office, her cheeky smile refusing to leave her face.

Scarlett walked down the street feeling light and full of

happiness, turned the corner, and saw Emily and Scott arrive home, immediately feeling the change in her mood. Things had been awkward between the three of them, and all Scarlett knew was that she needed to get out of that house before things got any worse. She grimaced at them, walked into the house, and all but ran to her room, sitting on the bed and sighing, happy that she had gotten passed them without having to talk.

"Hi," Scarlett said to Scott when he peered around the corner.

So much for my lucky escape, Scarlett thought to herself. Scott had taken Emily's side in this silent argument, but Scarlett didn't blame him.

We aren't the same people we were all those years ago, and I mean, I wouldn't want to risk losing all this either, she said to herself, looking at how Scott was clearly uncomfortable.

"Hey, so, I am just going to come straight out and say it, Emily wants you out of the house," Scott said. Scarlett could tell it was as awkward for him as it was for her, and it made her smile.

"Yeah, don't worry, I actually got paid today, so I'll be able to get out of your hair in a few weeks," Scarlett replied, a questioning look on her face when Scott pulled a face.

"Yeah, um, she kinda means, like, right now," Scott said, making Scarlett's eye go wide. She sighed, fell back on the bed, and felt her eyes begin to well up.

"Is this because I didn't want to fuck her the way she wanted? This is such bullshit," Scarlett replied, wiping her tears and getting up, going to her cupboard and taking a bag out. Scott just nervously walked out of the room and shut the door on Scarlett as she began to throw clothes into her bag as she cried.

Typical, everything has to go right, and then everything just goes wrong. I should have just let her fuck me, Scarlett said to herself, knowing that she had nowhere else to go. She sat on her bed, trying to push her tears back down before she left the house.

I can't let her see me cry. I'm not going to give that bitch the satisfaction, she thought, wiping her tears and taking some deep breaths. She got up, walked to the cupboard, and packed a couple of tins of food and packets of cookies before giving Emily the finger as she headed to the door.

I can't let myself be homeless. They'll find a way to put me back in there, I just know it, Scarlett thought, opening the door and looking back at Scott. She knew that this would be the last time that she spoke or saw him again, and she wanted to remember. She wanted to remember him as the boy she had grown up with, not the man who let his woman kick her out of the house because she had turned her down sexually.

I guess it's true. You don't finish with everyone you start with, Scarlett thought as she continued to look at Scott, who was looking apologetically at Scarlett as she slammed the front door behind herself.

"What a fucking bitch," Scarlett said out loud as she began to walk up the street. She didn't know where she was going, all she knew was that she needed somewhere safe to sleep for the night.

Oh fuck, Rachel, Scarlett suddenly thought, remembering that she had organized to see Rachel that evening. Scarlett made her way to a sidewalk bench and sat down. She knew that she was in the middle of a panic attack by the way her palms became sweaty, and she wanted to run away from everything.

I could, turn my phone off, hitch a ride out of town and change my name and start a new life somewhere else, Scarlett thought, smiling when she knew that she wasn't actually going to do that. Starting over had been significantly harder in practice than it was in theory, and the task of re-starting over made her uneasy.

Or I could be a grown-up, message Rachel what is going on. If I'm really lucky she'll let me stay with her and if not then that's also cool, but either way, we aren't going to go anywhere tonight, Scarlett decided, taking out her phone and dialing Rachel's number.

"Hi baby," Rachel answered, surprised that Scarlett was ringing her when only a few hours ago they had spoken.

"Hey, so, I'm not trying to get out of hanging out with

you, and I'm not asking you for any favors. But the people that I was staying with kicked me out, and I have nowhere else to go so I can't hang out with you tonight because I need to find a place to stay for a while," Scarlett explained, smiling to herself that she felt like she could handle this situation.

"Oh, sweetie," Rachel said, wondering if it would be too much to offer Scarlett to stay with her.

She wanted to take things slowly, you asking her to stay isn't slowly! Rachel thought to herself, biting her lip as she thought.

"I have an idea, and you can turn me down without me losing any interest in you, alright. Do you want to stay with me for a few nights? We can keep things going slowly, but I don't want you on the streets or in a shelter," Rachel replied, hoping that Scarlett would take her up on the offer.

"I don't want to sleep in the same bed as you, and I really don't want anything to happen. Getting out of prison has proven to be harder than being in there. At least in there, everything was predictable, and I knew what the deal was, out here, everything is so unstructured and unpredictable," Scarlett said, starting to cry. She felt so pathetic.

"Oh, baby. Don't cry. It'll be okay. Mommy is going to make everything alright. Where are you, send me your location, I'm coming to get you, alright?" Rachel said, getting off the couch and grabbing her keys.

"Okay. Thanks, Rachel," Scarlett replied between sobs,

hanging up and sending Rachel her location. Scarlett put her phone back into her pocket, placed her bag between her feet, closed her eyes, and waited for Rachel to pick her up.

"I feel really embarrassed, thanks for this," Scarlett said, feeling like the damsel in distress that was just saved by her princess charming as she sat in Rachel's car, playing with the hem of her shorts. Scarlett felt like one of the adult videos she had watched where some young, helpless girl gets picked up by a hot mature woman and then fucked the moment she gets taken to the woman's house.

"It's no trouble, I just hope that you aren't put off by my house, it's pretty basic, like nice, but nothing fancy," Rachel said, surprising herself that she felt insecure about her place.

"I just got out of jail, so like, as long as there's no one jumping me in the shower, it'll be amazing," Scarlett replied, realizing that it was the first time that she had acknowledged the truth of what had happened to her in the last week of her sentence.

"Did you just?" Rachel asked, stopping when she saw Scarlett's smirking face.

"Yeah, I did. Progress," Scarlett replied, laughing and reaching out to hold Rachel's hand.

"You know, I think it's really nice that you let me set the pace for everything. I kinda didn't think that that was something that I was allowed to do. I hope that you don't think that I am bratty or something because of it," Scarlett said, noticing the knot in her stomach, worried that she wouldn't be what Rachel wanted and that Rachel would kick her out as well.

"No, I don't think that at all. What I think is that you are trying to protect yourself, which I think is very wise. But in time, you'll learn that you can trust me, even though I bent the rules so that we could have this," Rachel replied, placing her hand on Scarlett's thigh and gently squeezing. Scarlett looked out the window and closed her eyes as she felt herself slowly relax.

This is nice. It might not have been how I thought it would go, but the plan is still working. I'm safe, I think, and Rachel is gorgeous, Scarlett thought, smiling as she felt the warm afternoon sun on her face.

"We're here," Rachel announced, pulling into the driveway. The cottage style house made Scarlett smile.

This looks like the types of homes in those fancy country magazines, Scarlett thought as she looked out the window at the white wooden cottage with the green garden and cobblestone garden path. The lavender on the front porch and the red and pink roses on the window sill made Rachel's house look like a postcard.

"You were worried about this?! This is cute," Scarlett said, making Rachel smile. She was happy that Scarlett liked her place.

"Come on, let's get you inside," Rachel said, unbuckling Scarlett's seat belt before heading toward the front door.

"What?" Rachel said, turning around to see that Scarlett was standing in front of the car.

"Don't you think it's a bit weird?" Scarlett asked, kicking the stones with her shoe. Rachel smiled and thought for a moment, unsure of what to say.

"Maybe if you didn't want me, it would be weird. But I've only ever given you what you needed and wanted. Is it so bad that I want to look after you?" Rachel questioned, placing her hands on either side of Scarlett's face and tucking her hair behind her ears.

"I guess not," Scarlett replied, stretching out her arms and holding onto Rachel, relaxing into her just as Rachel released her.

"Alright then," Rachel stated, taking Scarlett's hand and walking her through the front door. Rachel kicked her shoes off by the door and continued to walk Scarlett through the house and into the front room bedroom.

"You can put your things down here if you like," Rachel said, turning to look at Scarlett, who was smirking at the stuffie on the bed.

"I thought you might like it," Rachel said, her fake innocence making Scarlett shake her head.

"You're trouble," Scarlett replied, dropping her bag and sighing. She sat on the bed and thought about how she felt like a passenger to her life, that somehow, someone else was always driving the car, and she was just there reacting to their control.

"I think I need a shower. I'm really tired," Scarlett said, looking up at Rachel, who smiled down at her.

"Do you want me to run it for you?" Rachel asked, feeling herself slip into Mommy space. Scarlett just shrugged her shoulders and looked at the ground.

"What is it, baby?" Rachel asked, sitting down on the bed next to Scarlett. Scarlett shook her head, unable to decide what it was that was hurting her heart with such intensity.

"I don't know. I just feel sad," Scarlett said, beginning to cry. Rachel reached out and took Scarlett into her arms, slowly rocking her and holding her close.

"I know that everything seems a bit too much right now, baby. But it'll feel better soon," Rachel affectionately said, waiting until Scarlett's tears stopped flowing before she let her go.

"I think maybe I just want to shower by myself," Scarlett said, getting up and kicking her shoes off. She looked at Rachel, almost asking for permission as she put her hands in her pockets and deeply inhaled.

"Whatever you need, sweetie," Rachel affectionately said, getting up and kissing her forehead before walking out the door.

Scarlett walked into the bathroom and shut the door behind

her, sighing.

This is my life now, Scarlett thought to herself, looking around the bathroom, smiling a smile of relief. She thought back to the times where she would shower with her back to the wall, worried that somebody was going to try and hurt her.

No one can hurt you now, she said to herself. She turned the water on, stripped her clothes off, and waited for the water to become warm.

I can't let myself care. I just can't fucking care about them, she thought, standing under the water and feeling the guilt of finally looking after herself. She thought back to her family, always having to scrape together money for food, clothes, she remembered how cold her hands and feet used to be, the cold seeping into her bones, and how she would sleep with her knees to her chest to try and stay warm. She felt guilty for leaving them behind, feeling like an imposter in Rachel's house.

I should have gone back to them. I shouldn't have stayed with Scott, Scarlett thought. She remembered how whenever she had tried to ring them while she was away, they'd never ask how she was, only ever telling her drama that had happened and how drunk this person had gotten or that someone at a party had stolen their cigarettes.

I guess that's not the life I wanted either, Scarlett said to herself. Scarlett felt embarrassed about where she had come from, trying to figure out how she was going to explain who she really was to Rachel.

What will she think when she finds out? Yeah, she knows that I must have had a rough start by the fact that I ended up in jail, but what if I'm too trashy for her, Scarlett thought, washing her body and seeming to gasp under the water as her nervous system tried to regulate itself. She hadn't noticed that she was sitting on the shower floor until she heard the knock come from the door.

"Scarlett?" Rachel questioned, opening the door and cautiously peering in.

"Are you alright?" She asked, seeing Scarlett slowly standing up. Scarlett wrapped a towel around herself and ran her fingers through her hair.

"Yeah, sorry," Scarlett replied, making Rachel smile, relief in her eyes.

"You don't have to be sorry. I was just worried, you've been in here a really long time," Rachel explained, opening up her arms to Scarlett, who snuggled in close to her.

"Come on, do you want me to look after you tonight?" Rachel asked, walking Scarlett into her bedroom.

"Yes, please," Scarlett softly said, feeling herself slipping into her little space. That was all she wanted, somebody to take care of her, to make sure that she had everything she needed and to do everything for her.

Wow, I'm really clingy and needy, Scarlett thought, smirking to herself. After so many years of being alone, having someone who wanted to look after her made her head spin.

"Alright, little one," Rachel said, putting up her hair and taking a few things down from her cupboard shelf. Scarlett knew she was feeling little, as she sucked her thumb, happy when Rachel took her thumb out of her mouth and replaced it with a paci.

"Mommy's sweet girl," Rachel cooed, taking the towel away and sliding a diaper under Scarlett.

"Let's get you all ready for bed. I can't have my pretty girl falling asleep without a diaper," Rachel said, powdering Scarlett, who reached for her.

"Hold on, sweetie, Mommy is almost done," Rachel smiled, she loved how needy and clingy Scarlett was and fastened the tabs tightly around her waist. She reached for a light blue onesie and quickly dressed Scarlett, before taking her back to the bathroom and drying her hair.

"There, all ready for Mommy cuddles," Rachel said as she ran her fingers through Scarlett's hair and felt her head fall into her chest.

"This is nice," Scarlett softly said, holding onto Rachel like she held all the answers to every question Scarlett could ever have.

Chapter 9

Scarlett stayed in Rachel's arms all night, having panic attack after panic attack until she finally fell asleep in the early hours of the morning.

"My sweet girl," Rachel whispered, kissing Scarlett's forehead after holding her for hours, her tears soaking the top of Rachel's shirt as Scarlett stirred in her sleep, exhausted after feeling her heart slowly begin to heal. Rachel gave Scarlett everything she was looking for, but it came at a cost. The cost was honesty. Scarlett couldn't pretend everything was fine with Rachel, and as Rachel had soothed her broken, fragile heart through the night, Scarlett knew that Rachel was the woman she had always wished to find.

"Good morning, pretty girl," Rachel said as Scarlett blinked her eyes open. Scarlett's tears had sealed her eyes shut and rubbing them, Rachel smile and led her to the bathroom.

"Let Mommy wash your face," Rachel said, kissing Scarlett's cheeks as she took a washcloth and dampened it with warm water. Gently rubbing Scarlett's eyes clean, she opened them, their sparkly blue hue seducing Rachel without Scarlett even having to try.

"I have to go to work today," Scarlett said, biting her lip

and looking down at her onesie and diaper.

"I guess you can't go like that, can you?" Rachel laughed, smiling, and nodding her head as Scarlett began to undress, looking at Rachel for permission.

"Do you want breakfast before you go?" Rachel asked, trying to hide the fact that Scarlett's naked body drove her wild as Scarlett walked back to the bedroom and started getting dressed for work.

"No, I'll get something there," Scarlett called, putting on her lingerie and turning to face Rachel.

"Don't look at me like that," Scarlett giggled, Rachel, crossing her arms over her chest and leaning against the wall.

"I can look at you any way I want to," she seductively said, making Scarlett roll her eyes.

"Not if I don't let you," Scarlett replied, her cheeky smile encouraging Rachel. "Well, that is true, but would you really want Mommy to not be interested in you?" She questioned, walking forward and wrapping her arms around Scarlett, and throwing her down on the bed.

"Mommy," Scarlett giggled, pushing her off and sitting next to her.

"I can't right now," Scarlett added, the seriousness in her tone telling Rachel all she needed to know.

"Alright, baby," Rachel said, reaching out to tuck a strand of hair behind Scarlett's ear.

"I've got to go," Scarlett said, standing up and pulling

her jeans on.

"Do you need a lift?" Rachel asked, wishing that she was able to look after Scarlett more than she was letting her.

"No, it's cool, thanks, though, maybe tomorrow? I've got a late shift, and I kinda hate working them because they feel more dangerous than working a day shift," Scarlett explained, grabbing her bag and standing by the front door as she buttoned up her shirt.

"Well, that's because they are, so yes, I'll drive you to work tomorrow," Rachel said, feeling Scarlett suddenly wrap her arms around her neck and hold her tightly.

"See you later," Scarlett said, kissing Rachel before she left.

Scarlett walked down the street and towards her work, feeling all loved up from the night before.

Oh, I could have stayed in her arms forever, she thought, as she remembered Rachel's gentle stroking on her back and the way she fit perfectly against her body. Scarlett pushed the doors of the diner open and smiled as she walked toward the back.

Life is good, even if I have these fucking dishes to do, Scarlett said to herself, signing and rolling up her sleeves, beginning her shift. Little did she know, as she had passed through the diner, she had caught the attention of the warden, who was having brunch with one of the guards.

"Was that?" The guard said, Esther's eyes sparkling with delight.

"Yes, it was," she replied. This wasn't the usual place the warden came when she wanted to have vanilla pancakes, but her usual joint was closed for renovations.

"It's always so strange seeing them in the real world," the guard said, smirking when Esther got up and cracked her neck.

"Where are you going?" The guard asked, already knowing the answer. Esther just turned and looked at them, winking and turning back to begin to walk into the back of the diner.

"Hi," Esther said, Scarlett, turning around, her mouth gaped open as though she had just seen a ghost.

"What are you doing here?" Scarlett asked. Her words surprised not only the warden but herself as well.

Careful, Scarlett said to herself, unsure of her level of safety.

"I saw you come in, and I thought I'd say hi," Esther replied, putting her hands in her pockets.

"I see you've kept yourself out of trouble," Esther added, coming up behind Scarlett and wrapping her arms around her.

"You can't do that to me anymore," Scarlett said, slipping out from her gasp and wiping her wet hands on her apron.

"You weren't complaining last time," Esther said, clearly offended.

"Last time, I had no choice. It wasn't exactly an even power dynamic," Scarlett replied, annoyed that she could feel Esther getting to her.

"You should leave," Scarlett said, putting her hands on her hips. Esther looked at her, standing in front of her, being empowered, and didn't like it.

"Do you think you're better than me now or something? We aren't on the same level. You'll always be a shit kicker, having to work shitty jobs because you're trash. You came from trash, and you'll die trash. You were only ever good for a fun time. That's all you'll ever be good for," Esther said before leaving Scarlett, just as the tears she was trying so desperately to keep from falling, escaped her eyes.

Don't listen to her, don't listen to her, Scarlett told herself, feeling herself have another panic attack. She took off her apron and grabbed her bag, rushing out of the diner as her boss yelled at her for leaving, but she couldn't hear the words he was shouting as she ran out onto the street. Scarlett could feel her heart beating in her throat. She felt like she was going to be sick as she pushed past the people and felt her head spin. She knew that she needed to get home. She knew what she wanted.

"Mommy!" Scarlett frantically yelled as she opened the

door to Rachel's house and dropped her bag and then herself to the floor.

"Baby?" Rachel questioned, the concern and compassion in her voice bring Scarlett to tears.

"I'm sorry, I'm so sorry," Scarlett sobbed over and over. Rachel had questions, hundreds of them, but she knew that Scarlett wouldn't be able to answer any of them until she had calmed down.

"Can Mommy look after you?" Rachel softly asked, holding Scarlett's tear-stained face in her hands. Scarlett nodded, feeling more pathetic than she had ever felt in her life.

"It's alright, little bunny, Mommy knows what you need. You're a good girl, come here," Rachel said, picking Scarlett up and taking to the couch. Rachel set her up with blankets and her paci, smiling when she sat next to Scarlett

"Do you want anything else?" Rachel asked, enjoying how Scarlett pawed at her breasts.

"Yes, Mommy," Scarlett timidly replied, allowing Rachel to position her and letting her suckle.

"Don't try to tell Mommy yet," Rachel said, seeing Scarlett begin to try and talk. Rachel rocked Scarlett until her sobs ended, and her eyes closed, body relaxed, and began to feel heavy.

"Mommy's going to look after you, sweetie. I think you should give work a miss for now," Rachel said, smiling down at Scarlett, who cuddled into her.

"I saw her," Scarlett softly said, moving so that her face was in the crock of Rachel's neck. Rachel stroked Scarlett's back and held her tight on her lap.

"Who did you see, baby?" Rachel asked, leaning back against the couch, enjoying how it felt to hold Scarlett.

"Esther, the warden from jail," Scarlett whispered. Rachel could feel herself becoming defensive and protective, already hating where this conversation was going to lead.

"Do you want to tell Mommy what happened?" Rachel asked. Scarlett nodded her head and looked up into Rachel's loving eyes.

"I started my shift, and she was just there. Like she just appeared out of nowhere," Scarlett started to explain. She liked that Rachel didn't ask any questions; she just held her and listened, making her feel safe and loved.

"And then she started to say all this stuff about how I'm nothing and that I'm only good for sex," Scarlett said, feeling her tears begin to fall onto her cheeks.

"Oh baby," Rachel replied, kissing her tears away and rocking her.

"I'm happy you came home to Mommy," Rachel said. She knew that she would be able to support Scarlett for a few months while she found a new job, she sure wasn't about to let her go back to the diner now that the warden knew where she worked.

"I know it's the middle of the day, but I think you need

Mommy to look after you," Rachel said, beginning to take Scarlett's uniform off.

"You aren't going to need that anymore. I don't want you going back to the diner, baby. Do you understand me?" Rachel said, her stern words making Scarlett's eyes go wide.

"You don't have to be scared of Mommy. You just have to follow Mommy's rules, alright?" Rachel said, standing Scarlett up and waiting for her to nod her head before taking her into the bedroom.

"I'm happy it's the weekend," Rachel said, diapering Scarlett and putting her into a pink fluffy diaper cover and a white shirt, a pink bow in her hair, and her pink paci in her mouth.

"You're going to stay Mommy's baby for the rest of the weekend," Rachel lovingly said, as Scarlett touched the front of her diaper.

"Yes, that does mean that you'll wet your diaper for Mommy," Rachel added, reading Scarlett's mind.

Chapter 10

"Mommy," Scarlett whined. It had been three hours since she had been put in her diaper, and Rachel had been waiting.

"Well, if you just use your diaper like a good girl, Mommy will change you," Rachel replied. She had put a movie on for Scarlett, who was cuddling in next to her and would bury her face in her lap at every scary part.

"We could go to the art gallery and have a picnic if you'd like, sweetie?" Rachel asked, just as the movie ended. Scarlett's eyes went wide, making Rachel laugh.

"No, I would put you in something a little more discrete," Rachel laughed. She ran her fingers through Scarlett's hair and wondered what it would take for Scarlett to wet her diaper.

"I don't wanna," Scarlett whined, shaking her head from side to side and pouting. Rachel liked seeing this side of Scarlett. It was one thing to have a good girl. It was another to have a girl who was confident that the relationship would be fine if it got tested.

"You don't want to be a bad girl for Mommy," Rachel whispered, sending shivers down Scarlett's arms.

"Exactly, good idea," Rachel added, seeing Scarlett's eyes go wide with innocence once more and her diaper become wet.

"Let's get you cleaned up and ready to go out," Rachel said, taking Scarlett's hand and leading her to the bedroom. Rachel put out a changing mat and snapped her fingers and pointing to the floor.

"Lay down for Mommy," Rachel commanded, happy when Scarlett followed her orders. Rachel looked through her cupboard. Scarlett's clothes hung next to hers, the collection of adult baby outfits, just discrete enough that no one would be the wiser unless they were someway kink inclined.

"Those, Mommy," Scarlett said, pointing to the pair of baggy overalls.

"Please, Mommy," Rachel corrected, enjoying the blushing checks she gave Scarlett.

"Oh, you don't have to be embarrassed little baby. Mommy's not mad. But I'd be a bad Mommy if I didn't teach you to use your manners," Rachel said, coming to where Scarlett was laying down and kissing Scarlett's forehead.

"Please, Mommy," Scarlett softly replied, smiling when Rachel began to change her diaper.

"Mommy, I can't!" She was suddenly exclaiming and wriggling on the mat when she saw Rachel take down a diaper.

"Oh yes, you can, and you will," Rachel replied, playfully spanking Scarlett's thighs.

"Lift up for Mommy," Rachel said, seeing Scarlett obey her.

"Good girl. Mommy was going to put this big vibrator into your little pussy and make you have that inside of you while we were out if you hadn't stopped being naughty. Lucky for you, you remembered your manners," Rachel said, beginning to lube a small buttplug.

"But Mommy, you said I was good," Scarlett said, her eyes going wide. Rachel leaned forward and kissed Scarlett on the nose, enjoying how her heavy breasts pushed into Scarlett's tummy.

"I know you were good. This isn't a punishment, baby. This is something to enjoy," Rachel replied, pushing the tip into Scarlett and getting turned on by her soft moans as the plug filled her. Rubbing her fingers over the clear crystal at the end and pushing it into Scarlett, Rachel went back to diapering her. Scarlett felt it immediately, the sensation of the plug, making her clit tingle, and she reached down to touch herself, making Rachel smirk.

"No baby, we don't touch ourselves there," Rachel said, taking Scarlett's hands away as she arched her back, wanting her clit to stop throbbing.

"Oh, is somebody a little bit horny now?" Rachel said, enjoying watching Scarlett's clit harden. Scarlett nodded her head and reached for Rachel, warming her heart.

"Not right now, baby. But if you are a good girl for me,

on the way home, I'll give you a special reward," Rachel explained, making Scarlett bring her arms down to her chest and waited for Rachel to finish diapering her. Next, Rachel pulled on the overalls, some pink socks, and a pink t-shirt along with yellow Converse sneakers and put Scarlett's hair in a messy ponytail.

"What a sweet little girl you are," Rachel cooed, rubbing her breasts and captivating Scarlett.

"Mommy knows you like these," Rachel said, taking Scarlett's hand and leading her back out into the lounge room, enjoying that the plug in Scarlett's ass and the diaper made her walking slightly difficult.

"People are gonna know Mommy," Scarlett whined for the second time as she watched Rachel get her bag and keys.

"Baby," Rachel warned, she loved the look on Scarlett's face. A mix of arousal and fear.

"Get in the car," Rachel said, deciding that would punish Scarlett on the way to the art gallery.

"Mommy!" Scarlett exclaimed, feeling Rachel pull on her overalls.

"Shh, Mommy doesn't want to hear you," Rachel replied, putting her hand down Scarlett's diaper and sliding the vibrator between her pussy lips and turning it on.

"Now they might know," Rachel said, dressing Scarlett once again and beginning to drive away. Scarlett moaned and pawed at herself, wishing that she could be fucked the way she needed and craved.

"I was going to take you to the art gallery, but I don't think we'd make it inside," Rachel said, reaching across and groping at Scarlett's breasts at a red light.

"So this is what I'm going to do, we are going to find a quiet spot, and I'm going to stop the car, open the back door and push you down on the seats and strapon fuck you till your legs give out," Rachel said, beginning to drive off. Scarlett could hardly hear a word she was saying as she was teased, closing her eyes and pushing her head back against the seat, wanting more.

"I'm going to take these hard nipples as a, yes, Mommy," Rachel laughed, knowing that Scarlett was ready and willing to be fucked.

"Oh, Mommy," Scarlett moaned as Rachel unbuckled her seatbelt and got out of the car.

"Get your ass over here," Rachel growled, opening Scarlett's door and pulling her from her seat. Dragging her around to the back seat and pushing her against the leather, Rachel pulled down Scarlett's overalls, ripped off her diaper and took the vibrator and plug from her body. Spat on her strap on and slid it into Scarlett. Putting a paci into her mouth, Rachel pulled out of her just to push back in, Scarlett's arching back and twerking ass encouraging Rachel with every thrust.

"Yes, bounce that ass for me, baby," Rachel moaned, cracking her neck and pushing Scarlett down as she fucked her. Rachel had parked behind a sporting field, a place she knew well, and smiled to herself as she looked down and enjoyed the image that greeted her.

"Such a good girl," Rachel cooed, feeling Scarlett's pussy tighten and then flood, her body shaking. Rachel slowed her pace, knowing that Scarlett would not be able to take much more. Although she had only cum once, Rachel was acutely aware of the psychological toll the kink played on Scarlett.

"Mommy," Scarlett softly said, Rachel, pulling out of her immediately, knowing that she had reached her limit.

"Mommy's here," Rachel said, taking her strap off and collecting their things and putting them in a bag.

"Mommy will sort those out later," Rachel said, putting a new pull up on Scarlett and dressing her once again. Scarlett went to get back in the front seat, Rachel grabbing her arm and pulling her back into her.

"Not so fast," she said, sitting in the back seat of the car and pulling Scarlett onto her lap.

"Open that pretty mouth for Mommy. This is your reward," Rachel explained, Scarlett instinctively beginning to nurse. Rachel stroked her hair, sweeping it out of her face, and smiled as she felt Scarlett grab at her.

"Such a sweet little girl," Rachel affectionately said, closing her eyes and leaning against the seat in contented bliss.

What neither of them realized is that somebody had been

watching the whole time. Esther had been following Scarlett from the moment she had left the diner and put a tracer on Rachel's SUV. She had traced them to the field, and had taken photos and of the whole encounter.

"This will fucking show you to say no to me, you little bitch," Esther said as she slowly got up from her hiding position and began to walk away, her sinister plan in motion.

Chapter 11

Esther went home to her modest place in the suburbs and uploaded the content to her laptop, making copies of the photos and printing them out. She didn't have to search very hard to find out the Rachel had saved a tidy little nest egg for herself, and Esther planned to take her for every dollar of it.

"That'll teach you to play with things that are mine," Esther bitterly said as she wrote a note outlining what she wanted.

$50,000 in cash left at 81 Samsom Drive-by Wednesday or the world gets to see just how personal you make your sessions with clients.

"I can hardly wait," Esther said out loud, laughing as she placed the note and photos into a yellow envelope and sealed it. She knew that Rachel had the cash, and she knew that she wouldn't want to be disgraced and lose her license. Esther smiled to herself, poured herself a drink, and went online to find a woman for the night, wanting to celebrate her wicked plan.

"Hey, little one, Mommy's home," Rachel called from the front door. She walked in, saw Scarlett's blocks on the floor, and smiled, knowing that her baby had had a nice day. Rachel had told Scarlett to only focus on her online course, which meant that she was able to work around her own schedule. But what it really meant was that for 5 hours a day she studied, and all the other times, she was Rachel's baby.

"Mommy, I'm in here," Scarlett replied, popping her head up from the couch. Rachel undid the cufflinks from her blouse and walked to the living room, pouring herself a drink from the bar before sitting down on the couch next to Scarlett.

"Mommy, you're silly," Scarlett laughed, snuggling into Rachel, loving the smell of aircon and perfume.

"It was a long day, sweetie. Some people are fucking stupid," Rachel said, annoyed that her clients didn't do what she told them to do.

"It's like, they don't even want to become better, they just want to stay in this toxic little cycle of fucking up their lives," Rachel explained, finishing her drink and exhaling as the liquor burned her throat. Scarlett sat next to her waiting for her to feel better.

"It's okay, Mommy. They are just stupid," Scarlett replied, watching at Rachel turned her head and looked at Scarlett's mischievous smirk.

"You know you're not allowed to use naughty words," Rachel warned. Scarlett knew perfectly well what she was and was not allowed to do, making her giggle.

"But you said it, Mommy," Scarlett replied as

innocently as she could. Rachel smiled, tempted, but refusing to take the bait.

"Do you Mommy to punish you tonight? Hey? You've had all day without me, and you're going to try to use my frustration as an excuse to be naughty?" Rachel asked, loving the game that Scarlett had begun. Scarlett giggled, snuggled into Rachel and kissed her neck.

"Maybe," she softly said, getting lost in the embrace that Rachel greeted her with.

"I love you," Rachel whispered, feeling Scarlett's heart skip a beat. Scarlett looked up at Rachel, her surprised face, melting Rachel's heart.

"I don't want to be rough with you tonight," Rachel added, unphased that Scarlett didn't say it back. Rachel knew that it would probably take years before Scarlett felt comfortable to allow herself to feel that deeply. Although she didn't want to therapize Scarlett, Rachel had often found herself analyzing what she was saying or doing.

"Did Mommy make you speechless?" Rachel laughed, seeing her baby girl completely disarmed and nodding her head slowly. Scarlett rested her head against Rachel and closed her eyes.

"You've ruined all my evening plans," Scarlett quietly said, smiling up at Rachel.

"I planned to get you all worked up and for you to take it out on my pussy. But now all I want is to be clingy and needy," Scarlett whined, be secretly delighted that Rachel felt this way about her.

"Maybe Mommy can make up for that?" Rachel asked, deciding that she was going to take Scarlett out for burgers and shakes instead of using her cunt for the evening.

Rachel couldn't sleep. She wasn't sure if it was the amount of take out she had eaten or the fact that her job had become completely unfulfilling. She carefully got out of bed as to not disturb Scarlett and tiptoed through the house to the kitchen to make herself a cup of tea. Sitting on the couch, she sighed as she thought about her life with Scarlett, knowing that she finally felt complete. She got up and opened a window, smiling as she heard the birds beginning their day. She loved taking moments like this. They always seemed like the world was stopping and allowing her to catch up. Putting her mug of tea on the coffee table, she crossed her legs and wrapped a blanket around her shoulders.

I guess this is life now, she thought to herself, closing her eyes just as she heard glass shatter in the kitchen. Gasping and getting up, a knot tightened in her stomach as she heard tires screeching down the street, and she ran into the kitchen to see a yellow envelope wrapped around a brick.

"Rachel, are you ok?" Scarlett fearfully questioned, running around the corner but stopping when she saw the shards of glass covering the floor and the broken window.

"The fuck?" Scarlett added, assessing the situation. Rachel turned around and looked in shock.

"Baby don't come in, there's glass everywhere," Rachel said, wanting to make sure that Scarlett was safe. Rachel bent down to pick up the brick and undid the elastic band that secured the yellow envelope.

"What is that?" Scarlett asked, Rachel, shrugging her shoulders and looking scared and confused. Scarlett hadn't ever seen Rachel look afraid before, and she bit her lip, knowing that now was the time to be tough.

"Here, give it to me," Scarlett said, stepping forward and taking the envelope from Rachel's shaking hands.

"Come and sit down," she added, taking Rachel's hand in hers and leading her back to the couch and placed her mug of tea in her hands.

"Drink this," Scarlett said, wrapping her arms around Rachel, who began to laugh in shock.

"You must think I'm a mess," Rachel said, shaking her head and wiping a tear away.

"Nar, I'm just a little more used to this type of stuff happening than you are," Scarlett replied in a loving tone. Scarlett began to open the envelope, her fingers ripping the paper.

"What?" Rachel asked, seeing Scarlett's face go white. Scarlett handed her the photos, getting up to go to the fridge and get a drink.

"Fuck," Rachel said, reading the note and wondering who would want to do this to her.

"Fuck, alright," Scarlett replied, taking a swing of whiskey straight from the bottle.

"Hey, put that down and come here," Rachel said, seeing Scarlett being to give in to her old vices.

"You know who did this, right?" Scarlett said, the furry in her eyes heightening Rachel's caution as she watched Scarlett pace back and forth.

"Come here, sweetie," Rachel lovingly said, seeing Scarlett shaken and distressed, snapping her out of her own distress, wanting nothing more than to comfort Scarlett. She stopped pacing and looked at Rachel.

"But you do know, don't you?" Scarlett said, sitting next to Rachel and looking at her with those wild and cautious eyes Rachel had first fallen in love with.

"No, I don't. Tell me who you think it was," Rachel said, positioning Scarlett comfortably in her arms.

"It's obvious, that fucking bitch," Scarlett blurted out, annoyed that Esther was still trying to manipulate her life.

"We don't know that for sure," Rachel said, looking over the note.

"I don't even know what I'm meant to say about this," she sighed, passing the note to Scarlett. Reading the note, Scarlett frowned before looking up at Rachel with fear in her eyes.

"She can't be serious!" Scarlett yelled, taking Rachel by surprise.

"Baby, if it is her, she just threw a brick through my fucking window. I think whoever this is, they are pretty damn serious," Rachel angrily replied, startling Scarlett.

"Oh, baby, Mommy's sorry. Come here," Rachel quickly said, changing her tone and holding onto Scarlett firmly, as Scarlett tried to push her away.

"Don't push Mommy just because I made you scared. It's alright," Rachel said, feeling Scarlett relax and begin to cry.

"I know it's scary. But Mommy's here and I'm not going to let anything bad happen to you," Rachel reassuringly explained. Scarlett looked up at her and bit her bottom lip, snuggling into her breasts before closing her eyes.

"I don't have that kind of money," Scarlett whispered, making Rachel smile.

"I do," Rachel cheekily said, deciding that she wasn't going to pay it despite the huge threat to her career. Scarlett sat up, looked at her in surprise.

"Okay but, I still don't think that you should pay it," Scarlett slowly replied, understanding the weight of what she was saying.

"I mean. I don't care about people finding out about me. Like, I don't do anything special. But you! You are going to lose everything you've worked for if you don't pay her, but then if you pay her, what's to stop her from demanding more?!" Scarlett said, getting herself into a frenzy and making Rachel laugh.

"Easy there tiger," she laughed, kissing Scarlett's forehead and thinking.

"We should probably go to the police. Just because I'm not going to pay her, doesn't mean I don't still want her caught," Rachel said.

If I don't pay her, she will probably become more violent. She knows where I live. She might come after Scarlett again, and next time it will be far worse than the first time, Rachel thought, feeling angry as she imagined what Esther would do to her out of spite and revenge for not getting her way.

"I don't really want to stay in the house tonight. What if she comes back?" Scarlett fearfully questioned, looking at Rachel and wanting her to protect her more than she had ever felt in her life. Rachel thought for a moment. It was four in the morning, and the thought of going back to sleep made Rachel feel uneasy as a gush of wind came through the broken window and sent chills down her spine.

"Come on, get your coat, we are going to the station," Rachel declared. She had no desire to see her perfect girlfriend put in any more dangerous and compromising situations, and was fearful that Esther would come back if it was even Esther at all.

"Hello. I'm Victoria," an Amazonian looking woman said, extending her hand to Rachel and then Scarlett.

"Hi, I'm Rachel, this is Scarlett," Rachel said, sitting down on the chair that Victoria gestured toward.

"So, you've had a bit of a rough night?" Victoria said, raising an eyebrow at the yellow envelope that Rachel had in her hands. Rachel looked at Scarlett, who bit her bottom lip and nodded her head.

"Yeah, we have. Um, so, this came with a brick, and it was thrown through my kitchen window and um," Rachel said, feeling embarrassed about her love of the MDLG kink for the first time.

"It's okay, take your time. But just know that there's no judgment about what's in here," Victoria kindly said, smiling at both Rachel and Scarlett and assessing their dynamic.

"May I?" Victoria asked, Rachel, nodding her head, surprised that she felt so out of control. Usually, Rachel felt in control, her sensual energy empowering herself, and her confidence in her ability always to know how to deal with a situation fueling her fire. But not right now. Right now, she felt as though she was completely stripped of any power she had thought she had, any security she had built around herself, and as she looked at Victoria, any control she had in her life. Scarlett sensed that Rachel was struggling to process what was going on and placed her hand on her thigh. Victoria took the envelope and flicked through the photos, trying not to get turned on. She had sensed that Rachel and Scarlett had some sort of kink to their relationship, but she was pleasantly delighted that their interests were so aligned with her own. She read the note and slowly looked up.

"You've got yourselves a nasty stalker," she said, smiling kindly at Rachel, who found herself blushing, much to her dismay.

"Look, it's okay, if it makes you feel better," Victoria said, tilting her head and shrugging her shoulders and nodding her head in the way that told Rachel and Scarlett everything they needed to know.

"Oh, that actually does make me feel a lot better," Rachel said, deeply exhaling, only realizing that she had been holding her breath at that moment.

"So, now let's nail this person. I hate kink-shaming at the best of times, but this is just cruel," Victoria said, enjoying the change in energy in the room and the way Rachel and Scarlett both relaxed.

Victoria had suggested that they collect their most treasured possessions and go to a hotel for a few days while she investigated. So Rachel and Scarlett had gone back to the house and began to pack their bags.

"I feel like I do this way too much," Scarlett joked, making Rachel's heart hurt.

"I'm sorry, princess," she said, kissing Scarlett's

forehead and holding her tightly. Scarlett smiled against Rachel, loving the sensual smell of her perfume and loving embrace. It always made her feel loved, the way Rachel held her. It was the combination of fitting perfectly into her and the placement of Rachel's arms.

"I didn't mean to make you sad," Scarlett replied, realizing that Rachel had no intention of letting her go.

I just never thought my life would be like this. I'm about to potentially lose my career for a girl I've known for the shortest amount of time. I mean, I don't hate it, I just never thought it would happen, Rachel thought, stroking Scarlett's hair and softly laughing to herself.

"You didn't make me sad, baby. I'm just surprised that this is my life. I thought it was getting a bit boring, but I didn't need this level of excitement," Rachel joked. Scarlett felt the familiar knot in her stomach begin to tighten as she thought about the possibility of Rachel leaving her.

What if I just come with too much baggage? She thought to herself, annoyed that just when everything was going right for her, something or someone had to come along and ruin it for her.

I should just go and let Rachel get back to her life. She doesn't need me bringing her down and holding her back by being with me, Scarlett thought, grabbing her bag and waiting for Rachel by the door.

"Ready?" Rachel asked, noticing the fake smile across

Scarlett's face.

"Yeah," Scarlett replied, trying to convince Rachel but failing to do so.

Maybe she's just exhausted from the night, Rachel thought to herself, knowing that that wasn't correct. Rachel didn't have the energy to try and figure out what was distressing Scarlett, but she made a mental note to come back to it, especially if Scarlett stayed faking her happiness.

"Let's go," Rachel added, opening the door just as the emergency repair trades began to work on her window.

Rachel drove to the hotel, checked in, and held Scarlett's hand as they walked to their room, noticing that Scarlett pulled away from her halfway down the corridor.

"I think I'm going to go take a shower," Rachel announced, dropping her bag by the side of the bed and watching as Scarlett looked out over the city from the window. Victoria had told them to stay away for the week, estimating that that is how long it would take her to build a solid case around Esther, so Rachel had booked the penthouse suite for Scarlett and herself.

"Baby?" Rachel questioned, coming over and wrapping her arms around Scarlett, just to have her push her away. Rachel was exhausted, and she had to pause before responding to Scarlett's agitated manner.

"Do you want to talk about it? Do you know the words?"

Rachel asked, softening her tone and reaching out to touch Scarlett's cheek. Scarlett's angry eyes glaring back at her made Rachel understand that this was a trauma response.

"I know it feels like bad things are always happening and that you can't get away from your old life, but look at this great place. This is proof that while bad things can still happen because that's life, you are in a position to be less affected by them now," Rachel lovingly explained, seeing Scarlett sigh and become more relaxed.

"I just feel like, if it wasn't for me, you wouldn't have to go through this. And yeah, this is cool, but I only have this because of you. If I was on my own, I'd probs let her do whatever because what would my options be?" Scarlett replied, feeling her eyes lose their anger, just for the sadness she carried to begin to show.

"Well, first of all, my life was boring before you. So if you think that I am giving you up, you are crazy. And second, you're right, but I want you as mine, so just enjoy what I have to give you. Let me spoil and protect and nurture and love on you," Rachel playfully said, making Scarlett smile.

"Why do you even want me?" She asked, shaking her head and shrugging her shoulders.

"Like, I'm not even that good," Scarlett added, making Rachel smile. Rachel took Scarlett's hand and led her to the lounge, sat her down, and looked into her eyes.

"I want you because you trigger in me something that I

love. It's that neediness when you feel little that I adore, the way you are always trying to be such a big girl when you aren't little and how when I am sad you come out swinging, wanting to take on the world. You give me joy and peace and love, and I'm not sure what else I could ask for," Rachel said, taking Scarlett by surprise. She wasn't used to hearing those words, let alone directed at her, and their unfamiliarity made her nervous and on edge.

"Come on, let Mommy take care of you, honey. I can tell that you are overstimulated, and I need to get you settled and into bed. Even though it's morning, we had interrupted sleep, and you need a little bit of quiet time to relax and rest," Rachel said, opening her arms to Scarlett, patiently waiting as Scarlett decided if she was going to submit.

"My good girl," Rachel said, feeling Scarlett relax into her, giving herself to Rachel and smiling against her chest, knowing that Rachel was all she wanted. Rachel took Scarlett's hand and led her to the bathroom. Scarlett's eyes were softening as the familiar nightly routine began even though it was mid-morning, and she found herself in the shower, getting gently washed by Rachel's loving hands.

"Do you ever get sick of looking after me?" Scarlett softly asked, her insecurities creeping back in as she looked into Rachel's exhausted eyes.

"What? No!" Rachel said, turning Scarlett around and washing her back.

"It's just that," Scarlett said, stopping when she saw the look on Rachel's face.

"Here. That's enough of that silly talk," Rachel said, pushing Scarlett's paci into her mouth and taking her out the shower and beginning to dry her.

"Stand there while Mommy has a shower," Rachel said, snapping her fingers and smiling as Scarlett blindly obeyed her.

"Oh you know how to please Mommy, don't you," Rachel said, washing herself quickly before getting out of the shower and slapping Scarlett's ass playfully, making her walk back to the bedroom and lay down on the bed, expectantly.

"I know little bunny," Rachel replied, to seeing Scarlett's grabby hands. Quickly diapering Scarlett, Rachel dressed her in her dino onesie and pulled the blankets back, watching as Scarlett scurried under the covers. Rachel put on her panties and climbed into bed, pushing Scarlett's blankie into her chest and laughing at how she grabbed at it as though it was a lifeline.

"Mommy's sweet little girl," Rachel said, wrapping her arms around Scarlett, who quietly snuggled into her.

"Sweet dreams beautiful girl," Rachel whispered, as she felt Scarlett become heavy against her.

Chapter 12

Rachel woke up, the afternoon sun beaming through the cracks in the curtains. Getting out of bed and walking out onto the balcony, she shielded her eyes and felt the cool air against her skin, grounding her.

How should I move on with my life, Rachel thought to herself, sighing and draping her body over the rail.

What do I like the sound of that's not a therapist. Like, what am I even any good at? I could go and retrain, do something different? Maybe I don't even want to stay in this town. We could go anywhere, do anything, she reflected, watching the world continue to spin around her.

I have some really big decisions to make because it isn't just me anymore, Rachel reflected, thinking about how her decision would change not only her life but also Scarlett's.

I wonder if she'd even want to go with me. What if she wants to stay here, what if it all just gets too much for her? Rachel began to think, sitting down on the outdoor furniture and beginning to plan what her new life would entail.

"Hi, do you want one?" Scarlett asked hours later, pouring herself the smoothie she had just made.

"No thanks, baby, it looks yummy, though," Rachel replied. She had gone out that afternoon, taken a walk, and collected the newspaper. Going to the park, Rachel had sat and watched the water features in the pond, read her newspaper, and contemplated her life. She had come home just as Scarlett was waking up, enjoying watching her beautiful girlfriend toss and stir, waking up just as the lights of the city began to flicker and glow.

"I've been thinking about what we should do, little one," Rachel said, folding the newspaper on the kitchen bench and looking at Scarlett intensely. Scarlett took a sip of her smoothie, raising her eyebrows, sensing the seriousness of the conversation.

"Because I'm not paying that bitch, and I don't care if I lose my license, I want to start a life somewhere new. With you," Rachel said. Scarlett surprised that Rachel was prepared to walk away from everything she had built in the city. It was one thing not to pay Esther. It was another thing entirely to up and run.

"Where would we go?" Scarlett asked, happy to be leaving the city behind.

"I only have a few weeks left of probation, I can't leave before it's over," Scarlett explained, fearful that Rachel would leave her behind. Rachel smirked, stood up and walked around to where Scarlett was standing, wrapped her arms around her and kissed the top of her head.

"Of course we can wait until you have finished that sweetie, I can't imagine leaving without you!" Rachel exclaimed, knowing that setting themselves up in a new town was going to be no small feat.

"We will need to find a new spot, so start thinking about where you want to live little bunny," Rachel called down the hallway as she headed to the bathroom for a shower. Scarlett stayed standing in the kitchen, wondering how she had managed to get this lucky, and walked over to her laptop and began looking at real estate by the beach.

"What if she follows us?" Scarlett asked, curled up in Rachel's arms. Rachel and Scarlett had spent the better part of the last three days looking at properties online and finding a real estate agent. Rachel had decided to rent out her place and had been organizing how to do that with their real estate agent.

"I've never done anything like this before," Scarlett said, feeling overwhelmed by the task. Rachel smiled for her. This was not something that scared Rachel in the slightest, but she could understand why Scarlett found it intimidating.

"Baby, it's really easy. We'll rent out my place, and we will move to a new town, by the beach, and rent a property there to see if we like it," Rachel explained, wrapping her arm around Scarlett, who snuggled into her immediately.

"What's going to happen if we can't find a place?"

Scarlett asked, her little voice melting Rachel's heart.

"Mommy's got you, honey, you don't need to worry about not finding a place," Rachel replied, checking the time on her phone.

"Let's stop for the day. What do you want to do?" Rachel asked, understanding that Scarlett needed some time to relax after their day of planning. Scarlett thought, shrugging her shoulders and looking around the space.

"How about Mommy takes you for ice-cream?" Rachel asked, smiling as she saw Scarlett's eyes light up.

"I thought that would get your pretty smile back on your face," Rachel said, standing up and taking Scarlett's hand in hers.

"Don't look at me like that," Scarlett teased, loving how Rachel's gaze landed on her body.

"But you're such a cute, little thing," Rachel sensually said as she lovingly stroked Scarlett's face, making her gasp when she firmly slapped her cheek.

"I want to explore this body before we go, sweetheart," Rachel whispered, taking the pink bunny Scarlett was cuddling and gave her red cheek kisses with it.

"Good thing, bunny is here to kiss you better baby because Mommy isn't going to today," Rachel explained, getting up and going to her bag she had left at the door. She opened the bag, winking at Scarlett, who just giggled and took out two black silk ties and a strap on. Rachel and Scarlett had discussed taking their relationship to the next level and for their sex life to become rougher, and Scarlett was excited to see what Rachel had in store for her.

"I wonder what fun I can have with these," Rachel teased as she dropped the ties on Scarlett's body and began to fasten the harness of the strap on.

"Play with yourself," Rachel instructed, grabbing at Scarlett when she hesitated and leaving red finger marks on her skin, causing her to gasp.

"Oh, you thought I'd be gentle? Silly little girl, you aren't listening to Mommy, are you?" Rachel said, placing her larger hand on Scarlett's neck and squeezing until she was gasping.

"Start playing with yourself little one, you'll want to get nice and wet for Mommy or what I'll do to you will hurt even more," Rachel explained taking Scarlett's left hand and tying it above her head, gently slapping her tits until Scarlett was playing with herself at a pace which satisfied Rachel.

"Good girl," Rachel said, sitting back and stroking the big black dildo she had claimed as her own. Scarlett loved that Rachel always knew how to turn her on, and she giggled, finding it hard to be serious, which made Rachel give her a sideward smirk.

"Oh, you think it's funny, baby?" Rachel said, grabbing Scarlett's ankles and pulling her forward, making her gasp as she felt the tip of the cock against her pussy.

"Not so funny now, is it?" Rachel whispered as she slowly entered Scarlett, being gentle with her and watching for her cues. For the last few days, it had felt like the world was closing in on them, and Rachel cracked her neck as she began to fuck Scarlett, happy to have a release for her frustration. This is what she needed, and as much as she hated herself for using Scarlett as her fuckdoll, she knew that as long as she was gentle, Scarlett would find enjoyment from it as well.

"I'm not going to hurt you, little girl," Rachel said, feeling Scarlett begin to resist her. Rachel knew that she didn't have much time left before Scarlett reached her limit, and she fucked her aggressively with a need and desire she had forgotten she could feel. With the harness from the strap on rubbing against her clit, Rachel came just as Scarlett pushed her away, panting and smirking and satisfied.

"Good girl," Rachel cooed, reaching out to stroke Scarlett's hair, only to be pushed away again.

"Okay, little one," Rachel laughed, understanding what Scarlett needed. Rachel went to the kitchen, made up a bottle, and found Scarlett's blankie before coming back into the room. She took off her strap, lay down on the bed, and let Scarlett snuggle into her, feeling her grabby hands and short breath against her chest.

"There there, Mommy's here," Rachel said, holding Scarlett until her frowning forehead smoothed over.

"That was really fucking close," Scarlett complained,

Rachel smirking and letting Scarlett slap at her.

"I know, but it didn't go across the line, did it?" Rachel replied. She would usually have never let Scarlett be so bratty, but she knew that she had danced close to the edge, and if giving Scarlett a few expectations in her behavior was what she needed to feel better, Rachel was happy to oblige.

"Come on, Mommy needs to get you ready," Rachel whispered, seeing that Scarlett was feeling better. Scarlett's eyes grew wide, and her the innocence of her eyes told Rachel that while she may have needed to use Scarlett like a whore, Scarlett needed her Mommy.

"Oh, has my little girl missed this?" Rachel cooed, seeing Scarlett becoming little before her eyes. Nodding her head, Scarlett battered her eyelids at Rachel as she was diapered and dressed in a baggy pair of jeans and a tight-fitting t-shirt.

"It's cold, Mommy," Scarlett said, shivering as the sun went behind some clouds and the room becoming darker.

"I know, Mommy's got your hoodie," Rachel said, sitting Scarlett up and helping her put on her pink hoodie, kissing the top of her nose and making her giggle.

"The ice-cream shop is probably closed by now!" Scarlett whined, making Rachel raise an eyebrow.

"Then I'll come up with a solution, have I ever let you down?" Rachel questioned, liking that the answer was no, as Scarlett shook her head.

Chapter 13

"So, what happens now?" Rachel asked Victoria as she and Scarlett sat in the police station after Victoria had called them in. It had been a week since Esther had tried to blackmail them, and the drop date had come. Victoria had been waiting in place for Esther or anyone to come and collect the money that had been demanded, but with no one showing, it was hard to make a case. Victoria passed Rachel and Scarlett the coffees she had made, before sitting down in her chair.

"Well, the problem is, all the evidence we have for her is circumstantial. We can't actually tie her to anything because there were no fingerprints. The note was printed from a computer and not handwritten so we can't do a handwriting match, and the location was a public place that no one turned up to. There's nothing personal about case that could link it to her," Victoria explained, making Rachel and Scarlett annoyed.

"Our plan is to move to the other side of the country and start a new life there. What are we meant to do if she follows us?" Rachel asked, before taking a sip of her cappuccino. Victoria slowly nodded her head. This was the part of the job she hated. When all the circumstances pointed toward one person, but no evidence could tie them to the case.

"I think getting out of here would be a great idea. And if she does send these photos to the psychology board or whoever it is that you answer to, if you don't care about losing your ability to practice, then she's got no power. You can just get on with leading and rebuilding your lives," Victoria explained. She was happy that both Rachel and Scarlett seemed unphased and content with accepting that their lives would never be the same.

"Thanks for all your time," Rachel said, seeing that Scarlett had finished her espresso, extending her hand toward Victoria. Getting up, Victoria walked around the desk, shaking Rachel's hand before shaking Scarlett's.

"I'm sorry that we couldn't get her and lock her up," Victoria replied, knowing that she'd be keeping an eye on Esther for a long time yet.

"Well, that was kind of pointless," Scarlett angrily said as they walked back out onto the street. Rachel laughed, she loved that Scarlett could seem sweet and understanding one moment and bitterly furious the next.

"I know, but it is what it is, so let's just keep doing what we are doing, and hopefully, she won't be able to follow us," Rachel said, shrugging her shoulders and giving a Scarlett a curious look.

"What?" Rachel asked, taking Scarlett's hand in hers.

"You just seem so chill about this when it's taking

everything in me not to smash her face in," Scarlett innocently replied, making Rachel laugh.

"That wouldn't be a good idea. This one is much better," Rachel said, taking out the photo of the location they were planning on moving to.

"Oh my gosh, baby, come here and look at this," Rachel laughed from the makeshift desk in the living room. There were boxes all over the house, and she was standing with her laptop on a stack of boxes. The removalist people were going to be arriving at any moment. Esther, at least being true to her word, had sent the photos to the board of Psychology, and as Rachel read their email, suspending her immediately, she laughed. As Rachel laughed from behind the screen, she was happy that she had terminated her license to practice days earlier. Scarlett came out of the bedroom with what Rachel was hoping was the last bag left in there.

"Have you got everything, little one?" Rachel asked Scarlett as she walked over to her.

"Yeah. What is it?" Scarlett asked, gasping when she read the email from the board of directors.

"Wow, that fucking bitch!" Scarlett exclaimed, happy to be leaving this town behind for good.

"They say they want to investigate, but I honestly can't be bothered trying to convince them that I should stay. It was fun, but I'm ready for something else," Rachel said, closing her laptop screen.

"So, it's official, you have to find a new job," Scarlett laughed, still surprised that somebody would be willing to uproot their entire life just so they could still be together. She had half assumed that Rachel would leave her. After all, it was because of Scarlett that Rachel was in this mess, to begin with, or so she believed. Rachel had a completely different outlook on it, and no matter how many times she tried to convince Scarlett that it wasn't her fault, she refused to believe her. So Rachel had just decided that she was going to have to continue to show Scarlett rather than tell her.

"I already have a few ideas. I'm thinking, maybe opening up a café?" Rachel suggested, just as the removalists arrived.

"We can talk about the plan later," Rachel said, turning to greet them. She and Scarlett had discussed that they would both take a month to settle in before finding jobs. Rachel had enough money tucked aside and was more than happy to use. She had planned a month of full-time baby and Mommy time, and could hardly wait to get set up and begin their fun.

"Well, here's to a new adventure," Scarlett said, watching as the people began to pack their boxed belongings into the back of the moving truck. Rachel winked at her before wrapping her arms around Scarlett.

"Don't worry. Mommy's got you, honey," Rachel replied, knowing that their adventure together was just beginning.

The end... not quite!

To receive your free Baby Fox Coloring In, visit the link:

www.tinamooreauthor.com

Who is Tina Moore?

Tina Moore has enjoyed the lifestyle of a Mommy Domme for several years. She began secretly exploring kink and BDSM in her youth and found her love of being a strict Mommy Domme in early 2000. Tina Moore slowly became more comfortable and confident through making friends in the community and exploring the lifestyle and now openly celebrates being a Mommy Domme to her little.

Before becoming an author, Tina Moore worked in the finance sector, but it was through the encouragement of her current little that she took the leap and wrote her first MDLG book, Nancy's Little One.

From then on, Tina Moore continued to combine her experiences and desires, as well as the sweet and naughty things her baby girl does, to bring you tantalizing and salacious stories about both MDLG and DDLG relationships and the ABDL littles and middles who enjoy them.

Follow her on:
Instagram @tinamoore.kdp

www.ingramcontent.com/pod-product-compliance
Lightning Source LLC
Chambersburg PA
CBHW030654190726
48286CB00001B/17